PRAISE FOR *SUNSHINE AND SPICE*

"Aurora Palit delivers hilarity, heat, ᵃ family dynamics in *Sunshine and Spi* perfectly balanced Dev's grumpy s from the inside out was utter romaⁱ Aurora writes!"

—Jessica Joyce, *USA Today* bestselling author of *You, With a View*

"Packed with hilarity, charming banter, and the most memorable, and meddling, side characters, *Sunshine and Spice* is a slow-simmering rom-com packed with chemistry and heat. I was rooting for Naomi and Dev as they learned to love their culture as much as each other . . . and I wanted all the South Asian delicacies that Aurora Palit lovingly described. *Sunshine and Spice* is a fantastic debut!"

—Farah Heron, author of *Jana Goes Wild* and *Accidentally Engaged*

"In Aurora Palit's *Sunshine and Spice*, hearts sizzle and cultures collide as a woman cut off from her Bengali culture has to fake it for the opportunity of a lifetime. Palit's debut is sexy, witty, and warm, and you'll cozy right up to her grumpy hero with a gooey center!"

—Nikki Payne, author of *Pride and Protest* and *Sex, Lies and Sensibility*

"Funny, steamy, and bursting with character and playful banter, Aurora Palit's heartwarming debut about family, acceptance and finding love where you least expect it hooked me from the very first page. An absolute must read!"

—Sara Desai, author of *The Marriage Game* and *To Have and To Heist*

"A hilarious and heartfelt debut. *Sunshine and Spice* balances blazing chemistry between its two leads with witty, thoughtful commentary on how intercultural differences shape the classic opposites-attract dynamic. Poignant yet joyful, this book is sunshine/grump perfection."

—Regina Black, author of *The Art of Scandal*

Sunshine and Spice

AURORA PALIT

BERKLEY ROMANCE
NEW YORK

BERKLEY ROMANCE
Published by Berkley
An imprint of Penguin Random House LLC
penguinrandomhouse.com

Library of Congress Cataloging-in-Publication Data

Names: Palit, Aurora, author.
Title: Sunshine and spice / Aurora Palit.
Description: First edition. | New York : Berkley Romance, 2024.
Identifiers: LCCN 2023052725 (print) | LCCN 2023052726 (ebook) |
ISBN 9780593640180 (trade paperback) | ISBN 9780593640197 (ebook)
Subjects: LCGFT: Romance fiction. | Novels.
Classification: LCC PR9199.4.P3427 S86 2024 (print) |
LCC PR9199.4.P3427 (ebook) | DDC 813/.6—dc23/eng/20240126
LC record available at https://lccn.loc.gov/2023052725
LC ebook record available at https://lccn.loc.gov/2023052726

First Edition: September 2024

Printed in the United States of America
1st Printing

Book design by Daniel Brount

If you've ever felt like you don't quite fit in,
this book is dedicated to you:
you are worthy and deserving of love.

Sunshine and Spice

chapter
1

f Naomi was in need of Darjeeling tea bags, a Ganesh bobble-head, or tantric sex pills, she was in the right place. The tightly packed aisles of Gia's Bazaar were a mayhem of imports from India, cheap knockoffs, and the odd head scratcher, like a small wicker basket overflowing with brown Jesus keychains nestled between bottles of Fair & Lovely face cream.

Naomi would have to save examining the peculiar selection of inventory for later. She was twenty-two minutes late for her job interview, and the uncharacteristic tardiness was giving her palpitations. After a quick lap through the deserted store confirmed that she was alone, dread threaded up her spine like ascending black keys on an out-of-tune piano.

What if this awful first impression lost her the job? Or, worse, what if the potential client had deemed her a no-show and moved on to the next prospect? Naomi leveled her gaze on a particularly stern-looking brown Jesus in a bid to calm her shivering heart. She tried to rally, to "pull herself up by the bootstraps" as her step-father would say, as she had countless times before.

But she couldn't ignore the whisper of doubt in the back of her mind, not when it was as persistent as the smell of dust and cardboard lingering on the shelves around her. Not when, after recently starting her own brand consulting business, staying afloat hinged on securing a new client.

This client.

Competition was fierce in Kelowna, with larger firms looking to capitalize on the popular tourist destination's many gentrification efforts. Naomi couldn't afford to let anything slide through her fingers; there was no room for anything less than perfection, not at this crucial point in her career. Naomi hastily swiped her forearm across her forehead, her eyes widening when she saw the thin residue of sweat on the cuff of her sleeve. She needed to get a hold of herself. She couldn't fall apart now, not when she was two rent payments away from dragging her ass back to—

A light tinkling at the back of the room distracted Naomi from what she was sure were the beginnings of her first-ever anxiety attack. The welcome noise was punctuated by a sharp sneeze and unintelligible muttering.

Curious, Naomi ducked behind a tower of ladies' stockings—*Now with lifting action!*—and peered around the side. A South Asian lady stood behind the cash register, her back to Naomi, impatiently untangling a beaded curtain of seashells and tiny brass bells that hung from a doorframe. She appeared to be losing the battle as one of the bells slipped off the string and skittered across the floor.

"Bah!" The lady scoffed, relinquishing the tangled strings with a dramatic flick of her wrist so they clattered mockingly in return. She turned to crouch behind the cash register.

It wasn't the ideal time to make an impression—never mind a tardy one at that—but being caught lurking behind control-top pantyhose was a much worse fate. Naomi smoothed the front of her blazer in an attempt to smother the flutter of nerves flapping snow angels in her stomach. Meeting new clients always filled her with a roiling mixture of adrenaline and uncertainty. If she was going to overhaul a family's livelihood, she needed them to like her. And trust her. She needed her clients to forget that she was a relatively new name in the brand consulting field, to see past the snug cut of her gray blazer that, while a little tight over the shoulders, had been forty percent off and too good to pass up.

Naomi pressed her shoulders back, pasted a polite smile on her face, and headed to the counter. At the sound of her approaching footsteps, the woman stood slowly. Her dark brown eyes flicked to Naomi's hands and, finding them empty, moved over her blazer with suspicion.

Silently reassuring herself that she'd removed her jacket's clearance sale tag long ago, Naomi stuck out her hand. "Hi, I'm Nao—"

"I don't need life insurance."

"Wait, pardon me?"

"Whatever you're selling, I'm not interested." The woman's hands fluttered like a flock of agitated birds.

"But I'm Naomi Kelly."

Unimpressed, the lady glanced at Naomi's hand, still outstretched in midair, before meeting her gaze again with zero recognition on her face. The edges of Naomi's hastily stitched confidence began to fray.

"I'm here for my interview with the owners?" Naomi's voice faltered, and she lowered her hand slowly. "The Musas recommended me?"

Silence.

"A woman named Aashi arranged this meeting?"

When the woman's lips pursed, Naomi's mind made frantic

leaps and bounds through her memory; this *was* Gia's Bazaar, right? She'd read the sign outside correctly, hadn't she?

"I'm the brand consultant," Naomi blurted out.

"Oh! The Brand Lady!"

Brand Lady? Naomi tried not to wince as the woman assessed her again with narrowed eyes.

"You are not what I expected. 'Kelly' is not an Indian name, but you look South Asian."

Naomi managed to hold on to her smile before it pulled into a grimace. She was all too familiar with where this was going. If it wasn't "But where do you come from *really*?" from Canadians who could trace their family trees to settler times, it was people of color wanting to know where she belonged, the depth of her cultural roots. It had been bad enough bearing such scrutiny in her small, homogenous hometown, but the city of Kelowna was much larger and contained a sizable South Asian community by comparison. Here, curiosity barreled in from both sides. Naomi had been fielding questions since moving here four years ago, but she had learned, rather quickly, that there were right and wrong answers.

The South Asians in Kelowna were, for the most part, a formidable group: educated, traditional, proud of their roots, and wealthy, with many of them working white-collar jobs or owning one or more lucrative businesses. They didn't look too highly on those who didn't share the same values, and Naomi—the result of an unplanned pregnancy of a high school dropout who had fled her family and Bengali community for a rural, predominantly white town—did not represent the Indo-Canadian dream to which they aspired for their children. Her mother had never bothered to attain her GED; her white stepfather was a plumber. Naomi, at least, had gone to college but a technical one and, to a community that valued careers in STEM, there were very few bragging rights attached to her marketing management diploma.

Luckily, Naomi had long ago perfected the art of dodging questions about her past. "I get that a lot."

"I'm familiar with a lot of South Asian families in this area, but I don't recognize you. Do you live around here? Are you related to the Vissanjis? Are you West Indian?"

They always tried to place her.

"I'm from Alberta," Naomi replied, her voice as bland and harmless as low-fat vanilla yogurt. "I don't have any family here." It wasn't the entire truth, but it was usually enough to deter follow-up questions. In Naomi's experience, the South Asians of British Columbia were not too invested in the goings-on of her prairie province, thank goodness. But when the woman squinted at her appraisingly, Naomi rushed to add, "I'm looking for the owner, Aashi?"

The lady, although several inches shorter than Naomi's five feet, four inches, drew herself upward and lifted her chin so her weighty stare came from high above. "No, this is my store. I am Gia Mukherjee." As an afterthought, she raised her hands in front of her breastbone and pressed her palms together in a traditional Hindu greeting, but there was no warmth there. "I had my sister call you because she said she had heard of someone who could help the store. But from what she told me, I expected someone familiar with our community. Someone with more . . . experience."

Naomi's jaw clenched. The South Asians in Kelowna were a tight-knit circle and—for many reasons—Naomi was very much an outsider. And reminded of this fact all too often. But she refused to allow such a weak excuse affect her career. And even though most of the products in the store were unfamiliar to her, the desire to walk out didn't materialize. Instead, her spine reared upward in response. *This lady doesn't know you. Prove her wrong.*

It was time for the pitch she'd practiced for hours in the mirror—the one that always earned her at least a glimmer of respect at networking events and job interviews.

"I've been working as a brand consultant for over four years. Most of my previous work has been as one of the top-performing consultants with Adams and Ridge Solutions; however, I recently started my own company to connect with small business owners—"

"So you've never worked with a store like this before."

Startled by the interruption, Naomi shut her mouth and forced herself to smile. Forget the pitch, it seemed that the first order of business would be to win this passive-aggressive tennis match.

"Your sister seemed plenty impressed by my experience when she called me to set up this interview," Naomi said, dousing her voice in syrupy sweetness.

"I haven't heard your name before." A hard backhand.

Naomi lifted her chin—she knew her way around the court. "Really? That's surprising—I completed the Musa family's rebrand. Perhaps you just didn't know it was my work?"

Her opponent's eyes widened, and the arrogance on her face dropped a notch. "Oh?"

Naomi readied herself for an epic overhead smash: "Are you familiar with their store, Soul Cloth?"

At Gia's small nod of acknowledgment, Naomi could hear the applause thundering against her eardrums. Match point.

Gia might not have been aware that Soul Cloth was Naomi's handiwork, but the store's transformation from overstuffed, synthetic fabric store to ethically sourced African arts and crafts emporium spoke for itself. Located one door over from Gia's Bazaar, the family-owned store now thrived on steady foot traffic.

Thanks to Naomi, the Musas were one of the handful of business owners who had survived the gentrification sweeping through many of the older neighborhoods in Kelowna. Not all businesses in the strip mall housing Gia's Bazaar and Soul Cloth had held their ground, though: the Liu family had been the first to flee, a gourmet cheese shop now stood where the old halal meat market had been, and Deol Jewelers had migrated south in search of more affordable pastures. Hipster money was rolling in, and old businesses were shuffling out. Gia was late to the game, but from the way the owner was assessing Naomi now, it was clear she wanted a piece of the action.

And so did Naomi. She needed a big win, and soon, if the pile of overdue notices stuffed into her desk drawer had anything to say about it. Perhaps it had been too impulsive of her to do the Musas' rebrand at cost, an ill-conceived attempt by a twenty-six-year-old bleeding heart to give a struggling family a chance in Kelowna's changing economy.

But she could never regret the decision to take a pay cut to help them fulfill their dreams.

The warm, balmy weather might have lured Naomi to Kelowna, but it was the sea of colorful faces, each one with a different story to tell, that had convinced her to stay. Providing the Musas with the opportunity to keep their culture, and their livelihood, alive in the community was well worth six more months of ramen and scrambled eggs.

"Have you worked with the South Asian community before?" Gia asked.

Naomi hesitated, aware that she should tread with caution. "This would be my first time."

Although she was still finding her footing in Kelowna, Naomi was determined to make a name for herself. She didn't really have any other choice—unless she wanted to return to her parents' home, tail tucked between her legs, proving to her mother that trying to make her own way among a community that would reject her was indeed a mistake.

She'd choke down a *year's* worth of bargain-bin canned food to avoid that.

"Most of my customers are South Asian," Gia said. "It's important to me to retain them. Are you familiar with the products we carry?"

"Not all of them, but I'm a fast learner. I didn't know much about the Musas, and I was able to capture their vision for them." Casually, Naomi moved her left hand behind her back and crossed her fingers, as if the childish habit made up at all for the half-truths she was spouting now. Sure, Mr. Musa's natural interest in collecting African artifacts and art had easily lent itself to the redesign of the now-popular store, but there was no way his family would've gotten to that lucrative point without Naomi's help.

"Is three months enough time?" Gia asked.

Yes. Everything in Naomi eased as a bolt of confidence puffed into her chest. She'd done it. The Musas had been the perfect drop shot, her secret weapon to winning the game. "Of course," she replied, tucking her gloat away for later. Maybe she'd even splurge on cheap sparkling juice and pretend it was champagne. "Three months is more than enough time to develop a business concept to turn things around, no proble—"

"No. Three months to complete the job. My store has been quiet long enough; I'd like to reopen in three months." Gia cocked an eyebrow. "Besides, if you are as *capable* as you say you are . . ."

Frissons of sharp, hot panic crept up Naomi's neck. *Three months?* Even at her previous corporate brand-consulting job, where funds, resources, and labor had been endless and at her disposal, three months was a minuscule amount of time. It was a sliver of what Gia's Bazaar would need, if the fine layer of dust coating everything around them was any indication. But did she really have a choice? Since the Musas' rebrand—which she had completed over a month ago—Naomi had lured exactly zero new business. The market was too hot right now, Kelowna too connected.

Small business owners might be fighting to stay afloat, but they wanted established consultants, larger PR firms with a contingent of guarantees attached to their name. Or, worse, they wanted something—or *someone*—familiar to guide them into the capitalistic death match.

Naomi examined the firm set of Gia's lips. She might share the color of Gia's skin, but she was a stranger to the older South Asian woman. A nobody.

"Three months," Naomi repeated. She nodded once. Twice. "I can do it." On her third, forceful nod, she received a stroke of genius and hastened to add, "But a condensed timeline will cost you more than the fees your sister and I discussed."

"As long as I am satisfied with the results, I have no problem with that."

At Gia's easy acceptance, the demands started to spill forth. "I'll need full access to the store according to my schedule."

"Okay."

"And you'll need to close down the store so we can expedite the work."

"No problem."

It *sounded* like a win, but Naomi's shoulders slumped forward. Under any other circumstances, she would have been thrilled to have received such a quick succession of agreements. Yet the tilt of Gia's chin, the barely there lift of her left eyebrow . . . Naomi felt like she was gambling with candy at a high-stakes table in Vegas. Gia, and perhaps Naomi, too, had made this rebrand about something more than understanding the market and making sound business decisions. Bets had been placed and there was no way Naomi was going to fold.

She couldn't.

There was little time for celebration, however empty it felt, because Gia suddenly shook her head. "I'm still interviewing candidates," she said. Naomi couldn't hide her sharp intake of breath. "But I'd like to see your plan for the store this Friday at nine o'clock *sharp*." She angled her head meaningfully, alerting Naomi that her tardiness had not gone unnoticed. "Then I will decide who will be rebranding my bazaar."

"Friday it is," Naomi said. It was tempting to stick her hand out and shake on it; however, the potential for embarrassment should Gia ignore the gesture again had Naomi gripping the handle of her purse instead. The faux leather squeaked in her hand's sweaty grip.

Ignoring the faint ringing of alarm bells in her head, Naomi switched her bag to her other hand and attempted a self-assured, trustworthy grin. "I'm going to *dazzle* you," she added.

Gia's lips quirked in a fleeting smile that was anything but trusting. "Friday it is."

chapter
2

"Dev, asho na!"

Dev Mukherjee gritted his teeth from where he sat propped against his bed frame with his laptop and glared at the ceiling above him. His mother had called for him twice already, her voice growing shriller each time. Her growing neediness wafted through the floorboards, thick and pungent like pan-fried cumin.

Lately, every corner of the house seemed to reek of it.

Moving back to his childhood home after his father's passing had made so much sense eight months ago: his mother had been grateful for his company, his employers had agreed to him working remotely, and he was no longer surrounded by jovial flip-flop-footed tourists of Penticton, jacked up on warm weather and wine while toting their sand-filled clutter around town. Granted, the tourist situation in Kelowna wasn't much better, but at least people here were realistic, downtrodden by the rising cost of living.

However, since secretly quitting his job as a senior manager of a prestigious firm's tax division six weeks ago, his convenient, rent-free living situation had lost most of its luster.

"Dev! Come upstairs!" his mother's voice called again from above.

Frustration climbed Dev's spine. The first few months after his father's death had been distracting, for both Dev and his mother, Gia. While he had been busy tying up loose ends, his mother had been a social butterfly: volunteering to babysit her granddaughters, accepting dinner invitations from her friends, embarking on touristy adventures organized by her sister, Aashi.

But once the desire for distractions had passed, Gia's grief had turned inward, and her home became a protective nest. Now she rarely left, preferring to host friends and family in the comfort of her well-worn slippers. When she wasn't socializing, she was summoning Dev at multiple intervals of the day to force-feed him curry, ask what he was doing, and request his company for a never-ending marathon of Bollywood movies.

Her loneliness sought him out every day.

"Devdas!" Gia's voice was reaching the edges of a hysterical pitch that, during his childhood, was often punctuated by a half-hearted whack from a wooden spoon. And even though he was now a grown man, he wouldn't put it past Gia to whoop his thirty-one-year-old ass. Dev didn't bother saving the findings of his fruitless job search before pushing his computer aside.

Following the rich aroma of chai, Dev entered the kitchen to find his mother, Aashi, and another older Desi woman sitting at the kitchen table. They all stared at him like predators in various stages of the hunt: Aashi sparkled with anticipation, the stranger examined him shrewdly, and his mother was self-assured, ready for the kill.

Dev's footsteps slowed to the tentative shuffle of a fawn in an open field.

"Dev, this is Veera Auntie." Gia gestured for him to take the seat beside Aashi, which positioned him in prime staring-contest position with the newcomer.

"Namashkar, auntie," Dev murmured, inclining his head respectfully. The standard greeting fell from his lips, always at the ready for the many nonrelated aunties and uncles parading through his mother's home. "Kamon acho?"

"Oh no, son," Veera responded in English. She waved off his inquiry of how she was doing with a hearty chuckle and opened the folder in front of her to jot down a few notes. "I do not speak Bengali. But that was very courteous. Well done." She turned to nod her approval at a beaming Gia. "Well done, indeed."

"He is a good boy," Gia said with a proud smile. "Very well-mannered."

Veera nodded again, her pen flying across the page.

What the shit? Dev threw a panicked look at Aashi, the only adult in the room he could rely on as an ally. She blithely smiled back.

No help there.

His mother clapped her hands together, the gold bangles lining her wrists clinking together with excitement. "Veera is a matchmaker..."

Oh no.

"...for you, son!" Gia threw her hands above her head as if the idea had come from the heavens directly. Veera nodded, confirming her role in this divine intervention.

The fires of hell might as well swallow him whole right now. "Why?" Dev asked, hiding his clenched fists beneath the table.

Gia looked at him, eyebrows drawn tight. "It's high time you thought about marriage."

He'd already thought about marriage, *had* thought about it for a long time: after a lifetime of seeing the Desi community's version of wedded bliss, Dev had decided long ago that marriage was not for him. He didn't want a wife, preapproved by his mother—and the community—based on a list of attributes that were more about social obligation and status than love. Nor did he wish to risk the alternative of going against the grain, as many a friend of a friend of a friend had by choosing to marry someone outside their family's accepted standards, being looked down upon as a result, and forever whispered about behind steaming cups of chai and butter biscuits.

He'd rather be alone.

"I don't need a matchmaker," Dev said. "I can find someone on my own." Dev didn't add that finding a wife was the last item on his priority list, penciled in some place after dying.

As if on cue, the three women threw back their heads and cackled, reminding Dev of the three witches his grade-eleven English class had read about in *Macbeth*. He felt like his sixteen-year-old self, too: powerless and at the mercy of meddling adults. It was a feeling that had never entirely disappeared, part and parcel of being a respectful and dutiful Bengali son.

"Men never think they need a matchmaker!" Veera laughed. "Never!"

"Don't worry, Dev," Aashi said. "We will find you a nice girl."

"No, I don't—"

"What kinds of things do you want in a match, Dev?" Veera eyed him over the rim of her wire-framed glasses.

"Educated," Gia answered for him. "And Hindu."

"Nurturing," Aashi chimed in.

"Not too tall." Gia nodded in Dev's direction. "Definitely not taller than him."

"But not too short. We want tall grandchildren," Aashi added.

"And from a good, respectable family," Gia finished.

Because God forbid his future wife be considered on her own

as an individual. Lineage was as important to his mother as thoroughly rinsing the grains of basmati rice she served with almost every meal.

"Do you want a Bengali bride?" Veera asked as her pen frantically scratched across the paper.

Dev tried again. "No, I—"

"I agree with Dev," Gia interrupted, nodding her approval. "A Bengali girl would be great, but Dev would like any *good* Indian girl. I'm open-minded to my future daughter-in-law."

Dev choked back a scoff. As far as his tradition-loving, stubborn mother went, that was as open-minded as she got.

"Radius?" Veera asked.

"*What?*" Dev craned his neck, trying to get a glimpse of Veera's scribblings.

"Well, of course we want a girl with a nice figure," Gia said.

"No, no." Veera shook her head. "I have clients from all over the province." She paused to wink at Dev. "I'm *that* good. Do you care where she's from?"

"Someone local or from one of the surrounding areas," Gia replied firmly. "I want Dev to settle down nearby."

Aashi tapped her finger against her chin. "But most important, she should be kindhearted. Dev is the cool type, he needs someone warm."

Dev shot his aunt a look. "I'm not 'the cool type.'" He turned to his mother. "I'm not looking to get married, Mom."

Gia rolled her eyes at the matchmaker. "You're not getting any younger, Devdas. Your older brother is married, now it is your turn. Do you want people to think there's something wrong with you?"

At the Mukherjee family's catchphrase, Dev dropped stony eyes to the table's plastic-covered, green gingham tablecloth. He had been silenced with "what people think" his entire life, had been swayed too many times by his parents' concern for the larger South Asian community's opinion about everything under the sun. So entrenched were his parents in maintaining appearances, Dev had never figured out how to turn them away from such a stupid and superficial argument.

And yet he was part of the problem, wasn't he? His father had been a renowned surgeon who had demanded excellence from his family: Gia, for her part, had been an obedient wife, always at the ready to propel her husband's career forward. At their parents' insistence, Dev's older brother had become a mechanical engineer, and his younger brother was currently in law school. Dev was no different: he had curtailed his goal to pursue an MBA for an accounting designation instead because tax accountants were more desirable in the business community. More credible as far as designations in business went.

And boring as hell.

"Thirty-one is a little old," Veera confirmed. "But he is an accountant, and his father was a surgeon. Those are very attractive qualities. He has nice hair, is trim, pleasing face . . ." She lowered her voice conspiratorially. "He's a good height compared to most clients. Taller than average, but not so big that the girl should worry about her wedding night."

If that particular pitch was meant to sell him on the matchmaking scheme, Veera was failing. To his horror, both his mother and his aunt turned to him with new, critical eyes. God only knew what they were thinking.

"I'm not interested in meeting a wife," he snapped. *Ever.*

Gia clicked her tongue. "You're always so grumpy about everything. No woman wants a bad-tempered old man for a husband. Try to be charming, for goodness' sake."

"Listen, Dev." Aashi placed a reassuring hand on his arm. "Don't think of this as coercion into marriage." Dev swallowed a skeptical snort. "Try to see this as an opportunity to meet new people. You don't have to say yes to the first girl you meet. We're just asking you to try something new."

Had he been alone with his aunt, Dev might have revealed his desire to never marry, to avoid following in his parents' footsteps at all costs. And his aunt, who was twelve years younger than his mother and the only parental figure he felt close to, would listen. And maybe respect his opinion, even though she likely wouldn't agree.

But one look at his mother, whose eyes burned with the flames of the matrimonial fire on his wedding day, confirmed that his confession would bear no weight in this conversation.

"It is every mother's dream to see her sons settled into happy unions," Gia said, clutching a fist to her chest, as Dev was sure she'd seen in many Bollywood dramas. "I will help my son any way I know how."

"And I think it will be very easy to keep an open mind about these girls," Veera assured him, waving a fat pink folder in his direction before pushing it toward Gia.

Gia's eyes widened in delight as she began sorting through what appeared to be a collection of résumés. Her hands flew as she began muttering first impressions, more to herself than the other three people in the room who watched in silence. "Too plain. Crooked nose. Oh, very cute! Wonderful lineage. Too skinny . . ." Gia was ruthless as she sorted pictures into three piles like a seasoned farmer might sort melons.

Dev gaped, but Veera nodded as if Gia's methodology—"too tall for Dev. Too busty. Divorced at twenty-eight, my goodness!"— made perfect sense. Aashi, the supposed voice of reason, didn't comment as she listened with interest. Dev's heart sank as the sound of profiles shuffling into place foretold his fate.

"Mom, this is ridiculous," Dev said.

"What's ridiculous is this makeup," Gia said, holding a photo up for her sister to see. "There's something about a girl with this much powder that I do not trust."

"Mom—"

"Dev, relax," Gia said with a careless wave of her hand. "You can trust me."

"These Canadian-born children often forget that parents know best," Veera said, adjusting her sari as she stood up. Despite her petite frame, she had a commanding presence, which Dev guessed was instrumental for forcing people down the marriage aisle.

"Send me a text of which girls you'd like Dev to meet," she instructed, shouldering a large purse before gathering her folders.

"It's so much better when these profiles offer a full-body shot," Gia commented, squinting at a profile in her hand.

"I encourage all my clients do so, but for some reason, many of them decline," Veera answered with a shrug as Aashi escorted her out of the room.

Dev eyed his too-cheerful mother as she continued sifting through the profiles Veera had left her. His entire life, he had witnessed his parents adhering to baffling cultural beliefs he would never fully understand. In his opinion, their traditions were as tired and dusty as the suitcases they had used to emigrate from India to Canada thirty-seven years ago; it was unwanted baggage, yet another thing on a long list of what had made him different from the kids at school.

While his classmates had hustled off to hockey practice and sleepovers after school, Dev had been expected home to study, eat a family dinner, and then complete extra-credit work, which, given his private-school education, was always an option. The world his parents surrounded him with—tutors, friendships with other Desi children with like-minded parents, the newest laptop model—was all to get ahead, to rise above something Dev never quite understood. The white kids at school never seemed concerned about such things, even those from more conservative families. But everything in Dev's life siphoned back to his parents' upbringing, to a country they'd left behind but could never forget.

This matchmaking scheme, though, was on a whole new level of weird and old-fashioned. And with or without his mother's knowledge, Dev was determined to put a stop to it.

Abruptly, he stood and moved to his mother's side, pulling the folder away from her and snapping it shut. "I'm not interested in being set up for marriage."

Gia's sigh overflowed with impatience. "We talked about this, Dev."

Dev scoffed. Not even at gunpoint would he call what had transpired in front of Veera Auntie a conversation. But rational conversation, where everyone had their say and weighed each other's arguments, wasn't a Mukherjee family strength.

"Just give it a try," Aashi added, coming back into the room. "After all, your mother and I *both* had arranged marriages, and look how our lives turned out."

Dev knew she was talking about the wealth and comfort they had found after years of struggling as immigrants in a new country whose snow-covered mountains were as foreign to them as seeing a sex shop nestled between a Subway and a used bookstore. For people like Gia and Aashi, marriage had been the life raft for them to embark on such a journey, to wade into uncharted waters and start a new life.

But as far as Dev could remember, the marriage between his parents was fraught with a peculiar tension, something he could never find in after-school programming or the family unit in his elementary social studies textbook. He had never seen his parents kiss or show any kind of affection. They just lived together, a family bound by efficiency and obligation and the shared understanding that tradition was the be-all and end-all.

It was a life Dev would never willingly choose for himself. But how could he explain this to his mother, especially when she turned large, expectant eyes to him and said, "Yes, Dev. Please try. Who knows how much more time I have? I want to see you settled."

Dev sighed. If he was going to usurp her ridiculous plans, he would have to resort to the tried-and-tested method he imagined most first-generation offspring relied on to circumvent their parents' expectations: secrecy and scheming.

"If I agree to give this a try, will you butt out?" Dev laid his hands flat on the tabletop and tried to look complacent.

"Oh, of course, of course," his mother answered. "It is, after all, *your* choice in wife."

"Okay, good—"

"But keep in mind," Gia added with a narrowed glance. "She must be good enough to be *my* daughter-in-law."

"*Didi.*" Aashi cut in as her eyes darted to where Dev's hands were curling into fists. "How did interviews with the brand consultants go?"

Gia shrugged. "It was all right. Some stood out more than others."

"Did you meet the girl I called? Naomi Kelly?"

Dev watched his mother's face shrivel with disapproval. He'd seen that face many times before: when he received anything less than an A in school or when an auntie opted for a daringly low-cut blouse to pair with her sari at a traditional event, Gia's face pinched tight like a raisin.

"I don't know what you were thinking with that one," she scoffed. "I'm not sure she has what it takes for my bazaar. And has no one ever taught her not to argue with her elders?"

Aashi's eyes widened. "She seemed so sweet on the phone. Did you find anyone you'd like to hire?"

"Not yet. I asked two of them to present their ideas on Friday so I can decide who would be the best person for the job. Which reminds me," Gia said, turning to Dev, "I have to babysit the girls tomorrow, so I need you to mind the store."

Dev's eyebrows lifted at the news. He hadn't realized his mother had reopened the bazaar. When his father had suffered a stroke, Gia had closed it down to provide round-the-clock care for his rapidly decreasing health. And she hadn't seemed too interested in picking things back up after his passing.

"Mind the store?" Although he hadn't stepped foot in the bazaar for several years, he doubted it was a hot spot of activity. "Mind the store for . . . customers?"

Gia huffed. "You could do some dusting and tidying."

"Is it too much trouble for you to take a day off work, Dev?" Aashi asked sympathetically.

Using work as an excuse would be an easy way out of a task that Dev would rather shave his face with a chipped, rusted straight razor than do. But he couldn't bring himself to outright lie to them. He had hidden many smaller things from them in the past, but leaving his lucrative, respectable career as a tax accountant at a large, corporate firm was not a minor, forgettable event, like quietly dating a non–South Asian while knowing she would never meet his family.

His parents had played a large role in navigating his career path; the desire to change lanes would not be welcomed with open arms. Especially when he was *still* unemployed. And mooching off his mother.

Besides, Dev was the one his mother counted on. The one who *everyone* counted on. It was the consequence of having a less-than-stellar social life, he supposed.

"Yeah, sure," he said. "I'll mind the store."

When Gia beamed, Dev cringed. It was a smile he was all too familiar with, one he'd seen every time her children bent to her will. *She's grieving*, Dev reminded himself. *She needs your help*.

"That's my son," his mother said, flipping the pink matchmaking folder back open. "Now, let's get back to business."

chapter 3

As Naomi reached the front entrance of Gia's Bazaar, she paused to glance down at her outfit. Buttoned or unbuttoned, her black blazer looked stiff and uptight paired with her second-favorite pair of dress pants. Usually Naomi opted for something more comfortable and lived-in for on-site research for prospective clients—something that was easy to move in so she could dive into unearthing a business's hidden gems. But since her disastrous first meeting with Gia, Naomi couldn't shake the doubt lingering in her mind. Or Gia's cold, skeptical gaze.

Relax. You don't look like you sell insurance, she reassured herself. Since leaving the bazaar the day before, Naomi had been indulging in a lot of silent pep talks. She had two days to come up with an idea that would blow Gia away, and if she didn't come up with something soon, she was at risk of running out of empty platitudes to reassure herself.

Under normal circumstances, Naomi would have brainstormed a whole list of ideas to use as jumping-off points for the owners to help create a vision for their business. But that wouldn't hold up this time, not if Naomi was in direct competition with another brand consultant. She needed an idea to end all ideas—a proposal with the power to stock her fridge for the next few months and keep the creditors at bay. She needed an idea that would clean-sweep the podium and bring a tear to Gia's eye. No, not just a tear. She wanted Gia to *weep* at her genius.

Much to Naomi's delight, Gia's Bazaar was deserted again, and the intimidating owner was nowhere in sight. After all the guarantees she'd made the day before, if she could conduct her research entirely unnoticed, all the better. Her conscience couldn't handle any more half-truths or attempts at faking a confidence that was barely skin-deep.

As if she could leave her guilt at the door, Naomi jogged toward the cash register and surveyed the store. The aisles were jam-packed with miscellaneous items as far as the eye could see. Where should she even start?

At the familiar tinkling of the beaded curtain behind her, Naomi whipped around, ready for a rematch with Gia. Instead, she found herself face-to-face with a tall, broad-shouldered guy staring back at her in surprise. Even though he looked a bit droll, assessing her presence with a rainbow feather duster hanging from his hand, he commanded her attention. He was gorgeous, if a person was into the tall, dark, and brooding type.

Which Naomi definitely was.

Like Gia the day before, his eyes immediately dropped to her hands. And just like then, when he found them empty, he looked at her with suspicion. It was a terrible sense of déjà vu.

"Hi," Naomi said, powerless against both the flirty smile spreading across her face and her hand reaching forward.

He scowled in return and made no move to return the handshake. "Not interested." Naomi's hands flew to clutch the lapels of her jacket; she had known the blazer was a mistake.

"Excuse me?"

"I'm not sure what you were told, but I'm not looking for any-one right now." His voice was deep and velvety, reminding Naomi of tangled sheets before sunrise.

Naomi shook her head, confused. "I'm sorry, who are you?"

The guy rolled his eyes. "Dev Mukherjee."

Realization sank through Naomi, dragging her bones down-ward. He looked like he might be related to Gia—her son, maybe. They shared the same dark chocolate eyes, unsweetened and hard. Had Gia sent Dev in to tell her she was no longer being considered for the redesign?

Maybe she had changed her mind and was sending this ran-dom guy to do her dirty work.

"I'm sorry you wasted your time," he continued, gesturing at her carefully chosen ensemble. "I can tell you take this whole thing very seriously. But you shouldn't have bothered."

This whole thing. As if she could just abandon her desire to win the contract to the bazaar. As if it were no big deal. Naomi set her jaw. "I was under the impression you would give me a chance to prove myself."

"Forget everything you've been told. It's not going to work out."

Dev braced his hands on the countertop, his exasperation clear. The lines of muscle curving up his tense forearms did little to distract Naomi from her growing indignation. It was one thing to lose a job, but to be dismissed so rudely by a surly stranger with a serious lack of social skills?

Even Naomi had her limits.

"But your mother told me she'd give me a shot!"

"Are you seriously playing the mother card?" Condescension

dripped from Dev's full lower lip. "Will all of you be this determined? Because, just a tip, guys don't respond to desperation."

"Desperation?" Naomi repeated, her voice rising. A hot rush of shame and anger burst through her, burning her professional composure into a crisp. It was clear that this guy had never had his credit card declined at the grocery store.

"I'm *not* desperate," she said, even though she totally was. "But I might be the best fit."

"That sounds pretty presumptuous of you."

"Did your mother tell you to be rude to me? Is this some kind of test?"

Dev narrowed his eyes in response. "Look, I'm sorry if you've been making the rounds and no one's taking the bait—"

"The bait!" Naomi squeaked.

"Sorry," he said, holding his hands up, looking more defensive than contrite. "That was a poor choice of words. I'm sure your résumé is great and you have a ton of attractive qualities. And you're certainly nice to look at—"

Naomi looked down at her outfit in confusion. "What?"

Dev continued as if she hadn't spoken. "But I'm just being straight with you. You're not what I'm looking for."

There it was. Gia was sticking to her ludicrous list of criteria and had decided to cut Naomi loose. All of Naomi's fears bubbled to the surface, sour and hot: somehow Gia had gleaned that she wasn't South Asian enough for her tastes. When it came down to value, Naomi's qualifications, previous success, and passion for the job would never measure up to what she lacked.

Thank goodness she hadn't told Gia that she, too, was Bengali. Although it was a card that Naomi *always* kept close to her chest, somehow she knew that this rejection would have hurt a lot more if Gia knew about her cultural heritage. Especially since, other than knowing that her grandparents had emigrated from India forever ago, Naomi's mother had chosen to keep all knowledge of language, culture, and family traditions to herself.

Despite the disappointment simmering in her chest, Naomi swallowed the many choice words dying to land a knockout punch. She couldn't afford to make a scene even though she suspected nothing would feel better than to put Dev Mukherjee in his place. She would find another way to impress Gia, with or without researching the bazaar, because come hell or high water, Naomi was determined to present an outstanding idea on Friday.

Naomi settled for a dark glare before turning on her heel and storming toward the exit.

She was almost at the door when it swung open and a cheerful-looking lady bounced in.

"Are you Naomi? My goodness, you are even prettier in person!" She grabbed Naomi's hand and pumped it in an enthusiastic handshake. "I'm Aashi."

Hopped up on adrenaline, Naomi couldn't do much more but hold on to Aashi's hand for dear life.

"Give it a rest, Mashi," Dev called from the register.

Without releasing Naomi's hand, Aashi turned to Dev and raised her eyebrows. "Give what a rest? I've wanted to meet Naomi in person for a while now."

Naomi shook her head, confused. "Wait. I thought your name was *Aashi*," she said to the woman whose hand she clutched.

"Oh, Mashi is what all my sister's sons call me," Aashi explained. "It's a cultural thing."

"Right, of course," Naomi croaked, her hand growing clammy under Aashi's strong grip.

Luckily, neither Aashi nor Dev noticed her blunder. "Did Mom come up with that backstory or did you?" Dev asked his aunt.

"Backstory?" Aashi frowned. "Why would I need a backstory?"

"You only read her profile yesterday," Dev said, shaking his head in irritation.

"Yesterday? What are you talking about? I interviewed Naomi last week . . ." Aashi trailed off and burst into laughter. She *still* hadn't let go of Naomi's hand, forcing Naomi to stand awkwardly beside her as the other woman's entire body thrummed with unrepressed mirth. But it was a small price to pay when Naomi caught a glimpse of Dev's face.

He looked mortified. His mouth flapped open and closed a few times, not unlike a voiceless sock puppet, before he finally mumbled something in a foreign language.

A rapid-fire exchange occurred between Aashi and Dev for a few long seconds before Aashi started laughing again. This time, though, she pulled Naomi into a hug.

"Oh my goodness," Aashi chortled into Naomi's shoulder. "Did he try to fire you? I'm so sorry for my nephew, don't mind him. He mistook you for—"

"*Mashi!*" Dev said sharply.

Aashi's grin was wicked. "He mistook you for someone else." She giggled and wiped her eyes.

As her world righted itself, Naomi stole a glance at Dev, who, to her delight, looked ready to crawl into a dark hole and die. Good. Served him right.

Turning back to Aashi, Naomi nodded as she tried to gather her wits. "I'm so pleased to meet you." And she was. Even though her nerves were still frazzled, everything about Aashi warmed Naomi's soul, from her easy smile and lingering laughter to her reassuring grip as she tugged Naomi toward the cash register.

"This is my nephew Dev." Aashi's impish smile was back. "But I guess you've already met."

Dev let out a strangled groan. Buoyed by Aashi's energy and the relief that she was still in the running to rebrand the store, Naomi managed a weak smile. When Dev stared back sullenly, she reached for something—anything—to temper the lingering tension between them.

"So you work here?" she asked.

"No."

"Oh, so you pitch in every once in a while."

"Not really."

"Do you help out with the store in any way?"

"Nope."

They stared at each other in silence. When Naomi realized her cheek muscles were straining to maintain a polite smile, she turned to Aashi, who was watching them with an amused gleam in her eye.

"I wanted to do a bit of research today," Naomi said, more to Aashi than her stoic nephew, "to help me come up with some ideas for the rebrand." When she heard Dev sigh, she quickly added, "Nothing intrusive. You won't even notice I'm here."

"Doubtful," he muttered.

"Nonsense," Aashi said. "We'll be happy to help you poke around, won't we, Dev?"

Silence.

"Come, let's take a walk around," Aashi said, ignoring Dev's lack of enthusiasm. Naomi fell into step beside her, willing herself not to glance back when she heard the rustle of Dev following behind. She could feel his intense gaze boring a hole into her back.

They meandered through aisles of miscellaneous everything, some with English words marked across the packaging, others not. While Aashi kept up a steady stream of chatter, Naomi fought to maintain a poised expression on her face as self-doubt settled in her chest. Whoever won the contract would have to overhaul this place from the inside out, but the piles of neglected products were failing to inspire insight into the bazaar's hidden potential.

Naomi would have to dig. "So, how did Gia come to own the bazaar?" she asked.

"Oh, it's kind of a romantic story, actually." Aashi beamed. "My sister was having a hard time acclimating to living in Canada. This was before they started having kids. I mean, I was here, too, but on a student visa, so I was very preoccupied with my studies. Gia was lonely—"

"Because my dad was obsessed with his surgical career and didn't have time for anything else," Dev interjected in a flat voice from behind them. He was like an umbrella on a sunny day.

"So he bought her the bazaar as a surprise. Something to help pass the time and adjust to her new life."

Naomi cocked her head and reached for a random bottle off the shelf. She couldn't read the writing, but the kid grinning at her from the label suggested that whatever was inside was delicious. "Did it work?"

Aashi nodded while Dev shook his head. Baffled, Naomi-whipped her head between the two of them before settling on Aashi.

"It did, but not in the way it was intended," Aashi explained gently. "Gia didn't care much for sales or business, but it didn't matter. Her husband's income was more than enough for the family. What mattered was that she was one of the only South Asian stores at the time and the Desi community came for the import items from India. She started making friends, practicing English . . . She loved being in the store. It became a haven for her."

Naomi gave the bottle in her hand an experimental shake. It rattled. Pills. "That story *is* kind of romantic," she mused. When

Dev let out a faint grunt in response, she shot him a sideways glance. "So, what happened?"

Aashi hesitated and turned to Dev.

"My dad had a stroke last year, and my mom turned all her energy toward caring for him instead," Dev answered stiffly, his eyes riveted on the bottle in her hand. "The business wasn't turning much of a profit to begin with, so my mom closed shop for almost eleven months. And then, when she reopened after my father's passing, the neighborhood had undergone a one-eighty and the few people who had once frequented the bazaar had moved on."

"It makes sense, I suppose," Aashi mused. "A huge part of the bazaar's lure was Gia. She treated her customers like guests. Like family. When she stopped coming—and the surrounding businesses jumped ship—there was no reason to come down here anymore."

Naomi barely registered Aashi's explanation. She couldn't tear her eyes away from Dev, whose face had remained cool and composed while talking about his father's death. And although nothing about Dev invited physical touch, Naomi found herself resisting the urge to reach out and pat his shoulder or . . . *something*. She tightened her fingers around the bottle instead. "I'm so sorry, Dev."

A shadow flitted across Dev's eyes, and all at once he appeared both vulnerable and distant like a lone blackbird flying across dark gray clouds. His lips parted but before he could respond, a synthesized version of a popular Taylor Swift song sliced through the air.

"Oh, excuse me," Aashi said, reaching into her purse and pulling out a jeweled cell phone case. "That's my eldest's ringtone." With an apologetic nod, she shuffled to the next aisle, phone to her ear.

The moment broken, an uncomfortable silence descended upon Naomi and Dev. Once again, Naomi struggled for something to ease the tension. Normally, the right words—a light joke, a kind compliment—were easy for her to find. However, under the scrutiny of Dev's gaze, she felt rattled.

She settled on jiggling the bottle again. "This kid looks happy," she remarked, turning the label to face Dev. "I wonder what these pills do?"

Dev lifted a dark eyebrow. "You don't know?"

"Should I crack open this bottle and find out?"

Dev eyed the bottle for a long moment before meeting her eyes. "That's Hajmola," he said. "They're all-natural tablets to help with digestion and to control flatulence." Dev's mouth twisted slightly, and the hint of a dimple flickered in his right cheek. "You're welcome to try as many as you want if it'll help you with your research."

The tips of Naomi's ears burned, and she cleared her throat, aware that Dev was watching her every move.

"You've never had Hajmola before?" Dev remarked. "Every brown kid I've ever met has had this jammed down their throat at least a dozen times."

The heat of humiliation slid into cold trepidation. There it was: that subtle reminder that separated her from the likes of Dev and his mother. They were talking about something completely insignificant—a stupid herbal remedy for children—but it was like a bucket of cold water thrown in her face. She was not like them.

Nor was she one of them.

Naomi replaced the bottle on the shelf, shuffling backward when Dev stepped forward to line the bottle up next to the others, as if its placement mattered in a store that hadn't received a single customer since she'd stepped inside.

"My family favored home remedies," she replied, the words sounding empty in her own ears, and she hastened to add a truth to her lie. "Besides, you can't get this product in the small town I'm from."

"Your parents didn't stock up on them whenever they visited home?"

For as long as Naomi had been alive, her mother had never taken her "home"—whether that was the house she grew up in or her family's place of origin. Not even the world's most sought-after meditation retreat could tempt her mother to India. But there was no way Naomi was going to reveal that information to Gia's son. It would be an additional strike against her, yet another reason she was unfit for the job. Turning away from the stomach pills, Naomi pointed toward a folding table and a stack of upholstered chairs pushed into the corner next to the cash register. "What are those for?"

"Gia used to set up a table and a few chairs in that corner every morning," Aashi said, rejoining them as she tucked her phone in her purse. "She'd invite her friends to join her for tea and a snack, which was usually whatever mishti she had made that day."

"*Mishti* means 'dessert' in Bengali," Dev supplied. Naomi waved him off, not wanting to interrupt the picture Aashi was painting.

"So many patrons became loyal customers and friends after tasting those sweets," Aashi chuckled. "And my sister's chai is out of this world. But when my brother-in-law had his stroke and required constant care, the setup was unnecessary. Without Gia here, it's a waste of space." Aashi paused to nudge her nephew. "Remember, Dev?"

"Yeah, there's nothing my mom loves more than gossip and feeding people."

The smile on Aashi's face was wistful. "My sister loves to play hostess." She traded an unreadable glance with Dev before brightening again. "As much as I've loved this trip down memory lane, I have to run and take my daughters to high school orientation. Can you believe fall will be here soon?"

Naomi shifted, resisting the urge to roll her eyes. She'd purposely gone without air-conditioning all summer to cut down on costs, but she would never admit out loud why she was more than ready for a cool autumn breeze to sweep through the city.

"I hope we were able to help you with your research," Aashi continued. "Dev can answer any more questions you have. It was great to meet you in person, Naomi." She paused to give her nephew a pointed look before squeezing Naomi's upper arm. "Good luck."

Naomi bit her lip as she watched Aashi exit the store. A quick glance at the bottle of digestive pills suppressed any urge to put forward further inquiries about the Mukherjees' business. She also wasn't sure how nice Dev would play now that his aunt wasn't in the sandbox.

"I think I'm good for now," she said.

"Did you want me to ring up the Hajmola?" he asked with a straight face.

The cool fabric of Naomi's blazer provided little relief against her heated neck. Oh, she so badly wanted the last word. It was immature and unnecessary, unworthy of the professional standard she held herself to. But the desire to end things in an abrupt, mic-drop kind of way—and throw *him* off-kilter for a change—was strong. Naomi settled for a tight, close-lipped smile before whirling around and making a second attempt at a haughty exit. But just shy of the door, she couldn't resist turning to where Dev had moved back to the cash register and taken the rainbow duster back in hand.

"Dev?"

"Yeah?"

"Who did you think I was when I first walked in?"

He ducked his head and busied himself with quick, jerky sweeps over the counter.

"No one important."

chapter
4

W hy am I here again?" Dev asked as he followed his mother and aunt into the bazaar early Friday morning. Two trips to the bazaar in one week were, in his opinion, two trips too many, and yet he dutifully joined them at the front counter, where Gia surveilled the shop with a critical edge in her eye. Out of his periphery, he noticed Aashi averting her gaze, and his pulse immediately picked up.

"Does a mother need a reason to spend time with her son?" Gia complained.

"Yes."

"For God's sake, Devdas, I'll never understand your strange sense of humor. And do you have to dress like you're on your way to clean out the garage?"

Glancing down at his T-shirt and basketball shorts, Dev bit back a rude retort. His mother had waylaid him on his way to the gym, insisting he come to the store instead. "Would you prefer I hide in the back?"

Gia ignored his sarcastic offer and exchanged a quick glance with her sister. Even though Dev had witnessed their telepathic communications before, something shifted in his gut. "Aashi and I are going upstairs now," Gia said in a robotic voice. "You stay here."

Dev threw his aunt a questioning glance, but she had already made a beeline for the beaded curtain separating the bazaar from a hallway leading upstairs. "Don't worry about how you look," she called over her shoulder. "Just be yourself."

How he looked? Baffled, Dev turned to his mother and gestured at the empty room behind them. "What do you want me to do?"

"Just mind the store," she said impatiently, as if the world were suffering from a shortage of brown Jesus keychains and a mad rush was about to start. "And try to look professional and charming," she added after giving his clothes a defeated look. Like her sister, she bolted after that particularly unhelpful piece of advice.

Dev glowered at her departing back and leaned against the counter. He didn't understand his mother's motivations at the best of times, but this was downright weird. He could hear her furious whispers to Aashi as they made their way up the narrow wooden stairs to the apartment above the store, where he and his brothers had spent many hours of their childhood while their mother worked below. The studio apartment hadn't been used for years.

He was still staring at the beaded curtain, lost in thought, when the entrance opened. Dev turned to find Naomi walking in, an oversized black sketchbook tucked under her arm. She was wearing a stiff-looking blazer again, but underneath she had opted for a soft pink sweater that brought out the rosiness in her cheeks.

Not that he noticed. It was just that she was so . . . Bright. Bright curious eyes, a lit-up smile. Even her annoyance sparked. The way she was bounding over to him now was a ray of sunshine bouncing off ocean waves.

He hated the beach, especially on a sunny day. Too crowded.

"Greetings," she said with a cheerful little wave.

Hyperaware that he looked ready to embark on a thorough garage spring cleaning, Dev scowled. "What are you doing here?"

"Today's my day to present my idea for the store," Naomi replied, gesturing toward the book under her arm. When she realized Dev was staring at her white-knuckled grip around the book's edges, she let out a nervous chuckle. "Are you helping Gia decide which direction to take?"

Dev scratched the back of his neck. Was that why his mother had dragged him here?

Naomi didn't give him a chance to answer as she continued, her voice pitching a notch higher than before. "I know I'm ridiculously early, but I didn't want to take any chances today."

Before Dev could ask what she meant, the entrance swung open again. Both Naomi and Dev turned to see a young woman decked in a bright pink salwar kameez step inside and eye the bazaar curiously. When she spotted Dev at the counter, she straightened the sequined dupatta around her neck before gliding in their direction.

"Dev?" the girl asked. Her voice was as airy and gauzy as the fabric swirling around her legs when she came to a stop before them.

"Uh . . . yeah?"

"I'm Larisa," she said, sticking her hand out with a wide smile. As if on autopilot, Dev reached out and shook it, earning him a narrowed glance from Naomi. "Veera Auntie told me I could find you here."

Dev's eyes widened, and he dropped her hand. Unable to stop himself, he aimed a hard glance at the ceiling above them, where his mother and aunt were likely lying on the floor, ears pressed to the hardwood.

"If you're free, I thought you might like to get a cup of coffee?" Larisa asked, all sugary and sweet despite Dev staring at her as if she had sprouted an extra set of teeth.

"With you?" he blurted out.

Beside them, Naomi let out a strangled cough, and a slow flush climbed his neck. Professional and charming, he was not.

Larisa threw her head back and laughed gaily. "Of course with me, silly!"

Dev threw a panicked look in Naomi's direction. Whatever she read on his face had her taking a small step forward in Larisa's direction.

"Hi, I'm Naomi Kelly," she said to her, also sticking her hand out for a handshake, which Larisa ignored. "I love your outfit."

"Are you . . ." Larisa tilted her head in Dev's direction, traces of her sunny smile fading incrementally. "Are you here to see Dev?"

"Not—"

"Yes." Dev interrupted. When Larisa's eyes narrowed, he nodded frantically.

"Is this the first time you've met?" she asked.

Naomi shook her head. "Uh, no, we've met before, but . . ."

"Sometimes once is all it takes," Dev said, scraping together what he hoped was a fond smile in Naomi's direction. Her eyebrows furrowed in response.

"We don't really know each other, though," she finished.

"But feelings can change," Dev added.

To his ears, his voice sounded hollow and wooden, but understanding dawned on Larisa's face followed by an uncertain frown. "Veera Auntie didn't mention that."

Naomi's brow wrinkled. "Who is—"

"Sorry," Dev said. Awkwardly, he leaned across the counter and placed a rigid hand on Naomi's forearm. Although she stiffened under his touch, she didn't pull away. "She did take me by surprise, but . . ." Dev trailed off and tried to adopt a manly version of smitten.

He'd never felt so foolish in his life. "But I'm really happy to see Naomi again."

Naomi frowned. "You . . . are?"

"Of course," Dev said through gritted teeth. He softened his tone for Larisa. "I'm sorry, but looks like my morning is spoken for."

Larisa's lips twisted to one side. "All right, I see how it is," she said in a clipped tone. In a whirl of pink, she turned on her heel and stalked out.

Once she had vacated the store, Naomi stared incredulously at Dev's hand still resting on her forearm until he let go. "What was that about? Who was that?"

"She was no one impor—" Dev coughed when he realized he had described Naomi in exactly the same way when they'd met.

"Dev?" Naomi prodded when he didn't continue.

Dev scrubbed a hand over his face. Even though matchmaking was not an uncommon occurrence in the community, admitting the truth made his teeth hurt. "My mom hired a matchmaker for me."

"To . . . to find you a girlfriend?"

With a snort, Dev shook his head. "To find me a wife." When Naomi gaped at him, he couldn't tamp down his impatience. "C'mon, you know how brown parents get when their kids reach a certain age." Once a person's education was complete, marriage in the Desi community was as natural a next step in life as a baby's first laugh.

"Of course," Naomi replied quickly. "But you don't want an arranged marriage?"

Dev curbed his tongue before a rude retort could slip past his lips. He remembered that Naomi had grown up in a small town; maybe they did things differently in the boonies. Maybe, without a large population of South Asians gossiping around her, she hadn't grown up with the hot, bitter tang of cultural expectations breathing down her neck.

Still, she hadn't passed judgment on him, or mocked him for being single enough to warrant the need for matchmaking, and for that, at least, he owed her an explanation. "It's not necessarily an arranged marriage," he replied, aware that he was paraphrasing his aunt. "More like a family-led dating service."

"Wow. I didn't even know this kind of thing happened in North America." Naomi shook her head. "Let alone that there are matchmakers in Kelowna!"

"Yeah, well, we want to keep our population afloat."

"I'm guessing your mom didn't check with you before arranging for Larisa to come here? I can't believe she'd do that."

Dev wished he could agree, but Gia Mukherjee had been steamrolling his life since birth.

She, along with his father, had forced him into piano lessons, out of soccer so he could concentrate on his grades, and, when he had received his CPA designation, to accept a job in a firm that happened to be owned by one of his father's patients.

"Bengali mothers tend to be controlling," he said.

"I wouldn't know." Naomi's mother's parenting style had been the polar opposite: free-spirited and noninvasive to the point of being not present.

"Count yourself lucky."

Naomi lips lifted into a rueful half-hearted smile. It was tempting to admit that she shared Dev's heritage—in this moment, the revelation would likely bond them together, and Naomi's natural inclination was always to endear herself to others, to try to blend into whatever situation came her way.

But there was no way Dev could know, especially after she'd hidden the truth from Gia as well. Because they'd have questions about her family, her ancestry, her upbringing, and these were answers Naomi didn't know. And would likely *never* know thanks to her mother's refusal to discuss spaces that harbored such negative memories.

And though she tried to fight the feeling, Naomi was ashamed of herself for not knowing these vital parts of her, parts that made a person whole. People loved origin stories, but in this, Naomi had little to share, and the little she had was so dark and mysterious—even to her—that she preferred to keep it close. Hidden.

Instead, Naomi fidgeted with her sketchbook and diverted the conversation: "Your mom thought you'd respond well to an ambush?"

"She's never been too concerned about how her sons might react to these kinds of things."

"Yeah, but someone like you, especially."

"What do you mean?"

"C'mon, Dev . . . You're kind of . . ."

Dev schooled a neutral expression on his face as he waited for what was surely coming next. *Cold. Blunt. People repellent.* He'd heard it all before.

"Reserved," Naomi finished gently.

"I know how I am," he muttered. He might be the dependable, responsible son in the Mukherjee household, but it had been pointed out to him, many times over, that he was not sociable like his older brother, Neel, or laid-back like the youngest, Dhan. He was the awkward middle child, serious and reserved. Like his father.

No matter how hard Dev tried, he couldn't escape genetics. The few times he opened his mouth and heard his father's words come out made his skin crawl, his stomach dip and twist. No matter how much he bit back his criticism, how carefully he tried to honor his mother's expectations, and how consistent he was in putting his family's needs first, some things he couldn't change.

It stung a little, though, to know that Naomi had written him off in the same way.

"So, what will you tell your mom?" Naomi asked.

"About what?"

"Larisa will probably tell the matchmaker what happened." A faint blush splashed across Naomi's cheek. "You made it look like we're a match. It's going to get back to your mother."

"She's going to be pissed, but she'll know we're not dating."

"Because she's considering me to revive the store?"

"No." Dev shook his head. "My entire life, my mom has made it clear that I would end up with a traditional Desi woman. Hopefully Bengali, too."

Naomi's face hardened. "What makes you think I'm not a 'traditional Desi woman'?"

Dev thought back to their conversation about arranged marriage, one of the oldest South Asian customs. The level of pressure he was experiencing from his family seemed completely foreign to her. "Are you?" he asked.

"Well, no," she admitted before notching her chin higher. "So, what? You've only dated South Asians because of that? It's not weird to you to choose a life partner for yourself within your mother's parameters?"

Dev sighed. This was the most annoying cultural factoid to explain; he'd never encountered a white person who got it. But finding common ground with Naomi, at least when it came to his particular cultural roots, wasn't easy, either. Despite the shared color of their skin, it was like they were from two different planets.

"Where did you say your family came from again?" he asked.

"I . . . I don't see what that has to do with *your* dating history."

"I'll get to that. I think my mom said you're West Indian?" Dev studied Naomi's almond-shaped eyes and high cheekbones before lingering on her full lips. All the West Indians he'd known tended to come from more open-minded families that had learned to bend and sway with the cultures they immigrated into as opposed to resisting them with all their might.

"I'm Indian," Naomi replied flatly.

"From . . . ?"

"India."

"Which part?"

"The north," Naomi replied. In a tone that brooked no further argument, she added, "Does it matter?"

Dev shrugged. He supposed it didn't. He had known that different ethnic groups valued their own unique beliefs and traditions, but in his experience, there were usually common threads weaving first-generation children together. From the expectant arch of Naomi's eyebrow as she waited for him to answer her original question, her family must have operated under very different rules.

"I've dated non-Desi girls before," he said, holding up his hand when Naomi looked triumphant. "But I've never brought one home to meet my family." Dev didn't add that he'd never brought home a girlfriend before, in fear of the conclusions his parents would undoubtedly jump to in their dramatic way. It was why he had avoided dating someone from his community; had rumors begun to circulate, his mother would have booked their wedding venue before their third date. "Since my older brother married a

South Indian two years ago, he kind of set a bar for the rest of us. Marrying outside the general culture would crush my mom."

The consequences of committing himself to the wrong person had been dangled in front of him his entire life. He was damned if he did and damned if he didn't. "Either you obey your parents and marry someone from their preapproved list, or you end up with an outsider and risk cutting yourself—and your new family—off."

By the end of Dev's explanation, the light in Naomi's expressive eyes had dimmed. It wasn't pity, the typical response from even the most open-minded friends, but something deeper, bowed, and stormy that came from somewhere inside her. At least they both understood this facet of the culture in the same way.

"I guess, eventually, you have no choice but to marry someone in the community, then," Naomi said.

Dev scoffed. "Or not."

"But you just said—"

"I know." Dev ran a hand through his hair. His feelings about his future weren't something he liked to voice out loud, especially not to a near stranger he had used to save his ass earlier. In fact, the spontaneous act alone was so out of character that he should probably shut his mouth immediately.

But there was something about the openness in Naomi's face, the lack of judgment in her inquisitive honey-brown eyes that made him want to confide in her. The urge to lean into the feeling was unfamiliar but surprisingly pleasant and reassuring, too. She deserved the truth; after all, she hadn't blown his cover in front of Larisa.

"If marrying my mom's choice of bride or being disowned for choosing my own life partner are my options, then I'm not getting married." There. He'd said it and the ghosts of his marriage-minded ancestors hadn't swooped down to rattle his bones.

"Ever?"

"Ever."

He expected ridicule. The dismissal that he was immature and foolish, as was often his parents' response to the few times he'd tried to go against the grain. After a career fair in junior high, Dev had contemplated the idea of becoming an elementary school teacher only to have his father dismiss him as unambitious and lazy.

You'll have a family to provide for and a community to give back to, his dad had said. *Start thinking like an adult, Devdas.*

But Naomi cocked her head to the side and studied him carefully. "But you don't *know* that they'll disown you. Maybe your mom can learn to accept the person you choose?"

His stubborn, self-righteous mother? *No way in hell.* "Is it worth the risk?"

With a bitter laugh, Naomi shrugged. "I guess not. So, what are you going to tell your mom about Larisa?"

As if on some demonic cue, Gia's voice sounded gaily from behind them. "I thought I heard voices!" she said, sailing through the beaded curtains with Aashi close behind. "Dev, won't you introduce me to your friend—" Gia stopped short when she saw Naomi. "Oh. It's you." She craned her neck in search of her future daughter-in-law. "Did anyone else come in the store today?"

A lifetime of lectures stilled Dev from airing their dirty laundry in public, but he was powerless against the edge in his voice. "Why? Were *you* expecting someone?"

Aashi coughed while Gia avoided answering by rifling through a small basket containing an assortment of expired chanachur, a popular South Asian snack.

The front door of the bazaar swung open again, and Dev steeled himself for a second attack even though every nerve ending advised him to run away. Deterring hopeful-looking brides-to-be was exhausting.

But the woman who walked in was the polar opposite of Larisa. She was tall and willowy, looking downright lethal in a perfectly tailored pantsuit. Everything about her was sharp, from the determined look in her eyes to the blunt cut of her chin-length hair. She looked like the kind of woman who would eat him for breakfast in one razor-toothed bite.

But the real shocker was Naomi, who, just shy of the newcomer stepping into earshot, breathed, "Cynthia."

chapter
5

With one arm, Naomi hugged her sketchbook into her side as Cynthia Kumar approached, smelling of expensive perfume and looking like she had the bazaar's contract in the bag.

Which she probably did. Cynthia's dad was somewhat of a business mogul in the South Asian community in Kelowna and the surrounding area, and Cynthia had lived here for most of her life. Naomi had met her in the British Columbia Institute of Technology's marketing management program, where Cynthia, at every possible opportunity, had assured everyone that she would have a long list of clients waiting for her once her diploma was tucked in her pocket. So persistent was she in reminding her classmates of her guaranteed success in the industry, she might as well have lifted her leg and marked her territory on every South Asian business owner in watering distance.

And here she was in Gia's Bazaar, undoubtedly with a bladder full of entitlement. "Cynthia!" The disappointment over her first matchmaking attempt was long gone as Gia beamed at the second brand consultant.

"Auntie!" Cynthia sang back. She adjusted the strap of her suede purse before pressing her palms together. "Namashkar."

Gia let out a delighted laugh. "Someone's been practicing."

Cynthia threw Naomi a smug smile. "I may not be Bengali, but I know how important respect for your elders is."

Gia arched her brow in Naomi's direction. Strike one.

"Are these the only consultants we'll be hearing from?" Aashi asked.

"Yes." Gia nodded. "After you present your idea for my store, I'm going to deliberate with Aashi and Dev, and then we will let you know who is going to be the bazaar's Brand Lady."

"Me?" Dev asked. "You want me to be part of this?"

"Of course. You're a businessman."

"I'm an accountant."

"A successful businessman," Gia said, more to Cynthia, with a hopeful smile. From across the counter, Naomi detected a faint growl coming from Dev.

"Besides, Dev practically grew up here," Gia added. "I'm sure he's interested in the bazaar's potential, too."

"Nothing says potential like parking lot expansion," he said under his breath.

Naomi inhaled sharply to trap the rebellious giggle climbing up her throat.

"Why don't you go first, Cynthia," Aashi suggested.

Naomi moved to stand beside Dev on the other side of the counter and hugged her sketchbook to her chest. Cynthia noticed the movement and a small, condescending smile flickered across her face. Since meeting Cynthia, Naomi had always maintained a carefully cultivated professionalism around her, but it was more of a shield than a gesture of civility. Especially of late, the industry was a shark tank, and Cynthia was in a league of her own. She was a barracuda, the kind that could take down a killer whale, never mind a minnow flexing its new fins for the first time.

Striding closer to the counter, Cynthia pulled a slim black tablet out of her bag. With a few taps of her polished nails, a program Naomi recognized from her college design courses appeared on screen. It was an expensive app sought after by interior designers, one that Naomi would love to purchase for herself. One day.

Cynthia's voice reeked of self-assurance. "Auntie, with the way this neighborhood is going, you're going to see a serious influx of young people with disposable income in this area. Now is the time to capitalize on that. Tourists and locals alike have money, and they want to spend it."

Must be nice, Naomi thought dryly.

"People today want to experience authenticity. They want to connect to something bigger than them, to feel something real," Cynthia continued. "Which is why you should transform your store into a yoga studio that caters to that demographic." On the tablet, Cynthia pulled up a mock-up of the bazaar-turned-yoga-studio. She'd chosen a black-and-white color scheme with modern bamboo furniture and marble floors. It was like looking into a very rich person's loft, complete with a waterfall wall.

"Imagine an authentic yoga experience for people who chase luxury and trends," Cynthia explained. "A wholesome, soul-searching experience coupled with VIP treatment."

Tilting her head to the side, Naomi kept her face blank as Cynthia scrolled through color swatches, imported indoor flora, and potential theme nights. They weren't bad ideas—in fact, it would probably be a lucrative option for Gia's Bazaar—but she couldn't picture Gia in a space like that. It was so far away from anything currently in the bazaar, the polar opposite of Naomi's proposal.

Gia's, Aashi's, and Dev's faces gave very little away as they studied the images Cynthia was putting forward.

"Is that an LED chandelier?" Dev asked.

Cynthia nodded and flashed him a brilliant smile. "Ambience."

"It's certainly impressive," Aashi said.

"Any questions?" Cynthia asked in a voice that challenged anyone to second-guess her expertise. It was the tone of someone who knew her place in the world, who never worried about tucking an extra ace up her sleeve. Cynthia oozed the kind of confidence Naomi had to constantly reach for, never sure if it would materialize when needed.

As if they were a group of well-rehearsed synchronized swimmers, the Mukherjees and Cynthia turned in unison to look at Naomi. Cynthia's eyes flitted to her humble sketchbook, and she smirked.

"Whenever you're ready, dear," Aashi said kindly after a brief silence.

Naomi's fingers itched to open her book, but she forced herself to draw a deep breath instead. She could feel Dev's eyes transfixed on the side of her face, but for once his trademark intensity was kind of comforting; she'd underestimated the relationship-building power in being mistaken for someone's future wife.

"My proposal is that we should turn this place into an Indian-style café," she said. As soon as the words tumbled from her lips, Naomi felt that familiar rush of excitement and adrenaline. She might have been struggling to find work over the past month, but the rejection had not lessened her passion for her job in the slightest. It was this rush that had pushed her to strike out on her own, to do something that mattered for members of the community.

As she moved toward the store's dusty, neglected aisles, she felt in control for the first time since she'd been introduced to the bazaar. The newfound calm was a heady rush and added a little spring in her step. She had this.

"I'm picturing a place that's modern and earthy, but also bright in a way that reflects the rich culture. Wicker chairs, colorful cushions, low square tables," Naomi said while reminding herself to slow down. Her feet had other ideas. Jogging toward the wall-to-wall window by the store's entrance, Naomi turned to face her audience. "A long rectangular, family-style table could go here for larger groups wanting to meet over tea and sweets."

Naomi returned to the counter and positioned her sketchbook on its surface, taking care to make sure it was angled for Gia's line of sight. "The colors are just a suggestion," she said before opening her book to the tabbed page.

"Oh," Aashi murmured softly.

Across two pages, Naomi had sketched a vibrant scene: the walls were a bright cheerful teal, grounded by dark, peacock-green trim. In the back corner, a burgundy couch sat next to a miniature coffee table, warm and inviting. Yellow chairs dotted the room, welcoming people of all ages to relax and enjoy time with their friends and families. Naomi would never call herself an artist, but as she tried to survey her sketch with fresh eyes, she could almost hear the soft lull of voices and rattle of teaspoons against the mugs of patrons enjoying a respite from their busy lives.

Naomi drew her finger along the long, L-shaped countertop she'd drawn where the till stood now. "This could be one of those multitiered display cases you see in bakeries, so you can lay out what foods you have available that day," she explained. "We can make it as large or small as you want, depending on who is going to supply the food and how much variety you want to offer."

Gia gaze flew up from the book to find Naomi's. "Who will make the food?"

Drawing another deep breath, Naomi refused to look away. It was the part of her plan that she had been the most uncertain about, but under Gia's probing stare, she knew it was not the time to back down.

"I know you haven't quite decided how involved you want to be in the new space yet. But I think you should be involved." Naomi hoped she didn't sound as arrogant as the words sounded to her ears. "You're the one who built a community here, and I think you're capable of re-creating it. This . . . This could be your haven again."

When Aashi and Gia exchanged long looks, Naomi charged forward, no longer caring if her words tripped over each other. "The closest coffee shop is a fifteen-minute drive away. And so far, in this particular strip of stores, there are plenty of places to shop but nowhere to eat, except the rumored bubble tea place that's opening up across the parking lot, but I heard it's going to be pickup only."

When Naomi finally stopped rambling, she was aware that her breathing was ragged and harsh, as if she had completed the one-hundred-meter dash. She felt a strange buzzing in her chest, a combination of victory and panic. The urge to say more bubbled underneath her rib cage. She wanted so badly to say the right words, the ones that would convince Gia and her family that she was the right person for the job.

That they could trust her to do their business justice.

But she had no more to say. So she waited in silence, avoiding looking at Cynthia lest the buzzing in her chest dim.

"What kind of food would we serve?" Gia wondered out loud.

Even though she wasn't sure if the question was directed at her, Naomi jumped to answer. "Kelowna has several South Asian restaurants, but I haven't come across any place that specializes in Bengali fare." She chanced a quick glance at Cynthia before continuing. "I thought you could find a local bakery and bring in a selection of American and European desserts. But, Gia, you could make Bengali desserts. And chai. Something for everyone. Tourists, locals, and the South Asian community alike."

At that, Aashi muttered something to her sister in Bengali and the two of them fell into quiet conversation, heads bent over Naomi's proposal for the bazaar. For the first time, Naomi was struck by the similarities between the two sisters, something she hadn't thought possible after going head-to-head with the hard, unflappable Gia before seeking comfort in Aashi's cheerful reassurance. But the resemblance was there in the jet-black tint of their hair and the way their square-edged fingertips brushed tentatively over her sketch.

Naomi wasn't sure if they were saying good things about her idea or ridiculing the simplicity of her presentation compared to Cynthia's flash, but she refused to feel ashamed of her hand-drawn offering. Whether they picked her for the contract or not, she'd poured her heart into her sketch. Lacing her fingers together, Naomi found herself seeking Dev's eyes as if the answer could be found in his curmudgeonly gaze.

He was staring right back at her, giving nothing away as to whether she'd impressed his obstinate mother. But there was something there—respect, maybe. Grudging, yes, but respect all the same. Naomi offered him a tentative smile because, whether he realized it or not, he was part of this. When he had talked of his mother's love for hosting and feeding others, it had been the one time he had softened in the entire time she'd been in his acquaintance. That softness had fed her idea, inspired the confident strokes of her pencil on paper.

Dev smiled back, and Naomi felt her knees tremble.

The man had dimples. In both cheeks.

"We have much to discuss," Gia said, looking between Cynthia and Naomi. "Excuse us a moment."

Naomi and Cynthia were silent as Gia, Aashi, and Dev filed through the beaded doorway, but when Naomi heard the sound of ascending footsteps, she looked at Cynthia in confusion.

"There's an upstairs?" Naomi said, tilting her face to the ceiling.

Cynthia was busy scrolling through her phone. "There's an apartment or something up there." She glanced up and cocked her head toward Naomi's sketchbook, still flipped open on the counter in front of them. "This was a cute idea."

Cute. Hastily, Naomi closed the book and pulled it away. "Thanks."

"I mean, it's a little kitschy and small-town, but cute."

Classic Cynthia, queen of monochromatic colors, hard edges, and the backhanded compliment. And all Naomi could think to respond with was another robotic "thanks."

"I was surprised to hear you left Adams and Ridge Solutions," Cynthia commented. "You were doing pretty well there, weren't you?"

Naomi swallowed the desire to correct her. She had been one of the company's top performers, but declaring as much to Cynthia would be like dangling chum over the side of the boat into shark-infested waters. Instead, she affected a bored tone. "It was time to move on."

"Striking out on your own is pretty ballsy given the competition around here. How's that going?"

There was no way Naomi could admit to someone like Cynthia Kumar, with her family connections and designer purse, that it wasn't going well. Especially after her success with Adams & Ridge: For two years, her natural people-pleasing tendencies had been a perfect fit for a company whose motto boasted *Solutions done your way*. But the organization's ability to find those solutions hinged on clients who could afford its flash and panache.

Naomi had grown tired of rebranding large, faceless corporations. They all looked the same, wanted the same things. Leaving had been a no-brainer.

"It's great," Naomi lied to Cynthia, trying to look like a successful brand consultant whose cheap knockoff shoes *weren't* giving her blisters this very moment. "Business has been *so* busy."

"So, like, what kind of Bengali desserts are you going to recommend that Gia serve?"

Naomi bit her lip. "I . . . I hadn't thought that far ahead."

"Kelowna already has two well-known Punjabi dessert takeout places." Cynthia lifted a skeptical brow. "One of them was recently renovated and is super popular right now. My cousin was part of the construction crew."

"I'm not proposing Gia serve Punjabi-style sweets, though."

Cynthia rolled her eyes. "I know that, I was here during your cute little presentation, remember? But don't you think she should carry some of those desserts, too? They're well-known. You know, for the average Kelownian who doesn't know the difference between mattar paneer and shahi paneer, and always orders butter chicken when they get Indian food?"

The ragged, harsh breathing was building in Naomi's chest again. She knew Cynthia was trying to psych her out in classic barracuda warfare fashion, but she was inadvertently hitting all the right panic buttons. Before she could compose herself and hide her growing alarm, Cynthia's lips quirked.

"Oh, sweetie," she said, "you're in over your head, aren't you?"

Naomi was saved from having to find an appropriate answer by the clatter of footsteps making their way down the staircase. The noise provided a brief respite from their tense exchange but

Naomi's stomach shifted uneasily. Cynthia had successfully un-earthed the doubt Naomi had worked so hard to bury deep. Just moments ago, her ideas for the bazaar had seemed so abundant and fruitful, a meaningful way to connect to the Mukherjees' roots.

But what did she know of roots? Apple pie had been the dessert of choice in her household and she, too, like the average Gary and Deborah Kelownian, could not decipher between mattar paneer and the other paneer dish Cynthia had mentioned. Who was she to propose an Indian-style café? Especially to a family whose ad-herence to cultural values was planted deeper than Naomi could ever hope to dig with a busted trowel and a blank map?

"We've deliberated," Gia announced, clapping her hands to-gether and startling Naomi. Out of the corner of her eye, she saw Cynthia lift her chin expectantly. "And while both your ideas were very interesting directions to take the store, we've decided . . ." Gia's voice faltered and she looked to Aashi, traces of reluctance splashed across her face.

"We've decided to go with Naomi's idea," Aashi finished for her sister. "Congratulations, dear."

Naomi prayed that her lips were stretching into a smile and not a grimace as Gia rushed to Cynthia's side with soothing tones.

They liked her ideas; she'd won the contract. *And* beat Cynthia. She was employed again with the opportunity to devote the next three months to a project she could start from scratch while charg-ing more than her regular fees as she and Gia had previously agreed upon. She could keep her lights on.

But these realizations failed to inspire even the slightest glim-mer of euphoria. Naomi had everything she wanted but now all she wanted was to run away.

chapter
6

And this color scheme . . ." Naomi paused to suppress a yawn before opening a new tab on her laptop screen. Although she'd won the bazaar's contract earlier that same day, she felt like she'd lived a thousand hours since. Years, maybe.

Oh well. I'll sleep when I'm dead and debt-free, she thought, scrolling through the page with renewed determination.

"This color scheme would offset these countertops in a more subtle way," she finished, pointing to the screen.

Nick Santiago, her contractor-turned-best-friend, barely spared the screen a glance as he maneuvered his blue work truck into a parking stall. "Sounds good."

Naomi side-eyed his handsome profile. "Is that all you're going to say, Santiago? Are you even listening? I need your input."

As usual, Nick was unruffled. "Since when?"

"Excuse me?"

"Dude, we've done our fair share of projects together and you've never needed this kind of input from me." He leaned across her to pull the glove compartment open and grabbed his wallet.

"You're the most self-possessed and confident person I know when it comes to making decisions about things like theme and décor," he continued. "You point, I hammer. It's how we do."

Another yawn threatened to unhinge Naomi's jaw. "I know. But this project is . . . different." Since her victorious—but anxiety-inducing—win, Naomi had been combing over swatches, burrowing through design magazines, and falling down one rabbit hole after another. She kept second-guessing herself and spinning in circles as she looked for answers to what felt like the wrong questions.

All thanks to Cynthia. But deep down, Naomi knew there was more to the growing anxiety than a few snide remarks. She had oversold herself, had been too convincing that she could fake her way through this.

Nick drummed his fingers across the steering wheel. "Can we eat now?" When Naomi failed to respond, he turned resigned eyes to where she was scrolling through yet another Pinterest board. "They liked your pitch, Nae. Why are you freaking out? Is it the deadline?"

"Kind of."

"I told you, my crew and I can get it done in three months, don't worry." Nick studied her face. "Come on, tell me what's really going on in your head. But make it quick, I'm hungry."

Naomi shifted in her seat. "I feel like I'm swinging for the fences with a broken bat."

"You and your sports analogies." Nick half smiled. "English, please, for those of us who weren't forced to watch sports with our fathers while growing up."

"I liked it!" Binge-watching the Olympics with her stepfather had been an important tradition to Naomi, well worth being bleary-eyed and lethargic at school the next day. To this day, the smell of popcorn and strawberry licorice reminded her of those late nights, the pair of them on matching recliners, trading snacks back and forth.

"All work and no food makes Nick a bitch," Nick reminded her.

"What I meant is that I have the vision for what I want to do for Gia's Bazaar, but the parts of the picture aren't coming together like they usually do."

Nick looked more than a little puzzled, and she didn't blame him in the least. They'd met when Naomi had started at Adams & Ridge Solutions and had hit it off right away. Nick's easygoing charm and eagle-eye attention to detail were a perfect match for Naomi, who thrived on checklists, spreadsheets, and the look of pleasure on a client's satisfied face. Most importantly, Nick understood, more than anyone, why she'd left a cushy corporate job to work with locally owned businesses, to make her mark on the community by building beautiful and meaningful spaces in the ever-growing tourist town.

But even though Nick was her best friend, he didn't know about her past and why the contract to Gia's Bazaar had unearthed her insecurities. She'd never outright lied to Nick about her Bengali upbringing, or lack thereof, not like she had with the Mukherjees. It wasn't that Nick would care but . . . Something in Naomi's stomach fluttered with uncertainty. She didn't talk about her past with *anybody*.

"I'm sorry," she said, opening the passenger door. "I just . . . I don't feel like my plan is perfect yet."

"You'll get there. You always do."

"Yeah. I always do," Naomi echoed as she hopped down from the cab.

And she would. She had to. She had never shied away from solving her own problems before, and Gia's Bazaar was no exception. She needed to stop focusing on aesthetics and turn her energy toward authenticity. Unfortunately, unlike color palette and trending layouts, authenticity was not in Naomi's wheelhouse.

The bulk of her childhood memories centered on moments with her half-German, half-Ukrainian stepfather while her mother chased whims, fancies, and everything else she felt she had been denied growing up in a strict, conservative Bengali household. She'd embraced a life free of cultural expectations and had raised her daughter to do the same.

Naomi needed to find some kind of cultural barometer that would fill in the gaps her upbringing had left behind. And she needed to do it soon and under wraps, before Gia caught on and changed her mind about hiring her.

Her dwindling savings account was counting on it.

As Nick led her into the restaurant, Naomi finally registered where they were. "An Indian restaurant? Are you serious?"

Nick shrugged. "I'm craving tandoori, and you said I could pick if I paid. What's the problem?"

Naomi sighed. It was like her stepfather always said: *You can outrun your mother-in-law but you can't outrun your problems.* After a day of researching Bengali cuisine, customs, and couture, Indian fare was the *last* thing she wanted. But, with the bazaar haunting her dreams for the next three months, it couldn't hurt to try to become an expert on all things South Asian, at least until the check cleared.

"Sure," she said, "let's order all the paneer on the menu." The promise of cheese was enough to restore some of her trademark cheerfulness.

"And naan."

"And mishti," Naomi added shyly to herself as she followed Nick to an empty table. The Bengali word for "dessert" that Dev had taught her the other day felt strange on her lips, tentative and awkward. Just saying the word, even if under her breath, felt like a positive step toward the semblance of control, however small it might be. Maybe, one day, she would have the courage to say it out loud, as naturally as one would expect from a person with brown skin.

They were perusing their menus when Nick suddenly leaned forward with a peculiar look on his face. "Don't look now, but that guy over there keeps looking your way. Four o'clock." When she turned her head to look over her shoulder, Nick rapped her knuckles lightly with his fork. "Okay, first of all, I said *don't* look. Also, that's seven o'clock, not four."

"Is he good-looking?"

"Fuck yes."

Naomi's shoulder twitched with the effort of keeping her eyes on Nick. "How good-looking?"

"Well, he would be a lot hotter if he wasn't giving off a horror movie vibe."

With a grimace, Naomi refocused her attention on her menu. Nick's taste in men had always been questionable. "Not interested."

"No, I mean, he looks like he's about to be a serial killer's *victim*," Nick explained, glancing over her left shoulder. "He's looking at the back of your head again, and the dude's face is freaking out."

"What?" Ignoring Nick's advice, Naomi craned her neck over her right shoulder to see Dev sitting at a table with what was probably another potential bride. With his hands balled into fists on the tabletop and the grim line of his mouth, he did not look like he was in the throes of love.

"Do you know him?" Nick asked when Naomi turned back around.

"That's Dev."

"The stomach pill guy?"

Naomi rolled her eyes. Sometimes she told Nick a little too much. "Yeah. His mom hired a matchmaker to find him a wife, and I'm guessing he's on another setup."

Nick let out a low whistle as he studied the couple sitting a few tables away. "Since when does a guy who looks like that need help finding a woman?"

Although she couldn't fault her friend for ogling, it was Naomi's turn to rap Nick's knuckles with a fork. "It's a cultural thing," she told him, thinking back to Dev's explanation. Even now, she couldn't forget the helplessness in his dark eyes, heavy with the weight of family loyalty and a lack of options.

"Well, it doesn't look like it's going well," Nick commented, his eyes unabashedly riveted on the train wreck just a few tables away.

Resisting the urge to turn around again, Naomi lifted an eyebrow. "How are you so sure?"

"They're not talking, she looks irritated as hell, and Dev keeps looking over here like he's waiting for you to throw him a life raft."

"Should I go over there?"

Nick cringed. "I think it's too late."

Naomi whipped around in time to see Dev's date stand up, glass of water in hand, and throw its contents at his face. She then whirled around and stormed out, leaving a very wet and very despondent Dev behind. Naomi glanced around, her heart going out to him as several other patrons in the restaurant stared and whispered over the scene.

"If I were you, I'd go over there now," Nick said.

Naomi was already in motion. Grabbing her unused cloth napkin, Naomi made her way to him. She sat down in his date's vacated seat and silently handed him the makeshift towel.

"Thanks," he said in a low voice before scrubbing his face.

"That was quite the exit."

"Pretty sure she got that from a Bollywood movie."

Naomi watched as Dev attempted to dry the front of his shirt, a sour look on his face. "So, when's the wedding?"

Dev shot her a glare, but there was a faint twitch to his lips. "Very funny."

"What happened?"

Tossing the napkin on the table, Dev massaged his eyelids with his fingertips. "I don't know. I'm not good at small talk to begin with—never mind with strangers who inform me they want three kids in three years before we've even ordered an appetizer—and everything I said seemed to piss her off."

"Well, what did you say?"

"I don't know, normal things. I mentioned how ridiculous it is to pay for overpriced food that our parents cook all the time."

Naomi swallowed a smile. "Did she pick the restaurant?"

"Yes."

"Mmm. Go on. What else did you say?"

"She mentioned something about soaking up some final beach time before everything cools off and I told her I hate the beach."

"You hate the beach?"

Dev frowned impatiently. "It's always crowded, people litter everywhere, and don't get me started on those disgusting porta-potties."

Naomi couldn't help herself. She grinned. "And what led to her throwing her drink at you?"

This time, Dev had the decency to look embarrassed. "I . . . might have called her by the wrong name."

"Dev!"

"Cut me some slack! All my mom talks about anymore are

women she thinks I should meet. Larisa, Preity, Amika, Minu, Daisy, Sheenah . . . They all come from good families, have respectable jobs and shiny hair, love to cook, and are looking to get married in the next year. I can't keep them straight!" Dev shook his head, looking downright miserable. "I mean, I *kind of* knew her name might not be Preity but it's obvious that I need to find a better way to get rid of them. Something that won't result in waterboarding."

Although Naomi secretly agreed that having a drink flung at him was the least Dev deserved for that particular slip, Naomi couldn't ignore the flicker of sympathy in her chest as she took in his dejected face. Gia was a formidable opponent; Naomi couldn't imagine what it would be like to have someone like her as a mother. If Gia wanted to marry off her son, then Dev was definitely going to have to deal with a barrage of women parading through his life for the next few weeks. Or months. After all, Gia seemed like a woman with plenty of stamina. Dev would need to get a lot more creative at turning women away, lest one decided to hurl something much more dangerous his way, like a steak knife.

He needed an ace in his pocket—something that would protect him from a fate he clearly didn't want.

An idea was coming to her, half formed and fuzzy around the edges but enough to jolt her upright in her seat. Startled, Dev's head swiveled, as if the next potential bride was already descending upon him. At this rate, he'd need a shield: something to repel women in search of wedding bells and three children in three years.

"Something or some*one*?" Naomi mused out loud.

"What are you talking about?"

"*You* need a way to deter these women," Naomi said, her brain working overtime. When Dev nodded, her words picked up speed. "And *I* need help with the bazaar."

"You do? Since when?"

Naomi risked a quick glance over her shoulder to where Nick was happily digging into a complimentary basket of what looked like chips. He didn't seem too concerned about her whereabouts or that he was dining solo, but still, she lowered her voice.

"Listen," she said, leaning forward and beckoning Dev to do the same. When he obliged, she was momentarily distracted by his scent. Mint and something woodsy that reminded her of a quiet forest at night. Not what she would've expected from him, but also not displeasing, either. "I know everything there is to know about making the bazaar look good on the surface. But when it comes to what's underneath, I need help. Your mother's expectations far exceed what I'm equipped to do, but you're the perfect person to make sure I'm leading the redesign in the right direction. In the direction that *Gia* would approve of."

Dev tilted his head to the side. "And how are you going to help me in return?"

"My presence alone is a deterrent for brides on the prowl. Look what happened this morning!"

"With Lalita?"

"Larisa," Naomi corrected. "As soon as she saw I was in the picture, she retreated. It didn't take much else for you to get rid of her."

"I don't know . . ." Dev's fingers toyed with the wet napkin. "That doesn't sound like it'll work."

"Think about it. How easy is it going to be for these women to ambush you when you're busy working on the rebrand with me? Your mom might back off, too, considering she wants the job done in three months." With every word, Naomi found herself nodding more and more confidently. When a small cramp formed at the base of her neck, she forced herself to stop and settled for her most winning smile.

To her relief, Dev's face was thoughtful. Which was great, because Naomi was on a roll. "It's the perfect plan," she continued. "I'll get what I want, and you can avoid what you don't want." When Dev's forehead crinkled with uncertainty, she went for the ace in her sleeve. "And you said it yourself: your mom would never suspect something was going on between us, meaning she will have no idea that you're pulling a fast one on her." Naomi smiled and sat back in her chair. "It'll be seamless. A Michael Phelps gold medal sweep."

A dark cloud flickered over Dev's face, stormy enough to quell Naomi's barely contained exhilaration.

"What?" she asked. "What's wrong?"

"If we do this, people are going to talk about you."

"What do you mean?"

Dev shifted in his seat. "It's public knowledge that I'm on the marriage market, but you're not. The South Asian community doesn't really endorse casual dating, and if people see you're with me . . ."

Naomi shifted in her seat. As far as the Kelowna South Asian community was concerned, she was a nobody. And ever since her disastrous attempt to join her college's South Asian Student Association, Naomi had forced herself to be comfortable with her nobody status. She had quickly learned that there were certain unspoken codes in place for people hailing from the same mother ship. The international students were united by a shared language and a desire to re-create cultural events that reminded them of home, while the first-generation kids complained about their restrictive upbringings and rolled their eyes before attending all the activities hosted by the international students. Everyone had known their place and what to do.

Except Naomi, a second-generation Indo-Canadian who had been cut off from the same traditions these students came together to celebrate. Still, she had paid her fees and sat through exactly three meetings, where she had tried to feel comfortable in her own skin amid the bilingual teasing and Bollywood hits playing in the background.

It had been awful.

She would never fit in and never allow herself to care that she would forever be on the outside. But as a brand consultant, she wanted to be a somebody. And that somebody was not the person who slept with her clients.

But technically, she *wouldn't* be sleeping with Dev, and if people insinuated as much, she would know it was untrue. As would Gia, who would rather die than allow the rumor that her son was involved with some whitewashed, ethnically ambiguous brown girl to gain much traction.

Besides, was she really going to let the threat of a little rumor ruin the first job she had landed in too long? The dollar signs were already imprinted on her eyes, her wallet salivating in anticipation.

"I don't care," she told Dev. "I don't care what they say about me." If anything, it was motivation. Naomi would have to ensure that this rebrand was a monumental success—a complete turnaround that had people vying for her business card rather than speculating over her questionable methods.

"Your parents won't freak out if people start gossiping about you?" Dev sounded more flabbergasted than cautionary now.

Naomi was winning him over, she could feel it.

"They won't care," she said. *Because there's no way I'd ever tell them.* Especially not her mother, who would ditch even the most exclusive yoga oasis and drag her back home if she found out how deeply her daughter was submersing herself in the South Asian community. "So, what do you say?"

Dev ran a hand through his hair, grimaced, and then wiped his damp hand on his pants. "I'm in."

As Dev carried yet another set of folding chairs from Aashi's basement into her kitchen, he strained to hear the chime of the doorbell over the cacophony of clanging pots, a whirring blender, and two arguing sisters who shouldn't cook together.

Nothing yet. Dev glanced at the clock above the kitchen table: five minutes to seven.

Where was she?

"You need more green chili!" Gia admonished while rhythmically chopping eggplant into thick slices at the kitchen island.

Aashi waved a dismissive hand in the air as she stirred a large pot at the stove. "Too much gives me heartburn."

"It won't be tasty—"

From where she was stationed at the blender, his sister-in-law, Priya, threw Dev an exasperated glance before jabbing the blender back on high. But when the doorbell sounded in the distance, all noises ceased at once.

"I'll get it," Dev said.

"You keep bringing up chairs," Gia instructed, reaching behind her back to untie her apron. "I can get it."

Dev's brain scurried for a reasonable excuse to answer the door. Since striking the bargain with Naomi the night before, he had called his aunt to suggest she invite the brand consultant to her dinner party the next night as an opportunity for her to get to know the Mukherjee family for the bazaar's rebrand. A fan of Naomi and her work, Aashi had been happy to comply.

The threat of another matchmaking ambush washed away any guilt Dev might have felt from manipulating his aunt in this way, even as Aashi came to his aid again. Scooping a spoonful of sauce from her pot, she thrust it in Gia's face. "Let Dev get it. Taste this."

"It needs more chili—"

Dev ambled out of the kitchen but as soon as he hit the hallway, he bolted for the door. As he had hoped, Naomi was waiting on the other side and, after verifying that no potential brides were hiding behind his aunt's rosebushes, he ushered her through the entrance.

"Quick, get inside."

"Uh, hello to you, too," Naomi said with a nervous chuckle. "Why do you look like a cornered rat?"

"Gee, thanks."

"Sorry. You just seem . . ." Naomi studied his face. "Like you're down by two in the bottom of the ninth."

Dev lifted an eyebrow. "From rats to baseball metaphors. Interesting."

With an eye roll, Naomi waved her hand dismissively. "Never mind. Where is everybody?" she asked as she slipped her shoes off onto the plastic mat Aashi had lined the front entrance with for her guests' footwear.

"What do you mean?"

"Aashi said dinner would be at seven." Naomi gestured to her lone pair of shoes.

"Seven means eight according to Indian Standard Time. Seven thirty for the geriatric bunch." Dev threw her a dubious glance as they made their way to the kitchen. "I'm pretty sure that's a worldwide thing. Don't tell me the Desi community in Alberta is different?"

Naomi didn't bother with a response as they entered the kitchen, where chaos had resumed: Priya was blending, Gia chopping, and Aashi bustling between five large pots on the stove. But when his aunt noticed them, she immediately abandoned her work, arms extended with a big smile on her face, and shouldered her way past Dev to pull Naomi into a hug.

"Oh, you made it. I'm so glad!" Aashi said when the blender had died down again.

"Dev, the chairs," Gia reminded him, barely sparing Naomi a second glance. "And the folding table."

"And the serving dishes," Aashi said. "And paper plates."

"And extra garbage bags," Priya added as she peered into the contents of the blender.

Shyly, Naomi reached into her bag and pulled out a large re-sealable bag containing a dozen or so of the plumpest monster cookies Dev had ever seen. "I brought dessert."

Aashi smiled back. "That's so thoughtful, dear. Dev, take her downstairs and show her where I stowed the desserts for tonight."

Dev led Naomi to the basement, not bothering to acknowledge Aashi, who hollered at their departing backs, "Grab the plastic cutlery, too!" Having attended dinners like this his entire life, he knew the drill: show up early, help set up, and then hang out by the front door like a well-trained dog to trot the guests' coats off to the den. They all had their parts to play when a family member hosted dinner. A child himself, his younger brother, Dhan, always corralled the kids to the bonus room to watch a movie while the eldest, Neel, along with their uncle, played host to the men in the front sitting room in lieu of their father.

The honor of playing errand boy fell on Dev, the reluctant but silent butler attending to whatever his mother or aunt needed before, during, and after they hosted their friends. Even though it was the worst role of the three, he'd always accepted the responsibility as his: Neel bristled at taking orders and Dhan was too flaky to follow through.

When Dev opened Aashi's basement fridge to reveal a large bowl of prepared fruit salad, two boxes of store-bought mishti, and a punch bowl filled with homemade payesh—Bengali rice pudding—Naomi glanced at her puny bag of cookies and frowned.

"Your aunt said this was a family dinner."

Dev snorted. "That means immediate family plus several non-related aunts and uncles, including a sprinkling of senior citizens who will park themselves on the sofas all night and look like they're asleep until they hear some juicy gossip." Dev had been shuffled to dinners like this every weekend his entire life. He rarely attended anymore unless, of course, one of his family members was hosting. As a child, he had been insanely jealous of the other kids at school, whose weekends were spent loitering at the mall or going to the movies, while he had been at Mira Auntie's house, shoved in a room with kids aged four to seventeen, half watching some Disney movie while counting down until he could leave.

"Oh." Naomi stepped past Dev, close enough so the fleeting brush of her arm against the front of his dark green shirt raised pinpricks of awareness. When the tingle didn't immediately subside, Dev rubbed at the spot roughly.

She slid the bag into the fridge. "I didn't know." Naomi's voice was meek, all hints of her trademark cheerfulness squelched under the weight of a custom she hadn't anticipated.

Welcome to my world, Dev thought grimly.

Still, something about the tentative way Naomi nudged her humble contribution deeper into the fridge plucked at someplace unfamiliar in Dev's chest. It was a nettling tug, urging him to say something comforting.

Which, on his best days, he sucked at.

"No one's going to eat what you brought anyway," he blurted out.

"Great. Thanks."

Dev winced inwardly. "I mean, in a room full of Bengalis, you can't compete with homemade rice pudding," he said, flicking the bowl with his fingernail. "Even those boxes of mishti can't compete."

Naomi shot him a sideways glance. "Is rice pudding your weakness, too?"

With a scoff, Dev closed the fridge door with more force than necessary. "I don't care much for sweets."

"Why does this not surprise me," Naomi muttered behind him. Clearing her throat, she added, "I appreciate your aunt including me tonight."

Dev rubbed the back of his neck. "About that . . . I kind of told her to."

"Why?"

Despite having laid everything out for Naomi yesterday, Dev sensed a telltale heat creeping onto the tips of his ears. There was no other way to put it: "I wasn't sure who might show up tonight."

Naomi studied him, her lips rolled in ever so slightly and her eyes glittering with amusement. Even though he'd known her for only a few days, Dev knew this face all too well. She was trying not to laugh. At him. And for once in his life, he didn't mind.

"Are you . . . scared of Veera Auntie's bridal brigade, Dev?"

Her eyes were so luminous that Dev forced himself to look away. "Maybe."

"Seriously? They'd try to find you a love connection here? Tonight?"

"It's possible."

"In front of all their friends? What if it turned out to be another terrible match?"

Dev raised his eyebrows. What kind of world did Naomi inhabit where one's parents tried to spare their children from embarrassment? No wonder she was such an optimist.

"Maybe," he replied. "A lot of their friends have daughters."

Naomi fisted her hands on her hips. "You could've given me a heads-up. We're in this together, after all."

Dev leaned against the fridge and crossed his arms across his chest, more than a little startled by the kernel of pleasure blossoming there. It was peculiar—but pleasant—to think he had someone on his side. He was used to being on his own.

"You're right, I'm sorry," he found himself saying. "I panicked when I realized that there might be hopeful brides skulking around every corner of my life from now on."

"'Skulking'?" At Naomi's grin, the pleasure that had blossomed in Dev's chest a few seconds ago spilled outward into his veins.

"Skulking," he confirmed as he tamped his smile. Of all the Mukherjees, he had always considered himself the least dramatic, but it was kind of fun, plotting with his partner in crime.

And maybe Naomi thought so, too. She slapped a hand to her heart like a faithful knight. "Then I swear to protect you from their womanly wiles."

With a solemn nod, Dev turned to the stack of folding chairs and grabbed three to carry upstairs. Following his cue, Naomi grabbed two for herself and trudged along behind him.

When they returned to the kitchen, they found that Dev's brothers, Neel and Dhan, had joined the group. They flanked their mother's sides at the kitchen island, Neel crunching loudly on the vegetables she had painstakingly cut while Dhan leaned on his elbows, lazy and unaware that his unkempt, shaggy hair hovered dangerously close to the food.

Aashi clucked her tongue. "Naomi, you don't need to carry chairs. Leave that to the men. Why don't you help coat and fry the eggplant instead?"

Dev looked away as Naomi's front teeth raked over her lower lip. "I . . . I don't really know how to cook."

Mid-tomato slice, Gia's knife stilled. "Your mother didn't teach you?"

Naomi's face reddened. "No."

"How come?"

That uncomfortable tug was back in Dev's chest as Naomi's feet shuffled a little on the linoleum floor. "She's not much of a cook, either," she replied.

It was obvious that the answer didn't sit well with Gia. For a woman who clung to reminders of home as tightly as Naomi's wringing hands clung together now, such a revelation was unfathomable to her. After all, *she* had done her due diligence to adhere to the customs and traditions she had been raised by, even going as far to attempt a turkey curry when her sons' clamoring for a Thanksgiving dinner had gotten the best of her. Anything short of re-creating memories from back home was unacceptable in her eyes.

Those same eyes sought his out now. *See?* they said. *You want a life of hot dogs and hamburgers? This is why you need my help to find a proper wife.*

Priya dislodged the blender from its base loudly. "Why don't you help me over here, Naomi?" she asked. "I need someone to stir the pot while I pour this in."

As Naomi went to Priya's side, Dev retreated to the basement to bring the rest of the items upstairs, the guilt of abandoning Naomi to his mother's clutches mollified when he reminded himself that Priya would extend a friendly hand. His brother's wife had immigrated to Canada in her teens, and while she possessed many of the qualities Gia deemed appropriate for a proper, brown wife, she was also kind and patient with everyone who crossed her path.

How she ended up with his dickhead of a big brother, Dev would never understand. He hadn't realized Neel had followed him down until he felt the sharp sting of his meaty hand on his shoulder.

"Mom told me that she hired a brand consultant," his older brother said. "And that you're going to help."

Scooping up three more folding chairs, Dev grunted in response. But when he made a move to skirt around his brother, Neel shifted his bulk and blocked his escape.

"I gotta say, I was relieved to hear you're on the project, too," Neel continued.

"Why?"

"What's a whitewashed girl like her know about rebranding a Bengali business?"

Dev's jaw clenched. He'd always hated that word *whitewashed*. He'd been living in a kind of invisible hierarchy his entire life, positioning those who clung to traditions and old-world customs as the upper tier that everyone should strive to model themself after. Time and time again, his parents had compared him to his fellow brown peers, reminding him how he came up short against their accomplishments and talents. Hearing Naomi compared to what a true snob would consider the lowest of the low uncurled something thick and gray in his chest, a kind of smog that wrapped around his lungs.

"How do you know she's unqualified?" he asked in a curt voice.

"Who's unqualified?" their younger brother asked as he loped down the stairs to join them. He came to the kind of wavering halt that only rangy bodies with too-long limbs could master. Now the two of them blocked any chances of a hasty retreat.

Standing side by side with his brothers, Dev was struck, as he always was, by how similar they were. Appearance-wise, it was like comparing an apple to a banana: stocky Neel, with his trademark sneer and sharp crew cut, looked especially unforgiving next to Dhan, whose dreamy gaze and slack posture always gave the impression that he had just woken up. Yet they were so comfortable with themselves, like two soccer players on the field, one who had memorized the playbook and was determined to win, the other uncaring of how he might perform on game day but happy to go to town on the orange slices.

Meanwhile, Dev was always on the sidelines, aware of the rules but unsure how to play.

And probably wearing the wrong jersey.

"The brand consultant Mom hired is a coconut," Neel reiterated for Dhan's benefit.

"She's hot," Dhan said with a shrug.

"Doesn't change what's on the inside," Neel argued before

turning to Dev. "Trust me, you're lucky Mom hired a matchmaker. You don't want to end up with the wrong kind of girl."

Dev didn't want to end up with anyone at all, especially if it meant turning into an old-fashioned, judgmental asshole like his older brother. Or worse, their father. Although, judging from the arrogant gleam in Neel's eye, his brother was halfway there.

"Hopefully you'll end up with a good girl like Priya," Neel added.

"Oh yeah, I'm sure married life with you is her wish come true," Dev replied sarcastically. The chairs in his arms were beginning to weigh on him. "If you two would just move out of the way . . ."

"So you think the bazaar will hold its own in the neighborhood once Naina is done with it?"

"I think her name is Nandini," Dhan interjected. "Or was it Nadia?"

"Her name is—" Dev stopped midsentence. "Wait. Why do *you* care?" Although Dev had never shown much interest in Gia's Bazaar, his older brother had been the least caring and often dismissed its presence in their lives as *Mom's hobbyhorse.*

"Because if things turn out well, I'm going to take over the store."

Dev shook his head as he tried to picture barrel-chested Neel in an apron, peddling chai. "*You* want to run the bazaar?"

"No, I have a career," Neel said, affronted. "It'd be for Priya."

"Priya wants to work at the store?" Dhan shook his head, confusion wrinkling his forehead. "Isn't she a stay-at-home mom?"

"She's back at the library," Dev replied tightly. "Part-time." It had been apparent to everyone that the decision to return to work had been more Neel's than his wife's; Dev couldn't imagine Priya wanting to devote the time and energy it would take to get a new business off the ground.

"My wife needs to get out of that stuffy library." Neel rolled his eyes. "She can do better."

Shifting under the weight of the chairs, Dev stared at the idiot before him, wishing he felt taken aback at the turn of events. But he wasn't. Hadn't their father done the same thing by changing the course of Gia's life by gifting her with an Indian convenience store without any prior discussion? And now Neel was doing the same thing: making decisions for others, thinking he knew what was best. He'd gotten even worse since assuming his role as patriarchal head of the family after their father's passing.

"You're right," he said, passing another assessing look over his brother's ironed golf shirt and obnoxiously large watch. "Priya can do better. But why don't you let Mom decide what she wants to do with her store?"

"Trust me, Dev. Mom needs someone helping her run her life. She's been a mess without Baba."

"It's true." Dhan nodded and raked his hands through his hair. "Sometimes she leaves me *two* voicemails a day."

Since her husband's passing, Gia did seem a little unsure of how to spend her time. The majority of her adult life had been devoted to her family's care, and now—as a widow with adult children—she seemed lost. Two of her sons were (to her knowledge) settled in their careers, and the youngest was attending law school a five-hour drive away. She tried to fill her time with granddaughters and social visits, but more often than not, Dev walked in on his mother frozen in front of the television for hours on end. Or cooking late into the night, only to fill their freezer for some unknown purpose.

Dev knew his mother was still grieving, but making decisions for Gia wasn't right. He wanted to tell his brothers so, but they had never shown much interest in Dev's opinion—especially Neel. Besides, for all of his head-of-the-household crap, Neel was not above tattling to their mother at the barest hint of a perceived slight.

Still, the idea of the bazaar falling into his brother's graceless hands didn't sit right with Dev. It should belong to someone who *cared*.

When Dev shifted his weight again, Neel chuckled before leaning forward to help relieve him of his burden by taking *one* chair out of his grasp. "Geez, little brother," he said, turning toward the staircase where Dhan, empty-handed, was already on his way to the main floor. "Maybe you need to take a break from crunching numbers and lift some weights once in a while."

Dev glared at his older brother's retreating back. As if engineers were known for being in top physical condition—Neel's bulk was more rice and roti than muscle. But he refused to engage any more than he already had because, from the sounds of new voices upstairs, he would need all the patience he possessed to get through the next few hours.

chapter
8

Dinner long over, Naomi grinned as she listened shamelessly from where she sat alone on Aashi's staircase in the hallway separating the kitchen and family room from the living room at the front of the house. After a busy night of meeting a ton of blunt aunties, their jolly but indifferent husbands, and Aashi's shy preteen daughters, it was nice to have a moment alone to relax.

And eavesdrop, of course.

"Ooof, her laddoos were on full display!" an auntie jeered from afar.

"Mine would be, too, if they looked like that," Aashi replied. The ladies congregated in the family room shrieked with laughter.

Although Naomi lost track of the conversation when someone replied in Bangla, the answering chorus of playful jeers brought a smile to her face.

"Has anyone been to that new Punjabi sweet house yet? Their laddoos are first-class!" an elderly voice chimed in.

"As is the Bangladeshi chef they hired!" someone else said.

More hoots. So this was what Naomi had missed out on, growing up in a small redneck town that was more likely to witness a tornado on the horizon than another brown person for miles.

From her vantage point, Naomi could hear the low, thoughtful tones of the men—the *uncles*, she quickly corrected herself—in the living room punctuated by the raucous laughter of the aunties in the family room. The children had been shuffled off upstairs to watch a movie where, Naomi was sure, at least some of the younger ones must have fallen asleep. The leftover scents of clove, coriander, cumin, and who knew what else wafted from the kitchen. Her taste buds were still reeling from the homemade Bengali dishes she had sampled tonight.

Dev was right. It was hard to imagine paying for food at an Indian restaurant after the feast Aashi, Gia, and Priya had created that evening. And *her*, too, Naomi supposed. Sure, she had done very little and had been completely out of her comfort zone next to the other women's more competent hands and yet, even under Gia's critical, watchful eyes, it had felt inordinately nice to be part of something like that. Even helping the other women clean up after dinner had felt important. Significant.

A short vibration on her lap alerted Naomi to a new text message, and she glanced down where her phone was balanced between her thighs.

Nick: Hey Spy Girl. How goes reconnaissance?

Naomi's thumbs hovered over the keyboard as her mind sought an appropriate response. Although she'd mentioned attending dinner at Aashi's house to Nick earlier that day, she hadn't mentioned her agreement with Dev. And while keeping her friend in the dark left her uneasy, it wasn't the full reason behind her hesitation in answering. Naomi's feelings felt too big and raw to put into words properly. Or jokingly. She felt like she was sitting in a pool of new emotions that, while not entirely unwelcome, were overwhelming nonetheless.

Naomi: The food here is UNREAL.

Nick: Nab some in your purse for me!!

Naomi: Oh yeah, that'll get me invited back.

Nick: If you truly love me, you'll do it.

"What—" Dev said, rounding the corner from the living room into the hallway.

Naomi stuffed her phone into her pocket before lifting her hand to stop him in his tracks. "Let me guess," she teased before dropping her voice several octaves in an attempt to mimic the velvet timbre of his voice. *"What are you doing here?"*

Dev ducked his head as he sprawled on the stairs a few steps below Naomi. "I don't sound like that."

She thought she'd matched his cranky undertone quite well. "I'll keep practicing."

"The question still stands," Dev reminded her.

"I'm . . ." *Loving this.* "Taking it all in."

Although Dev looked puzzled, he didn't prod. Instead, he held up his phone—the latest model of a smartphone, Naomi couldn't help but notice—to show her that it was after eleven o'clock. "I think the dangers of my marriage-infatuated mother's scheming aren't going to surface tonight. You don't have to stick around if you don't want to."

"Are you kicking me out?" Naomi feigned puppy-dog eyes.

Dev rolled his eyes. "It's the weekend," he said matter-of-factly, like the old, crabby man he was. Naomi half expected him to pull a nickel out of her ear and encourage her to treat herself to an ice-cream cone. "I'm sure you have better things to do with your time."

"Like kicking up my heels with other young whippersnappers?"

Dev glared back.

Leaving was the last thing she wanted to do, but Naomi had no idea how to put her feelings into words. There was something captivating about the ease and familiarity of the women clucking away in a language she didn't understand, and the way the men, bellies full, sprawled out on couches, comfortable and at home with one another as they picked away at their teeth with toothpicks.

Even though Naomi's family had been the only mixed one in her small town, they hadn't been lepers. She had been to large family get-togethers with her stepfather's extensive family of beer-guzzling aunts, cowboy-boot-wearing uncles, and shrieking cousins. The Kellys had accepted Naomi and her mother as casually as they accepted that sometimes Great-Grandma Kelly would jab you with a knitting needle when she wanted you to straighten up.

But then a curious aunt would run her fingers through Naomi's coarse dark curls and marvel at the texture, or her cousin would make some stupid vow that this summer she would achieve a tan comparable to Naomi's dusky skin, and Naomi would feel something dark brewing inside her—a whispered hiss from deep within.

"I'm okay to hang out a bit more. I'm kind of feeling the vibe around here," Naomi said.

Dev glanced around, disbelief splashed across his face. The hallway was lined with pictures of Aashi's daughters, from kindergarten to present, in outdated gold frames. The conversations swirling around them were punctuated every few minutes by the flush of the main floor's toilet as it valiantly tried to accommodate the thirty or so guests in attendance.

"And what vibe are you feeling, exactly, on this Saturday night?" he asked, as if he expected to be on the receiving end of the perfect punch line.

"This feeling of fam—" The sudden lump in Naomi's throat

cut her off, both a warning and a mocking reminder of how out of her element she was. She knew Dev's family wasn't perfect—his chauvinistic older brother was proof of that—and yet their closeness with one another and with lifelong friends pulled forward the questions she had tucked away long ago. Had her mother not run away from her family, would she be enjoying this same closeness? Would she know how to prepare biriyani and payesh, guided by the hands of a doting grandmother whose protectiveness was as sharp as her tongue? What would it be like to be a strong branch of a larger family tree whose roots ran deeper than a rebellious daughter's rash decisions?

"This feeling of community," Naomi said instead, unable to keep the wistfulness out of her voice. "It's sweet."

Dev snorted and stood to lean against the staircase banister, his button-down shirt stretching over his chest as he crossed his arms. "Sweet?" His voice dripped with skepticism. "They do this every single weekend, Naomi. And it's the same thing over and over again. The house may change, but it's the same people stuffing themselves with the same kinds of foods and then moving to the same corners of the house to talk about the same things."

Naomi's eyes widened. Taciturn Dev could really get going when it came to a rant.

"The men," he continued, "talk about politics and the state of the world—even though they refuse to step out of their own communities and do anything about it—and the women cook and clean together while gossiping shamelessly the entire time. It's . . . it's . . ." Dev exhaled. "Suffocating."

Naomi fought to keep her smile in check. With everyone else, she always tried to get along, stay in good graces, but with Dev, she couldn't resist poking the bear. "What's wrong with good food and good company?"

"It doesn't feel too good when it's been shoved down your throat your entire life."

This time, Naomi was powerless against the bitter downturn of her lips. He had no idea how lucky he was to have this in his life, this particular brand of asphyxia. Loneliness was worse. Being on the outside, fated to forever pick the lock with a hairpin that was always either too short, too thick, or too hopelessly curved to gain entry to whatever was inside was a far worse fate. But she didn't know how to tell him that as the swirl of voices circled them, together but apart.

In the end, she didn't have to because a small, elderly woman ambled toward them, a mischievous smirk on her prune face. She began rolling her wrists above her head, sashaying in small, shuffling steps. "Sajna, kya yeh mera pehla, pehla pyaar hai," she sang with a warble, finishing with a darling little shimmy of her shoulders.

Charmed, Naomi grinned back, but Dev blushed. "She doesn't understand Hindi, auntie," he said. "And she's not Bengali." He turned to Naomi to explain: "That was a popular song from *Kabhi Khushi Kabhie Gham*, a famous Bollywood movie."

"Not Bengali? But you're so pretty." The old lady peered into Naomi's face. "What are you?"

Naomi cleared her throat. "My family lives in a different province."

"Province, schmovince," she answered with an impatient bobble of her neck. "I mean, where is your family from? What country?"

"India." Under the old lady's curious but kind gaze, Naomi bit her bottom lip and backed up a step. One of the gold picture frames on the wall dug into her shoulder.

"She's a brand consultant. My mother hired her for the bazaar," Dev said, a hint of sharpness in his voice.

"And you don't speak your mother tongue?" The woman looked at her with concern. "How do you talk to your relatives back home?"

"We're not that close," Naomi said tightly.

"Oh dear, that's awful."

"I disagree," Dev muttered.

"What's that, Devdas? I didn't catch that." The elderly woman seemed immune to the sudden coolness that had descended upon them. "Well, no matter. Who needs flowery talk? After all, they say music is the language of love," she said as she glided past them to the bathroom, humming and swaying her hips in her peach sari. She shot them one last cheeky grin over her shoulder before shutting the door.

"I'm doomed," Dev said darkly, shaking his head.

Naomi huffed a sigh of relief. "The matchmaker is going to send both the young and old, huh?" When Dev slouched moodily against the banister, Naomi thought that, at this rate, the shimmying old lady had a better chance of attracting a match than he did.

But Dev didn't rise to the bait. Instead, he drove his hands through his thick black hair. "That old lady is just a taste of what you're going to have to deal with over the next few months."

"What do you mean?"

With surprising grace, Dev pushed himself off and angled his chin to the bathroom door. "I mean this weird obsession with love and marriage and romance." Dev spat out the last word like it was rice pudding poison. "It's like when you reach a certain age, a wedding is the be-all and end-all."

"The expectation to get married isn't just a South Asian thing," Naomi pointed out.

Dev snorted. "Maybe not, but I'm still doomed. God forbid I want something different than what the community decides is appropriate or what my parents based their lives around. Get married to someone who ticks all the boxes or choose for yourself and risk being a leper . . . Those are the only two options."

"Oh, it can't be that bad," Naomi said with a chuckle. "You're exaggerating."

"Sure. I love joking around about my bleak future."

"Dev, Prince of Doom and Gloom," Naomi teased. She gestured to the closed bathroom door where the elderly woman's faint humming warbled behind rushing water. "She's harmless."

Dev responded with a dubious glance. "Don't let the sappy lyrics convince you otherwise. This community is obsessed with matrimony. Don't get swept up in the idea that an arranged marriage is the answer to all my problems. Don't forget our deal."

A high-pitched shriek followed by a chorus of giggles from the women's area was enough to mask Naomi's sigh of resignation. Dev was wasting his breath. Being in the presence of people who shared the texture of her hair and color of her skin wasn't enough. Nor was secretly knowing she came from the same roots, could claim the same Bengali heritage even if it refused to claim her.

It was never enough. She couldn't understand the sappy lyrics, nor could she go home and re-create the complex flavors she had tasted tonight. Even after Dev's explanations—and rants—Naomi could barely wrap her head around the customs motivating Gia to go as far as to hire a matchmaker for her very unwilling son. There wasn't any danger of getting swept away, not when, even in her element as a brand consultant for the bazaar, doing what she loved, she was barely hanging on by her fingernails.

Getting swept up in the South Asian community was the last thing Naomi would allow to happen.

chapter
9

Dev's forehead creased as he pulled into an unfamiliar strip mall in West Kelowna. He glanced at his phone: the pin Naomi had sent him indicated he was in the right spot, but she hadn't divulged exactly where to meet her. For a brief, shaky moment, Dev allowed a fleck of doubt to wriggle into his brain. Since he'd struck this deal with Naomi, it had been there—nestled in the back of his mind like a stubborn speck of pepper between his teeth—reminding him that she could change her mind at any moment. For no reason at all.

Never mind that baring his fears of marriage to her had been completely out of character for him; the real shock was that she'd stuck around. Stuck around *and* agreed to help him. Dev kept waiting for the other shoe to drop, for Naomi to inform him that the rebrand of the bazaar aside, helping him wasn't worth the trouble. *He* wasn't worth the trouble.

When he finally spotted Naomi leaning against her silver Toyota, looking happy to see him as he made his way to her, Dev had to steel himself against the relief that washed over him. *She could still change her mind*, he reminded himself, but as her smile widened, as open as the sun, the caution flew from his mind as did the rest of his self-preservation.

Had a person ever had this effect on him before? On a Monday morning, no less? In the crowded parking lot of old cars straddling white lines, she was hard to look away from and he awkwardly averted his gaze to the ground before she noticed.

"What are we doing here?" he grumbled, shoving his hands in the pockets of his windbreaker.

Although her eyes narrowed, Naomi's smile refused to wilt. "Research." She turned and led the way to a cheerful-looking storefront in the middle of the row of shops: Sweets That Make You Singh. Just shy of opening the entrance door, Naomi noticed his reluctance and beckoned him forward.

Dev grabbed Naomi's arm before she could swing the door open, taken aback by the delicate contours of her wrist. So far, she'd shown herself to be so capable, a woman who refused to give up without a fight. Everything about her was unbending, steel strength, but her fragile wrist said otherwise.

He gentled his grip and tone. "Why are we here?"

"This place used to be Sweets of Punjab, but a few years ago, they decided to modernize and expand their clientele." She lifted her chin. "I want to see their spread and what's popular on the menu."

By Dev's estimation, the only thing that could make a Monday worse was a trip to a Punjabi sweets store. He'd visited them enough times over the course of his life. But he held his tongue because it was becoming clear to him that around Naomi, he was especially prone to sticking his foot in his mouth. He'd already known he was rarely, if ever, the most charming person in the room, but in her presence, it was as if everything short-circuited and his baser, blunt instincts kicked in.

Even now, the embarrassment of ranting about marriage because a little old lady had broken into a brief song-and-dance pressed between his shoulder blades, uncomfortable and sharp. And as Naomi stared at him with expectant eyes, her other hand on the door handle, Dev reached for something easier, and more familiar, to soothe the pinch.

Good old crankiness.

"We had to come all the way to West Kelowna to do this? There are plenty of Indian restaurants and sweet shops closer to the bazaar."

Naomi pulled open the door. "I felt we needed to get away from the bazaar—and that neighborhood—for this."

Dev hesitated a brief second before following her inside. Sweets That Make You Singh was not what he had expected. It was a standing-room-only Indian desserts shop. And busy, if the swell of eager voices was any indication. People of all different backgrounds were lined up at the register, eyeing rows upon rows of colorful sweets winking from behind glass display cases. A giant chalkboard announced boxed assortments with clever names like "Treats to Woo Your Mother-in-Law," "She Said Yes," and "Last-Minute Potluck." It was gimmicky, but it worked.

"Isn't it great?" Naomi beamed. In the bustling, happy chatter of the store, her eyes were as bright as the pink chum chums advertised as the "Sweet of the Day." Despite adding waiting in line to his pet peeves list, Dev found himself moving closer to her.

"It's all right," he allowed.

Naomi leaned her ear toward him. "I'm sorry, are you *agreeing* with me?"

"Maybe." Perhaps it was being away from Gia's Bazaar, but in the bright and whimsical dessert store, he was feeling lighter and at ease with Naomi by his side.

Not that he would ever admit that to her.

"And here I thought I'd never see the day." Naomi's smug grin was surprisingly endearing. "Dev Mukherjee agreeing with the Brand Lady."

"Okay, you made your point." Dev forced a scowl to hide his smile. "And as you can probably see, the gulab jamun and laddoos are flying off the shelves. Are we done here?"

"Not until I get something delicious to eat."

"Fine. But it's a pass for me," Dev replied, even as a robust gulab jamun caught his eye.

Naomi nudged him with her elbow. "Really? Because you're staring at that mishti like a sprinter eyes the finish line."

Noting that Naomi had remembered, and correctly pronounced, the Bengali word for "sweet," Dev lifted his eyebrows. "Someone was paying attention."

"I'm full of surprises," she said with a wry smile.

"What's with the sport references, anyway?"

"What?"

"This is the third time I've heard you randomly compare something to a sport."

A faint blush darkened Naomi's already rosy cheeks. "My stepdad and I used to bond over the Olympics. You learn a lot about different sports when you're glued to the screen for sixteen days straight." She shot him a sideways glance. "I know it's weird. He does it, too. My stepdad, I mean."

Dev paused to bury any traces of wistfulness in his voice. "Are you close to him?"

"Yes, I am."

They fell silent, two statues in a fidgety line. Although Dev knew he had, once again, said the exact right thing to lead them down the wrong path, this time felt different. The insurmountable edges of awkward regret failed to appear. He felt oddly comfortable falling into contemplative silence with Naomi. Even more strange was the urge to lighten the mood and return them to a place of easy banter. To spark the light in her eyes again.

"I have a thing for sports, too," he said. The words sounded stunted in his ears, but at Naomi's grateful smile, he felt his chest expand.

"Really?"

"I don't think I'm as well versed as you are, but I'd love to work for the business side of a professional, or semiprofessional, sports team." The second the words left his mouth, Dev blinked, startled. He'd never admitted that out loud to anyone before. Even to close friends, he had glossed over his reason for leaving his accounting firm, citing a *desire for new opportunities* to bullshit his way out of follow-up questions.

"That'd be cool. Is there a need for accountants in that industry?"

There had better be or he'd be trapped in his mother's house forever. "Someone has to manage the money." *And the stats*, Dev added dreamily to himself. Not that he'd ever admit *that* aloud.

"So, what's stopping you?"

Dev scoffed. "Bengalis are pretty conservative when it comes to career paths. The preferable ones are medicine, law, and engineering. Business school was acceptable to them as long as I got a CPA because taxes were familiar ground to them." He cocked an eyebrow at her. "Are your parents as extreme?"

Naomi sidestepped his question. "It's funny, isn't it? How what we want can be so different from what our parents want for us."

"I think every first-generation kid raised in North America feels that way."

Naomi's chuckle was low and tinged with sarcasm. "Well, at least we have that in common."

"What do you mean?"

Naomi's face clouded over for a brief moment before she flashed another grin and clownishly threaded her arm through his. "Oh, Dev. There is so much you have yet to learn about me."

Before Dev could retort, they had reached the front of the line. Although waiting to buy South Asian desserts was the last way he wanted to spend his time, vague disappointment misted over Dev. He was joking around and enjoying it.

Maybe Monday mornings weren't so bad after all.

"Are you here for the class?" a jolly-looking woman asked, beaming at them from behind the register.

"What class?" Dev asked.

The woman's eyes flicked to where their arms were still linked. "The cooking class. It's starting in a few minutes."

"Oh n—"

"What are you making?" Naomi interrupted.

The woman pointed to the tray of gulab jamun that had caught Dev's attention earlier. Naomi turned to him, bright, shiny, and eager.

"No."

"Come on," she cajoled, tugging on his arm. "It will help me get an appreciation for Indian cuisine."

"I saw the heap of food you put away at my aunt's house; I think you've got the appreciation part down pat."

"Dev." Naomi drawled his name with exasperation. "Don't you want to learn how to make plump, juicy gulab jamuns?"

Women like Naomi shouldn't be allowed to say words like *plump* and *juicy* in public spaces. Especially while standing so close that even with the thick, sugary fumes of the confection store around them, her scent overwhelmed him. Coconut and something light and fresh—like sunlight warming the sand beside a calm ocean in the morning. When he failed to answer, Naomi elbowed him again.

"Consider this as part of our deal? Please."

Although making the stupid dessert had nothing to do with researching for the store, it was clear Naomi really wanted to do this. Dev could feel himself relenting, but it was the saleslady who hammered the last nail in his coffin.

"These classes are very popular, and there's only one spot left this morning," she said. "It'll be thirty-five dollars for both of you."

At Dev's resigned sigh, Naomi stepped in front of him and pulled out her wallet. "Count us in."

As the cashier pushed the PIN pad in Naomi's direction, she gave Dev a long once-over. "Do I know you?"

Probably, Dev thought glumly.

But before he could respond, she snapped her fingers in recognition. "You're one of the boys from Gia's Bazaar." Her eyes flicked to Naomi with new interest.

Naomi, bent over the PIN pad, didn't notice the gleam in the woman's eye, but Dev did, and something in his gut tightened. His agreement with Naomi had seemed like a no-brainer after having a drink tossed in his face, but as this woman's eyes bounced between them, he had the sinking realization that maybe he hadn't thought this one entirely through.

"Enjoy the class," she said with a knowing smile.

What have I gotten us into? Naomi tightened the strings of her pristine white chef's apron and glanced around the industrial-sized kitchen located directly behind the sweets store. Six other couples were in attendance, most appearing to be in their mid-twenties to late thirties. Surrounded by premeasured cups of flour, sugar, and oil, every person in the room seemed either horny, in love, or, sickeningly, both.

Except Dev and Naomi.

She blamed the sugar for this rash decision. The cloying sweetness clinging to the air in the bakery's front room had brainwashed her, brainwashed them both. A sickly-sweet seduction that had loosened their tongues and reservations, forcing the stress of the rebrand and the threat of potential brides to take a back seat to the rich, tempting desserts surrounding them. And Dev's company had felt different today. Comfortable.

Irresistible.

Besides, Naomi *really* wanted to make gulab jamun. However, one glance at Dev now, who scowled like a seasoned criminal in a violent prison movie, told Naomi that this spontaneous turn of events might have been a colossal mistake on her part.

"I can think of worse ways to spend the day," she joked weakly.

Unmoved, Dev lifted an eyebrow. "Like?"

Naomi's gaze trailed to a couple to their left: she and Dev watched in silence as the petite blonde dipped her finger in the cup of sugar for her partner to suck off with exaggerated tongue action. When Dev turned back to Naomi, he looked pained.

"Uh . . ." Naomi shrugged. "Like watching a movie with your grandparents with multiple sex scenes?"

"What kind of movies did you watch with your grandparents?" Dev asked in disbelief.

"All right, lovebirds!" The woman who had sold them their spot called from the front of the room and clapped her hands. "Welcome to Sweets That Make You Singh's couples' cooking class."

Naomi detected a faint groan from her cranky partner.

Oblivious, the instructor continued. "Today we are making gulab jamun, a traditional dessert that is very popular in our store. First, we will make the syrup. You will need to add four lightly crushed green cardamom pods into your pot with the sugar and water."

Dev snatched up the cardamom pods lined up on the tray of ingredients in front of them and tossed them into the empty pot.

"She said they need to be lightly crushed!" Naomi picked them out and pressed them firmly between her fingertips as she had seen Priya do at the dinner party. She felt an unexpected burst of pride as the spice's shell cracked between her fingers, releasing an earthy-sweet scent.

With a huff, Dev dumped the rest of the required ingredients in the pot before glowering at their instructor.

So much for lightheartedness, Naomi thought, casting a sideways glance at Dev. His arms were folded across his chest. Naomi couldn't help herself—her eyes automatically sought the firm cut of his forearms. At least there were certain perks to his sulking.

Once the class had finished making the syrup, the instructor led them through creating the dough. "Gulab jamun dough is very delicate, so when you roll it into balls, try not to overhandle them. Be delicate and gentle." She expertly worked the dough between her hands. "See? Think of your balls as smooth, perfectly shaped little babies."

At the workstation in front of Naomi and Dev, a couple that looked eerily alike gazed starry-eyed at each other and giggled. Dev scowled at their dough and made no move to follow the instructor's direction.

With an impatient huff, Naomi reached into the bowl. "For a

guy whose mother is well-known for her cooking, you don't seem to know your way around the kitchen."

"Why should I? Just because I grew up eating it doesn't mean I love it."

Naomi's temper flared. "You could at least try, considering I'm going to be playing defense for you for the next few months."

"Why? *You're* not going to be cooking for the renovated café."

Annoyed, Naomi pursed her lips and focused on smoothing the dough between her hands. Dev watched her for a moment before shoving a hand that was anything but delicate and gentle into the bowl and fisting an alarming amount of dough. Jerkily, he began forming a large ball.

"That's too big." Naomi held up her own donut-sized creation for comparison. It was, as the instructor had said, a perfectly smooth baby.

He responded by slapping more dough onto the ball.

Speaking of babies. Naomi kept her thoughts to herself as she finished rolling the rest of the dough. As instructed by their teacher, Naomi turned on the stove to heat their oil. She eyed Dev's ball warily. His creation loomed over hers like a third-grade bully preying on defenseless preschoolers.

Dev caught her stare. "It's fine," he insisted.

As the class waited for their oil to reach optimal temperature, their teacher provided a brief overview of the store's history and the cultural significance of Punjabi sweets. Dev's loud sigh whistled with irritation.

"Let me guess." Naomi meant to be playful, but sarcasm soured her words. "You already know the history of gulab jamun."

Dev lifted a puzzled brow. "Gulab jamun is a Punjabi dessert. I'm Bengali."

Outwardly, Naomi rolled her eyes, but her insides bristled. Although she couldn't blame Dev completely—he didn't know about her upbringing—having her lack of knowledge of the culture thrown in her face over and over again stirred ugly feelings in her chest.

Their instructor stepped in before Naomi could give in to the dark, shadowy mess inside her. "It's time to deep-fry your balls!" she called from the front of the room. Naomi and Dev traded exasperated looks. "Be careful, the oil will be very hot."

Dev passed the slotted spoon to Naomi.

"Sure, I'll fry them," she said sarcastically.

"Remember," the instructor called over the hiss and crackle of hot oil popping through the kitchen. "You want to treat your babies with the utmost tenderness. You created them! Use a soft touch!"

After carefully dropping her neat little balls of dough into the oil, Naomi scooped Dev's giant contribution and wrestled it into the oil. To her dismay, the damn thing didn't break.

"Oh my," the instructor commented as she passed by their workstation. "Your balls are awfully uneven."

"It's a problem of his," Naomi said with a mischievous glance at the ever-stoic Dev. "Runs in his family."

"I'm proud of my balls," Dev replied, straight-faced.

The instructor shrugged in confusion and moved on.

Gingerly, Naomi used the slotted spoon to roll Dev's giant monstrosity so it would fry on all sides. Another euphemism was at the tip of her tongue, but as she pulled her eyes away from the pan to shoot Dev a sly look, she felt a piercing burn on her thumb.

"Ouch!"

Dev grabbed the slotted spoon from her hand and tossed it on the counter. "What? What's wrong?"

"I think some oil jumped out of the pan onto my thumb."

Moving closer, Dev cupped her hand gently in his and examined her thumb. "I don't see anything. Does it still hurt?"

The brush of Dev's fingers against hers was soft and warm as he carefully examined her hand. He turned her thumb this way and that, examining her skin with a gentleness that belied all his earlier grumblings. Whatever pain had triggered her nervous system only moments ago disappeared, replaced by a thrilling kind of burn where Dev's skin brushed against hers.

His touch would be etched on her cells long after the class was over.

"You smell like cardamom," he murmured, his head still bent over her hand.

Something in Naomi's chest hiccuped.

"It doesn't hurt anymore," she whispered, kind of wishing it did. He gave her a long look before dropping her hand and grabbing the slotted spoon to finish the deep-frying himself.

Several minutes later, each couple had a plastic container of gulab jamun swimming in syrup in front of them. Despite herself, Naomi was proud of their work. Even Dev's creation looked nicely toasted and delectable.

"We could've bought these instead of doing the class," Dev grumbled, untying his apron.

"But it was an experience!"

"That resulted in you burning yourself."

"Does anything bring you joy, Dev? Besides accounting and giving me a hard time?"

He tossed his apron on the counter. "Nope, that's about it."

Naomi fought the urge to crack a smile. Something about this man kept her on the precipice between laughing and screaming into the abyss.

"Now, usually we would let the gulab jamun sit for a few hours to soak up all that delicious syrup and double in size," the instructor said, holding a tray of perfect, uniformly shaped balls in the air like the Olympic torch. "But I always tell my class to try one right away to enjoy the fruits of their labor." The instructor offered a cheeky wink. "In fact, I encourage you all to feed one another as a romantic ending to a labor of love."

Dev shook his head with a grunt, but Naomi considered the bowl in front of her. Impishly, she reached for the massive ball and lifted it to Dev's lips with a challenge in her eye.

He scoffed. "No, thank—"

Before he could finish, Naomi thrust her hand forward, forcing the gulab jamun into Dev's partially opened mouth. Never one to half-ass anything, she didn't stop there. Naomi smashed the entire ball against his face, enjoying the sumptuous squish of deep-fried dough on the palm of her hand. Shell-shocked, he stared at her, but she could only focus on the mess of gulab jamun smeared on his face. His nose and chin were covered, too, casualties of her vengeance.

The rest of the dessert fell onto the floor with a delicious *plop*.

Under his alarmed gaze, Naomi stared at Dev, the victim of a dessert hate crime. It was comical. And horrific. Naomi prepared herself for the worst, her fingers curling in anticipation, sticking to her palm thanks to bits of syrup-soaked, fried dough on her skin. Would Dev renege on the deal? Or worse, consider her actions a fireable offense?

And then, to her shock, Dev threw back his head and laughed, his dimples deepening wonderfully. Several other couples lingering in the room stared in astonishment, but Naomi found herself grinning in delight. Surrounded by his unfiltered laughter, her mind wandered back to those precious few moments when Dev patiently bent over her hand, concerned for her well-being, and although the burn was long forgotten, her right hand started tingling. The desire to lick away the remnants—as well as the imprint of the scrape of his jaw against her fingertips—crept into her mind, silent and tentative but so very present all the same.

As she swiped a striped dish towel off the counter, Naomi cautioned the warmth stirring in her core not to spread too far. *He's Gia's son*, she reminded herself. It was a personal rule not to get involved with clients, an important one given her brand consultant network's penchant for gossip. Unfortunately, Naomi's professional rules seemed a lot murkier when it came to Dev.

One thing was becoming very clear, though: Dev was not as salty as he seemed. There was some sugar there, too, and maybe Naomi should consider going on a diet.

chapter
10

Later that week, Naomi stood shoulder to shoulder beside Dev at the bazaar's counter, watching Nick and his construction crew gut the store, with a huge grin on her face. Dev was frowning.

Quelle surprise.

It didn't take a rocket scientist to figure out that Dev was not a champion for change. For that reason, and the countdown to Gia's three-month deadline looming over her, she had kept Dev away from the bazaar so Nick could get a head start. Smashing a deep-fried ball of dough in his face had simply been an unexpected perk to her plan.

Dusty aisle by dusty aisle, the store was transforming into a blank slate for new beginnings and reimagination. In the growing emptiness of where knickknacks, display stands, and faded posters of Bollywood movie stars had once been, Naomi saw possibilities. An empty canvas just waiting for color, texture, and meaning. Naomi *loved* this part.

Buoyed, she nudged Dev and lowered her voice. "Why so serious?"

He turned to glare at her. "How—"

Bang! Bang! Bang! Bang! The methodical pounding of a sledge-hammer drowned out his comment. Dev snapped his mouth shut and directed a glare at the plaid-wearing offender. When the noise stopped, he tried again.

"How long do—"

Bang! Bang! Bang! Bang!

Naomi unsuccessfully checked her smile and used the mind-numbing noise as an excuse to lean into his face and shout, "What?"

At the next bout of silence, Dev's words rushed out. "I said, how long do we have—"

Bang! Bang!

Naomi threw back her head and laughed maniacally until Dev grabbed her upper arm and pulled her closer. He pressed his lips close to her ear. "How long do we have to endure this racket?"

She froze, her side pressed to the front of his chest. For a guy who was frosty at the best of times, the heat seeping from him was a mystery in itself. His breath dusted over her, sending a minty shiver spiraling downward from her earlobe to her core. When he didn't step away, Naomi turned her face toward him, their noses a hairbreadth away. His chocolate eyes had darkened into rich, velvety fondue, and, for a wayward nanosecond, they snapped downward to her lips before meeting her eyes again.

"Well?" he asked, his voice pitched lower as if inviting Naomi to lean closer. His warm breath fluttered against the sensitive skin behind her ear, and while Naomi fought to remain still, she couldn't stop her toes from curling inside her shoes.

Before she could answer, Nick stepped to the counter. He had that shiny, elated sheen of a contractor high on the thrill of a remodel. Naomi reclaimed her space and smiled at her friend. From the corner of her eye, she saw Dev stiffen.

"We're going to make a lot of progress today," Nick reported, inadvertently answering Dev's question. "Give us a week, maybe less, and we'll have this place emptied out." He hooked his thumbs onto his tool belt and turned to Dev with an easy smile. "I think we'll be able to meet your three-month deadline, no problem."

"That's great," Naomi chimed in when Dev failed to answer. Or refused, given the stony look in his eyes. His trademark scowl was back. "Thanks, Nicky. There's a reason why I always call you in for a job."

"We have done our fair share of redesigns together. You're practically my work wife." Nick jerked his thumb in Naomi's direction and addressed Dev. "The stories I could tell you about this one."

"I bet," Dev said, his voice short.

Nick turned back to Naomi, undaunted. "We will need to firm up our materials, colors . . ."

Naomi nodded and reached into her bag for her notes. She pulled out a typed list she'd made for Nick the night before and slid it onto the table. Dev sidled closer to take a look, and as sharp as a starting gun, Naomi was keenly aware of his proximity.

If she backed up half an inch, she'd be pressed against his solid frame, and the knowledge drizzled a slow, sweet burn through her veins.

"A few things are missing, but this looks solid. Gives us a good idea of where to start," Nick said, folding the list and tucking it into his back pocket. "What would I do without you and your anal-retentive ways?"

"Install a mirrored dance floor?" Naomi teased.

"Hey! The owner of that bar wanted original ideas—"

"Right, and you just love an opportunity to—"

"It'll be hard to meet your deadline if you don't get back to work." Dev's voice interrupted their banter.

As usual, Nick was unbothered. "You got it." He smiled at her again, winked at the ever-stoic Dev, and ambled off to consult with his crew.

Dev's brow was furrowed as he watched Nick walk away. "Did he just . . . wink at me?"

"Yep."

Dev turned to her, his mouth agape.

Naomi bit her lip and swallowed a chuckle. "He's always had a thing for brooding, grumpy guys." She didn't add that Nick might not be the only one.

"He's gay." Gravy-thick realization coated Dev's voice.

"I wouldn't get your hopes up. He's been dating that guy with the sledgehammer for almost six months."

A small, private smile crossed Dev's lips so quickly, Naomi could have blinked and missed it. But she didn't. She had grown curiously attuned to those rare, quiet smiles and the wink of his dimples. It helped that those smiles, as fleeting as they might be, were the perfect time to capitalize on Dev's good mood. She reached for her bag again, ready to seize the moment with a deep discussion on fabric swatches. Behind the whack of hammers and shuffling of construction boots, she thought she detected the sound of the store's front entrance opening, but Naomi didn't bother to look up until she heard Dev hiss, *"Shit."*

Swatches forgotten, Naomi snapped her head up to see a young South Asian walking—no, stalking—toward them. She was a woman on a mission. She barely glanced at the half-demolished store around her and, lucky for her, her feet seemed immune to the dangers of stray nails and loose debris as they sought their target: Dev.

Naomi lifted an eyebrow and turned to him.

"Get ready," he whispered out of the corner of his mouth.

"What?"

He whipped his face toward her, urgency darkening his eyes. "You said you would deter potential brides; that includes the ones who come to do battle."

Oh right. It had been all too easy for Naomi to forget her end of the bargain and focus on the job, especially since none of the matchmaker's contingent of potential brides had surfaced for several days. It had been remarkably pleasant, pouring all her energy into the bazaar with Dev by her side, as baffling a realization as that was. He was like a shadow, gloomy and at times foreboding, but he was always there. Dependable.

But now it was her turn to deliver. If Dev could good-naturedly take a gulab jamun to the face in the name of research, then surely Naomi could fool this matrimony-minded panther making her way toward them into believing that she, too, was in the running as a potential South Asian daughter-in-law. Even if that was the furthest thing from the truth.

"Dev?" the girl asked shortly.

"Uh, yeah?"

However, with charm like that, maybe Dev didn't need her help after all.

"Jasminder Dhaliwal," the girl said. "I'm here to see if we're a match."

"Well—"

Jasminder pulled out her phone and glanced down at the screen. "I've reviewed your profile at length, and a lot of your qualities match what I'm looking for."

Despite herself, Naomi leaned forward. "Such as?"

"I'm interested in someone with a good education, solid lineage . . ." Jasminder gestured toward her phone again. "A secure job, the potential for upward mobility, and no kids."

Naomi turned to Dev with raised eyebrows. After seeing him

play with one of the aunties' toddlers at Aashi's dinner party, the information that he was antichildren took her by surprise; however, when she thought about it, Dev tended to err on the side of aversion when it came to, well, everything.

"You don't want kids?" Naomi asked.

Jasminder waved her phone impatiently. "No, no. It says he *does* want kids but that he doesn't already have them."

"It does?" Dev looked alarmed. "My profile says I want kids?"

"Don't you?" Jasminder said, frowning as she scrolled through her phone.

"I . . . I . . ."

"Can I see his profile?" Naomi asked. When Dev angled his head warningly, she cleared her throat. "I mean, can I *review* his profile again?" Jasminder handed her the phone.

While Naomi was well aware that an awkward silence had descended over the three of them, she was powerless against the lure of reading Dev's matchmaking profile. No middle name, thirty-one years old, five-ten . . . It took less than one swipe to reach the bottom of the page. How peculiar it was to sum up a person's marriage potential on one, maybe two pages, as if Dev's education, salary, religion, and parents' and grandparents' names were enough to ascertain what kind of husband he would be. She'd gleaned very little from skimming his bio. Nothing that mattered, anyway.

And yet these were the things that meant everything to the Gias, Jasminders, and Larisas of the world. These were enough for him to be a worthwhile candidate on the marriage market. It was a baffling punch to the gut knowing that Naomi would never measure up to these standards. That her diploma from a technical college, her struggling career, and the fact that she didn't know her biological grandparents' histories would be marks against her, earning her a big, fat red stamp: undesirable.

There was little time to wallow in this realization, though, as Dev cleared his throat as if his lungs were in a choke hold. When Naomi's gaze met his, he looked ready to jump out of his skin as his eyes darted to where Jasminder stood and back again.

Oh right.

"Well, Dev has all the qualities I'm looking for in a man—I mean, husband, too," Naomi said as she slid the phone back to Jasminder.

Jasminder cocked her head expectantly.

"And . . ." Naomi tried to sound territorial. "I got here first, so . . ."

"So?" Jasminder looked between Dev and Naomi, unimpressed.

"So I'd like to get to know Naomi a little better," Dev offered.

"But maybe if you get to know *me*, you might feel otherwise," Jasminder reasoned.

Naomi wet her lips and darted a glance at Dev, but the panic creasing his forehead was enough to alert her that he was fumbling. It was up to her to run the ball even if Jasminder seemed capable of filling every spot on the defensive line.

But Naomi and Dev had agreed on a game plan, and with the beginnings of the bazaar's rebrand happening right before Naomi's eyes, there was no way in hell she wasn't playing to win.

"He's not interested," Naomi informed Jasminder, whose eyes narrowed in challenge. *Bring it,* Naomi thought darkly. Her next paycheck depended on her ability to get rid of any and all potential brides, and when it came to keeping her lights on, Naomi was prepared to tuck her head down and charge.

"And how would you know?" Jasminder asked. "Are you his girlfriend?"

Dev opened his mouth to answer, but Naomi beat him to it. After all, she had rent to pay.

"Yes," she said, startling herself with how easily the word tumbled from her lips. Or perhaps the real surprise was how seamlessly she was learning to toe the line between the truth and the lies. The knowledge was an uncomfortable weight and she quickly added, "I mean, kind of."

Jasminder turned to Dev. "What's that supposed to mean?"

"It means," Naomi said before Dev could answer and further botch up what was already turning into one hell of a hack job, "that we're still figuring things out." She moved closer to Dev and slid her arm around his trim waist. When Dev failed to shift his arm so it encircled her shoulders as a socially competent person might to accommodate a side hug, Naomi was left pressing her nose into his firm biceps. She rolled with it, smooshing right in, and batted her lashes up at him. "Aren't we, honey boo boo?"

"Right," he said faintly.

"Right," Naomi cooed with enough assurance for both of them. It looked like she was going to have to sell this on her own. Naomi straightened her fingers, which were currently wrapped around his waist as if she were preparing to jab someone in the throat before drilling them into his side. As she'd hoped, Dev's arms jerked up and she leveraged the free space to snuggle right in. It was an added bonus to learn that Dev's preference for loose, casual clothes was not doing justice to the body underneath.

"So . . ." Jasminder studied the pair, her skepticism ebbing away. "You're spoken for."

"He is," Naomi confirmed.

"You're her 'honey boo boo'?"

Naomi could feel Dev's full-body shudder, and she grinned to herself.

"Yes," he said. Naomi could practically taste his bitterness on her tongue. "I'm her . . . 'honey boo boo.'"

Naomi gazed up at him, trying to look docile and adoring and whatever else a filly who had found her stallion might look like. A small, nagging voice in the back of her head warned her of the potential consequences of what she was setting in motion, but she ignored it. Besides, she couldn't bring herself to slide her arm away from the firm lower-back muscles that were finally relaxing in her hold.

It was too late now.

Jasminder tucked her phone back into her purse and shook her head. "Well, this is a surprise." Unlike Dev's previous failed matches, though, she looked more bemused than irritated.

A frisson of guilt wormed its way up Naomi's spine. "I, that is, *we* are sorry to have wasted your time."

But Jasminder seemed none the worse for wear. She shrugged and, now that arms had been laid down, seemed to notice the construction crew behind her. They were packing up for the day, the small group of workers quieted by a long day of hard labor. Naomi and Nick were going to expect a lot out of them in the next few months, but it would be worth it.

She wasn't going through with all of this for nothing. But tucked securely against Dev's side, her arm so relaxed around his waist, it was as if it had been there before and would happily go there again, and she couldn't help but wonder who was *really* benefiting from their deal.

"Well, you never know," Jasminder commented, almost as if she were speaking to herself. "You can read all the profiles in the world but who knows who you'll meet in person."

"Or whom your mother will sic on you next," Dev murmured under his breath.

Naomi jabbed his side again, although more gently this time, and searched for something comforting to say to Jasminder. She might not understand the method, but she understood the desire to find a match, a person one could belong to.

But she knew better than anyone that there were no guarantees that feelings, no matter how deep they might seem to run, would last. After all, her biological father hadn't stuck around. Even though he and her mother had fled to the prairies to raise their daughter, it had sustained him for only three years before he'd run off for something bigger and better out east. He was no better than her grandparents, who, after Naomi's mother had exited their lives, seemed perfectly satisfied with an estranged daughter. And granddaughter. They had never sought her out, as if they had swept away their feelings, leaving behind zero crumbs for Naomi to find her way back.

Forever was a flighty promise at best.

"I have to say, I am surprised," Jasminder continued. "I would not expect the two of you to be a match."

When Naomi stiffened, Dev tightened his arm around her shoulders. *Here it comes*, she thought grimly. *Don't react.* What was it about her that people like Jasminder, or Gia for that matter, could take one look and know something was lacking? That she wasn't the kind of person one would consider a suitable partner for a person like Dev, who, apparently, was the catch of the day? Was it the wildness of her curly hair? Her clothes? Or were *authentic* South Asians gifted with a third eye that could suss out the riffraff from the roses?

Jasminder stared down at her phone, her face wistful. "I told the matchmaker I wanted a genuine kind of guy, someone with a solid job who was reliable, mature, and not too flashy. A serious, no-nonsense type of man."

Naomi glanced up at Dev, who was listening attentively. He *was* all those things. The whole package. A catch.

But Jasminder shook her head at Dev, puzzled. "I never thought she would try to set me up with a 'honey boo boo.'"

chapter
11

Waterfront Park always delivered. The peaceful lake shimmered cobalt blue, trees lining the pathways stood full and tall, and the sun's rays had chased away the morning chill a couple of hours ago. It was unfiltered, surreal. Spirit-lifting.

Unfortunately, with yesterday's events playing a loop in her mind, Naomi might as well have been sitting in a landfill. What had she been thinking? At the time, snuggling into Dev's side, playing the part of doting girlfriend, had been the easiest option, a no-brainer like sliding on a pair of fluffy slippers after a grueling day.

The aftermath, though, had sent her crashing through the trees. Once Jasminder had left the store, "Honey Boo Boo" had turned to Naomi with horror etched across his face. The triumph of a successful charade had dissipated quickly, and Naomi, at a loss for how to explain the new, rocky terrain she had stumbled them into, had done the most cowardly thing possible.

She'd fled. Nick's crew had finished packing up for the day, providing Naomi with the perfect excuse to dash out the door like a world record was on the line.

But it was a new day, and with the sun toasting her legs and the rush of sugar from a sprinkled donut fading away, she knew it was time to face the music. With a resolute set of her shoulders, Naomi pulled out her phone and hit the call button, worrying her bottom lip as it rang.

"Well, look who it is."

Naomi relaxed back on the weathered park bench, allowing the familiar baritone on the other end of the line to soothe some of her tension away. "Hi, Dad."

"Happy Saturday," Eric Kelly replied. "Where are you today, sweetheart?"

Every Saturday, Naomi chose a park or nature sanctuary to unwind and decompress after a long workweek. The outdoors called to her, a trait she had inherited from her stepfather. When he had visited last month, she'd dragged him to Kasugai Gardens, laughing as the retired plumber lumbered through the peaceful Japanese-inspired gardens, in cargo pants and work boots, no less.

He was a simple guy, her stepfather. And her best pal.

"I'm at Waterfront Park." Naomi closed her eyes and smiled at the sun. "It's lovely."

"It's cold and gray here," Eric informed her, his voice cheery and unbothered. Born and raised in the same rural small town he was living in now, he was a man who was used to cloudy, cool skies for eight months of the year. He didn't mind living in a place with over five burger joints to choose from but no Thai or Vietnamese options. Or that the extent of "Culture Day" at school involved maybe a handful of students whose Ukrainian or German grandparents sent traditional dishes, while everyone else claimed to be Canadian and that was that.

Naomi's mother had refused to allow her to participate in Culture Days, much to her teachers' disappointment.

Still, despite their respective preferences for where they called home, Eric was Naomi's rock.

"What have you been up to?" Naomi asked.

"Everything is fine, just fine. The Campbells down the street had a basement flood emergency yesterday, so I spent most of the day there."

"Dad, you're supposed to be retired."

"Oh, come now. They're my neighbors," he chuckled. "Besides, I would never pass up the opportunity to—what do you kids say these days?—'flex' my skills."

At her stepdad's admission, Naomi forced a smile even though he couldn't see her. It was probably best that he was the neighborhood's unofficial on-call plumber: her mother was not a homebody. Supriya "Sue" Kelly lived for adventures and new experiences, which included signing up for whatever classes she could find, planning lengthy soul-searching trips, and changing jobs every few years.

"Hang on, sweetheart," Eric said. "I think your mom is home from her aerial class and the garage door is stuck again. I'll be right back."

Naomi immediately moved her phone several inches away from her ear as, predictably, her stepdad dropped his phone on the nearest hard surface with a clatter. As she listened to rustling and her parents' muted voices, a large family gathering at a nearby picnic table caught her eye. Adults chatted while unpacking coolers and bags of Tupperware while children scrambled about in what looked like a hysteria-induced game of tag. A balding grandfather sat at the rapidly filling picnic table, holding a baby and smiling at the kids shrieking around him.

It was a familiar scene for Waterfront Park and, at face value, served to enhance its picturesque views: the family was happy, comfortable, and so . . . together. A familiar ache hollowed Naomi's chest.

"Naomi?" Sue chirped into the phone. As usual, she didn't wait for a greeting before launching into a detailed description of her escapades. "You'll never guess what I learned today . . ."

Usually, Naomi absorbed her mother's tales with the same ease with which she accepted the odd, chilly breeze during her Saturday outings, but today she couldn't stop sneaking glances at the picnicking family, their noisiness momentarily stifled by a shared meal.

"There I was, dangling in midair, ribbon riding straight—"

"How come you never taught me to cook Bengali food?"

"—up my . . . What?" Sue paused. In the span of that single-syllable word, Sue's voice plummeted from cheery to wary. "Why?"

Naomi didn't miss the undertone in Sue's tone, the warning that rusted floodgates were better left untouched. Her mother never talked about her upbringing. When she had fled her family—a newborn on one arm, a flight-risk boyfriend who had taken her virginity on the other—she hadn't just escaped that chapter of her life; she'd thrown it in the shredder and set fire to the scraps.

It was a topic Naomi had learned to avoid at an early age, an easy feat in her homogenous community where the pressure to fit in with her white classmates was encouraged by her mother as well. As if embracing the present was a foolproof way of replacing the past.

"Did your parents not teach you how to cook traditional

foods?" Naomi pressed. "Do you have a favorite Bengali dish? Do they?"

"Naomi, what is this about?" Sue's impatience reminded Naomi of the day she'd returned home from elementary school, crying, because a classmate had used a red marker to draw a dot on Naomi's forehead without her consent. Her mother had rolled her eyes, irritated that her eight-year-old daughter would shed tears over such a trivial matter that could be easily washed away with soap and a rough cloth.

Naomi hesitated, torn between suds and water or lamenting over the abrasions the scrubbing had left behind. *Why don't I know my grandparents? Why can't we talk about them? Would they want to meet me?* There were too many questions lodged at the back of Naomi's throat, and after so many years of letting sleeping dogs lie, she had no idea where to start.

"Did something happen in Kelowna? Did someone say something to you?" her mother demanded.

Naomi straightened. She had known that her grandparents lived in Nanaimo, a city several hours away, but it had never occurred to her that any indirect connections to them could be made. Her social circle in Kelowna was small and, until recently, hadn't consisted of any members of the South Asian community.

"No, of course not," Naomi said. "I—"

"You don't mind what anyone says to you," Sue said with the kind of passion she normally reserved for realigning her chakras or showing up the perky blonde at spin class. "They can be so nosy and judgmental." Her voice rose a pitch. "Why you choose to live so close to them, I'll never understand."

Whether Sue was referring to other South Asians or Naomi's grandparents, Naomi wasn't sure, but at the shivery timbre in her mother's voice, she instinctively sought to pacify her. "No one said anything," she said. "I was just curious." Naomi's eyes looked to the family gathering again. The grandfather was now cuddling the sleeping baby while listening to what a young girl, maybe five or six, was telling him. They shared the same dark hair and serious expression. "Sometimes I wonder what they're like." And how she'd fit with them. Whether they'd like her and if she'd see a piece of herself in them.

"Count yourself lucky you don't," Sue said. "They are the least open-minded people I've ever met. They'd expect you to do everything their way, no matter how backward or old-fashioned."

Naomi thought of Gia. "And if I didn't live up to their expectations?" she asked softly.

"Then they would never accept you," Sue snorted. "They never accepted me. I got out rather than live a lifetime of never-ending criticism and disappointment."

Naomi wanted to argue, to express her disbelief that something as simple as personal choice and living one's life could escalate to abandonment and grudges that tore a family apart. But then she thought of Dev. Maybe Gia wouldn't sever ties with disobedient children, but given Dev's adherence to her wishes, Naomi imagined the alternative would be very bad.

Which was why her decision to position herself as Dev's fake girlfriend was ludicrous. She had everything Gia would disapprove of: a rebellious mother, scandal, and an estranged family.

As if sensing her discomfort, Sue's voice softened. "Trust me, honey. I raised you so you would never have to know the sting of rejection."

But she did, didn't she? Her father had left her, her grandparents wanted nothing to do with her, and since getting mixed up in Gia's Bazaar, she had felt it in a hundred different ways.

For a moment, she thought her mother might say more about

where she came from, about the people Naomi longed to know. They rarely talked about Sue's past, but when they did, Naomi gathered all the tidbits she could, tucking them away to examine, turn over, and preserve. Instead, Sue fell back on the same habit that had saved her from countless difficult situations. She retreated.

"I need to squeeze in a shower before book club. I love you, Naomi."

"I love you, too, Mom."

Dev brushed his hands against the sides of his joggers and glanced around his new living quarters. Not terrible. The original furniture, while outdated, was still in good condition and, aside from a few dishes and new bedsheets, Dev would require very few additions to make this place livable for the next few months. Citing the bazaar's remodel as his excuse, Dev already felt a thousand times better about his decision to move into the apartment above the store, despite his mother's protests and guilt-tripping sighs of woe.

"But who will double-check that all the doors are locked after I've fallen asleep on the couch? Who will run to the store to grab me yogurt when I'm in the middle of cooking?" she'd asked.

"I lock the doors from an app on my phone and you can still call me for cooking emergencies," he'd replied, but when he'd looked up from packing his meager belongings, there had been real trepidation in Gia's eyes.

Even before his father's passing, he'd always been the one taking care of his mother in small, often insignificant, ways. His older brother had idolized their father, while his younger brother had been too flaky. It was Dev who had noticed the work Gia put in appeasing a workaholic husband, the loneliness she felt within the walls of her own home. So he'd sat with her through marathon Bollywood sessions, fumbled his way through the Indian grocery store when she'd put in a long day at the bazaar. Helped clean up after dinner, even though his father scoffed because it was "woman's work."

Gia wasn't one to say thank you, but Dev was always the first person his mother turned to for help.

He needed some space, even if said space was a tiny studio apartment, complete with a bathroom housing the tiniest shower known to man. The main room couldn't have been more than six hundred square feet and consisted of a queen-sized bed, a small kitchen with enough counter space for very careful knife wielding, and a love seat turned to face a TV set from the nineties. But at least now he had the privacy to find a new job and get himself his own, more permanent place. It was a small step toward reclaiming his own life, a one-fingered salute to everything that had been predetermined his entire existence.

A soft chime sounded in the apartment, alerting Dev through the security system that someone had entered the bazaar below.

"Hello?" Naomi's voice called from downstairs.

Dev stuck his head out the door. "Up here." He shouldn't have been nonplussed at Naomi's arrival—she had texted him this morning asking if they could meet, even though it was Saturday, her self-imposed day off—and yet his hands grew clammier with each approaching footstep on the rickety staircase.

"Oh wow," she said once she stepped through the door. "Are you living here now?"

Dev scratched the back of his neck as he glanced around. Although he felt a peculiar sense of accomplishment for moving into this meager apartment, he frowned, embarrassed, when he realized how the empty walls and old-school furniture might look through Naomi's eyes. "I moved in this morning," he said. "But it's temporary."

"Can I snoop around?"

Dev cast a wary glance at his tight living quarters. "Uh, sure."

"Did your family live here at one point?"

"No, we grew up in Glenmore," Dev said, referring to one of the more affluent neighborhoods in Kelowna. "But this was the perfect solution for cheap babysitting. When we were old enough to not need constant supervision, my mom would stick us up here while she worked downstairs. There's only one way out and not much up here for us to get into trouble." He nodded at the chipped coffee table in front of the love seat. "We used to cram around that table and do our homework."

Naomi moved to stand beside him and smiled at the makeshift living room. "You and your brothers must be pretty close." There was a thread of wistfulness in her voice, reminding Dev that Naomi was an only child.

"We were, but we're very different from one another. We get along now, for the most part, but I wouldn't say we're close anymore." It was hard to find common ground with Neel, who embraced everything their parents had forced upon them, while Dhan seemed unaffected, likely thanks to his fondness for hotboxing.

He gestured to the stove behind them. "This is where my mom would often make treats and chai for her friends downstairs. And us, of course."

"So . . . Did you pick out that comforter yourself?"

Dev folder his arms across his chest. "How about you stop stalling and tell me why you're here."

Naomi moved so that her back was against the stove and she was facing Dev. She took a deep breath. "I wanted to apologize."

"Apologize? For what?"

"Thanks to me, everyone is going to think you have a girlfriend." Naomi's light brown eyes widened. "That's the last thing you need."

"That's *exactly* what I need."

"Do you have to be so sarcastic all the time? I'm trying to apologize."

Dev reached forward to place his hands on Naomi's shoulder. "I'm not being sarcastic."

"Wait." Naomi tilted her chin and examined Dev's face. "You're serious?"

Dev grinned. "I needed someone to keep the women away, and you came through." At the time, Naomi's snaking her arm around him and staking her claim had nearly bowled him over, but after some thought, he realized she'd provided him with the perfect cover. Word spreading that he had a girlfriend was the ideal repellent against his mother's marriage-making schemes. Surely now, fewer girls would seek him out, much less approach him, if he was already spoken for.

It was perfect. And Dev couldn't deny that being linked to Naomi wasn't a hardship: she was smart, warm, beautiful, and fun. He would never admit so out loud, but even with her propensity for poking fun at him at every turn, she was surprisingly easy to be around. Dev liked being in her company, even though she was constantly shoving paint samples, design magazines, and baked goods his way.

"But . . . you don't want a girlfriend," Naomi protested.

"And technically, I don't have one." In Dev's eyes, that was the real beauty of their situation. He wasn't *technically* lying, just skirting the truth, which was something he'd done his entire life in order to circumvent, at least somewhat, his parents' strict rules and impossible expectations.

Dev watched in amusement as Naomi wound a curl that had escaped her ponytail around her finger. Not for the first time since meeting her, he had the unexpected desire to give that same curl a tug and watch it spring back into place. Another part of him wanted to feel the softness of that curl between his fingers.

The realization was more than a little unnerving, so he quickly added, "We should probably come up with some ground rules."

"Ground rules?"

"Yeah. The more we look like a couple, the less likely girls are going to be interested in meeting me. But we should be in agreement about what that looks like for us."

"So you don't stiffen up like a corpse when I touch you?"

Dev rolled his eyes. "Right, because you calling me 'honey boo boo' was so natural. Let's scrap that nickname, by the way."

Naomi chuckled. "If we want to look like a couple, you're going to need to get used to certain things."

"Like?"

After a slight hesitation, Naomi took a step forward so that her body was half an inch away from his. They weren't touching and yet the air suddenly seemed a little too thin for Dev's rapidly compressing lungs. Naomi lifted her hand and, after a moment of hesitation, placed it on his chest in the barest brush of contact. Dev wanted to joke that she needn't treat him like he was a wild animal, and once his heart stopped galloping, he planned to do exactly that.

Once she saw that he wasn't going to push her away, Naomi's hand flattened against him with confidence. "I won't overdo it, but we should share casual touches like this." When Dev didn't respond, she cocked her head, half playful, half unsure. "You should give it a try, too, honey boo boo."

Dev had had girlfriends before, and flings and one-night stands, and yet his palms began to sweat at the idea of touching this decoy girlfriend in front of him now. When Naomi raised her eyebrows expectantly, he lifted his hands to waist level, pausing for a brief second before ever so gently resting them on her hips.

A faint blush was creeping onto Naomi's cheeks. "We don't need to be a handsy couple or anything, but we do need to look comfortable with each other," she said in a low voice. She cleared her throat, and a half smile quirked her lips. "Still, a little notice before you decide to jam your tongue down my throat would be appreciated."

Although he knew it was his cue to laugh, every nerve ending directed Dev's gaze to Naomi's lips instead. When she parted them, he was powerless against leaning forward, his neck all too happy to curve to accommodate the difference in their heights. He was vaguely aware of the insistent press of her hand on his chest, but it wasn't pushing him away. Rather, it was like she was drawing him forward. The scent of coconut and late-summer sunshine filled his senses. The roar of waves rushed to his ears.

He could learn to like the beach.

Dev was suddenly aware that they were very alone in a too-quiet apartment. For the first time in many days, there was no persistent banging of a sledgehammer, no intrusive Mukherjee family members sticking their noses where they didn't belong. No wedding hopefuls skipping in his direction, matrimonial bells echoing their steps.

There was only the two of them, sharing the same oxygen between her parted, cherry pink lips and his. Somehow Dev knew she wouldn't taste like a cherry, though. She'd be a smooth, salted caramel bourbon: rich and full-bodied. And there was no way in hell that one taste would be enough to satiate the ache in the pit of his stomach.

The ache of wanting. Dev wanted to be around this woman whose endless optimism should have grated on his nerves. He wanted to step closer and imprint the contours of her body onto his, to feel the scorch of her luminosity on his bare skin.

He wanted to kiss her.

"That's . . ." Naomi swallowed, and Dev fought the urge to slide his hands upward to cup the sides of her graceful neck and feel the flex of the delicate muscles there. "That's more believable."

Under Dev's long, silent look, Naomi pressed her lips together and stepped back, her fingers sliding away slowly. He would feel the burn of her fingertips long afterward. Her cheeks were rosy like an August sky at dawn, and it would've been too easy for Dev to lean into her again. Instead, he braced his hands on the counter behind him and willed his body to calm down.

Dev forced a nod. "Okay, good. Right," he agreed. His brain was doing that short-circuiting thing again; he desperately wanted to lighten the mood, to erase the startling heaviness between them. "At least I didn't jam my tongue down your throat?" Dev closed his eyes in mortification. He would do well to learn that for a guy like him, silence was always the safest option.

But when he risked opening his eyes to see Naomi's expression, her gaze was glued to the floor, her face unreadable.

"Right," she said. She pressed her fingers into the shallow nook between her collarbone and Dev's mouth went dry. "At least we didn't do that."

chapter 12

thought you moved out?"

Dev faltered on the staircase and almost face-planted, much to the amusement of Aashi, who was stooped in front of the back door of his mother's home to remove her sandals. She waved a handful of herbs at him, fresh from Gia's garden.

"I did," Dev said, holding up a black laptop charging cord. "I forgot this."

"I see." She eyed him from head to toe. "I don't think I've ever seen you so . . . *alive* in the morning."

Dev paused midstride and swallowed. Aside from going to the gym every morning, there usually wasn't much else propelling Dev forward early in the day. Let alone someone. But lately, the too-bright rays of early-morning sunshine and mid-September's crisp chill was having an entirely different effect on him.

He was *eager*, for God's sake.

"Got a store to save," Dev croaked, shoving his hands into the pockets of his windbreaker and hunching his shoulders forward.

"Mmm." Aashi raised an eyebrow before nodding toward the kitchen. "Come, join me for some tea and biscuits."

"No, thanks. It's too early for sweets."

Aashi smiled to herself. "That's interesting. I always find something sweet is exactly what's needed to get a person out of bed."

"What's that supposed to mean?" But his voice lacked conviction as his mind drifted to the smell of coconut tinged with sugar the closer he was to Naomi's skin, most potent along the curve of her neck.

With a cheeky bounce in her step, his aunt ignored the question and made her way toward the kitchen. "Come, sit with your mashi for a while."

"I really should get going . . ."

"Please, putro?" Aashi insisted with wide, plaintive brown eyes. "Spend some time with your poor old aunt."

Dev rolled his eyes but followed, accepting the tin of cookies his aunt handed him from the pantry before seating himself at the table. A few minutes later, Aashi handed him a cup of tea and sat across from him. Dev took a sip before staring into his mug with surprise. "Green tea? I thought homemade chai was the only way to go."

It had been both a running joke and a sore spot growing up in the Mukherjee household: at every opportunity, Gia and Aashi had clung to old-world traditions no matter how much Dev and his brothers clamored for North American convenience. Like making chai from scratch regardless how pressed they were for time or grinding their own spices rather than relying on curry powder from the grocery store.

"Don't get me wrong, chai runs in my veins," Aashi said. "It may be labor intensive, but it's calming. And the scent of spices in the air? That first sip of milky, golden perfection? That's home."

Dev eyed the watery tea in front of him doubtfully.

Aashi chuckled at his expression. "But green tea is easy and convenient. Healthier." She paused to top up her cup. "There's a time and a place for each, and either way, you get a cup of tea."

Someone needs to inform my mother of that, Dev thought, taking a tentative sip of his tea. It was neither rich nor sweet, but it *was* refreshing.

"So, the bazaar seems to be eating up all your free time," Aashi said, cupping her mug between two hands and examining him over the rim. "You've been working on it every day."

It was true and, in addition to moving out and spending the precious free time he had scouring online job postings, Dev had seen very little of his family in the last few weeks. He'd clocked in plenty of hours with Naomi, though, accompanying her to a variety of design and furniture stores, hanging around the bazaar with Nick and his construction crew, and, his favorite, poring over one of her many spreadsheets.

He could barely admit to himself how much he liked sitting beside Naomi, their heads bent over her beautifully organized columns, working together to ensure that everything lined up. Especially then, the temptation to tug on one of her springy curls gnawed at him. His unsatisfied fingers always tingled afterward, a pleasant reminder that he would be tortured by the same temptation dangling in front of him the next day.

But sitting across the table from his aunt, he could admit that he kind of missed his family, even as Aashi examined him with a cat-that-ate-the-canary grin teasing her lips.

"It needs a lot of work, in case you haven't noticed," he said.

"Mmm." Aashi hummed again before taking a long sip of tea. "I'm sure Naomi and Nick can handle things without you."

"Naomi needs my input."

"Mmm."

"I want the bazaar to succeed," Dev protested weakly. As soon as he heard the words, he realized they weren't completely untrue. With every deliberation over roman or roller shades or the never-ending conversations about the merits of oak versus walnut, he found himself more and more eager to see the finished product. The business had been in his family for thirty-five years, almost like a fourth child, sucking all of Gia's attention. Dev had never cared much for the store, had even at times felt the faint traces of resentment when he and his brothers ate half-heated frozen curry for dinner while their mother tended to customers, their father spending his waking hours, and then some, in the operating room at the hospital.

But now, for the first time, Dev could see himself in the bazaar and imagine what his contributions might mean for its success. *He* had ended the accent wall debate between Nick and Naomi, and had broached the idea that they broker a deal with Sweets That Make You Singh to provide some of the desserts not in Gia's wheelhouse. He was making decisions and seeing them come together. Sure, they were the insignificant pieces of the overall puzzle, but still, he was part of creating the big picture.

His father would roll over in his grave if he were to learn this was how his son was occupying the bulk of his time after quitting a lucrative job. Yet Dev didn't feel the sense of shame or guilt he might have a year ago. Being part of something from the ground up was satisfying. Having a say, however inconsequential the matter, was growing increasingly important to him.

Of course, if he never had to listen to Naomi insist on the differences between Chantilly Lace and White Heron again, he wouldn't complain. There were only so many paint samples—all in the same glossy shade of white—that a man could take.

"For someone who has spent most of his adult life avoiding the bazaar, you're very cozy with it now," Aashi said. "Why, you're even sleeping there."

Dev's eyes narrowed. Aashi knew of, and likely secretly supported, his decision to move out of his mother's home and into the apartment above the store. But she was doing a laughable job of hiding her knowing grin behind a flower-patterned teacup.

He eyed his aunt. "What are you getting at?"

"I'm merely suggesting that while it's very noble of you to spend your holiday helping your mother with the store, you don't have to work yourself to the bone. You should find time to relax."

In response, Dev dragged the cutlery canister sitting in the middle of the table closer toward him and began sorting the overabundance of spoons, forks, and knives. Telling his family that he was using vacation time from work to help with the store had been, in his opinion, a quasi lie: they just didn't know he was on a *permanent* vacation. But keeping his unemployment status a secret, especially from Aashi, curdled his stomach. His father had been staunch in his expectations about his sons' career paths: unemployment was for the lazy; pursuing anything outside of medicine, law, or engineering was a waste of one's talents; and climbing the ladder was a measure of one's success. Dev wasn't ready to admit that he had no intention of returning to the world of taxes, not when he had nothing else lined up for the future.

"I'm enjoying the remodel," he said, wincing when the mishandling of a fork resulted in a pinch to the pad of his forefinger.

"Mmm."

"I'm doing this for Mom—"

"What about me?" Gia bustled into the kitchen, peeling off her gardening gloves as she moved toward the sink. Dev's fingers lost their grip and the crash of several teaspoons falling from his grasp onto the table jerked him upright in his seat.

"Dev was telling me about all the time-consuming changes he's making to the store," Aashi said, earning her a warning glance from Dev.

"Satyi?" Gia said over the sound of rushing water. "Really?" she repeated once she'd turned off the tap.

"Oh yes." Aashi slipped a wink in Dev's direction. "It has given Dev a new spring in his step."

"Well, that doesn't surprise me," Gia mused, staring out the kitchen window above the sink. "It's a special place."

"It's going to be even better than before," Aashi commented as Gia sat down beside her. When his mother rubbed her wrists—a giveaway that her arthritis was flaring—Dev stood and went to see if the dishwasher needed emptying.

"I'm almost afraid to see what this girl has done to my store."

At the faint squeaking sound of his jaw clenching, Dev forced himself to relax his grip on the dinner plates he was pulling out of the dishwasher. His mother hadn't stepped foot in the store since hiring Naomi. It was like Gia had washed her hands clean of the fate of the bazaar, diving headfirst, instead, into orchestrating her second-born's death march toward the wedding altar. Or more apropos, toward the sacred, matrimonial fire, since nothing short of a weeklong series of traditional wedding-related activities would do for someone like Gia.

Still, there were the odd moments that Gia managed to make her digs—a sly comment about the Brand Lady's lack of knowledge about Bengali culture or a derisive sniff when Naomi's name was mentioned. Every time, Dev's jaw tightened in response, a troubling tic for someone who ground his teeth at night. The soreness in his jaw was nothing new, though: raised in a household where children were meant to be seen (seen studying, to be exact) and not heard, he was well versed in keeping his arguments to himself. Besides, Gia wasn't one for listening or changing her mind. Speaking up against one's elders was also considered the ultimate sign of disrespect, even when a paternal grandmother came to visit for the summer and demanded her grandsons be pulled out of outdoor swimming lessons because their skin was growing too dark. Dev hadn't much enjoyed jumping into the freezing pool every morning, but still.

He considered himself a pro at swallowing his arguments and grimly accepting whatever fate was decided for him, but holding back when it came to Naomi was threatening to give him lockjaw.

"I'm sure the rebrand will be lovely," Aashi said. "Dev has been working by Naomi's side day and night."

"Well, then, you deserve a night off. I expect you to attend Garba tomorrow night," Gia said. "The Patels invited us."

Dev paused from where he'd been lining up mugs in the cupboard with military precision. He hadn't been to a Garba dance celebration since college. It wasn't even a Bengali tradition, but far from home and with a relatively small population of South Asians to contend with, it wasn't abnormal for the Desi community to celebrate whatever custom was available to them if it provided some kind of connection to the world they'd left behind.

"Why?" Dev asked. "Are you going?"

"No, I'm going to Saisree Auntie's house for dinner," Gia said as she gestured for him to bring her a mug. "Your brother and Priya are home with the girls, who have a cold. And you know Dhan," she added, "he's so busy with university."

"If no one else is going, why do I have to go?" Dev complained, resuming his seat at the table.

Gia glowered at him. "It's been a full month since we hired Veera's matchmaking services, Dev, and you've made zero matches! Zero!"

"And what do you think that means, Mom?" Dev asked dryly.

"It means that you're not trying hard enough. In the span of a month, I met your father, got engaged, and had my wedding!" Gia leaned back in her chair so she could address the ceiling. "Why I have been cursed with such a difficult son, I'll never know."

"What does this even have to do with going to Garba?"

Gia sucked her teeth. "A *slow*, difficult son," she amended. "How do you expect to meet a wife if you don't put yourself out there? These kinds of events are the perfect opportunity to find your match."

At this rate, his mother would probably deem bumping into someone at a restaurant bathroom as the "perfect opportunity" to find his future wife.

"Veera Auntie said lots of the girls on my approved list will be there," Gia added. "And that the women will likely outnumber the men ten to one. It'll be like you're on that show . . . What is it called?"

"*The Bachelor*," Aashi supplied, and Dev shuddered.

Gia pointed a cookie at him accusingly. "Take this seriously, Dev. I don't want to hear from Veera that you are disinterested and difficult. Turn on the charm, son. Act like you want to find a wife."

He'd heard enough. Pushing his chair away from the table, Dev stood up. "Well, I better go. The sooner the day's work is done, the sooner I'll get to meet my dream girl."

His mother was immune to his sarcasm. "Finally, some enthusiasm!" she said, before looking upward again and nodding her approval at whatever higher being she was addressing.

Aashi, however, heard him loud and clear. "Yes. You wouldn't want to miss your dream girl," she said to his departing back.

chapter

13

"Here we are!" Naomi sang, swinging the door to Magic Hat Imports open before ushering Dev inside with a grand sweep of her arm.

Dev cocked an eyebrow and made no move to leave the sidewalk outside the store's cheerful signage. "Another cooking class?"

The rasp of Dev's roughened jaw against Naomi's sticky fingertips flitted across her memory, and she forced a smirk. "No, I won't put you through that again. And I promise not to smash anything in your face while we're here." With gusto, Naomi gestured into the store once more. If Dev found her bravado peculiar, he didn't comment as he brushed past her into the store.

Still, she should probably tone it down. Usually, researching and shopping for décor was one of Naomi's favorite parts of a rebrand. She loved digging around for the personalized touches and unique items that would pull at the client's heartstrings and add to a customer's lasting impression. But when it came to the bazaar, her instincts were nowhere to be found.

Cold sweat, however, she had aplenty.

Dev didn't get very far into the store before he came to a dead stop. "Holy shit."

"I know, right?" Naomi looked around, a sliver of cautious optimism threading through her. "Isn't it great?"

His eyes widened in shock. "This place looks like the original setup at the bazaar."

Naomi cocked her head to the side. "What do you mean?"

"It's a junkyard!"

Magic Hat Imports *was* a little cramped. It was an odds-and-ends décor store, the kind of place where a mounted singing trout could be found next to a dainty hand-painted music box. It had a little bit of everything and stacks of nothing: the perfect starting place for someone with a broken compass.

"Trust me," she insisted. "It's an organized chaos."

Dev's eyes were riveted on a life-sized clown statue proffering a platter of wrapped candy. "It's terrifying."

Naomi patted his shoulder, gently removing her hand—with supreme willpower—before it lingered too long on the smooth cord of muscle there. "I'll protect you. Follow me." She turned left and led Dev past wicker furniture, a bin dedicated to ironic doormats, and baskets of fake exotic flowers to a dimly lit corner.

"Ta-da!" Naomi said, holding her arms out wide.

Dev's brow furrowed. "What am I looking at here?"

Swallowing against the lump of uncertainty in her throat, Naomi turned to the shelves dedicated to imports from India. "I thought this might be a good starting point for the bazaar."

"Why?"

The confusion in Dev's voice flooded Naomi's cheeks with heat as she stared at the items before her. She wasn't suggesting they fill the Mukherjees' café with everything before them, but surely a few hidden gems could be found amid the Ganesh lamp, the jeweled and sequined throw pillows, and the wooden carving of the om symbol. She sometimes received items like these from her grandma Kelly at Christmas: chai hot chocolate mix, paisley-printed scarves in colors that never matched anything in her wardrobe, and scented candles with bizarre names like Eastern Dream or Masala Mist.

Her stepfather's mother's ancestry might have traced back to Germany and Ukraine, but it had been her attempt to connect with Naomi, a well-meaning attempt to find common ground in her granddaughter's South Asian culture. At the time, Naomi had thought it was sweet, even as she had awkwardly accepted the odd gifts. But now, with derision shading over Dev's face, she wasn't so sure.

Naomi couldn't hide the tentativeness in her voice. "What's wrong with this?"

"It's stereotypical. We don't want the café to look like something out of *The Simpsons*. I'm not even sure these are actual imports from India," Dev said, shaking his head at the display. He lifted one of the throw pillows and showed her the tag. "Made in China."

A bead of sweat slipped down the back of Naomi's neck. "Well . . ."

Oblivious, Dev scoffed as he placed the pillow back on the shelf, lining it up perfectly in a row with the others. "Besides, my mom is too much of a snob to get behind any of these tourist-type knickknacks." A maniacal grin spread across his face. "They would drive her crazy."

Naomi forced a chuckle. "Well, what kind of stuff would she gravitate toward?" When Dev shrugged, Naomi tilted her head toward the rest of the store they hadn't yet explored. "Maybe we should just wander a bit and see if anything jumps out?"

With a dubious nod, Dev started down the next aisle and, after a brief hesitation, Naomi turned on her heel and went the other way. She needed a moment to quell the nervous flutter in her throat, the privacy to wring out the moisture pooling at her collar.

She supposed she should be grateful that she had Dev on her side to help her avoid these potential pitfalls. It would've been a million times worse to slip up like this in front of Gia. Yet Naomi's lungs felt like they were turning themselves inside out as she meandered down the aisle in a daze, her hand pressed against her chest. It wasn't so much that she had screwed up in front of Dev but more that this kind of mistake had happened at all. Why hadn't she recognized the wrongness of the South Asian section of Magic Box Imports? Why couldn't she just get it right?

"Yikes," Dev's voice called from the next aisle over.

Naomi swallowed several shallow breaths before answering. "What?"

"I'm in Tiki Town." Dev said, sounding aghast. "How about you?"

Despite herself, Naomi managed a small smile and looked around her. A Cheshire cat money bank grinned back at her. "*Alice in Wonderland* hell."

Her lungs puffed comfortably again when Dev chuckled from afar. "You're missing out on leftovers from Grandma's estate over here," he called over the tall shelves.

With a giggle, Naomi moved forward more determinedly, trying to match her pace with Dev's. "I'm in Peacock Paradise."

"Peacocks? Stay right there."

In a few moments, he was by her side again, nodding slowly at the peacock-themed paraphernalia in front of them. "This might actually be perfect."

Naomi eyed a large statue of a mean-looking brass peacock and frowned. "You're kidding, right?"

Dev followed her line of sight and snorted. "Not the stuff here exactly, but my mom has a thing for peacocks. I think her grandma used to keep a few at her compound in India."

Although nothing on the shelf screamed taste or café appropriate, Naomi nodded, the last remnants of tightness in her chest easing. "I could look into some peacock-themed mugs. With matching napkins, maybe. They'd have to be custom-ordered, though."

"She'd like that," Dev confirmed. "She loves coordinating patterns." A wry smile spread across his face. "She used to dress my brothers and me alike when we were kids. Even now, for larger events, she tries to color-coordinate us."

Naomi swallowed a giggle and looked at the brass statue again. "Your great-grandmother raised peacocks, huh? That's pretty cool. Did you ever see them?"

"Of course I did." Dev punctuated his exasperation with an eye roll. "We used to fly out to India every winter break. It sucked." His eyebrows lifted expectantly. "You know how it is."

Naomi couldn't bring herself to admit that she'd never traveled to India, let alone been welcomed into any blood-related family member's home. No one had fussed over her fluctuating weight, pinched her cheek fondly, clucked their tongue over her choice of hairstyles, or a dozen of the other acts she'd seen the aunties dole out at Aashi's dinner party.

Whether he expressed envy or not, she didn't want Dev to know about everything she'd missed out on—all the missing pieces that added to her loneliness. It was too mortifying, too pathetic, especially after her initial ideas for decorating the bazaar had fallen flat.

"Well, we didn't go *every* winter," she lied. "But yeah, I know what you mean."

"Your vacations were probably better than mine, though. While my dad took my brothers to play Nintendo at various relatives' houses, my mom insisted on dragging me to all her favorite childhood haunts: overcrowded beaches, questionable food stands, sweltering movie theaters, you name it."

Naomi could imagine a young, scowling Dev being dragged around crowded streets, his mother forcing him to enjoy relics of her past, not really caring if he didn't. He had likely balked every time a new cultural artifact was shoved in his face—or down this throat.

It sounded wonderful to Naomi. But out loud she said, "Sounds awful."

"Yeah, well, no one else wanted to go with her." With a sardonic smile, Dev began moving down the aisle again. "You know, I'm glad they hired you and not some random."

"What do you mean?" Naomi asked as she fell into step beside him.

"Like, I know you're not Bengali and your family isn't as bonkers as mine, but it's nice that you get it," he said. "It just makes things easier, you know? It can be really hard talking about this stuff with people who didn't grow up in the same way."

Naomi ignored the sudden pulse of her heart in her throat and nodded as if she knew exactly what Dev was talking about. As if she held claim to the experiences that shaped a South Asian person, that bonded them together and defined their existence. As if she were the real deal.

"Since we're on the subject of family," Dev said, his voice hesitant. "I need to ask you something kind of weird."

Naomi's thudding heart dropped into her stomach as, inside her worn-out sneakers, her toes curled and flexed, as if debating running away. Maybe Dev suspected she'd been lying all along. Maybe this was the moment that all the lies Naomi had strung together for the Mukherjees unraveled, right here in the whimsical teapot aisle at Magic Box Imports. Her palms were hot and sweaty, while her fingers tingled numb with cold. Anticipation warring with dread.

"I feel really bad for asking," Dev continued. "Even though I shouldn't."

Just say it. But there was no way Naomi could voice the thought out loud, not when her brain was flipping through the many scenarios that could play out. Should she lie again? Admit the truth? Beg for Dev to keep her secrets to himself?

When she didn't respond, the tips of Dev's ears seared red. "I need you to come with me to Garba."

"It's not what you thin—" Naomi stopped, her tongue pressed to the roof of her mouth. "What?"

"I need you to come to Garba," Dev repeated, his voice dropping with his eyes. "With, uh, with me." As the silence stretched between them, he rushed to add, "I know I'm asking for a big favor, but my mom hinted that she expects me to meet a lot of potential matches there."

Naomi was reeling over the request. Cool relief shimmied through her limbs, and yet she was a little disappointed that Dev hadn't called her out. A part of her wanted to believe that he'd understand and try to help her anyway.

With a start, she realized she didn't want to have secrets with him, as necessary as they seemed.

"I know it's a big ask," Dev repeated, his discomfort etched on his face.

"I'm not sure I have anything suitable to wear," Naomi blurted out.

A slow smile stretched across Dev's face, framed by deep dimples. "We can fix that."

"I don't think this is such a good idea," Naomi said as she and Dev approached Lotus Fashions.

Dev jerked the front entrance open. "You said you needed something to wear."

Feet frozen to the sidewalk, Naomi nervously glanced at the glass storefront before her, housing mannequins in vibrant, flowy couture, splashed with sequins and heavy, gold-embroidered borders. They were stunning, impossible to look away from. Naomi had walked past these storefronts many times in Kelowna, but never had she dared to enter for fear that the haughty looks on the mannequins would be replicated by the salespeople inside.

When Dev caught Naomi's expression, he let go of the door and hustled to her side. "What's wrong?"

Naomi chewed on her bottom lip. "Getting a new outfit for this Garba thing seems like overkill, doesn't it?"

"You said you didn't have anything suitable to wear," Dev pointed out with a shrug. "You don't have to wear anything brand-new."

Naomi averted her eyes to the cracked sidewalk underneath. When she'd told him she didn't own anything suitable for Garba, he's assumed she didn't own anything fancy *enough*. She'd decided not to correct him because the truth was, she didn't own any type of traditional clothing. Nothing. And the idea of entering a store like Lotus Fashions filled her legs with ice, her blood slowing in her chilled veins.

"You can wear anything you want," Dev said. "You'd look good in anything."

Despite herself, Naomi shot him an amused glance, his pink-tinged ears bringing a small smile to her face.

"I mean," he said hastily, "you'll be fine in whatever. I just need a buffer."

Naomi gave the storefront mannequins a tortured look. "Maybe you could hide behind a really tall plant or something?"

"Please, Naomi," Dev said. "I need you there."

Sighing, Naomi brushed past Dev and led the way into the store.

It was worse than she could have ever imagined. There were a few circular racks of outfits, but the majority of the fabrics were on ceiling-high shelves built into every wall. Long counters separated the clothing from the customers, preventing them from browsing independently, making a discreet purchase, and hustling out the door.

Before Naomi could ask Dev what they were supposed to do, a woman who looked to be about her age called from behind one of the counters. "Welcome! What are you shopping for today?"

A nudge from Dev pushed Naomi to approach her. "Um . . . I need something for Garba."

"Oh, wonderful!" the woman said. "What are you thinking? Sari? Lehenga? Sharara? Anarkali? Do you have a preference for fabric type? Color?"

"I mean, anything here would be fine." Naomi gestured at the rack of clothing in the center, earning her a vehement shake of the saleslady's head.

"Oh, no, no, no. Those would *never* do for something like Garba," she said with a solemnity that had Naomi pressing her lips together and looking at Dev helplessly.

"What do you recommend?" he asked.

"A lehenga will look so beautiful while she's dancing and will be easier to move in." The woman turned to examine the tower of shelves behind her. Before Naomi could pipe in that she wasn't planning on doing any dancing, she continued, "And her skin tone would look fabulous with something bright. Orange, maybe? Pink?"

When neither Dev nor Naomi responded, she turned and looked at Dev with critical eyes. "What color are *you* wearing?"

"Oh, uh, I don't kno—"

"Then perhaps matching outfits for you two today," the saleslady said. She turned back to the shelves.

"I'll wear something I already own," Dev said, his voice flat.

"Color?"

"Blue."

"Like navy blue? Sky blue? Cyan, aquamarine, cobalt, peacock—"

"Turquoise," he interrupted as he crossed his arms over his chest. Naomi hid a smile—it was obvious that he was losing whatever little patience he had.

"And what style? Bandhgala? Kurta? Kurta with a vest? And if so, what's the design on the ve—"

Dev's sigh could have shaken the rafters. "Just a kurta."

Behind the saleslady's back, Naomi elbowed Dev, mouthing *Be nice* when he scowled at her.

"I have the perfect outfit," she replied. To Naomi's relief, she bypassed a rickety-looking ladder and pulled out a clear package with golden-yellow fabric inside. When she brought it to where they stood, Naomi could see that the contents had a turquoise design embroidered throughout. "The skirt is a nice A-line and the dupatta is turquoise, too," she added when she saw Naomi's interest. Silently, Naomi filed the word *dupatta* away to look up later. And how to wear a lehenga while she was at it.

As Naomi ran her hand over the plastic-wrapped outfit, the saleslady nodded. "Do you want me to open it?"

"It should be fine," Naomi said.

"You're going to look fabulous." She smiled fondly at them both. "I love it when couples match and I think it's so sweet that your husband came to help you pick something out."

Naomi shook her head. "Oh, he's not—"

It was Dev's turn to elbow her in the ribs. "Sounds great," he interrupted, pulling out his wallet. "We'll take it."

A delicious thrill shot up her spine, and she turned away to hide her reaction. "Whatever you say, honey boo boo."

chapter
14

I t was like stepping onto the set of a Bollywood movie. People of all ages, regardless of gender, wore a rainbow of colors and textures, glittering sequins, and shimmery threads that caught the light as they whirled on the makeshift dance floor, flawlessly finding their dance partners to tap their dandiya sticks together. They were in a community hall with chairs pushed off to the side to make room for the eager dancers. And everybody, young and old, was joining in.

Naomi stood against a wall with Dev, the swirl of hues before her imprinting a kind of beauty she knew she'd see again whenever she closed her eyelids. Overcome with an emotion she couldn't name, Naomi turned excitedly to look at Dev who, unsurprisingly, was stoic, his intense gaze on the dance floor before them, both seeing and unseeing. He, too, seemed to be in some kind of trance, but Naomi doubted the magic of Garba was affecting him in the same way.

Or maybe he was adopting an antisocial face to keep the bridal wolves at bay. It seemed unnecessary, though: they'd arrived about twenty minutes ago, and aside from the odd friendly nod or hand-shake from an older uncle or auntie, no one had approached Dev with fluttering eyelashes and a silky pout.

Kind of a shame, Naomi thought as she eyed Dev, looking trim and, well, unbelievably hot in a fitted kurta. She wouldn't mind risking a few casual touches here and there, in the name of pre-venting any potential matches, of course.

"Isn't it wonderful?" Naomi asked Dev.

"What?"

"The dancing!"

Dev shrugged, reminding Naomi he had attended these types of events his whole life. He didn't know how fortunate he was to have unbridled access to this, the thumping beat of the dhol vi-brating through the soles of one's feet, anchoring them to a rich, vibrant history.

"What's the meaning behind Garba, anyway?" Naomi asked.

Dev shrugged again. "Beats me."

"No, seriously, tell me."

"I really don't know." Dev waved at the crowds of people around them. "And a lot of people here probably don't, either. There are so many meanings behind everything, so many customs . . . It's not unheard of to go with the flow and experience the moment for what it is."

This was news to her. Naomi's brow furrowed as, for the first time, she took a moment to look around, to *really* examine her sur-roundings. As expected, most of the participants were South Asians, but there was the odd non–South Asian, too, including white people dressed in traditional garb, laughing and having a good time. All types of languages floated in and out of her ears, including English—sometimes accented, sometimes not—and whatever the dialect, it didn't deter people from connecting with one another.

It wasn't what she had expected at all.

When Naomi turned back to Dev, he was watching her face, his expression soft but unreadable. She opened her mouth to say something, but nothing came out.

"Want to dance?" Dev asked.

It would be a night of shocking revelations, it seemed. "What?"

Dev gestured to the dance floor. "Do you want to dance?"

"I . . . I don't know how."

"Just go with the flow."

Naomi's heart curled inward. *Go with the flow.* As if it were so easy, so seamless. But maybe, with Dev at her side, it could be. Did she want to take that chance? It was on the tip of her tongue to decline, but her feet were already shifting beneath her, seeking rhythm. She wanted to dance. To try.

"Okay."

When the music paused, Naomi followed Dev onto the dance floor, accepting the dandiya sticks a departing girl passed to her. They lined up with the other partners and Naomi listened carefully as Dev explained the footwork. As the opening notes of the music started again, she nodded, trying to exert confidence as her brain sifted through the hastily memorized steps.

If this was the scene in the movie where the wallflower heroine stepped onto the dance floor for the first time to become a graceful, sensual force to be reckoned with, then Naomi was no heroine. She flailed about, dizzying herself and only sometimes successfully meeting someone's sticks when offered to her.

But surrounded by people of all ages, including the odd senior citizen who shuffled gaily to the beat of their own drum, Naomi stopped caring what she looked like. She was by far one of worst dancers and yet, when she caught the eye of another dancer, they smiled back, encouraging and nonjudgmental. The onlookers clapped and chatted around her and if anyone was staring at her, she didn't feel the weight of self-consciousness she had expected to feel upon stepping into the community center.

Naomi stopped caring and started *feeling*. Her sense of rhythm might've been nowhere in sight, but the music filled her limbs anyway, circling her pounding heart, excited and full.

It was a heady feeling, belonging.

Even more of a revelation was her dance partner. It was obvious that Dev knew what he was doing as he moved effortlessly across the floor. His feet were light, his body loose-limbed and agile, and his smile so wide and easy, Naomi was transfixed.

Garba was like magic, and Dev knew all the tricks. Every graceful bend of his body to the rhythm thrumming around them was like a perfect illusion, and Naomi couldn't look away if she wanted to. And she wanted much more than that. The desire to draw closer to him spilled through her, thick like caramelized sugar. She wanted to blanket herself in the woodsy freshness that clung to him and feel his warm skin against her own. She wanted to fold her curves around his hard edges.

She wanted to taste him.

When the last few chords of music drew to a stop, and a breathless Dev came to a stop in front of her, the pleasure on his face pierced her chest.

"So?" he said. "How do you feel?"

Feelings of belonging and joy lingered in Naomi's limbs, but as she studied the man in front of her, his face flushed and dark chocolate eyes bright, desire flooded her senses, sharp, raw, and addictive.

What would it feel like to kiss those perfect, sulky lips? To wrap herself up in the heady combination of pine and mint. To press up against a man who was as quick with a sarcastic remark as he was to slide the protective sleeve from his coffee cup onto hers when he noticed her shifting the hot drink from one hand to the other. It would likely be the kiss to mock all others, including her first one, which had taken place at a crowded high school party with her first everyone-is-pairing-up-you-should-too boyfriend, their friends chanting "kiss" while toasting them with red Solo cups.

Without a doubt, Naomi knew that a kiss from Dev wouldn't be a throwaway activity at some party. It would be an event in it-self, a moment to return to over and over again long after it was over.

Naomi studied his mouth now, the beautiful curve of his full lower lip, the dusky pink tint. She wanted the dandiya sticks back in her hand, a water bottle, anything to keep her from reaching for him.

He just looked so solid. And dependable. And kissabl—

"Naomi?" he prompted.

"I feel good," she murmured. "But maybe a drink?"

Resisting the urge to fan her heated cheeks, Naomi leaned against one of the walls inside the community center, using all her willpower not to watch Dev's departing back as he went to fetch them drinks. She needed to collect herself, to cool down the up-roar of feelings vying for attention inside her now that she was safe from Dev's overwhelming nearness.

A few stumbles around the dance floor and Naomi was spell-bound. Garba, she was learning, was more witchcraft than magic.

"I didn't think I'd see you here," said a familiar voice.

Naomi turned to see that Cynthia had sidled up beside her. For once, Naomi was relieved to see her: Cynthia was the cold dose of water she needed, as frigid as the ice-blue lehenga she wore, shot through with silver thread.

"You look gorgeous," Naomi said, her voice cautious.

Cynthia preened. "My mother brought this back for me on her last trip to India. Don't you love it when they bring back the goods?" She fluffed the dupatta pinned artfully to her shoulder. "I saw you on the dance floor."

Here it comes, Naomi thought, bracing herself for a rude remark about her dancing, the clumsiness of her presence in a place where she obviously didn't belong.

"You looked good out there," Cynthia said instead. "The cut of your skirt is perfect for Garba."

Surprised, Naomi offered Cynthia a smile, performing a little spin. "Thank you. I know I was a bit of a mess."

Cynthia waved a dismissive hand at the crowded dance floor, where skirts whirled like flowers opening for the sun. "Some of the people here have been learning this dance since they were toddlers. Some of them compete in Garba competitions."

"Really?" Naomi raised her eyebrows even though the information shouldn't have shocked her, given everything she'd learned about the culture so far from Dev. "Have *you* done that?"

For once, Cynthia's smile was guileless. "I can't figure out these steps to save my life," she said, unashamed and unapologetic. "I come to these things to network, shake hands."

Had Naomi needed convincing that this nicer, approachable version of Cynthia wasn't a figment of her imagination, that would have done it: she always had a bottom line.

"I haven't seen you at any events like this before," Cynthia continued. "And I go to a lot of them. I didn't think they were your thing."

Naomi bit the inside of her cheek. This morning, she, too, had been convinced that they weren't her thing. That they would've taken one look at her and turned her away at the door. But in her yellow dress, dupatta slightly askew, and her feet already restless to fumble their way back on the dance floor, the idea of carving a place for herself did not seem entirely impossible. A tiny sliver would be nice—something that, if she nurtured and shaped in the right way, could grow into something even the mighty Gia would approve of.

At the thought of Gia, Naomi automatically looked for Dev in the crowded room. He was standing near the water coolers, two disposable cups in hand, chatting animatedly with a woman in an emerald-green sari. For once, he wasn't throwing her panicked eyes, but still, her feet forgot all about dancing and sought to be at his side.

"If you'll excuse me, there's something I have to attend to," Naomi murmured.

Cynthia had set her own sights on someone else across the room. "Me, too. Gurpreet Singh is here. He's opening a restaurant on—"

Naomi barely heard her as she strode toward Dev. He didn't acknowledge her when she moved to his side, her arm pressed against his. His companion did, however, and turned to Naomi with curious eyes.

"Hi, I'm Mandy," she said in a friendly tone. Her eyes flitted to where Naomi's body joined Dev's.

A brief glance at Dev gave nothing away, so Naomi shifted away from him slightly. "I'm Naomi."

"I saw you guys on the dance floor," Mandy said. She reached out and poked Dev's wrist.

He didn't recoil, and Naomi frowned.

"He used to be *my* designated Garba partner," Mandy added with a little laugh.

"Mandy and I have known each other since childhood," Dev added. "I didn't know you'd be here, though. I thought you moved to Toronto."

Naomi bristled at the familiarity in Dev's tone, and she had to remind herself that Mandy was an old friend, not a woman on the hunt. Still, she found herself pressing closer to Dev again in a not-so-gentle reminder that she was there.

For the sake of their agreement, of course.

"It's my grandfather's eightieth birthday," Mandy replied. "My whole family gathered for the event." Her face lit up. "You should come!"

"We'd love to!" Naomi blurted out with a big, fake smile. "That's so sweet of you to invite us. Can we bring anything?"

Mandy was polite enough not to correct Naomi, but her eyes darted between the pair of them uncertainly. "But Veera Auntie said . . ."

Beside her, Dev stiffened and his fingers tightened on the cups in his hands. "You know Veera Auntie?"

"Yeah, my parents introduced me to her a few days ago," Mandy confirmed.

Despite herself, Naomi was impressed. Veera Auntie, it seemed, was the businesswoman to know in Kelowna. Naomi could rebrand a thousand businesses and never be as sought after as a woman orchestrating happy endings.

The pointed end of Naomi's elbow found Dev's ribs sharply enough to jostle him and slosh some of the water in the cups over the edge. "Yeah," Dev echoed. "We'd love to come to the birthday. Text me the details."

"Sure," Mandy said. "I will." Naomi could tell, though, from the disappointment in her eyes, that said text would not be forth-coming.

Mission accomplished.

As Mandy excused herself and wandered away, Dev turned to Naomi with a rueful smile and offered her one of the drinks. "This could get complicated," he said. "Mandy's an actual acquaintance of mine and now she thinks you're my girlfriend."

Naomi accepted the cup, ignoring the delicious little bolt that shot through her when her fingers brushed his. "Except she'd be making a false assumption because technically, you never said I'm your girlfriend."

Realization dawned over Dev's face, inviting the stitch of dimples in both cheeks. Naomi wrapped both her hands around her cup to prevent herself from doing something *really* embarrassing, like poking the tip of her finger in one of them.

"You pretended like she was inviting us both to her grandpa's birthday," he said in awe.

"We didn't technically lie." Naomi couldn't keep the smugness from her voice as she turned Dev's words back on him.

"I know you don't have a ton of experience with this whole sneaking-around-your-parents'-back thing, but you're fitting right in."

Naomi moved to Dev's side, turning so they were both facing the dance floor again. The sweep of colors before her eyes was still dazzling, but Naomi was pleased to realize that some of the mystery from before had faded. It was still magical, but maybe Naomi had a trick or two up her sleeve as well.

Maybe she could be part of the magic, too.

chapter

15

Drops of rain were scattering from the dark October sky when Dev and Naomi left Garba. With a frown, Dev squinted across the crowded parking lot to where his black BMW was parked on the other side of the lot.

Fuck, he thought, as if on cue, a light rumbling gurgled in the distance. *Thunder. Figures.*

Behind them, the door to the community center swung open and Cynthia stepped outside, a small black umbrella tucked under her arm.

"It always rains when I wear dry clean only," she joked by way of greeting.

"There wouldn't be room for two more under that thing, would there?" Naomi asked as Cynthia popped her umbrella open.

Under the canopy of what looked like a miniature, travel-sized umbrella, Cynthia smiled helplessly. "I wish, hon. Let me know if you need the name of a good dry cleaner. I can get you the friends-and-family discount," she said before hustling into the parking lot.

Dev cursed under his breath as they watched her depart.

"Suddenly parking far away from everyone else to avoid dings on your car doesn't seem like a good idea, does it?" Naomi teased with her bare arms crossed tightly against her chest.

Well aware of how ridiculous it now seemed—he had thought so many times as a child when his father had insisted on doing the same—Dev waved a dismissive hand at the rain, which had already transitioned from scattered to insistent. "It's worth it." Still, neither of them moved from their precious, dry shelter.

"Even now?" Naomi asked, as a crack of thunder mocked them from above.

Dev turned to scowl at her, but when he noticed Naomi rubbing her arms, he clasped her hand in his instead. "C'mon, we'll run for it."

"Whoa." She laughed as she teetered after his long legged stride. "Heels, remember?"

Dev came to an abrupt halt and shook out his damp hair. Crouching, he gestured to his back. "Hop on."

"Really?" Naomi asked with a delighted grin. "I wouldn't want to impose," she added, but already she was gripping his shoulder with one hand while trying to gather her long, heavy skirts in her other so she could climb on.

"Today, Naomi," Dev said through gritted teeth after her third unsuccessful try. By now, the beginning of an all-out shower was underway, and the fabric of his kurta was wet and sticking to his skin, rough and itchy. *This* was why he never wore traditional clothing unless absolutely necessary. Yet as he watched Naomi struggle with her skirt, the long length of turquoise bracelets tinkling on her arms and her soaked curls spiraling over her ornately decorated blouse, he had to admit that the traditional clothing was undeniably appealing to look at. Even while wet.

A drop of water snaking its way downward across the few inches of smooth flesh between the hem of Naomi's top and the waistband of her skirt caught Dev's eye, and he painstakingly averted his gaze. *Especially* while wet.

Since childhood, he'd been dragged to traditional events like Garba. Dev was more than well acquainted with the gaudiness, the heaping of heavily spiced foods, the cacophony of drums, music, and jubilant South Asians trying to outdo one another. These events were like visiting the bottle depot: the same people were always working the sorting bins, the process never changed, and without a doubt, one walked away disappointed with the fruits of their labor while relieved to cross that annoying chore off their list.

In another month or two, they'd be back and it would be the same damn drill.

But nothing could have prepared Dev for tonight. In her brightly colored dress, a smile permanently etched on her face, and practically vibrating against the beat of the dhol, Naomi was more than her usual, bright self. She was *brilliant*. Several times, Dev had caught her adjusting the dupatta around her neck so it rested just so and twisting her hips from side so she could watch the graceful swirl of her skirts around her ankles. The fact that he'd contributed to her obvious pleasure by doing something as insignificant as buying her that dress did weird things in his chest.

When Naomi finally hoisted herself onto his back, Dev could feel the bunched fabric of her skirts creating a thick barrier between them, preventing her legs from finding a suitable angle over his hips. Already she was slipping off. Without thinking about it, Dev cupped her smooth, supple calves in his hands and gently pulled her as snugly against him as he could. He thought he felt her muscles flex in his grip, but he couldn't be sure. His fingers might have twitched slightly, too, unable to resist luxuriating in Naomi's soft, warm skin.

Maybe Dev wasn't sure of anything anymore.

"Hold on tight," he said before he shot out into the dark parking lot, zigzagging his way when cars were too tightly packed to ensure Naomi's safety when they squeezed past. He waited for her to complain about the bumpy ride or, at the very least, urge him faster in an attempt to save her brand-new, dry-clean-only outfit. But she surprised him.

Naomi laughed the entire way, the musical notes of her joy seeping past his itchy kurta, more persistent than the rain, sinking bone deep. Her laughter, and the tinkling of the bangles on her arms wrapped around his chest, would be imprinted on his eardrums for a long time.

And he wouldn't mind.

When they reached the car, Dev immediately cranked the heat, adjusting the vents so they pointed at Naomi, who was shivering. Water streaked across Naomi's face, her haphazard curls dripping, and her gauzy dupatta clung to her neck like a wet plastic bag.

She looks absolutely beautiful, Dev realized with a start. But outloud he blurted, "You have raindrops in your eyelashes."

Naomi looked startled for a moment, but then she laughed and blinked a few times, causing the liquid there to shiver off her lashes and onto her cheeks. Without thinking about it, Dev reached forward to brush the moisture away, but at Naomi's sharp intake of breath, his knuckle froze against her cheek, his hand opening as if independent of his brain to caress the side of her face. With her smooth skin against his palm, Dev couldn't help but press his fingers against her cheekbone, mesmerized by the delicate curve he found there. He gave in to temptation and soothed the fullness of her bottom lip with his thumb, half shocked and half enthralled that he was *touching* the mouth that was as quick to tease him as it was to laugh with him.

The plumpness of her perfect, pink bottom lip felt like silk, her warm breath an electric current shooting through his nervous system.

He almost pulled away when Naomi's eyes widened but couldn't bring himself to do so, not when she nuzzled into his hand and leaned toward his seat. Dev met her halfway, flicking his eyes to her lips and back up again, seeking permission. She leaned infinitesimally forward, close enough that her breath tickled his bottom lip, and nodded hypnotically, her almond-shaped eyes never leaving his.

That was enough for Dev. He pressed his lips against hers in a quiet invitation, stopping just short of exploring her full, soft mouth. But when a sigh drizzled from her mouth to his, Dev couldn't resist moving his left hand to cup the back of her head and deepen the kiss. Naomi's mouth opened under his, accepting his attention and, if her tentative hand finding its way to the underside of his jaw was any indication, asking for more.

Everything in Dev was eager to fulfill Naomi's quiet request. Lightly, he grazed his tongue along the inside of her lush, lower lip and was instantly rewarded by the slide of her tongue against his.

Salted caramel bourbon.

But so much better. Like quenching one's thirst and awakening one's taste buds at the same time. He'd never get enough of this, not with the smell of coconut and sunshine rushing his senses and one of Naomi's stray, damp curls tickling the underside of his jaw.

Both of her hands moved to the front of his kurta, her hands balling the material in her fists so she could pull herself closer.

Dev's body was happy to accommodate, but once he did, a sharp rasp—like nails scratching over rough burlap—sliced the air.

They broke apart and looked down to where the sound had emanated from. Naomi's bangle was caught on the fine threads of embroidery on Dev's shirt.

"Oh my God," she gasped. "I'm so sorry."

Dev stared at Naomi's balled-up fists, frozen in midair between them. They looked so small anchored to his shirt by a few loose threads. Those fragile, stubborn strings tethering her to him caused something to shift inside his chest, something he couldn't quite identify but that was achingly comforting.

Carefully cupping her wrist to hold her hand steady, Dev gently unwound the threads to free her jewelry. Naomi pulled back and pressed her fingers against her lips. The only sound between them was their breaths—hers shallow, his ragged—chasing each other.

"I ruined your outfit."

Dev glanced down at the loose threads on his kurta and shrugged. "I don't care."

Shyly, Naomi stared down at her own dress, still waterlogged. "I must be on a roll tonight seeing as I've ruined this outfit, too."

"You can do whatever you like with it. It's yours."

"But . . . but you bought it."

"Yeah, but I bought it for you." An awkward silence descended upon them at Dev's admission, and he immediately felt a telltale heat creeping onto his ears. "I mean, I bought it for you because that lady at the store assumed I was your husband." And just like that, the silence grew even thicker, creeping over him and leaving behind the burn of full-body mortification. "It would've been weird *not* to pay," he babbled. "Besides, I'm not going to wear it."

"Well, thank you." Naomi's words were so soft and shy, Dev

wanted to lean closer to feel the sweetness of them on his skin. Worried that he might do just that, he gripped the steering wheel with both hands and forced himself to stare out the windshield instead. The rain was already starting to let up. *Figures.*

When he didn't respond, Naomi cleared her throat. "I think you've earned a morning off from helping me with the bazaar. Why don't you sleep in tomorrow?"

"I can't. I've got a game at seven in the morning."

Naomi quirked an eyebrow. "A game?"

Dev scratched the back of his neck sheepishly—the welcome reprieve from his scratchy collar against his skin was almost better than sex. Dev shot a quick glance at Naomi, who watched him curiously, beads of moisture trailing her collarbone. *Almost.*

"Yeah, some of the guys and I get together on Sundays and play basketball at the Y. We're trying to get back into it after slacking this summer."

"'The guys'?"

"Some of the guys I went through the CPA program with," he admitted. "We're . . . uh . . . We're not very good."

"You guys are all accountants?"

"Well, yeah."

When the corners of Naomi's mouth flickered with a poorly repressed smile, Dev glared at her. He had the overwhelming urge to wipe her mirth away with his mouth.

Instead, he frowned and maneuvered the car out of the parking stall.

"Accountants on the court shooting hoops," Naomi mused. "You guys play pretty early for a Sunday morning."

Distracted by the traffic as he merged onto a busy street, Dev replied, "We have to get our game in before the legit guys show up and claim the court."

He didn't need to glance at Naomi to know she was grinning. The car had heated nicely thanks to the vents on full blast, but the knowledge that he had made her smile washed a different kind of warmth through Dev, the kind that soothed away some of the rough edges that were all too familiar to him. He knew she was probably holding back laughter at his expense.

But he didn't mind.

chapter
16

The following morning, Dev sat on the bleachers and watched with a morbid kind of fascination as Garrett Rooney, an auditing and assurances accountant who towered over their basketball group by at least five inches, dribbled with determination toward the unguarded basket. He was going for a dunk. He always went for a dunk.

And he always biffed it. Despite his six-foot, four-inch frame, Garrett's spindly legs never seemed to secure enough air time for him to make contact with the basket's rim. With his eyes squinting in concentration, he followed his usual formula: he traveled illegally, attempted a mighty leap, and, with giant hands outstretched, missed the bottom of the net by several inches. The ball slipped from his hands to ricochet off the back wall of the gymnasium.

But, as usual, the rest of the guys, most of whom were under five-seven and would never dare to attempt such a feat, clapped Garrett on the back with a chorus of "good try, man" and "so close, dude" platitudes. Likewise, Garrett nodded gratefully while eyeing the basket with a glint in his beady eyes. He would try again.

As the guys resumed floundering across the court, Dev leaned back and shook his head as he took a swig of water.

"Dude has heart," his closest friend of the group, Prakash Talwar, said from where he sat beside him. Before enrolling in the CPA program, they had met at the University of British Columbia and immediately bonded as two sheltered brown kids having moved away from home for the first time. Together they had learned how to operate laundry machines, which libraries were the best for late-night studying, and where—for the ultimate moment of weakness—to find food that reminded them of home.

Dev laughed. "He's clueless."

"At work, too." Prakash shook his head. "No self-awareness, that guy."

They watched as Harry Tsai weaved his way down the court and successfully shot a three-pointer. He was the shortest and most talented of their motley group, and head of the forensic accounting department at Prakash's firm. He found Dev and Prakash on the sidelines and waved them over.

When they both declined, he shot them an unimpressed look before turning to rejoin the laughable hustle of the other players.

"I know my excuse," Prakash said, pointing to his ankle wrapped in a sporty-looking brace. He had required ankle surgery in high school and could only play for a minimal amount of time before needing increasingly long breaks. "What's yours? As one of our more skilled players, you and Harry run circles around these guys until the college crew gets here for their pickup game."

It wasn't high praise, given the level of talent on the gym floor. Still, Dev half smiled. "I didn't get much sleep last night."

"You're still unemployed, right?" Prakash leaned in, his voice lowering with excitement. "Wait, did you land the job yet?" Prakash was the only one in the group who knew of Dev's real reason for leaving his firm. As Penticton was Prakash's hometown, he knew many of the accountants at Dev's well-known firm, and so Dev had told him the truth as a fail-safe. Besides, he trusted Prakash.

"I've been checking, man," Dev replied with a rueful sigh. "None of the professional or semiprofessional sports teams are hiring for positions I want. But I'm going to keep trying."

"Your family know yet?"

"Nope."

"Shit." The word conveyed everything: a Sikh Punjabi from a very traditional family, Prakash knew exactly why Dev was leaving his family in the dark. "You're not panicking and staying up late combing for work, are you? I can help you out if you're low on funds."

Dev's chest tightened pleasantly, and he threw his friend a grateful look. "No, I'm good."

"So, what's got you losing sleep?"

Tipping his head back for a swig of water, Dev stalled. Although Garba had always been one of the few cultural events he enjoyed, it had never left him on a peculiar adrenaline high before, with the echo of the dhol pulsing through him every time he had tried to drift off to sleep last night. Well, the drums and the delicate clink of turquoise bangles jostling together against his chest.

When Dev's face reddened and he didn't answer, Prakash smirked. "Or, should I say, *who's* keeping you up at night?"

Hastily, Dev lowered his voice and told Prakash about Naomi, the brand-consultant-turned-buffer-turned-fake-girlfriend. Since his brain still felt rain-muddled from the previous night's events, he decided not to mention Garba. And the parking lot.

Prakash was grinning like an idiot when he finished. "So, you like her."

"It's not like that." Dev's protest sounded feeble in his own ears.

"Dude, I've known you for a long time. I know when you like someone." Cockily, Prakash tossed his water bottle in the air and caught it with a loud *thwap*. "And it sounds like you've got it bad."

"Fuck."

"What's the big deal? You finally like a brown girl." Prakash raised his hands, palms up, toward the ceiling. "Your mother will rejoice on the hilltops."

"She's not the right kind of brown."

"I thought you said your family doesn't care if you marry a non-Bengali."

"No, I mean, she's not the kind of brown girl you bring home to your family."

Prakash's forehead wrinkled. "Tattoos? High school dropout? Divorcée? Single mom?"

"She's not in touch with her roots," Dev said glumly.

Prakash winced, familiar with the ramifications. A brown person who failed to uphold any cultural identity whatsoever? Unspeakable. There was an unspoken hierarchy of authenticity, and despite everything that drew Dev to Naomi, she was on the bottom rung in his mother's eyes.

"Ah, whitewashed," his friend said with a sigh. "That sucks, man. My parents can't seem to trust people who stray away from the culture . . ." Prakash was silent for a moment before he snapped his fingers. "What's the big deal? Just go for it in secret. You've done it before."

It was a normalized thing, younger generations hiding relationships—especially unsuitable ones—from their families so they could enjoy dating without the added stress of dealing with parental interference. Immigrant South Asians, particularly those with arranged marriages, did not understand casual dating. And the idea that their children might be engaging in premarital sex was never talked about, as if forced ignorance signified it wasn't happening.

It was ridiculous. But it was a burden that all the first-generation kids bore.

"It's not like you want to get married eventually," Prakash added, leaning his elbows onto the bleacher behind him. "You've always been anti-marriage."

"That's true," Dev said slowly. He *could* apply the same set of rules to Naomi as he had in the past: a mutually agreed fling between two people who wanted to continue operating independently with an understanding that there would be an end date.

Yet Dev wasn't so sure he wanted to hold himself back from Naomi and all that inexplicable warmth that radiated from her, lighting everything and everyone in her path.

Maybe it was just infatuation—he'd known her for only a little while, after all—and when the bazaar's completion date rolled around, these feelings could fade. His past relationships usually did at the three-month mark.

A small part of Dev wondered what Prakash might say if he mentioned these confusing thoughts, but he immediately tamped down the urge. Dev never talked about this kind of stuff with anyone, and although Prakash was a good friend, there was no way Dev could reveal this side of himself without making things awkward and embarrassing them both. No, it was better to keep the words—and his feelings for Naomi—lodged in his chest in the hopes that eventually they would just go away.

But when the realization that he'd be seeing her later that day brought a faint smile to his lips, Dev stood up abruptly, his skin suddenly two sizes too tight.

"You wanna get back in the game?" Prakash asked, standing up at a more languid pace and stretching his back.

On the court, Harry was eyeing them again, more insistent this time. Behind Harry's back Garrett aimed a sloppy pass at Ben Fields that nailed the recipient flat on his face. Even that looked a lot less painful to Dev than dealing with his own feelings.

"Yeah, let's go."

When Dev returned to the bazaar, Naomi was waiting outside the door, looking unusually antsy.

"What?" he asked wearily, his eyes dropping to his feet. Since their kiss, he wasn't entirely sure where to look. The gentle caress of her rain-soaked curls against his cheek was still etched in his mind, as was the sweep of her lush, dark eyelashes when her eyes had fluttered close as she'd leaned into him. He'd never forget how her perfect, pink lips had looked when they'd pulled apart—wet, swollen, and addictive.

Dev didn't dare let his mind wander to what might've happened had they not been interrupted by the catch of her bracelets against his kurta.

"I have something special for you waiting inside," Naomi said, oblivious to the dangerous turn of his thoughts.

Dev grabbed the towel draped over his shoulder and wiped his forehead. Despite the earliness of the day, he could already feel the humidity. The sudden heat had nothing to do with the beautiful woman beckoning him forward, practically shimmering from excitement.

"It's too early for strippers," he said.

Naomi rolled her eyes as she laughed and pulled the front entrance open. Dev stepped inside, momentarily taken aback, as he always was, despite having worked on the rebrand every day for over a month.

Oak floors gleamed against freshly painted teal walls. Gone were the tired-looking shelves, and without the overcrowded aisles of wall-to-wall junk, the room was airy, open, and dust-free. Nick had built custom floating shelves along the far back wall, where Aashi had agreed to lend her pottery collection for display. Aside from the long L-shaped display counter, there had been no furniture in the room. Until now.

In the corner next to the pottery wall sat a burgundy couch and a small table painted the exact same color as the walls. Equally sized wooden chairs surrounded the four sides of the table, which also housed a large wooden bead maze.

"What's all this?" he asked as Naomi fussed with positioning the chairs just so.

"Whatever happens to this café," Naomi said, contemplating her work before adjusting one of the chairs again, "it's clear that family matters a lot to your mother. And you. And while I know you don't have the best childhood memories of this place, you mentioned that you guys had a little craft table in the corner to keep you guys busy while your mom worked. I thought this would be a nice touch. It's a nod to the bazaar's history."

An image flitted from Dev's memory. He had been eight or nine on summer vacation, coloring at a plastic kids' table in the corner with five-year-old Dhan. His little brother, an artistic child, had barely looked up the entire time they were there, so consumed by his drawing. But Dev's focus kept returning to his mother, chatting and laughing with customers. She had brought a large

container of sandesh with her and happily offered the popular
Bengali sweet to anyone who glanced her way. It was a memory
he'd shared with Naomi several weeks ago, a careless remark when
they'd been at one of the many furniture stores she'd dragged him
to, arguing over table heights.

He looked at Naomi in surprise now. "I can't believe you . . ."
Words failed him. It wasn't just that she'd listened to him and
committed something so small to her memory. She'd folded the
moment into the bazaar's rebrand and her thoughtfulness made
Dev's rib cage expand, his chest impossibly full.

When he trailed off, Naomi shot him a nervous glance. "It's a
really good idea," she said defensively. "Cafés aren't always kid-
friendly, but this little corner will elevate your business for parents. And up your sales, too, since you're selling desserts." When
he didn't answer, she relented. "We can get rid of it if you want. I
know it wasn't part of my initial design, but—"

Dev placed a hand on her shoulder. "It's not what I expected,"
he said. "But it's perfect."

When her body relaxed under his hand, Dev didn't immediately let go. He didn't want to, not when he wanted so much for
Naomi to understand that he didn't have the exact right words to
explain the sudden catch in the back of his throat. How could he
express how good and *right* it felt to be standing there, with her,
between the walls that had housed the better part of his childhood? How, for the first time, he could look around the bazaar
and see light and history and the ways in which his mother carved
a life for herself in this country?

He didn't have the words, but he knew he didn't want to stop
touching her with the same certainty that there was no way he
would be sick of Naomi when the three-month deadline passed.
He would never step foot in the bazaar without thinking of her,

regardless of who claimed ownership in the end. She was etched in every detail of the café: the vibrantly painted walls, the comfortably rounded corners of the glossy white display counter, and the very carefully selected solar shades hanging at the windows. She would be there, too, when a patron curled grateful fingers around a steaming cup of chai in the middle of winter, and when a relieved mother curled up on the couch with a magazine, her children busy coloring at the kids' table and feasting on gulab jamun.

It *was* perfect. A place for sweet tooths and seeking comfort and trying new things. Dev's mouth was dry as he watched Naomi straighten the coloring books and crayons. He wasn't sure why watching her complete such a mundane task made his fingers itch to touch her again, but this time, in that sweetly curved hollow of her lower back, but he knew one thing:

He didn't want these feelings going away anytime soon.

chapter
17

S tanding under the green-and-white-striped awning of
Belmont Heights, a senior-living apartment complex, Naomi
examined the ancient intercom outside the dirty glass doors with
a frown.

"Are you sure we're at the right location?" she asked Dev.

He took a few steps backward to read the address on the awning. "I think so."

They were there on business. Kind of. Word had gotten out
about the bazaar's remodel, and among the excited chatter and
well-wishers, an old friend of Gia's had reached out asking if there
might be room in the future café's menu for her homemade samosas. It wasn't the first offer Gia had received, but it was the only
one she had insisted Dev follow up on.

And Naomi, whose taste buds still remembered the amazing
spread at Aashi's dinner party, had tagged along. After all, if they
were impressive enough for Gia to send Dev on a house call, then
they must be pretty damn amazing.

"So? Are you going to buzz up?" she asked, nudging Dev's ribs with her elbow.

Dev grunted. "I hate these types of things."

"What's that?"

"The only reason we're giving this lady a chance is because she's a friend of the family. It's nepotism."

Naomi nudged him again. Since their kiss the day before, something else was in control of her synapses whenever Dev was around. A brush of lint off his forearm here, a playful nudge into a firm shoulder there.

"Your mom asked you to check it out to see if it's the right fit for the bazaar. She isn't giving her the job, no questions asked. Besides, who knows, maybe this is going to be the best food you've ever tasted in your life."

"They're just samosas."

Just samosas. Naomi swallowed the urge to touch him again—this time with a hearty shove. He didn't know how lucky he was. Instead, she forced cheer into her voice. "Just dial."

Dev raised a quizzical brow but did as she ordered, peering at the yellowed list of resident codes before finding the correct number.

They waited at least a half dozen rings before a small voice croaked. "Um, yes. Speak?"

Dev shot Naomi a pointed look before leaning into the crackling intercom. "It's Dev Mukherjee."

"Ki?"

"Dev Mukherjee."

"What? Ki?"

Naomi pressed her lips together and swallowed a giggle when a faint growl rumbled from Dev's chest.

"Gia's son!" he yelled.

"Oh! Gia! Good. Good." After several heavy breaths, the line went dead and a faint buzz alerted them that the door had been unlocked.

"I already know this is going to be awkward as hell," Dev muttered under his breath as he held the door open for Naomi.

As she brushed past him, Naomi shot him a quick look. The past twenty-four hours had been awkward as hell. They had yet to discuss what was arguably the best kiss of her life, and while Naomi rarely shied away from the kinds of conversation that would twist Dev's panties in a bunch, she couldn't bring herself to broach the subject. Not when the desire to ask him when they could do it again made her cheeks flush and her stomach roll tight like a cinnamon bun.

What if he said no? Naomi knew that in his bumbling, tongue-tied way, Dev would try to be kind, but his rejection would crush her. There'd be no bouncing back.

Casual touch was easier. Meaningless. And so, with a light punch to his biceps, Naomi led Dev to an elevator smelling faintly of mothballs and cooked cabbage. Although the apartment complex was clean, she was taken aback by the faded wallpaper and ragged carpets. She had assumed, given the Mukherjees' wealth and Gia's lofty opinions about everyone and everything under the sun, that Dev's family only rubbed elbows with people of their tier or higher.

Don't judge a weight lifter by their size, her stepfather liked to remind her before that particular Olympic event. Who knew what apartment suite was hiding behind that croaky, old voice? It wasn't like the bazaar had given much away about its owners when Naomi had entered it for the first time.

In this case, however, the proof was in the pudding. The home

Naomi and Dev were ushered into by a petite, elderly lady in a rumpled brown sari under what had to be at least three shawls was a reflection of the elevator they had vacated: worn out, dusty, and smelling faintly of cabbage and mothballs.

"Welcome, welcome," the old lady said, nodding with excitement. "Thank you, thank you."

"Nice to meet you, Mrs. . . . ?" Naomi hesitated. She looked too old to be labeled an auntie, which seemed to be Dev's default for any older South Asian woman.

The old lady pointed to herself. "Didu."

"Mrs. Didu."

The old lady chuckled, and Dev gently cupped Naomi's elbow with his hand. "*Didu* means 'grandma' in Bengali."

Naomi's cheeks heated as the old lady released a string of words in a language she didn't understand, and the blush crept to her neck when Didu began gesturing at her and grinning.

Dev cleared his throat, the pink tinge seeping onto his ears complementing Naomi's palette nicely. "She's congratulating me for having such a pretty girlfriend."

Naomi shook her head. "Oh, no, no. I'm the brand consultant."

Didu's eyes widened, and she clapped her hands together. "Oh! Brand Lady! *Asho, asho.*" She turned and led them across a small living space to a kitchen from the seventies, complete with checkered linoleum floors and cotton-candy-pink laminate countertops. The wallpaper was faded and peeling.

At Didu's shaky, sweeping arm, Dev and Naomi sat at a kitchen table with two mismatched chairs. Given Didu's basic command of the English language, Naomi knew she should take a back seat in conversing—which Dev would probably bemoan later—so as to not discomfort herself, or Didu, any further. But when she spotted the trio of ornate candles sitting on a wooden platter in the middle of the kitchen table, she couldn't stop herself from sitting forward in her seat.

"These are beautiful," she said, tracing the floral pattern on the cream-colored one with the tip of her finger.

Didu smiled and placed a plate of samosas on the table before placing a hand on her chest.

"You made these?"

The old lady nodded, pleasure creasing her eyes. She said a few words in Bengali and then turned to Dev expectantly.

"She says she hand-makes them and gives them to friends for Diwali," Dev translated. "They're all decorated with mehendi, which she does herself." When Didu said a few more words, Dev added, "She used to do bridal mehendi many years ago."

"Diwali . . ." Naomi murmured, racking her brain. "That's the festival of lights, right?"

"Yeah, it's in November."

Naomi shook her head as she examined the candles with new respect. They were gorgeous, the detail so intricate and masterfully crafted. "So beautiful," she repeated.

Didu responded by pushing the plate of samosas closer to Dev and Naomi.

Eager to taste a creation by the hands that could produce such art, Naomi chose one and took a hearty bite, Dev not far behind. They stared at each other as they chewed, Didu hovering at their side.

The faint ringing of a phone interrupted the tasting, and Didu held a finger up to signal her departure before shuffling toward the living room.

As soon as she was gone, Dev grimaced. "Something's wrong with mine. It tastes like the bottom of a compost pail."

"I don't think it's just you," Naomi said around a mouthful of mush and grit. She looked around for a paper towel or a garbage bin. "I need to spit this out."

The sound of crunching gravel emitted from between Dev's teeth. He'd found the grit that Naomi was already pushing to the front of her mouth in anticipation of ridding her palate of this culinary abomination.

"Quick," Dev gurgled, sounding less in command of his gag reflex. "She's telling whoever's on the phone that she has company."

Naomi jumped up and began swinging open the bottom cupboards lining Didu's modest counter space, unsurprised that the contents were those of a person living on a tight budget.

Naomi was more than familiar with this collection of generic brand names, dollar store cleaning tools, and bags saved from the grocery store. When a hidden garbage bin didn't surface, Naomi began pulling at the drawers.

"Napkins!" Pulling out two, she handed one to Dev before spitting in her own.

Dev's panicked eyes were riveted on the crumpled ball in his hand. "What do I do with it?"

"Your pockets!" Naomi shoved her own crumpled napkin at him as the unmistakable sound of Didu's shuffle approached. "Quick!"

"Gross," Dev muttered as he complied. Naomi pushed him back toward his seat while hoping that whatever rancid ingredients Didu had used in those samosas didn't burn a hole through Dev's pants.

They were reseated, albeit breathing heavily, when the older lady returned, slightly out of breath as well.

"So?" Didu asked, looking at Dev with undisguised hope on her face.

Dev cast Naomi a look of wide-eyed terror. Naomi shrugged back. For the first time in her life, she was grateful she didn't know a word of her mother tongue. Dev's face contorted as he reached for the right words to crush an old lady.

As he floundered, Didu patted his shoulder and nodded at the plate. "More?"

Naomi coughed as Dev shook his head frantically. "Thank you for the . . . delicious . . . snack, but I'm not sure these samosas are going to work with the menu we've planned." He then spoke in rapid Bengali.

It was like a train wreck, watching Didu's kind face fall into a deeply lined frown. She said something, a faint protest.

"She's listing all the other things she knows how to cook," Dev murmured out of the side of his mouth. The elderly lady's chin was starting to tremble, her voice breaking as she tried to convince them to give her a chance.

"I'm not sure what to do," Dev whispered to Naomi before responding to Didu in gentle tones, which seemed, at least somewhat, to pacify the distraught woman. Naomi was not surprised in the least with how careful Dev was with Didu, how patient he was with her warbled responses. He even reached out to pat her arm a few times.

Because that was what Dev did. Beneath that crusty exterior was a man who took care of others. Naomi's and Dev's lives might have revolved around the bazaar's rebrand and thwarting Gia's matchmaking schemes, but when needed, Dev never failed to do his family's bidding, whether it was giving Aashi's daughters a ride, providing last-minute babysitting services for his nieces, or joining his mother for a homemade lunch at her house.

Naomi leaned her elbows onto the table, hypnotized by the soft timbre in Dev's voice. His growl was sexy, but this, this was just as enticing, if not better. Dev might never have the right words, but that tone could lull a person into total relaxation, like the slow, consistent glide of wax melting down the side of a . . .

"Candle!" Naomi blurted out, cutting Dev off midsentence. Startled, both Dev and Didu turned to look at her. "We could sell the candles!" she said, gesturing to the center of the table.

Didu didn't need a translation for that. "Really?"

"It's genius," Naomi said, more to Dev. "These would be a lot more lucrative than samosas." *Especially samosas that could double as fertilizer.* "Local businesses do this all the time, showcasing local artists and selling their work. We can work them into the décor. Didu could supply according to demand. Year-round, not just for Diwali."

Dev nodded slowly and translated. Didu was as still as a statue as she absorbed the idea.

When he finished, she looked at Naomi for a silent moment before shuffling forward.

Naomi wasn't sure what to expect. A samosa to the face? A cuff to the back of the head for overstepping? She had no knowledge of Bengali grandmothers, but Grandma Kelly, for all her virtues, never shied away from pinching the underside of Naomi's forearm when she misbehaved.

But Didu placed dry, weathered hands on top of Naomi's head. "Mangala hoka," she said, a tremble in her words. "Anek mangala."

When Naomi turned questioningly to Dev, something flickered in his dark steady eyes. "She's blessing you," he said in a hushed voice.

Naomi wasn't sure how to respond, not with her throat thickening and tears threatening to make an appearance. Didu reached across her and pulled the tallest candle from the centerpiece. It was crimson with a swirling gold-and-pink leaf design.

Didu thrust the creation into Naomi's hands. "Thank you, thank you."

"No, I couldn't . . ."

"Thank you, thank you," Didu repeated firmly.

Naomi cradled the candle to her chest and pretended to inhale its scent while she tried to sort through the emotions playing rugby in her chest. Didu stood in front of her, her eyes soft and knowing, and Naomi was suddenly hyperaware of the ticking of the ancient clock hanging beside the fridge, the smell of cabbage and incense in the air, and the soothing, silky texture of wax on her fingertips.

"Naomi?" Dev's voice was low, concerned.

Naomi gently handed the candle to Dev as one victorious feeling rose above the rest and took command of every single one of her nerve endings. She didn't stop to think about cultural boundaries or how she might look or what was appropriate in this humble little kitchen with coupons and discolored dishcloths tucked in its drawers. She wrapped her arms around Didu and squeezed, and was gratified when the old lady hugged her back.

It was a quiet car ride home. Dev seemed distracted while Naomi couldn't stop glancing down at her candle. She'd been gifted by clients before, and much more lavishly at that—gift cards to expensive restaurants, décor from a million-dollar show home, even a handcrafted armchair once.

But this humble candle was in a league of its own, something Naomi would *never* sell no matter how stretched her finances were. She could still feel gnarled hands at the crown of her head, the weight of gratitude and kindness smoothed onto her hair.

When Dev pulled his vehicle into the spot next to Naomi's in front of the bazaar, he finally turned to her, his face indecipherable.

"What?" Naomi pulled the candle self-consciously to her chest.

"How do you do that?"

"Do what?"

He turned back to the windshield and flexed his fingers a few times around the steering wheel. "Whenever there's a problem or an awkward bump in the conversation or a potential bride with her claws out, you just . . . know what to do. You always have the right words."

Except with you. Under Dev's dark gaze, so steady and serious, Naomi experienced that same sensation of being turned inside out like she had in Didu's apartment after receiving the candle, but it was different this time: deeper, more intense, and almost mortifying. Because Dev had seen so many parts of her, and while he wasn't intimately acquainted with the darkest corners, he'd grazed against their edges and still, he looked at her now like she was something to behold.

Something beautiful, bright, and ethereal.

"I think you're better at it than you give yourself credit for," she managed after a long pause. "I saw how you comforted Didu back there. Even before I chimed in, you were helping her."

"Still . . . your idea is perfect. Exactly what we needed at the right time." A mixture of frustration and awe coated Dev's words. "You don't let anything get in your way, do you?"

Yeah, she was a real saint, manipulating others to get what she wanted. There was too much he still didn't know about her, things he would never understand and could likely never embrace. Maybe she should just tell him. *By the way, did I mention I'm Bengali? My grandparents don't want me, my mother loathes your culture, and*

most days I'm an impostor, but other than that, we're not so different.
How would Dev react?

But she couldn't tell him, not when he was looking at her with
soft, solemn eyes, his mouth slack and relaxed. And the usual guilt
associated with the knowledge that she had lied to Dev—and his
family—dissipated when Naomi thought back to Didu's threadbare throw rugs.

So instead, she shrugged. "I didn't want to leave without offering Didu *something*, nepotism or not." Naomi glanced down at her
candle. "You have to admit, it's so lovely."

"It is," Dev said in a low voice. When Naomi glanced up again,
his eyes were on her face, intense and fringed with sooty black
lashes.

Naomi stared back, vaguely aware that behind him, his window had started to fog. She was suddenly too warm, as if her skin
were lighting up from within. She wanted to curl into herself. Or
rip off her clothes. Something, *anything*, to relieve the jangle of
nerves buzzing through her.

Unlike Didu's kitchen, the silence settling around them wasn't
unpleasant; it was lush, like the undetectable whisper of the wind
whipping through the grass. After carefully placing the candle on
the floor, Naomi's hand rose of its own volition to press against
Dev's chest, her fingers desperate to learn the firm planes underneath.

Dev hesitated slightly before his fingers caught one of Naomi's
tight, black curls and tucked it behind her ear. Naomi closed her
eyes as his fingers skimmed over the sensitive skin underneath the
earlobe and down her jaw.

"You keep rescuing me." He paused and a faint blush seeped
onto his cheeks. "I like it."

"Me, too."

They shared a smile and, as if a starting gun had sounded in the distance, in one fluid movement Naomi leaned forward and Dev pulled her out of her seat and onto his lap. Naomi laughed breathlessly as Dev reached down to the automatic seat adjuster to slide his seat back before she settled her mouth against his. They both froze in that position, lips snug. Naomi let the sense of sweet relief wash through her, down to her toes, relaxing every muscle in its wake like a line of falling dominoes.

Dev recovered first, his mouth opening beneath hers, tongue seeking its mate. God, he was good at that, and Naomi was more than happy to comply. She loved the feeling of her chest pressed against his, his fingers digging into her lower back, her legs straddling his. Again, the desire to rip her clothes off materialized, but she'd settle for curling into *him*, cloaking herself senseless in peppermint woods.

Even though they'd kissed only once before, it was as if this meticulous man had memorized every secret of her mouth, every button to press so that she was powerless against rolling her hips forward against him. There wasn't much room in Dev's cushy vehicle, but Naomi persisted in seeking purchase against the rough seam of his pants, the straining hardness underneath. Well aware that her movements bordered on clumsy and frantic, Naomi couldn't find the self-control to slow down. Or care. Because the need for relief was too sharp, too close to slicing her in half if she didn't get it now. She wanted to consume this moment, consume him.

When he growled deep in his chest, Naomi pulled away with a breathless sound that was half laugh, half moan. She refused to be embarrassed by it, by the lack of control of her inner thighs clenching on Dev's lap. Or how, at the loss of contact, she couldn't resist leaning forward and nuzzling her nose against his.

"Dev?"

"Yeah?"

"Is that a balled-up napkin in your pocket or are you happy to see me?"

Although his dimples flickered to life, Dev's eyes were intense as always as they searched hers. Naomi's insides melted like hot candle wax, and she couldn't resist pushing a gentle fingertip into his left dimple.

"Naomi?"

"Yeah?"

"Do you want to go upstairs?"

Thank God. "Yes."

Wordlessly, Dev hit the power lock and led her inside, his hand in hers.

chapter
18

When they reached his apartment, Naomi stopped a few feet away from the bed, all too aware of how much space the simple queen frame occupied in the tiny studio.

As usual, Dev sensed her hesitation and gave her hand a squeeze. "We don't have to do anything you don't want to do."

He was giving her an out, unaware that the heat from his fingertips was electric, spiraling downward through her body, pooling into liquid heat, and Naomi knew, despite all the reasons they shouldn't, she wanted him.

Badly.

She lifted her eyes to meet his. "I think a part of me has wanted to do this since I smashed that gulab jamun in your face."

Dev's lips twitched as he pulled her closer. "It took almost a whole bottle of shampoo to get the syrup out of my hair."

Naomi ran her fingers through the hair at the base of his neck, transfixed by the silky slide of inky black strands over her skin. "I don't regret it one bit."

"Why am I not surprised?" His right dimple pulled a hit-and-run before his face straightened. "I've gotten tested since my last partner."

There Dev went again, taking care of her before she even needed to ask, and Naomi's heart began to skip. "So have I."

Dev's hands cradled the sides of her neck, his thumbs stroking back and forth across the base of her jaw in a lazy rhythm. "You're so different from anyone I've ever met. I can't believe how beautiful you are."

From the way he was drinking her in and the reverent sweep of his skin on hers, Naomi could do nothing but let go of the insecurities bubbling beneath her surfaces and believe him. The hair on her arms singed, her insides on fire. She felt seen. He was looking at something inside her, and although what exactly she wasn't sure, every nerve ending edged her closer to him. Before she could stutter a suitable response, Dev pulled her into the curve of his body and found her mouth with his.

His lips were controlled but commanding: every caress of his tongue was a question that demanded an answer, revealing her lips' secrets and vices. This perfectionist man, who watched her so carefully and solemnly whenever they were together, was determined to learn everything about her that night.

And master every new piece of information he gleaned.

She needed to regain the upper hand, some indication that she was in control, too.

With slow, deliberate steps, Naomi backed her way to the bed, unbuttoning her shirt as Dev followed, his eyes tracking every new inch of skin revealed to him like it was a luxury. When she peeled off her top, revealing a plain black bra, Dev closed his eyes.

"Christ," he said.

Naomi smiled as Dev leaned her back, deftly unhooking her

bra before her back hit the bed. She laughed a little as he pressed his firm body against her and felt him smile against her neck.

"What?" he asked, his voice muffled. He nipped the sensitive skin of her pulse in retaliation.

"I had no idea accountants were so smooth."

He nipped her again. "Calculators improve dexterity."

Naomi's chuckle skittered into a gasp when those skilled fingers found her breast. As Dev kissed a slow trail down the column of her throat, his thumb stroked over her nipple, softly at first and then more firmly when Naomi moaned. When her back arched against the mattress, he lifted his head and raised a mischievous eyebrow before gently tugging the puckered tip between his knuckles.

An impatient current shot straight to her core, and when Dev felt the telltale lift of her hips, he quickly replaced his fingers with his mouth while treating her other breast to the same sweet torture.

He hadn't been lying about the dexterity.

Naomi shifted her toes against the sheets in a bid to keep the growing need that dampened her panties at bay. She was vaguely aware of Dev's erection, hard and insistent against her leg, and a voice somewhere in the back of her mind told her to spring into action, to show her appreciation and reciprocate. But Dev's lips, tongue, and teeth worshipped her breasts so attentively, robbing her focus completely.

For once the people-pleasing voice quieted and her limbs grew heavy. Lethargic. He was going to take care of her.

Naomi swallowed a whimper. "Dev, please."

He slid back up her body for a scorching kiss as his hand glided over the curve of her belly to unbutton her pants. He slipped his hand into her panties, cupping her where she needed relief so badly. Naomi couldn't hold back a grateful hiss as her hips rose greedily to meet his palm.

Dev skirted his lips over her cheek to tickle the sensitive skin behind her earlobe with the tip of his tongue. Naomi's mind whirled with the implications.

"You're so wet," he whispered in her ear, using her slickness to soften his touch. "You're so perfect."

There was no way in hell Naomi could formulate an appropriate response. She could barely think. Didn't want to. All she could do was luxuriate in Dev's skillful fingers as he found her cleft. Like everything else he did, he was meticulous in testing what she liked, the subtle curves and grooves of her most private place. His fingertips memorized the exact pressure that urged her hips to jerk upward, that arched her back on the mattress as she climbed toward release.

"The way you're moving . . . fuck, it's so hot," Dev said brokenly, his eyes riveted to where his fingers worked her like a dirty secret, hidden from view in her panties.

His words were an aphrodisiac and Naomi swallowed a moan. "I'm . . ." She trailed off as Dev found her favorite spot, the one that pushed her over the edge every time. "Yes. Right there, Dev."

Dev responded by placing his thumb on the exact same spot to continue his torturous massage as he slid two fingers inside her. He groaned as Naomi grew wetter, his thumb pausing as he curled his fingers upward questioningly.

Naomi pressed her lips together and silently commanded her body to lie still, to control its greedy desire. She reached her hand out to palm Dev's erection, but he shook his head, that familiar impatience clouding his eyes.

"This is for you," he said. His eyes drifted to where his fingers were buried inside her. "Tell me what feels good."

But Naomi couldn't bring herself to say the words. Instead, she tried to shimmy her lower body a little, coaxing Dev's thumb to do what she needed. Whether he understood her or not, he applied more pressure and Naomi could have wept with relief.

"Fuck, that's sexy," he murmured as Naomi's hips rebelled, bucking with embarrassing eagerness to meet his rhythm. Naomi couldn't have stopped them if she wanted to; she was mindless to everything but the rush of heat swirling through her, beckoning her forward.

"What else?" he asked.

Naomi closed her eyes. With painstaking focus, he was coaching her body's responses, patiently searching through the hidden pockets for her pleasure, as if her satisfaction was all he cared about. She didn't feel rushed or like she would need to return any kind of favor. And yet a small voice inside her head cautioned her to hold a part of herself aloft.

She wasn't ready for him to know everything.

"What else?" Dev repeated. When she still didn't respond, he leaned forward and nuzzled her mouth with a light, coaxing lick.

On a slow exhale, Naomi opened her eyes to meet Dev's serious, dilated gaze. Here, at least, she desperately wanted to let go. To lay herself bare to him, free of all the hard, complicated things between them.

She took another deep breath. "Fuck me with your fingers and make me come."

And, of course, he did exactly as she asked, watching her carefully, so carefully, as her body flushed in response. The lush sound of his fingers pumping inside her, slick with milk and honey, was the only sound in the stillness of the apartment, broken only by Naomi's cry as she welcomed the waves of liquid fire cresting over her, all the way to her toes.

As the currents of pleasure slowed and softened like the last note of the sweetest love song, Naomi turned onto her side toward him, aware of his fingers still inside her. She blinked contentedly at him, basking in the expression of awe on his face.

She felt powerful.

"I *felt* you come on my fingers," he murmured, almost to himself, as he withdrew his fingers.

Naomi blushed.

"Do you—" Dev hesitated. "We don't need to . . ."

Naomi responded by detangling herself from him before pulling her pants and underwear off and tossing them off the foot of the bed. Dev's eyes darkened with fresh desire as he unceremoniously rid himself of his clothes, seemingly unaware of Naomi's hungry gaze roving over his body. She had known he was trim and solid, but his sleekly sculpted body astounded her.

After several beats, Dev glanced down at himself uneasily. "What?"

"Who knew all this was hiding underneath your nerdy accountant veneer?"

There was humor and light in his answering glare. "It's part of my charm."

Naomi wrapped her hand around his length, smiling wickedly when he closed his eyes with a sharp gasp. "Won me over."

"G-good." Dev's voice was faint as Naomi began stroking, unable to tear her eyes away from his vulnerability. It was so rare but so beautiful. And he didn't even know it.

"I want you inside me, Dev. Now."

His eyes flew open, glittering in the darkness of the apartment and questioning.

"I have an IUD," she said.

Dev leaned down and kissed her roughly; it was the first break in control he'd shown that night. And yet, even then, he took his time, using his tongue to explore hers as if he had all the time in the world.

If he always kissed her like this, Naomi would never leave this room, rebrand be damned. And right now, as her lips eagerly moved to match his, it sounded like a great idea. She was mildly disappointed when Dev pulled away to nibble her bottom lip but was immediately pacified by the gentle stroke of his fingers against her core, where she was unashamedly wet and more than ready for him.

Naomi's entire body tightened in anticipation for that first moment of contact, of her body's most intimate place stretching in that oh so satisfying way. Dev's hands found hers as he settled between her thighs and, after clasping her fingers tightly in his, he entered her slowly. They shared a groan.

"Fuck," he said through gritted teeth. "This is better than I imagined it would be."

Her sheath clenched at his gruff words, and Naomi couldn't help herself from saying, "Tell me." If sex was making this taciturn man talk, she was going to milk him for everything he was worth.

He shot her a searing look; he knew exactly what she was asking for, and yet he surprised her. "I want to draw this out forever..." He paused to withdraw very slowly before sinking into her again. "It's never felt like this for me," he added. Another thrust. "Ever."

Dev groaned again as Naomi experimentally rotated her hips. "Don't do that. I need a minute," he said, his voice pained.

"Why?" Naomi asked breathlessly, unable to hold back another wiggle. She felt delightfully full and every movement sent her nerves dancing, reawakening the same fire from earlier.

Dev buried his face in the crook of her neck. "It's been a while for me."

Her heart squeezed at the admission. Naomi freed her hands from his to wrap them around his back, loving the feel of strong muscles under her palm.

"Dev?" she said, arching her hips temptingly, which earned her a tortured look. "I like it hard. And fast."

He closed his eyes for a moment, a smile playing at his lips. Naomi made a mental note to kiss his dimples later. When he opened them again, the look in their dark chocolate depths clenched her heart again, among other things. "Have I told you already how perfect you are?"

Naomi's chest squeezed and she locked her legs around his back. "Fuck me hard."

Dev grasped her thighs, spreading her wider and angling her hips so he could sink deeper, and gave in to his carefully leashed passion. He tucked his face into her neck as his hips pounded into hers, the repetitive slap of their bodies accented by Naomi's moans.

With every demanding thrust, the edge sharpened and her toes curled, achy for a second release. She lifted her hips for purchase, selfishly seeking her own pleasure. But although she could feel herself growing wetter, the peak remained out of reach.

As if he could read her mind, Dev scraped his teeth behind her earlobe, prompting a shiver down Naomi's spine. "Touch yourself, sweetheart," he said. "I want to feel you come on me again."

Naomi didn't need to be told twice. She slipped her hand between them to where her body welcomed the attention. It didn't take much—half a dozen circles and she contracted around him in an echo of the orgasm she had experienced before. Dev held back until her insides relaxed, her body liquefying underneath him. Only then did he finally give in with a low growl, his muscles bunching underneath her hands, his hard torso pressing into her softness as he released inside her.

Their heavy, staggered breaths were the only sounds in the room as they lay still, Dev's body collapsed on hers. The warmth seeping from his skin was a welcome, reassuring blanket. The weight of him lying on top of her was a sharp reminder of what they had done, the lines she had intentionally crossed.

Naomi breathed in Dev's familiar scent and traced her fingers over his back. Her hand moved slowly but confidently as if it had already explored this expanse of skin, even though every curve and plane was new.

She wanted to know every inch. Memorize it.

Her mother had always warned her against mixing with the South Asian community. She'd been taught to believe they'd look down on her, equate her westernized upbringing to a lack of morals, a betrayal of roots.

That she could never fit with them.

But as her fingers slid over the dips and valleys of muscle, bones, and beauty marks, Naomi wondered if she could be the exception. Because this—their breaths falling in the same easy rhythm, legs intertwined—made sense to her. Something that felt this right couldn't possibly be wrong. Not when his skin warmed hers and his lips, curled into a smile, pressed faint kisses against the side of her neck.

Dev's life might be entangled in everything she'd been cautioned against, but he knew her. He knew what mattered; she didn't need to prove anything to him. And, more than anyone, he would understand why she'd keep certain parts of herself locked away. Of course he'd understand.

He had to.

chapter
19

Waking up next to Naomi was Dev's version of the perfect day at the beach: clean, isolated, and with none of those flying rat-birds squawking in the distance.

The scent of sweet coconut and sunshine infiltrated his senses—ripe, beckoning, and fresh. Naomi's slow, even breathing, still deep in slumber, was a hundred times more comforting than the gentle swish of a rolling tide breaking onto the shore. Her supple skin was the sunbaked sand, warm and smooth, inviting his touch. Dev wanted to bury himself in the soft expanse of her.

Beep! Beep!

The blare of his phone's alarm ruined it. Quick like a crab, Dev scuttled to his bedside table to shut it off. Naomi's stillness suggested she was still asleep, so Dev eagerly returned to his initial position, wrapped around her from behind.

He'd never been much of a cuddler before. In previous relationships, overnight stays had been rare. And the few he'd grudgingly accepted—never in his own bed—he preferred his space, on the left side of the bed, one pillow only, thanks.

But Naomi's smooth skin warming his front while he nuzzled into the soft, wayward curls that smelled like a fruity, tropical drink he'd eye with longing but could never bring himself to order? Paradise. He could stay there forever, tucked away with her in this tiny apartment, matching his breath to the slow, sensuous rise and fall of her stomach under the palm of his hand.

Naomi let out a soft moan, her back arching so her toes could find shelter between his legs. He'd been awoken several times over the course of the night by the icy little glaciers against his skin.

He didn't mind; it felt nice to be a source of warmth for a change.

"What time is it?" Naomi murmured in a rough, husky voice that blanketed Dev's eardrums in the coziest way.

Dev thought back to his phone alarm signaling it was time for his workout. "A little before six."

Naomi sighed and rolled to face him, causing a very pleasing mashing of things against other things. He *definitely* didn't mind that either.

As Naomi's eyes shuttered closed again, Dev studied her face, marveling at how the features he thought he'd known so well seemed different now. Because now he knew the sweep of those long, soft eyelashes feathering across his cheek, and the decadence of that pink bottom lip caught between his teeth. The hollows of her clavicle as she waited, on a sharp gasp, for what would come next after he slid between her thighs, her body tight with anticipation as he parted her with his fingers. When his eyes wandered back to Naomi's eyes, he found them watching him back as if her thoughts were not so different from his own.

Dev felt himself harden.

"We should talk about what happened last night . . ." she began.

And then he softened. *Don't be a jerk if she has regrets.* "Okay, sure."

"I think you should know something," she said. "When I met your mom—"

Well, that did it. Completely deflated, Dev flipped onto his back with a groan. "Can we not?"

"Can we not what?"

"Just once, let's keep my family out of it. I speak from experience—keeping them out of the equation is the way to go."

Naomi propped her head up on her hand and wrinkled her nose. "Well, then, let's talk about that."

At this rate, he'd never get hard again. His jaw, on the other hand, tightened with a noticeable squeak. "Please, let's not talk about my family right now."

"Not that," Naomi said, poking him in the ribs. "About your *experience*."

Naomi's tone might have been teasing, but drawled that way, the word carried a hint of caution. A gateway word to an epic argument. Yet Dev wanted to tell Naomi whatever she wanted to know. To convey—in a not-weird, casual way—that she could never be lumped with those women, the ones he never wanted anything more than three months with. He didn't want to define this relationship against his family's expectations, as he had felt forced to in the past.

Don't fuck this up, he coached himself. Now was not the time to blurt out the wrong thing.

"I've mostly just slept around." *Shit. Well done, Dev.*

Naomi's eyebrows shot up. "Oh?"

"I mean, I've never really done relationships in the past." Even prior to his mother introducing matchmaking hell into his life, Dev had never been interested in the idea of dating. Small talk? Planning romantic moments? Prolonged eye contact and the pressure to say the right thing at the right time? Dev cringed. No, thanks.

But as he cast a sidelong glance at the beautiful, luminous woman at his side, dating seemed less like a chore and more like an exquisite form of torture. He could learn to be a desirable boyfriend, to reciprocate those casual, affectionate brushes that Naomi doled out so easily.

With Naomi, he could learn to be warm.

A relationship with her would be anything but two people together for the sake of convenience. It would be lighthearted teasing and easy companionship. Laughter between kisses and the sweet anticipation of seeing that same familiar face every time he woke up.

It would be friendship . . . with lots and lots of nudity if Dev had his way.

"I guess I can understand why you've avoided actual relationships in the past," Naomi said. Her lips quirked. "Given everything with Gi—I mean, she who will not be named. It doesn't sound like you've had a ton of choices."

Dev didn't miss the thread of sadness in Naomi's voice. Under the covers, his hand sought hers and, much like it had throughout the night, he found it easily.

"This isn't like that." In the stillness of his apartment, the words were thick and everywhere at once. A fresh sheet of wet, heavy snow blanketing a quiet prairie field. "I want to do things differently with you."

So much for being casual. And yet Dev's chest felt light, his limbs pleasingly slack and relaxed.

"But all those things your family cares about and all those qualities Gia wants in your future wife . . . Do those things matter to you?"

"Look, I know you're not from a traditional Bengali family," Dev said. When Naomi averted her eyes, he rushed to add, "But I don't care. If anything, I'm relieved that we don't share the same culture. One meddling, overdramatic family is enough, don't you think?"

When Naomi's teeth worried her bottom lip in response, he squeezed her hand. "Seriously. I'm glad you are the way you are. I don't want the same things my mother wants."

He'd always wanted to escape the ironclad chains that bound him to his culture, believing that loyalty prevented him from doing so. But here, beside Naomi with nothing between them but rumpled sheets and streaks of dawn's rosy light, he could admit that something else had kept him reeled in.

Fear. He couldn't imagine life without his family. They might manipulate, steamroll, and annoy him, but they were *his*. His responsibility. His touchstone. His world. Who else would want him—a stoic, awkward, moody accountant who still didn't have his career sorted out?

But it was all a lot less scary with the thought of Naomi at his side. They were a team. Everything that had happened in the last few months had solidified that. He could count on her. She looked out for him and expected nothing in return.

He wanted to give her everything he had.

Maybe they'd stand up to his family together. Maybe they'd run away and leave it all behind. Whatever happened, he knew he could trust her.

Beep! Beep! Now it was Naomi's phone ruining the moment. Dev reached for where it lay next to his and passed it her way.

"That's my cue," she said with a grimace. "Although considering you get up before sunrise every day to go to the gym, I should stop complaining." She opened her email inbox and began scrolling. "We should probably get to work."

Dev slipped his arms around Naomi and squeezed. She relaxed

in his embrace and squirmed closer, her eyes darkening to burned honey even as she continued to scan her email, the device squished between them.

"That's nice," she murmured when his hand slid to the curve of her lower back to massage the muscles there.

"Uh-huh." Dev wasn't deterred. After several minutes, his ministrations wandered lower to her perfect ass, gently kneading. Naomi's body practically melted into the sheets.

"Nick's crew will be here soon," she said, her voice drowsy.

"Right." With a wicked smile, Dev brushed his finger over her already wet opening before pulling her tight to his erection. She moved restlessly, her hips angling to cradle him.

When he ground against her with a subtle tilt of his hips, the phone slipped from her hands. Dev grabbed it and reached over Naomi to place it on the far edge of the mattress.

"Seriously? Again?" Naomi asked breathlessly as he rolled on top of her.

Arms on either side of Naomi's head, Dev rested his weight on his forearms and enjoyed the luxury of studying her face. It was sappy and brought heat to the tips of his ears, knowing she was watching him watch her, but the contentment spreading through his chest erased his embarrassment.

"Dev?" Naomi prodded, her toes tickling his leg gently.

He nipped at the base of her jaw in retaliation. "What accountants lack in muscle definition, we make up for in stamina."

Naomi's laugh fluttered into a lush sigh as he trailed wet kisses downward, paying special attention to the curve of where her shoulder met the graceful line of her neck. He'd mapped this territory the night before, knew that the light graze of his teeth on this very spot would drive her heels into the mattress.

Sure enough, Naomi began to shift restlessly. Dev continued downward, trailing over warm skin, the perfect dip of her belly button.

When Dev's tongue found its way to the insides of her inner thighs, Naomi struggled to sit up. Dev laid firm hands on her stomach, urging her back down. He could tell it was hard for her to lie still, to not actively participate. To just receive and not give. But he wanted to take care of her, this vibrant, addictive woman who had rescued him countless times and effortlessly teased a smile from him despite his reluctance.

When Naomi grudgingly lay back down, it felt like the ultimate victory. And Dev was just getting started.

With intense focus, Dev explored her with fingers and tongue, lingering in spots when her hips lifted in agreement, sliding his fingers inside her when a low moan escaped her lips.

"Does this feel good?" he asked, slipping a second finger inside her.

"Yes."

Dev pumped his fingers several times. "Do you like this?"

"Yes."

"How about . . ." Dev curled his fingertips upward. He was rewarded by Naomi's entire body arching, her fingers tightening on the twisted sheets.

"That's better." Dev's fingers moved into the new rhythm as his tongue found her again, her sweet, earthy scent flooding his senses. So decadent. Like eating dessert barefoot on the shore, waves lapping languidly nearby.

"You're so sweet," he said against her, blowing a cool puff of air against her warm center.

"It feels so good," Naomi whimpered.

Dev cast a wry glance up the long line of her writhing body;

good wasn't enough. He wanted to do better. He knew, from the previous night, that Naomi liked to hear him talk, had felt her clench when he, for the first time in his life, had whispered the right words in her ear as he thrust into her.

"Tell me what you want," he said, letting his lips brush against her but slowing the glide of his fingers to a more teasing pace.

"I . . ." Naomi looked down at him pleadingly.

"Tell me." He wanted her to tell him what she needed. To not only receive pleasure but to take it from him, to demand the exact thing that would send her over the edge. He wanted her to use him, to think only of herself and the pleasure he wished to give her.

After a long pause where the only sound between them was the slow slide of Dev's drenched fingers, Naomi finally gasped, "Faster."

Dev was more than happy to comply. And as fresh moisture flooded his hand, he looked up at her again. "What else? Tell me."

Naomi's mouth pursed but no words came out.

"You can tell me," Dev said gently.

Her beautiful lips parted, her tongue darting out to moisten them. Dev swallowed a groan.

"I want . . ." Naomi's face flushed.

"What?"

"I want you to . . ."

"Naomi." Dev could see the uncertainty flitting across her face. He wanted to prove himself to this beautiful woman, to show her she could let go with him. She could be herself—demanding, imperfect, and wild—with him.

"You can trust me," he added with a certainty that rushed through his veins like adrenaline.

"I w-want you to suck my clit," she cried, lifting her hips to his mouth.

His adrenaline burst like wildfire, and he quickly complied, eyes watching Naomi's reaction carefully so he knew how much pressure she liked, how deep of a pull she craved. It wasn't long before her body broke on a sharp cry, squeezing his fingers so fucking tight that Dev couldn't help but press his own hips into the mattress, seeking relief.

When Naomi's breathing slowed, Dev crawled up her body, returning to his original position, arms on either side of her face, the perfect vantage point to study her. Her beautiful light brown eyes were half closed, her lips parted and pliant.

"We should shower," Dev said, punctuating his suggestion by nuzzling her nose with his. He couldn't resist rolling his hips into hers.

Naomi's eyes flew open. "The shower in this apartment is the tiniest one in the whole world."

Dev grinned back. "We'll make it work."

chapter
20

Two weeks later, Dev was halfway down the bazaar's rickety staircase when he heard the crash and skitter of something very breakable falling to the floor. Pulse pounding, he hurried the rest of the way and burst through the beaded entryway, well aware that the clatter of shells and tiny bells was an entrance fit for a hippie in a low-budget psychedelic movie from the seventies.

"Naomi, are you ok—" Dev stuttered to a stop when he saw that it was Neel who was responsible for the noise. Seeing his older brother frowning in irritation that one of Aashi's vintage ceramic teapots had dared to slip from his meaty grasp reminded Dev that he wouldn't be seeing Naomi until later that evening because she had a dentist appointment. The realization washed an unfamiliar sense of contentment over him.

It was nice knowing something so intimate as a person's whereabouts, even something as insignificant as a trip to a dental clinic. It was absurdly comforting: he knew where she was, and when he would see her again.

Too bad Neel, who kicked a few of the shards away with no intention of cleaning them up himself, was exactly the right person to bring him down. Dev grabbed a dustpan from behind the counter and began sweeping up the mess as Neel moved on, unapologetic, with his trademark douchebag swagger.

"It kind of stinks in here," his brother said.

"They did the final coat yesterday."

"Is that so?" Neel glanced around the room with a smirk. "Interesting color choices."

Dev rattled the contents of the dustpan, his eyes trained on the ceramic shards. "You better hope Mashi isn't mad that you broke this."

"They're junk."

But they mean something to her. Not that Neel would get it. Just like when he dropped his daughters off in their mother's care without any prior notice, as if Gia had nothing better to do.

Or when he showed up to family dinner over a half hour late, unperturbed that they were waiting on him. Neel *never* got it. He, too, had inherited some of their father's worst qualities, but, unlike Dev, Neel didn't loathe or fear them. He basked in them.

He always had, and it had set an indiscernible tone in the Mukherjee household. Neel trailed after their father like an impressionable puppy, their father barely noticing his firstborn's adoration—or anyone, really—as he obsessed over his career. Dev had quietly sided with Gia, doing the best he could for such a stubborn and critical woman. And Dhan had hidden away in his own space, separate from and seemingly unaffected by whatever tension brewed outside his bubble.

The three brothers had been close, once upon a time. But as Dev studied his older brother now, snapping pictures of various angles in the room on his camera phone, he could barely remember those days. He was more attuned to his level of annoyance, which had shot up from a casual everyday five to a simmering six.

"What are you doing?" Dev asked.

Neel ignored him and crouched like a wildlife photographer so he could get a close-up of the floor.

Seven and a half. Dev rubbed the bridge of his nose, where a headache was taking root. He wished Dhan were here. Although Neel tended to bully them both, Dhan's laid-back, quirky sense of humor helped soothe the jagged edges of Dev's irritation.

There wasn't much to photograph yet. Save for the couch and kids' area in one corner, the hand-built white counter, and the heavy wood family-style table with matching benches along the wall, the bulk of the furniture and décor had yet to arrive. Dev knew it was a source of stress for Naomi, whom he had heard mumbling words like *back order* and *discontinued* in her sleep.

Neel wandered toward the long, rectangular table and rapped his knuckles against it.

"Well, this'll have to go," he said. Neel peered down its length, which could seat ten adults, and shook his head.

"What do you mean?" Dev asked as he joined Neel's side.

"If we want to capitalize on this place," Neel said, "then we don't want the vibe that people should stay and hang out. A long high top along this window with cheap plastic chairs would be better. We want people to guzzle their drinks and then make room for the next customer." Neel's chest puffed as he expanded his hands to conceptualize his version of a masterpiece for his brother.

Dev frowned. "What about customers who like people watching?" he asked, nodding at the long window stretched across the wall.

"Uncomfortable chairs will take care of that," Neel said with a smarmy wink. "I'm not feeling that, either," he added, gesturing at the gleaming white display cases Nick had installed next to the cash register. "It's not necessary. It should be more like how the bazaar used to be: prepackaged, imported snacks. Like a convenience store."

Dev hid his fists by crossing his arms over his chest. Thank God his mother had decided to hire a brand consultant for the bazaar; Neel's ideas were god-awful. If his brother was looking for a grab-and-go kind of café, he was not going to be pleased when the cushioned wicker chairs and inviting throw pillows Naomi planned to toss on the couch arrived.

"Mom already approved the design," Dev pointed out.

"Yeah, well, out with the old and in with the profitable, bro," Neel smirked. "I called Mom last night and told her about my plans for the store."

"And what did she say? What were her exact words?"

"What could she say? You can't argue with logic."

More like, she can't argue with you. It wouldn't have taken much for Gia to give up against Neel, the de facto head of the household. Like their father, he tended to barrel through conversations and situations, and Gia was more likely to scuttle out of Neel's path rather than stand her ground. After all, she'd done the same with her husband many times, swishing in and out of sight to do her husband's bidding, regardless of how it affected her. It was what she'd been taught a "proper" Bengali wife should do.

Which was why Dev would never be able to comprehend why his mother believed he would want a similar life. His mother was looking for herself in a daughter-in-law—flexible, domestic, traditional—but he'd never seen Gia particularly happy with her marriage. Or satisfied. He knew she took pride in their hard-earned wealth, their sterling reputation in the community. But how could she not understand that maybe her middle son needed more?

He'd never seen his mother advocate for herself with his father, and if she couldn't do it with Neel, he would have to step in.

"So she agreed?" Dev pressed. "She said, 'Yes, the bazaar is yours to do as you like'?"

Neel bent at the waist to examine the underside of the table. "Not in so many words, but basically, sure," he murmured, distracted. "Who is your contractor? I need to have a word with him."

"Any changes you want to make should be taken up with Naomi."

With a snort, Neel straightened and folded his arms across his chest. "I'd rather take it up with the guy in charge." When Neel finally took stock of Dev's narrowed gaze, he smirked again. "Uh-oh, don't tell me Downer Dev is back."

At Neel's childhood nickname for him, Dev's jaw clenched. "What's that supposed to mean?"

Neel shrugged and moved toward the long white counters. "Everyone's been talking about how cheerful you've been for the past few weeks. All happy and shit. But I knew Downer Dev would make a comeback eventually."

"What?"

"Because I know you—"

"No," Dev said. "Who's been talking about me?"

"Mom and Aashi talk all the time about how you're acting different. They think you're in love or something."

Something cold fisted Dev's spine, and he straightened. "In love? With whom?"

"Dunno. Your future wife, maybe? They're calling the matchmaker a miracle worker."

The revelation was a lump of half-chewed, undercooked samosa lodged in his throat. Had he been acting different? Maybe
he hadn't grumbled enough when Gia had guilt-tripped him into
escorting her and her granddaughters to the local kangaroo sanctuary because she was unfamiliar with the area. It was possible
that the last time the topic of the matchmaker had come up around
the family dinner table, he'd made the mistake of shrugging off his
aunt's teasing too good-naturedly.

Shit. He *had* been acting differently. But his mother hadn't
cuffed him on the back of the head yet or called the firing
squad, so there was no way she knew the real reason behind the
improvement in his mood. Everything between him and Naomi—
everything real, anyway—was, so far, a secret for two.

But maybe that needed to change.

The idea of thwarting yet another potential bride had never sat
well with Dev, but it was no longer just another annoying part of
his culture that he wanted to avoid. The thought of faking a relationship with Naomi peeled a layer from his insides, flooded his
body with a chill that was both uncomfortable and nauseating. He
didn't want to pretend anymore, to subvert his family as if doing
so would fulfill him and get him what he wanted.

Yes. It was time for a change.

chapter

21

Naomi's fingers were flying over her laptop keyboard when her phone vibrated against her kitchen table. Normally she ignored incoming calls and messages when working after hours, but when she saw her parents' landline flash across the screen, she picked up.

"Hey, Dad."

"It's Mom, Peanut."

Naomi sat up straight. "What's wrong? Is Dad okay?"

"I'm fine, he's fine, everyone's fine," Sue Kelly assured her, and Naomi's fingers twitched to return to the keyboard. "I thought I'd check in."

Why? Check-ins were her stepfather's domain. Sue might swoop in for a word or two if she could pull herself away long enough from whatever project or hobby she was currently obsessed with. But when Sue didn't launch into a long-winded, detailed overview of her newest venture into self-discovery, a faint alarm bell rang in Naomi's brain.

"What's up?"

"You tell me. Eric has mentioned a few times that you've been very busy."

Naomi had been keeping her stepfather updated on every little detail that she was sure, thanks to Dev, would win Gia over. From the peacock-pattern mugs, a subtle tribute to Gia's favorite animal, to the splashes of plum accents throughout, Gia's color of choice, Naomi's confidence was growing as they approached the bazaar's deadline.

"He says you've been working too hard," Sue said, parroting exactly what her stepfather had mentioned during their last few phone calls.

"I only have two weeks left." Naomi's finger tapped against the edge of her laptop keyboard. She had twelve days, to be exact.

"And how much is there left to do?"

Ignoring the touch of urgency in Sue's voice, Naomi opened the master spreadsheet that haunted her dreams. Many of the larger tasks were checked off; however, she was in the final period, when subtle details and snowballing hiccups liked to play offense. And Naomi would roll over and die at Gia's feet before she let things go into overtime.

"We'll get there." These were the same words she repeated silently to herself when, in the middle of the night, she awoke in a cold sweat at the thought that the Fisher Chrome X-9 faucet she had chosen for the bazaar might go on backorder.

Sue paused, and Naomi heard Eric's low baritone in the background. When he fell silent, Sue was back. "Which park had you wandering around like a Disney princess and tree hugging this morning?"

Hearing what was unmistakably her stepfather's words fall from her mother's lips ignited something bitter and fiery in the center of Naomi's chest. Why did Sue even care? Up to this point, she'd shown little interest in her daughter's career, much less how she spent her free time on her days off.

"I'm not sure," Naomi replied, vaguely remembering that she hadn't stepped foot outside today. When her peripheral noted that six minutes had passed since beginning this phone call, Naomi cleared her throat. "Anyway, I should get goi—"

"We're worried about you," Sue said. "You're not acting like yourself."

"Why? Because I didn't hug a few trees today?" *Uh-oh*. That had come out snappier than intended. And from Sue's sharp intake of breath, her mother agreed.

"Working with this family hasn't been good for you," Sue said, speaking over Eric's muffled voice in the background. "I don't know what you were thinking, messing with these kinds of people. Nothing you do will ever be good enough for them."

Messing around. As if she were doing this on a whim and not building her career. Not busting her ass to make ends meet. But as Sue continued her tirade, Naomi sank into her seat instead. She'd heard it all before; had been on the receiving end of this rant her entire life. Although it had been a long time since Sue went off like this, the fact that her daughter had intentionally left the privacy and anonymity of a small, homogenous town to live among the community she had chosen to run away from twenty-six years ago had to chafe.

"My work will be good enough," Naomi said.

"You aren't cut from the same cloth, Naomi."

The same cloth, indeed. The Mukherjees were a rich tapestry, centuries of finely woven threads pulled tight, infallible. Naomi was threadbare, patchy at best.

Both Sue and Dev had warned her about not getting swept away by the South Asian community, and that was exactly what had happened. Somewhere along the way, though, things had shifted in a way that popped a kernel of uncertainty in Naomi's chest.

Something else was driving Naomi forward now, something that sandwiched her lungs whenever she thought of Gia's face upon seeing her renovated business. Would Dev's hand find hers as Gia took in the newly painted walls, gleaming surfaces, and heart-wrenching accents that breathed life and love into the café? What would Gia say then? What would Dev say about her work?

About *her*? Naomi shivered. Imagine if she let *that* little bomb drop to Sue.

In the background, Eric's calming monotone grew in volume, and after a faint rustling, Sue relinquished the phone. Naomi listened to her stepfather clear his throat into the speaker, the gruff scratch of his throat from over seven hundred kilometers away a soothing balm after Sue's litany.

"Are you all right?" His voice was so gentle that Naomi's heart quivered, reminding her of his clumsy hands fumbling for the pink box of Barbie Band-Aids whenever the tiniest of scrapes brought tears to her eyes. "I know your mother kind of lost her cool, but she's worried about you. We both are."

It was tempting to reassure Eric that he needn't worry, how her spare time was in the hands of someone she was interested in, someone who was making the unbearably long days bearable . . . even while sometimes being adorably unbearable himself.

But with Sue hovering in the background, Naomi wasn't interested in signing her death sentence tonight.

"I'm fine," she said.

"Are you sure, Peanut? Because you don't quite sound like yourself these days. This project sounds like more trouble than it's worth."

"I said, I'm *fine*." Eric fell silent and guilt flooded through Naomi. He did not deserve to be snapped at. She needed to do a better job at pretending everything was all right, that despite overdue bills, sleeping with her client, and a looming deadline for a very critical business owner, she was *fine*. Naomi was the master of holding it all together on the outside even in front of the people she cared for the most.

She loved her stepfather, but he would never understand what the bazaar's success meant for her. He'd grown up in the kind of community where the librarian who set aside his favorite books was also in a crochet circle with his mother and had been taught Sunday school by his grandmother. There had never been any doubt where Eric Kelly belonged in life, no uncertainty of where he fit and how. He was steady, dependable, and thoughtful, but he was also oblivious to what it was like to be on the outside looking in.

He was a lot like Dev, in a way.

"I'm fine," Naomi repeated with a determination that didn't invite further discussion.

Her stepfather's injured tone acknowledged that he heard her loud and clear. "Okay, sweetheart. I'll leave you to it. Just . . . Take care of yourself, all right? Your mother and I are worried."

Naomi's lower lip trembled. She wanted to apologize, but what if she said too much, revealed the darkest corners inside her, parts of her that she could barely bring herself to flicker a light on? No, she couldn't unload that on her stepfather right now. Not when the rebrand was almost done and she was *so* close. Instead, Naomi said her goodbyes and forced her attention back to the laptop.

When her phone vibrated again, Naomi spared her cell only the briefest of glances, so determined was she not to give into distractions again.

However, when she caught sight of Dev's name, she opened his text message.

Dev: I think I'm in your neighborhood. Can I stop by?

Naomi's eyes widened as paper-thin vulnerability fluttered along the edges of something thick and sweet low in her belly. Pleasure.

A few minutes later, a knock sounded at her door, interrupting Naomi's desperate attempt to tidy up. Naomi abandoned a half-folded throw blanket and flew to the door.

"I thought we were meeting at the bazaar?" she said as she let him in.

Dev's sharp brown eyes moved around her small one-bedroom apartment. She had forgotten how observant he could be and felt herself shrinking a little as she wondered what her apartment—nestled on the second floor of a tired building in a less affluent Kelowna neighborhood—would look like to someone like him.

Don't let him see your uncertainty, she reminded herself as she notched her chin upward, as if the thrift store throw rugs and chipped laminate kitchen countertops didn't bother her in the least. She moved to sit behind her laptop with a dismissive wave at the apartment. "I just need to finish some emails. Feel free to snoop." As if she wouldn't be watching his every move from behind the laptop she had yet to pay off.

Dev nodded and moved into her small living room, which was a mismatch of secondhand furniture and show pieces gifted to her from loyal service providers she had met during her corporate days. Her apartment was colorful and cluttered, and it lacked the understated qualities that belied a lifetime of taste and deep pockets; it was the complete opposite of how Dev had grown up.

"Are these yours?" Dev asked, holding up a few books from her bookshelf.

Naomi squinted in his direction and ducked her head when she saw the titles in his hand. They were Indian cookbooks, ones she had purchased recently on a whim but had not yet tried.

"Yes."

Dev grinned. "I thought you didn't grow up eating this stuff?"

He had been envious when she had revealed that her mother's knowledge of cooking anything, least of all Indian food, had been comical at best. Dev had seemed enamored with the idea of a lifetime of canned soup, grilled sandwiches, and burgers, unaware that such foods had barely satiated her craving for a home she didn't know.

"Sometimes I crave a big, fat gulab jamun. Don't you?"

"Believe it or not, I do," Dev said with a chuckle.

Dev moved to Naomi's living room end table and examined the collection of framed photographs there. "Who is this?"

Naomi craned her neck, but the arm of the sofa blocked her view. "You'll have to be more specific."

"This guy standing beside you at graduation."

"That's my dad."

Dev's eyes rose in surprise and, belatedly, Naomi realized she had never mentioned that her stepfather was white. "My stepdad," she admitted. "He's my stepdad."

"You never mentioned . . ." Dev trailed off. "What about your dad?"

"I never got a chance to know him."

She could tell from the downward turn of Dev's lips and his eyes clouding over that he was assuming the worst. "I'm sorry, Naomi."

There was no way to casually explain that her biological father wasn't part of her life because he had shown zero interest in doing so after abandoning her when she was a toddler as if it still didn't bother her twenty-three years later, so Naomi settled for a shrug and trained her eyes back to her laptop, trying not to type too aggressively and failing miserably. She could feel Dev's eyes on the side of her head for several long moments before he shuffled to a second bookcase stuffed beside her TV.

"Someone likes Keanu Reeves," he murmured. "You have . . . Wait. Hang on." Dev slid a DVD case off the shelf and waved it at her. "*Kabhi Khushi Kabhie Gham*? Really?"

Naomi's cheeks heated. It was the same Bollywood movie he had mentioned at Aashi's house, a title she had committed to memory after the elderly lady's suggestive song and shimmy. "I was curious."

"Did you watch it?"

"I . . . I haven't had the time," she replied. Or, at least, she hadn't had the time to watch more than the first half hour of a three-and-a-half-hour movie. Still, it filled her with a strange sense of purpose knowing she would finish the movie one day—and maybe try her hand at churning out an Indian dish from scratch. She could learn. And check things off the invisible cultural bucket list she kept adding to in her head.

"You don't know how lucky you are," Dev said.

"How do you mean?"

"I mean that, culturally, you get to pick and choose what you want to be a part of. No one is demanding anything from you or telling you what you want."

If he only knew. Naomi pretended to examine her screen as she chewed her lip. Without realizing it, he was offering her the perfect segue to confess her desire to connect with any semblance of culture. To discover the Bengali side of herself, if such a thing even existed. But how did one express a need to feel grounded to a person who felt suffocated six feet under?

Besides, at this point, the truth was embarrassing. Admitting she was jealous of his large, meddling family and the adherence to a culture that was, yes, overbearing, but also rich, and meaningful, and beautiful. Her envy was as silly as a tall, proud fir tree longing to be cut down and dragged into someone's home to be trimmed, decorated, and live out its days on display for one month, maybe two max.

But at least that tree would be surrounded by family and know its purpose.

"The best part is you're in complete control of your fate," Dev added, sitting down on her couch and leaning back with his hands folded behind his head. "For example, you might decide to master Garba and go on to become the best dancer out there. But whether you attend every Garba or never attend again, no one will care. No one expects anything from you. That must feel so good."

Naomi's heart plummeted. She knew that Dev was trying to compliment her situation and that he had no idea how he sounded, but she heard exactly what he *wasn't* saying. She could hone her skills, try her best, and attend events, but, in the end, no one would care. There were no expectations for someone who would never truly belong, who would always be on the outside, face pressed against some grimy window.

She would never be enough.

"Are you spending the night here?" As soon as the words fell from her lips, Naomi winced. She sounded impatient and accusatory.

Dev sat up straight, his forehead wrinkling. "Is that okay? I don't mean to presume. I don't have to if you don't want me to. Like, I want to but not if you don't want me to. I . . ."

As Dev babbled—his eyes wide and hands flat against his thighs, fingers splayed—Naomi softened at the sight of him clearly panicking with no clue how to recover. It was endearing and, even though he had said all the right words to pluck at the wrong strings, she wanted to rescue him. To ease his discomfort. She rose from the table and sat beside him.

"I'd like for you to stay," she said, placing her hand on his leg, which had begun to bounce.

He relaxed back on the couch immediately and offered her a relieved smile complete with the shy wink of his dimples. At least, Naomi decided as she brushed a chaste kiss on his right dimple while trying not to give in to the bitterness that had soured the moment earlier, if she couldn't win with the South Asian community, at least she could win at this.

Every time Naomi spent the night with Dev in his apartment, she could count on his hand seeking hers at various points of the night while they slept. Maybe it was a silly habit of his—born out of growing up with a security blanket or something—but she liked to pretend he craved her touch. Thrived on her closeness, like she did his.

As she lay in the quiet of her bedroom, away from traditions and mothers and fumbling half-truths that made her want to hide away in there forever, Dev's hand tucked against hers made her heart launch itself off a gymnastics vault, landing be damned. Too bad, at this rate, she was going to splatter all over the mat.

Why him? Naomi asked herself as she studied Dev. He was sprawled on his back and taking up more than his fair share of the bed. And snoring softly. Even in peaceful sleep, he looked a little grim. The fact that she had fallen for an accountant—and a cantankerous one at that—was baffling on its own. But his situation also represented everything about the community her mother had warned her against, had protected her from with an iron will that bordered on zealous.

And yet the sight of her hand loosely tangled with his on her colorful bedspread filled her limbs with a sense of contentment, satisfying and plush. Naomi had worked with various businesses in the past. No matter how much of herself she poured into her work, or how deeply connected she felt to previous clients, it had always been easy to walk away. Although she nurtured those businesses like they were her own, releasing them back to their rightful owners had never been a problem.

But this wonderful, heavy feeling sinking her into the mattress and making Naomi wish an hour were endless and a second could last a lifetime? This would be hard to walk away from when her work on the bazaar was complete. And it was all because of this man. This awkward, brooding, *aggravating* man.

But time was not on Naomi's side. Very carefully, she pulled her hand away and reached for her phone to find a message from Nick.

Nick: You gonna be late coming in today?

He'd punctuated the message with a gif of two people dressed as potatoes gyrating on a dance floor.

Naomi rolled her eyes. She hadn't so much *told* Nick of her new relationship—or whatever this was—with Dev so much as he'd just figured it out, as best friends often do.

She almost texted back a quick *no*, but the heat of Dev's body beckoned her to sink more deeply into her mattress, to forget about the pressing demands of the rebrand for a little while and just bask in this lovely little glow that surrounded them in the quiet of a cozy morning. It had been a long while since she'd had someone spend the night in her apartment, and with Dev snoring at her side, she felt a strange sense of security she hadn't felt with someone before. Suddenly, she wasn't bothered by her faded comforter or the deep scratches on her secondhand dresser.

Her response to Nick was simple and devoid of any guilt for putting off the bazaar: I'll see you at noon.

She was staring at Nick's answering text bubble when it registered that the snoring had stopped and Dev was lying on his side, head resting on the crook of his elbow, watching her.

"Well, that's not creepy at all," she said, Nick's impending response forgotten.

Dev's drowsy voice was the the rasp of dry leaves on a forest floor in late autumn. "How can you work first thing in the morning?"

"Says the guy who chooses to set his alarm for five thirty a.m. so he can work out at the gym without the 'beefcakes' watching his every move." Naomi waved her phone at him. "And while I wasn't working, that does remind me: We need to make some decisions about displaying the menu. Is your mom into chalkboard art? Or maybe she'd prefer—"

With a groan, Dev rolled onto his back. "Does it even matter at this point?"

Naomi's fingers clenched, but she barely noticed the crunch of her phone grinding against the chipped phone case. "What do you mean?"

"My older brother has gotten it into his thick skull that he's going to be running the place when the rebrand is done, and he has a different vision for the café. An asinine vision, but he's pretty sold on it."

White noise trampled Naomi's eardrums, and she paused a moment before responding. "What?"

"He wants a grab-and-go type of café. Of course, he has no taste, so . . ." Dev trailed off when the crunching sound emanated from Naomi's palm again. He looked at her warily. "What's wrong?"

"You're kidding, right? This is, like, your version of a practical joke?"

"Accountants don't joke," Dev said with a sardonic grin. "It overwhelms our circuit boards."

"Dev, seriously. Is Neel taking over?"

"Apparently."

"Since when?"

"He mentioned it to me a few months ago, but I didn't take it to heart because he's a douchebag. But then a few weeks ago, he stopped by the bazaar and . . ." Dev glanced at Naomi's face and snapped his mouth shut.

"Your *brother* is going to take over the business. Your *brother* doesn't like how it looks right now." Naomi paused. If anyone was short-circuiting right now, it was her. "And you're just telling me this *now*?"

"I . . ." Dev shook his head. "It's not a big deal, Naomi. The bazaar will stay in my family. And the changes he wants to make are minute, easy fixes."

Naomi pressed her hand to her chest, trying to decipher if the rapid rise and fall of her chest was the beginning of a panic attack or her soul trying to wrestle its way out so it could strangle one very clueless accountant. "I've been busting my ass to impress *Gia*, Dev. And now I'm finding out, with less than two weeks left, she's not even my client anymore? Are you fucking kidding me right now?"

"You still have the job, Naomi. Why is this freaking you out?"

"I have so much riding on this. The chairs are supposed to come this week. The concept for the redesign is all about community and closeness. I . . . The . . . The—"

"Hey." Dev reached for her, his hand firm and solid on her

knee. But when he extended his other arm to pull her close, she jumped out of the bed and stared at him incredulously.

"This is a big problem!"

Dev's eyes widened. "You're yelling at me."

"Yelling is better than killing, Dev!" Although her voice sounded too loud in her ears, Naomi was beyond caring. Beyond checking herself for someone else's comfort.

"This isn't your problem, Naomi. You did what you set out to do."

"If the client isn't satisfied with the end result, I might not get paid." Naomi's voice turned ragged. "I need the money, I have bills to pay. I—" Naomi caught herself before she blurted out something pathetic, like she was one more overdue notice away from having her power cut.

"I'll make sure you get paid."

"Great. The guy I'm sleeping with will make sure his family pays me even though I didn't fulfill my end of the contract. Just *perfect*." As soon as the bitingly sarcastic words slipped from her mouth, Naomi braced her hands on the edge of the mattress and focused her gaze on the floor while forcing herself to take deep, calming breaths.

Her lungs pushed back every attempt.

Naomi raised her head to look at Dev just in time to catch the familiar look of panic eclipsing his face. It was clear that he hadn't thought through the implications of Neel taking over the family business, and the realization somewhat mitigated the rising tide of anxiety and anger in Naomi's chest. An uncomfortable lump formed in her throat when she realized that the grumpy, cynical man sitting in her bed, staring at her in fear and completely unaware that he was sporting some serious bedhead, had become a puzzling soft spot for her.

She needed to sort the facts. "Okay, let me see if I understand the situation," Naomi said, lowering her voice and easing herself onto the edge of the bed. "Your brother wants to take over the bazaar."

Dev nodded, his eyes still scared. She couldn't blame him: she sounded eerily calm, her voice the exact cadence of the ominous music right before an innocent victim was slashed across the throat in a horror movie.

"If that's the case, why have you been helping redesign it according to what your mother would like?"

"I figured it was just Neel running his mouth, as usual. It didn't seem like a done deal."

"But your mom is going to sell him the café? She's made arrangements to sign over the lease? She's agreed to"—Naomi choked out the words—"the changes Neel wants despite what we've done?" To what she had painstakingly pieced together, forgone sleep for, and fucking sacrificed her mental wellness to accomplish?

"Not officially." Dev hesitated before adding, "I'm not even sure she would necessarily agree with Neel's vision. I wouldn't be surprised if he's trying to bully her into this."

"I don't understand. If Gia isn't on board, how do you know it's even happening?"

"Because it's what Neel wants."

"So?"

"So . . ." Dev's forehead wrinkled. "So my mom will give it to him."

They were having one of those moments that always made Naomi feel like she was talking to Dev from behind a two-way mirror. He was on the reflective side, oblivious that his behaviors—like accepting Gia's decree with a grumble and a helpless shrug or tossing the extra, unused napkins in the fast-food bag away instead of saving them for later—were being watched on the other side by a silent, baffled Naomi.

But when it came to her career, silence did not suit her. Naomi straightened. "You need to talk to her."

"To whom?"

"Your mother!"

"What? Why?"

"Because this is the kind of decision that needs to be crystal clear to everyone, Dev. We're not undoing everything we've done for someone's passing interest in running the show."

Naomi might have risked her self-worth for the bazaar, but she would put up one hell of a fight before she risked her career. Except, at this point, it wasn't really *her* fight, was it? It belonged to the man staring back at her as if her face were disintegrating before his eyes.

"Are you telling me that after almost three months of spending every waking hour on the bazaar, you don't care if someone waltzes in and changes everything?" Naomi asked.

Dev shrugged. "Story of my life."

Not this time, buddy. "You have no interest in the café's success?" she pressed.

Although he had opened his mouth to respond, something stopped Dev and he paused. When he finally answered, his voice was slow and careful. "Don't get me wrong, I'm proud of the work we've put in, but it's not like *I'm* going to work there when it's done."

"What about Gia?"

"What about her?"

"It's okay with you that your bullheaded older brother is going to take her bazaar away from her? You said he probably bullied her into it and that doesn't bother you?"

Like clouds drifting across the sun, Naomi watched triumphantly as Dev's complacency took a back seat to grim reluctance. Although she didn't understand the patriarchal garbage Dev seemed to operate within when it came to standing up to his brother, she knew, despite his grumblings, that he cared for his mother. Took care of her. And as far as Naomi was concerned, Dev was a co-captain in the rebrand, and while he might not be as invested in its future as she was, he at least owed it to Gia to go to bat for her if she couldn't do it herself.

"What would I even say to her?" Dev asked.

"What do you mean? Just talk to her."

Dev's hands fisted and released a few times, crumpling and uncrumpling her comforter in the process. "I don't know if you've noticed, but my mother and I don't really talk. She's not much of a listener."

A part of Naomi wanted to reach for Dev's flexing hand, but a sliver of irritation held her frozen on the spot, refusing to show even an ounce of empathy. The entire time she'd known him, she'd never seen him confront anyone in his family, not for anything important. The Mukherjees seemed to dance around conflict; they were more inclined to follow some ancient drumbeat created by their ancestors before them.

But Naomi's livelihood was on the line now, and she didn't care if she upset their rhythm. "This is going to sound like a bad cliché," Naomi said, "but the only thing you can do is speak from the heart. You know better than anyone what Gia's store means to her. If there's anyone she'll listen to, it's you, Dev. There's a reason she relies on you the most among your brothers."

Dev's nod was resigned but determined. "You're right. I need to say something."

Naomi nodded back. *Good.* She'd already done her fair share of jumping through hoops with the Mukherjees—it had been a never-ending series of tricks since meeting Dev's family.

Sure, not all her efforts were a success. As Dev had pointed out last night, in the end, her work would be forgotten about. But at least she'd tried, despite everything working against her.

It was his turn now.

chapter
23

"U h . . . Mom?"

Gia didn't look up from the sink, where she scrubbed at a frying pan like she was trying to erase the sins of the past. "Mmm?"

"Can we talk?"

"Mm-hmm, mm-hmm," Gia said, more to the pan in her hands than her son. "Talk."

Even though she was barely paying attention to him, Dev's leg began to bounce under the table. It had been jiggling all evening—from the moment he had stepped into his childhood home for Sunday night family dinner, and throughout a sumptuous meal of warm parathas, homemade daal, and chicken curry, and while waiting for his brother to pack his yawning daughters into the car.

Had Dev known that family confrontation would have this effect on his nervous system, he would have stretched beforehand because at this rate, he was overdue for a calf cramp.

Everyone had left, save for Aashi, and it was that magical time after a good meal with a few hours to spare before his mother hunkered down on the couch, ready to zone out while catching up on her favorite Tollywood soap operas.

"Mom," Dev said, wincing when, in an effort to raise his voice authoritatively, it sounded tinny and whiny instead. "I need to talk to you about something."

From where she sat across from him Saran-wrapping leftover fruit salad, Aashi stood up, her chair squeaking in protest. "Let me take over, Didi. This sounds important." The sisters traded ominous looks as they switched places.

Well, at least Dev had their undivided attention now.

"All right, Dev," Gia said as she settled into Aashi's vacated seat. "*Bolo.* Tell me what this is about." The look on Gia's face gave Dev pause. She was flushed, the corners of her lips twitching as if she was fighting a smile. Inwardly, Dev winced. If she thought he was about to announce he'd found his future wife, she was going to be very disappointed.

That was who he was, Disappointing Dev, letting people down since birth. After all, hadn't Gia lamented many times, out loud, to him, her family, and her friends, that she had prayed for a daughter after her firstborn?

"Let's hear it, son."

"I want to talk to you about the bazaar."

"Oh, this makes me so happy—" Gia broke off and blinked a few times before settling on the confused squint she reserved for teenage cashiers at the grocery store mumble-asking if she needed help carrying her groceries to the car. "The bazaar? You want to talk about . . . *the bazaar?*"

Dev couldn't resist, his leg momentarily stilling. "Well, of course. What else would there be to discuss?"

Gia's face pinched like an overdehydrated raisin. "Nothing. What about the bazaar?"

"Is it true that you're letting Neel take over?"

From the kitchen, the sloshing of soap and sponges halted as Aashi waited to hear Gia's answer.

"Why do you ask?"

"He told me."

Gia waved a dismissive hand in the air and Dev noticed, for the first time, that her wedding bangles—a traditional gift from one's parents and in-laws to signify her status as a married woman—were gone. "Oh, you know Neel. He likes to have his hand in everything. He's interested in the bazaar now, but he'll move on."

Dev thought back to the greedy look in his brother's eye and the plans he had concocted for his wife. Once the shininess wore off, Neel might move on, but Priya would be left behind to carry the burden. And Priya was nothing if not dutiful—especially when it came to family burdens like obnoxious, crappy husbands.

"I don't think so, Mom," he said. "I think Neel is pretty set on this. He's stuck on the idea."

Taken aback, his mother frowned. From a short distance away, Aashi had dropped all pretense of pretending to mind her own business. She was leaning against the counter, rubber-gloved hands clasped in front of her, as she watched them.

"Well . . ." Gia deflated like a balloon. "I mean, it's not like I have a head for business."

Dev stiffened. That sounded like something Neel would say. Or their father.

"If this is what my eldest son wants, who am I to deny him?" Gia added.

"But he's an idiot who only cares about himself!"

Gia raised a cautionary eyebrow. "Do not speak of your brother like that. He is doing what's best for the family."

It was his cue to back down, and under normal circumstances

he usually would have. Well aware of the extent of conflict resolu-
tion in the Mukherjee house, Aashi turned back to the dishes,
sponge in hand. But Dev could not dismiss Naomi's insistent face
from his mind, her eyes wide and charged with something he
didn't quite understand but had obviously meant the world to her.

He didn't want to let her down.

"I know Neel wants to do what's best for the bazaar," Dev said.
"But I think you're underestimating yourself. *You're* the one who
built a community there." For a moment, Dev stumbled when he
realized he was repeating something Naomi had said when she
had pitched her grand idea for the rebrand. He was even more
startled to realize how clearly the words rang when said out loud,
even from his less charming voice.

They rang with certainty. In the past, when arguing against his
parents' old-world logic, he had always found himself stumbling at
the crossroads between what he thought he wanted versus what
they deemed was best for him and his family. But right now, he
knew he was speaking a truth that, to his surprise, mattered to him.
This conversation *mattered* to him. He didn't want to be brushed
aside, as he had been so many times before when speaking his mind.

He wanted to be heard.

Dev reached deeper. "No one but you can rebuild that same
sense of community, Mom. Certainly not Neel. And you deserve
something for yourself, something that's all yours that you can be
proud of."

Gia stared at him, speechless. The room was silent, Aashi having abandoned her scrubbing again. Intimidated, Dev began to
ramble.

"No one cooks like you, Mom," he said. "Not that you have to
cook for the café, but you can choose what you—"

He stopped when his mother lifted her hand. When she finally spoke, her gaze was directed over his shoulder, into a future, or maybe the past, that was further away than Dev could reach. "You're not wrong. It is *my* store. And I have a legacy, too," she said slowly. "I'm . . . I'm going to think about this. I appreciate you trying to look out for me, though."

It wasn't flat-out agreement; hell, she had even figured out a way to admit he was right without actually admitting it—not that Dev expected to hear *those* words cross his mother's lips in this lifetime. But he felt strangely hopeful. All his life, he'd feared confrontation with his formidable parents, who, he had always assumed, would stick to a set of unwritten rules he didn't understand come hell or high water. But in the moment, he felt like he was talking to someone different. Like they'd made a major breakthrough in their relationship.

"Since you're in the mood to think about the unexpected," he ventured, "maybe we could talk about this whole matchmaking thing."

Gia sat up straight, a speculative gleam in her eye. Aashi dropped her sponge and hurried to join them at the table. "Yes?"

"I've met a lot of the potential matches now, and . . ."

"Go on."

"And I'm starting to wonder what would happen if I ended up with someone who wasn't on your list."

Lips parted, Gia whipped her head to look at Aashi, then back to Dev, to Aashi, and finally back to her son.

That's one calf cramp for me and whiplash for Mom, Dev thought as his leg began to bounce again.

"Did you have someone in mind, Dev?" Aashi asked.

They stared at him—their eyes intense and unblinking—and, under their scrutiny, Dev's courage waned and he blurted out the first thing that came to mind. "No, I'm talking hypothetically.

Would it be so bad if I picked someone according to my own list of wants?" When he realized what he had said, a pinch of uncertainty zipped across his chest. Had he meant to say that? It was the first time he had ever even hinted to his family that marriage was a desirable outcome for himself, that he was invested in a future with someone else.

It should have been liberating or triumphant, maybe. But as Gia shook her head, impatience bracketing her mouth, Dev averted his eyes to the tabletop. His other leg began a restless bounce in unison with the first. Great. He was sweating from the top up, performing a fucking Riverdance from the waist down.

"Dev, we've talked about this," Gia chided. "How can you not understand that I am thinking of your future from a place of experience? That I might have a better idea of what marriage means and what a successful union requires?"

Aashi cleared her throat. "Didi, we can't know that we would automatically disapprove of the kind of girl Dev might like."

Dev shot his mashi a grateful look, but Gia pursed her lips and shook her head again. "Dev is unrealistic. I could send a thousand girls his way, and he wouldn't like any of them. He doesn't know what he wants. He just knows that I'm wrong."

All the hope that had brewed in his chest earlier dissipated like wisps of smoke in the rain. Dev's temper flared in its wake. He could never be right, not in this family.

"I'm not arguing for the sake of arguing, Mom. I'm trying to tell you what I want."

"Marriage isn't just about *you*, Dev. That's not our way," Gia replied. "It's about our family, too."

"Can you at least understand why, from the way you're talking, the idea of an arranged marriage would be unappealing to someone like me?"

"'Someone like you,'" Gia mimicked, scorn bracketing her mouth. "I don't even know you anymore. First, disrespecting your elder brother, now this. You think you're *so* Canadian now, huh? You know, in so many ways, you're just like your father."

The words were like a punch to his gut, a hard jab that landed somewhere between his pancreas and large intestine. He'd received criticism from his mother his entire life, but this was different. This was brass knuckles.

Like your father.

Aashi eyed him with concern, but Gia continued, oblivious. "Your father always thought *he* knew everything, always wanted to do things *his* way. He never wanted my opinion, never thought I might have something important to contribute. He was so cold."

Dev lowered his gaze and allowed Gia's disapproval to wash over him, as it had so many times in the past. Except this time, it wasn't a quick rinse that he could pat dry later with an eye roll. This was soaking in like a bone-deep chill.

His entire life, he'd been the odd one out in his family. Not a day went by where Dev wasn't aware that he was awkward, aloof, difficult to deal with, and about a thousand other things that made his brothers smirk and his parents shake their heads. Forget trying to be considerate, generous, and kind. Forget warmth. In the end, he couldn't escape the one thing he'd promised himself he would never be.

Cold, like his father.

chapter
24

"Are you ..." Naomi flattened herself against the cool concrete wall of the community center as two little girls in red South Asian dresses ran past, shrieking with laughter and oblivious to the November chill. "Are you sure I'm not underdressed?"

Staring like a zombie at the people filing into the hall for Diwali, Dev barely spared her a glance. "You're fine."

Glancing down at her plain white blouse and black dress pants, Naomi bit her bottom lip. "But I—"

"Seriously, it's fine."

Naomi glanced at Dev's icy frown and tried for levity. "Maybe my *Lovesexy* T-shirt would've been more appropriate."

No reaction.

With a sigh, Naomi turned back to face the partygoers as well. Dev had been in a mood lately, somewhere between distracted and impatient—well, more impatient than usual. He still showed up to help her with the bazaar every day, dependable and involved, but the qualities that were so irrevocably Dev were shifting in a way that left Naomi uneasy. Instead of hilariously cynical, he was aloof. He was more prone to silence, too, where before she would have welcomed his sarcasm. He was at her side, but the important parts were fading, like the tearstained ink on a Dear John letter, folded and unfolded too many times.

When he'd informed her he was expected to attend a Diwali celebration, it had crossed Naomi's mind to decline. Toying the line between fake dating and real-time bed partners was starting to mess with her mind, and some distance from Dev, his community, and the lies wrapped around them was not unwelcome. Also, besides the lehenga she had promised herself she would dry-clean as soon she could afford the luxury, she had nothing suitable to wear.

But when he'd looked at her with those steady, chocolate-brown eyes, the smudged shadows under his eyes hinting at something more than fatigue, something from a place inside him that he kept under lock and scowl, Naomi hadn't been able to say no. And a small part of her was dying to see what Diwali was all about, too.

Even if, in a sea of rainbow fashion and ornate tinkling jewelry, she would look like a drab moth.

"Hey," Dev said, his voice as gentle as the surreptitious brush of his pinky against hers. "We'll make this brief. If yet another potential bride introduces herself, I'll fake stomach pains and run away. You won't have to do a thing."

It wasn't so much the consolation but the glimmer of the old Dev—*her* Dev—that made Naomi break out into a goofy grin. "Stomach virus?"

"With the potential for projectile vomiting. I'll store a chewed-up laddoo in the pocket of my cheek just in case."

Just like that, Naomi forgot both the strain of the past few days and the fact that she was horribly underdressed. She nudged his biceps with her shoulder, lingering an extra moment against the firm line of muscle. "Okay, let's go," she said, entering the hall.

The event was being held in the same community center as Garba, but if the previous event had seemed like a magical combination of music and joy, then Diwali was . . . It was . . . There were no words.

There was only light.

LED candles lined the room, offset by fresh flower garlands hanging from the walls, intertwined with soft white Christmas lights. In the center of the room were various designs—some floral, some not—beautifully painted on the floor. Among the patterns were tea lights that cast a soft soothing glow over the incredible splash of colors.

"Oh my God." Naomi stopped short of the entrance, aware that she looked like a slack-jawed tourist. "What are those?"

"What?" Dev asked. He followed her line of sight to the center of the room, where candles glowed. "Those are a damned fire hazard." He punctuated that decree with a disapproving shake of his head.

"You're such an old man," Naomi teased. The urge to kiss away his frown was overwhelming. "Next you'll say it's too loud in here."

Dev paused, his mouth tight. Then he broke into a self-conscious grin. "It *is* too loud in here."

Naomi rolled her eyes. "I wasn't asking about the candles. I meant the paintings on the floor. What are they?"

"Oh, that's rangoli. They're meant to welcome Laxmi, goddess of prosperity and good fortune." Dev cut her a questioning glance. "Diwali is pretty popular among South Asians . . . Your family doesn't celebrate?"

Naomi cleared her throat. "Not like this." Or ever, for that matter.

"We can take a closer look if you—"

"Hi, Dev!"

Naomi smirked at Dev before turning to face what had to be a potential wife sent by the matchmaker. Pity they hadn't had time to hit up the laddoo table so Dev could arm himself. But her cockiness dissipated when she found herself face-to-face with Mandy, Dev's childhood friend who she'd met at Garba. There was something different about her today, though—a firmness to her chin, a determined glint in her colored contacts.

"Hey, Mandy," Dev said, oblivious that the woman in front of him was on the hunt. "You're still in town?"

Mandy nodded and took a small step forward. "My mother insisted I fly back for Diwali. I was hoping to run into you tonight."

"You were?" Dev cocked his head to the side.

Naomi frowned. *Seriously, Dev? Get a clue.*

Ignoring Naomi, Mandy stepped even closer, the A-line of her hot pink lehenga skirt brushing the tip of Naomi's right shoe.

"Veera Auntie insisted I hang around a bit longer," Mandy confirmed. She placed her hands on her hips and raised an eyebrow. "Are you not happy to see me?"

If Mandy was trying for playful, someone needed to inform her she sounded downright predatory. Realization finally dawned over Dev's face.

About time, Naomi thought.

"Veera Auntie?" He wheezed.

"Veera Auntie," Mandy said with a meaningful smile.

Naomi straightened her shoulders, ready to insert her way into the bourgeoning tête-à-tête when Dev's next words startled her.

"Veera Auntie!" he exclaimed, stepping away from them both.

A small lady materialized at Mandy's side. Her baby blue sari was a stark contrast to the shrewdness in her brown eyes, further magnified by perfectly round, wire-framed glasses. She laid a wrinkled hand on Mandy's arm, but there was nothing gentle in the way she assessed Naomi, her eyes roving from head to toe and back up again.

Oh shit. Gia's scorn was laughable compared to Veera's, and Naomi shrank back. "Devdas," Veera said smoothly. "I believe you already know Mandy?"

"Y-yes."

"When Mandy informed me you two wouldn't be a good match, I was surprised given what your mother told me about your childhood friendship."

Dev paled, but he was out of Naomi's reach now. They hadn't planned for this, and surely Dev wouldn't have insisted Naomi join him tonight if he had known that Veera Auntie would be in attendance. As much as Naomi wished to offer even the smallest sign of support, there was no way a subtle brush of her pinky against his would go unnoticed under the matchmaker's watchful gaze.

"When I mentioned as much to your mother, she gave me marching orders to make sure Mandy had a chance to meet you again." Veera smiled at Mandy, the golden girl, who preened in response.

"My mother?" Dev croaked, and Naomi's body stiffened in alarm. Perhaps Dev would projectile-vomit after all, with or without prechewed ammunition.

"Well, of course," Veera said, gesturing over her shoulder. "She's right over there."

The flood of Diwali lights surrounding them was suddenly too much. What Naomi had once considered a dreamy, romantic glow became a harsh, buzzing spotlight shining directly on their little foursome. And Naomi was the unrehearsed understudy with zero knowledge of the script.

And when Gia sidled up, two friends Naomi vaguely recognized from Aashi's dinner party so many weeks ago in tow,

Naomi's eyes searched the room for a trapdoor she could disappear into.

"Dev, look, it's Mandy!" Gia sang, threading her arm through Mandy's free one. Naomi stared at them: Gia, Mandy, and Veera, an impenetrable offensive line of tradition, expectation, and authenticity.

"Yes, I know," Dev said, his voice tight. "Are you chaperoning the matchmaking now, Mom?"

"Is that the worst idea?" Gia shot back. "You don't seem to be making any progress."

"It's not unheard of for parents to help secure a match," Veera added.

"Dev? Naomi?" a familiar voice asked from behind Naomi. A new person joined the group, stepping neatly between Dev and Naomi. It was Jasminder, the second bachelorette who had walked into the bazaar in what felt like a lifetime ago. But Naomi remembered her well: she had treated the potential of matching with Dev with the severity of a job interview.

If the ghosts of Dev's past and present were making an appearance tonight, then Naomi would welcome the grim reaper's arrival to put an end to this agony.

Exactly as Naomi remembered her, Jasminder was as blunt as ever. With little preamble, she said, "Did I hear that you two secured your match?"

"No, dear." Veera shook her head. "He's still on the market."

Jasminder's brow wrinkled as she jerked her thumb at Naomi. "But he's her honey boo boo."

Dev's breath hitched, and the entire group turned to witness his short coughing fit until one of Gia's friends stepped closer into the fray.

"Ki?" she said in confusion. "Her name is Honey Boo Boo?" she asked, gesturing at Naomi. "What country is *that* from?"

"No—" Dev cut in.

"No." Jasminder's impatience was louder. "Her name is Naomi, and she and Dev are together. *He's* the honey boo boo."

"What is a honey boo boo?" the friend asked, turning to Gia.

"It sounds like one of those code words for drugs," Gia's second friend chimed in, casting a suspicious eye over Jasminder and Naomi. "Dev is not looking for a woman who does the drugs."

"None of my clients do drugs," Veera said, affronted. "I work with *good* girls." She nodded at Naomi. "*She* is not my client."

Embarrassment flooded Naomi's cheeks. She risked a quick glance at Dev, but it was in vain: his face was blank even though horror lurked in his eyes. She'd seen that look many times—every time, in fact, a potential bride had walked into his path, expecting promises for the future.

Dev was shutting down. And under Gia's and Veera's watchful eyes, Naomi could not possibly come to his rescue.

"I think what they're trying to say is Dev and Naomi are dating," Mandy said quietly. She threw Dev a questioning frown. "*Were* dating?"

"Dev is not dating anyone," Gia answered in a hard, clipped tone.

"You told me you were his girlfriend," Jasminder said to Naomi, her mouth curling downward, hurt. "Did you lie to me?"

One of Gia's friends clapped Gia on the shoulder. "It worked! Your son has found a match!"

"My sister is going to India this Christmas," the second friend added as Mandy whispered something in the matchmaker's ear. "She can bring back the wedding suits!" She turned to Naomi.

"You don't have to wear red anymore, you know. My niece wore shocking pink—"

"*Bas!*" Gia held up her hand, silencing them all, including the small crowd of gossip-hungry Diwali attendees who had gathered around, ears pressed forward. "That is quite enough. Naomi is not Dev's girlfriend. Beta, what is going on here?"

All eyes turned to Dev, who looked like an Olympic diver peering over the edge of the high dive while second-guessing his decision to eat sushi out of someone's trunk the night before.

Say something, Naomi silently implored. *Say anything.* But deep down she knew what she wanted him to say.

Tell them who I am. Tell them what I mean to you.

"We're not a couple," Dev said, oblivious to Naomi's silent plea. "We made the whole thing up."

Six sets of professionally threaded eyebrows shot way, way up. Naomi closed her eyes, as if doing so could erase Dev's revelation, erase *her* from this horrifying moment of feeling alone and exposed in front of too many judgmental stares. Her brain screamed at her to run, but her feet were rooted in place with the desperate hope that Dev would stand up for her.

Scratch that. She wanted him to stand *with* her.

"Why?" Gia asked.

"Because . . . I told you . . ." Dev's hands scurried in midair, gesturing at everything and nothing. "I don't want this."

"Not want marriage?" one of Gia's friends hissed to the other. "What's wrong with him?"

"Maybe *he's* the one on the drugs," the second friend replied.

"I'm not on drugs," Dev snapped. "I needed help getting rid of all the potential brides you were sending my way." For the first time, he looked at Naomi. "Naomi agreed to help me out."

"It was my idea," Naomi blurted out. "I asked Dev to assist me with the bazaar's rebrand in exchange for me standing in as his fake girlfriend." At that revelation, her audience's eyebrows practically disappeared into their hairlines, and Naomi's voice faltered. "It seemed like a good idea at the time?"

"A good idea? A good idea!" Gia's voice surged forward, growing louder and more forceful with every word. She glared at Naomi, her stare a thousand times more frigid than her son's could ever be.

"Mom, calm down," Dev said in a hushed voice.

Naomi valiantly tried to hold her ground. "I was trying to help your son."

"My son doesn't need help, especially yours," Gia said with a bitter laugh. "It's laughable, really!"

"It's true, dear," one of her friends said gently. "If Devdas is on the drugs, he is probably beyond your help."

"Jesus, I'm not on drugs!" Dev shot back.

Naomi barely heard them, so absorbed was she in the snide twist of Gia's face. There was no lie or truth anywhere in this world that would pacify Dev's mother now.

"*You* could never be a suitable match for my son," Gia said. Her eyes assessed Naomi's humble dress pants and blouse, so plain and out of place for Diwali, and she shook her head with disgust. "We want a good girl. A proper daughter-in-law. Someone who understands and respects what our people—"

"Don't you dare speak to her that way!" A furious voice said somewhere behind Naomi.

Panic spiked up Naomi's spine, leaving a trail of goose bumps in its wake, as the group turned to the community hall's entrance. Naomi was the last to round on the new, thunderous voice because she already knew who stood behind her. She'd know that warning tone anywhere.

It belonged to her mother.

Dev—and about two dozen other Diwali participants—
stared as a woman dressed in bohemian clothing ran to Naomi and pulled her to her side so the two of them stood somewhat
apart from the others. The muscles in his arm tightened and he
instinctively moved to steady Naomi when she stumbled, her face
tight with discomfort and something he'd never seen on her
before.

Panic.

But when Naomi's eyes met his, his legs betrayed him: they
locked in place, as if the fear in her gaze had poured concrete right
into his veins. An awkward silence stretched among the group before the stranger pressed the palms of her hands together and
bowed her head. "Namashkar," she said, more mocking than civil.
"I'm Naomi's mother, Sue."

Blood coursed through Dev's ears, drowning out the whispers
the announcement inspired around him. The woman standing
beside Naomi was her mother? Although Naomi was much taller,
and her skin several degrees warmer, there were obvious similari-

ties between the two. The curve of their foreheads, the high cheek-bones. The rigid set of their shoulders: Sue's challenging, Naomi's shocked.

Naomi's eyes were much lighter, though, and her neck, even with the tendons stretched tight, more graceful. Again, the desire to surge forward threaded through Dev's brain, but this time, the hard lines around Sue's mouth told him to stay back.

As the murmured conversations of onlookers grew stronger, Sue turned to Gia. "Perhaps we should take this somewhere else," she said in perfect Bengali. Switching to English seamlessly, she added in a much louder voice, "Somewhere we can speak in private." Ignoring the collective sigh of disappointment around them, Sue grabbed Naomi's hand and marched out, leaving Gia and Dev no choice but to follow.

When they were in the less public, but not entirely private, hallway between the main hall and the bathrooms, Gia turned to Sue with wide eyes. "Are you . . . Bengali?" she asked in English.

"Yes, I am," Naomi's mother responded in curt Bengali as if to prove her point. "And you are?"

"I'm Gia Mukherjee."

Understanding drew Sue's face tight, sharpening the already hardened lines in her face. "So you're Gia."

Dev's stomach clenched at the disdain in Sue's voice, but Gia's attention was fixed on Naomi. "But Naomi is not Bengali." Gia cocked her head to the side. "She's West Indian."

"No, she's not," Dev corrected. "She's North Indian."

"Actually, uh . . ." Naomi interjected in a small voice, shooting a fearful glance in Dev's direction before turning to Gia. "I never actually said I was West Indian. You assumed and I didn't want to correct you."

"*Hanh?*" Gia's head reared back. "Why?"

"I . . . I didn't wish to be rude, especially with the contract for the bazaar on the line."

Dev studied the side of Naomi's face, trying to read the uncertain lines bracketing the corner of her eyes. Why would she mislead his mother like that for something as trivial as the bazaar's rebrand? That didn't make any sense.

"What did I tell you?" The ferociousness in Sue's voice hurled Dev's train of thought off its tracks. "These people love to assume and tell you who you are. Who you can *be*."

"Hang on—" Dev began, but his mother cut him off.

"What is that supposed to mean?" Gia asked. She turned to Dev, her frown heavy with disapproval. "What kind of person hides who they are?" From her tone, it was clear it was a question Gia didn't need an answer to.

"She's not like that," Dev said. His voice faltered a little when, out of the corner of his eye, he saw Naomi stiffen, but he cleared his throat and continued, "I know her. I know Naomi."

"You don't know the first thing about her," Sue interjected.

"Mom," Naomi cautioned. "Don't."

Gia crossed her arms over her chest. "Maybe we don't know anything about you, but I know what it looks like—you hid the truth because you're *ashamed*."

"Ashamed of what?" Sue's voice was low and full of censure.

Dev's mother, however, paid no heed. Her accusatory eyes pinned Naomi with barely restrained disgust. "Ashamed of being Bengali."

"That's not it." Dev jumped in, but he couldn't stop himself from glancing at an uncharacteristically silent Naomi again with a raised brow.

When he turned to face his mother again, he could tell that Gia had reached her capacity for patience and understanding. As she had done many times before whenever even a whisper of doubt regarding her culture was uttered—whether it was over the purpose of ancient customs or their relevance in the world they lived in—she shut down.

From the stubborn pinch between his mother's eyebrows and the darkness of her gaze, it was obvious that Naomi had crossed some undefinable line for Gia. A sister who toed the line of old-world and new-world traditions for the sake of convenience? Sure. A cantankerous son who questioned his mother's every decision but ultimately fell in line? Fine.

But a person who *hid* the truth of her culture? Despicable.

When Gia spoke again, there was an awful finality to her tone. "Whatever the case, she deceived us all," she said. "You, me, Aashi . . . Veera Auntie, all those women . . . She's told so many lies."

"We're *both* responsible for the fake-girlfriend lie," Dev protested. His skin itched at where Naomi's gaze bore into the side of his face, but he kept his eyes on his mother. "I was miserable, and Naomi helped me out. It's my fault, too."

"This is exactly why you need my help finding a suitable wife," his mother replied, shaking her head. "Girls like this lead men astray. She isn't proud of her heritage. She is not our kind of people. Who knows what else she's hidden from us?"

Dev turned to Naomi, more than a little mortified at the pleading note strumming his words. "Tell her what you told me—you said you were North Indian when we first met," Dev said. "Naomi, tell her . . ." His pleas petered out when Naomi closed her eyes in defeat.

"I lied." With a deep breath, Naomi's eyes flicked to Dev's, their honey depths asking for something he had no idea how to provide. "My parents are Bengali."

"But you said—"

Naomi shook her head slowly. "I lied to you."

"Sweetheart, trust me, she's Bengali." Sue's voice dripped with the kind of contempt that soaked through Dev's pores, spreading the heat of humiliation over every possible surface. "Not that it's anyone's business," she added for Gia's benefit.

Gia scoffed and began speaking in rapid Bengali, her words razor-edged darts flying into the confines of the narrow, dimly lit hallway.

Dev clenched his hands, barely registering how icy his fingers felt curled into his palm. "Excuse me," he muttered. He didn't bother to wait to see if anyone had heard him before he turned and stalked out of the community center.

When Naomi joined him outside several minutes later, the curved edges of Dev's shock had given way to sharp, metallic anger, just barely coating the stomach-churning embarrassment underneath.

She'd manipulated him. It wasn't the lie about her heritage that chafed but the fact that she'd never bothered to share the truth about herself—even when he'd opened up to her, admitted things to her he'd never dared to say out loud to anyone else before—that stung. It was bad enough that, like everyone else, he'd believed all her lies and had played right into her hand; but worse still, he'd placed his feelings for her above everything else—the traditions, the expectations, his family—because he'd actually believed they could have the kind of relationship he never imagined he'd be privileged enough to find.

He'd trusted her to take care of his heart.

He was such a fool.

At some point during the disastrous evening, the sky had opened up to the same torrential downpour as their night at Garba. It was depressingly similar, Dev thought as he stared out into the crowded parking lot to where his black BMW was parked on the other side. Except this time, there was no teasing, no beckoning heat between them. No laughter punctuating the sweet clink of Naomi's bracelets against his eardrums.

There were only two people staring at each other, the hammering of raindrops a foreboding backdrop to the tension growing, even now, between them. Dev felt like he was looking at a stranger.

"Dev, I'm sorry you had to find out this way." Naomi took a small step forward but halted when Dev shuffled back. Hurt clouded her eyes.

"*That's* what you're sorry about?"

"I—"

"You manipulated me. Why would you . . . you . . ." The words deserted Dev as he thought back to the past three months. There had been countless times—maybe not at the start but after they'd grown closer and admitted feelings for each other—that she could have come clean about herself.

But she'd held back—allowed him to make assumptions about her so she could have a leg up with the bazaar. As realization dawned, Dev could've sworn icy claws had clamped around his heart; this whole thing was about her getting ahead. She'd used him to build her fucking career.

Meanwhile, he'd laid himself bare at her feet *like an absolute fool*. Dev turned to face the parking lot again, not sure if he was more disgusted with himself or with her. One thing was clear: she was no better than everyone else in his life, walking all over him so they could get what *they* wanted, his desires be damned.

"You let me go on and on about all the cultural shit I'm dealing with. You had every opportunity to tell me the truth, but you never said a word." When Dev risked a glance at Naomi and caught her wringing her hands and biting her lower lip, anger roiled dangerously in his gut. How *dare* she act like the injured party here.

"I wasn't trying to manipulate you," Naomi said softly. "I just . . . It's hard for me to talk about my heritage. I'm not like you. I'm *not* Bengali . . . not really."

Dev rolled his eyes. "Your mother is in there talking to my mom in perfect Bangla right now, Naomi."

"Dev, my mother looks like she belongs at a Burning Man festival. You don't know anything about her. Or how I was raised."

Dev shook his head, unconvinced, as bitterness flooded his senses. He'd shown her too many vulnerable moments in the last few weeks, and the memories embarrassed him now. Had she been laughing at him behind his back while playing angel of mercy to his face? Had she told her friends?

He couldn't fall down that rabbit hole right now, not when she was watching him so carefully and seeing every emotion that crossed his face. Taking a deep breath, Dev forced himself to think rationally. "Why did you lie to my mother?"

"I didn't want it to matter."

"What does that even mean?"

"Authenticity means everything to your family, Dev! I've seen the kinds of girls your mom thinks you should marry, and I know what she thinks about me." Naomi lifted her hands to her chest. "I don't have the same upbringing as you—I've never gotten to know my grandparents, or aunts and uncles, or anyone from the same gene pool. I didn't want it rubbed in my face, especially when I'd been hired to rebrand your family's business. If your mother knew I was Bengali, she would have had a certain level of expectations."

Naomi's voice thickened. "Those are expectations I'll never meet, Dev. She would have written me off."

"So you lied for the job." The acknowledgment hurt anew: all he'd ever been to her was a stepping stone in her career.

"I . . . I hid the truth." Naomi's gaze roved his face. "You wouldn't understand."

"Understand what?"

"What it's like to not belong . . ." When Dev snorted in disbelief, her face twisted. "Don't act like you're squeaky clean, Dev. You've lied to your mother plenty, and to the matchmaker, and all the girls who came to meet you."

"But I never lied to *you*, Naomi. There's a big difference." Dev snapped his lips closed before he admitted something truly mortifying, like how, for the first time in his life, he'd felt secure enough to open himself to someone—only to have her stomp all over him.

"You don't know the whole story."

A small part of Dev wanted to back down from the dark feelings simmering inside him—to hear exactly what Naomi had kept from him and why—but he was afraid to give in. Because focusing on his all-consuming anger was a hell of a lot easier; keeping everything inside, safer. Besides, Naomi had yet to apologize for lying, as if skirting around her identity was on the same playing field as thwarting his mother's attempts at pushing him into a marriage he didn't want.

And here she was, acting like he shouldn't be hurt by her deception. What was it about him that invited people to walk all over him? For months he had been acting like a guide, sharing his culture with her and explaining its baffling nuances as if its dictates—and his family's expectations—were something to be embarrassed of. How pathetic he must have looked in her eyes, complaining

about his family while toeing the line between servitude and sacrifice.

She'd acted like the worst kind of tourist, taking everything in
with polite, wide-eyed curiosity to his face and likely pitying him
behind his back. *Poor, weak-willed, gullible Dev. He's the Mukherjee
family loser.*

"And lying to me? What's your reasoning for that, Naomi?
Was this the plan all along? To manipulate me into helping you get
the job done? Is that all this was?"

Naomi's eyes widened. "*No*, of course not."

"Do you really expect me to believe that now?"

Ducking her head, Naomi dropped her eyes to the cracked
concrete. She looked so helpless that his heart squeezed, an ache
that was both sympathetic and a reminder that she had played the
shit out of him.

But there was no way he would give in to that sympathy, not
when Naomi had led him to believe that he could have more. That
a relationship built on friendship and warmth was possible for
someone like him, despite everything he knew about family and
the iron chains anchoring him to that inescapable fate.

She had done exactly what his mother had done so many times
before: manipulated him for her own means.

Naomi was watching him, her eyes roving over his face like she
was sorting through fragmented pieces of a puzzle. "What are you
thinking?"

Did it even matter? "I don't know who you are. I don't even want
to know why you chose to lie to me—" Dev cut himself off. *Careful*, he reminded himself. *Don't give any more of yourself away.* Dev
shook his head to clear his thoughts. He needed to salvage at least
some of his pride. "I've had enough."

"What are you saying? You don't want to see me anymore?"

Naomi's voice was flat. Lifeless. She sounded so unlike herself that in any other situation, Dev might have paused and chosen his words cautiously, but he was so damn tired of treading carefully around everyone in his life. If it wasn't his mother, it was his brother, and now it was Naomi, too.

If love meant jumping through hoops until the soles of his feet were bloodied and raw, he wanted nothing to do with it. "I'm saying that I just realized I've been fucking a stranger for over a month. So yeah, I'm done."

He barely caught Naomi's flinch as he stepped off the community center sidewalk and stalked into the parking lot toward his vehicle. He was halfway there when he felt her hand on his wrist jerking him to a stop.

The fire in Naomi's eyes was a clear indication that she wasn't going to back down. "You know who I am. You know the parts that *matter*. I'm sorry that you feel lied to, but I don't owe you shit. I don't need to *prove* who or what I am to anyone, and if this matters so much to you, to the point that you're calling me a stranger? Then maybe you're not the right person for me. Maybe you're exactly what my mother tried to protect me from."

"Hang on, *you're* mad at *me* now?"

"I admitted that I lied, but you'll never understand why. I bet you don't even *want* to understand." Naomi shook her head, rain flinging off her curls in every direction. "How are you any different than the rest of them? The people you constantly bemoan because they refuse to open their minds to anything outside of their narrow worldviews? Face it, Dev, you're just like them."

"I'm not like them." The words sounded uncertain in his own ears, and, despite himself, he couldn't resist a quick glance over Naomi's shoulder to see if anyone had trickled out of the community center to witness their argument. He owed the skies a note of gratitude, the heavy rainfall granting Naomi the privacy to stomp on his heart.

"Really? Because I didn't hear you telling any of them about our *real* relationship." Naomi laughed sarcastically. "Oh, wait, silly me. Apparently we're just *fucking*."

A fleeting sense of chagrin fluttered in Dev's chest. She wasn't wrong, but he had been so bowled over by the turn of events that in front of Veera, his mom, and her friends, the right words hadn't come. They never came when he needed them.

"I wasn't ready to reveal my personal life," he said stiffly. "Not to a group of people who would never understand." He winced when he realized he'd parroted almost exactly the words Naomi had used only a moment ago.

Naomi barked a sarcastic laugh, and Dev's shoulders hunched forward in response. "At least I define my own life, Dev," she said, "but I don't want to be with someone who lets other people's expectations dictate his life, especially if I'm always going to come up short. I refuse to live like that. I'm done with that crap. I deserve better."

Dev gritted his teeth. "They may not be perfect, but they're my family and we stick together. I'm not going to throw that away for . . ." He trailed off, but from the clouding of Naomi's eyes, she had heard him loud and clear: *she* wasn't worth risking his relationship with his family.

"If you can't respect that, then you're right—I'm not the one for you," he finished.

Hurt flitted across Naomi's face, followed by something so raw and vulnerable that the urge to rescind immediately flickered like a tentative flame in the blackest of storms. He ignored the urge, resorting instead to dwelling in the familiarity of that cold, dark place of his that kept women like Naomi at arm's length. That kept everyone at arm's length.

"So we're done?" she asked quietly.

Had Dev missed the words thanks to the deluge of raindrops around them, her face would've said it all. Naomi looked broken.

I don't know. No. Although his heart squeezed in quiet warning, Downer Dev wouldn't give in.

Dev turned on his heel and, after trying to swallow the lump in his throat, threw his parting shot over his shoulder. "We're done."

chapter
26

S o many choices," Sue mused. "Which one to pick."

Naomi shifted at her mom's side, the grocery store basket weighing more heavily with each deliberation Sue insisted was required for throwing together her "famous" spaghetti and tofurkey meatballs.

With jarred sauce, of course.

"Are we Bolognese babes tonight or hot marinara mamas?" Sue giggled and shook the jars of pasta sauce at Naomi. It was a game they had played when Naomi was younger, choosing their grocery items according to their moods or a weird theme Sue had invented. That was her mother in a nutshell, seeking adventure and playfulness in whatever she could find, including the grocery store.

But Naomi was sick of game playing. They'd been at Fine Foods for over thirty-five minutes and that was a half hour she would rather spend on her bed, under the soothing caress of all the blankets she owned, unashamedly pressing her nose into wrinkled pillowcases where traces of pine and mint still lingered.

God, she was pathetic.

The grocery store—and Sue's endless chatter—was probably a safer option. Because with mint and pine came the sequence of nightmarish events from the Diwali celebration the previous day. No matter what angle she took or scenario she played out in her head, the single damning fact remained that she had stood by, hoping Dev would rescue her from the South Asian community's judgment. From Gia's judgment.

She, the girl who solved her own problems her own way, had let them cut her open. She had just *stood* there, watching her skin split and the truths she had carefully hidden away bleed out for everyone to see. And ridicule.

Dev hadn't said a damn thing. But, even worse, neither had Naomi.

Pathetic.

Naomi eyed the perfect rows of jarred sauces. "I'll go get the spaghetti," she muttered, shuffling toward the next aisle, basket banging against her hip. But when Naomi saw who was also in the pasta aisle, she debated turning back around. She'd shed enough blood already.

"Naomi." Cynthia greeted her, her voice flat. "I didn't know you shopped here."

She usually didn't. Fine Foods was one of the more expensive grocery chains in Kelowna, a place that didn't offer a more affordable, generic option next to every brand-name item. But given Sue's penchant for long-winded decision processes, Naomi had pulled into the first grocery store she'd seen.

Too bad the fear of not being able to afford food for the next few months was ruining what could have been an extravagant shopping experience. Even if the rebranded bazaar lured in Indian royalty who paid in gold bricks, there was no way it would transcend Gia's disapproval of everything Naomi represented. Everything she'd ruined. Her reputation was toast.

Naomi glanced into Cynthia's half-full shopping cart. She held back an eye roll at the plethora of "Smart Choice" labels, organic stickers, and zero trans-fat guarantees Cynthia was stocking up on, and reminded herself that her last interaction with the barracuda had been civil. Friendly, even.

"Just picking up a few items for dinner," Naomi said, forcing a cheerful smile.

"I'm surprised you even have time for dinner. Isn't the deadline for Gia's store right around the corner?"

Naomi's eyebrows shot up. She had assumed the ridiculous timeline had been for her only, a tactic to discourage her from competing for the job. Under normal circumstances, it would have been a pleasant discovery to know that Gia, despite rooting for Cynthia, had treated them equally in that regard.

But she wasn't an equal, was she?

"I'm not worried. Things are going according to schedule."

A small, private smirk twisted Cynthia's lips as she considered the selection of noodles in front of them. "Oh, that's right. Why would you worry, anyway?"

Naomi's hand paused midreach from the cheapest package of spaghetti on the shelf. "What do you mean?"

"Oh, nothing."

"Cynthia, what is it?"

When she turned to face Naomi, the coy little smile was gone. Her lips pulled into a hard, grim line and she assessed Naomi like she was a rotting, bruised tomato at the bottom of the produce bin. "Well, I know I would worry a lot less about my clients' wishes if I were sleeping with one of them."

Everything, from the piped-in grocery store music, to the shuffle of tired parents grabbing last-minute items with newborns strapped to their chest, to the squeak of rusted grocery carts turning corners, faded away as a distinct ringing sound blared in Naomi's ears. "Wh-what?"

Although Cynthia lifted a perfectly shaped eyebrow in disgust, her voice was saccharine. "I suppose I don't know if you're actually sleeping your way to your paycheck, but the kiss I witnessed in the parking lot after Garba left little to the imagination."

Sleeping your way to your paycheck. Naomi's dry lips parted but no words came out. It was Diwali all over again.

Cynthia sniffed and turned back to the pasta. "I suppose you've got to do what you've got to do to keep your new little business afloat, but if I were you, I'd be more discreet."

"Have you been gossiping about me behind my back?"

"Honey, I don't need to. Everyone is talking about what happened at Diwali. Even I heard about it, and I didn't even attend. Fake dating? Getting chewed out by Gia?" Cynthia paused to toss a box of high-end, gluten-free pasta into her cart. "The community might not know what I know, but it's still not a good look for you."

Her throat tight and her mind alarmingly empty of a good defense, Naomi stared at the shiny packages of carbs in front of her. Even if her work on the bazaar paid out—and that was a big *if* at this point—there was no hope in salvaging her career in this city if people were talking about her. Fake dating was one thing, but what if word got out about the lies she told to secure the job? What if Gia decided to look into her family and discovered the real truth about Naomi's heritage?

Everything Naomi had tried to build for herself, everything she'd done to keep the damn lights on . . . a waste. Thrown out like trash because she'd crossed too many lines.

When Naomi met Cynthia's eyes, something inside her shriveled at the hint of pity she saw there.

"I was so wrong about you," Cynthia said when Naomi failed to answer. She turned her shopping cart around before adding, "You are not the person I thought you were."

With unfocused eyes, Naomi watched Cynthia walk down the aisle, staring long after she had disappeared from her line of sight. When Sue appeared at the end of the pasta aisle and beckoned her forward, it was like walking toward a mirage.

A grim, scowling mirage with steel in her eyes.

"*This* is why I told you *not* to get mixed up with these people," her mother hissed. "How many times do I have to tell you what they're like before you pay attention?"

"How much did you hear?" Naomi asked, even though her usual defenses were nowhere to be found. She wasn't embarrassed or irritated or even upset.

She was empty.

"I heard enough to know that you can't stay here. You're coming home with me."

"Mom."

"I knew I should have stopped you from moving out here. I knew—"

"Mom!" Naomi had lived through enough verbal beatdowns in the last twenty-four hours to last her a lifetime. She didn't even glance around to see if anyone was listening to the pair of them, raising their voices in front of specialty bags of chips with hipster names—Flaming Hot Flavor-Stache and Dill Pickle Remixed, whatever that meant—at Fine Foods, of all places.

More than ever she wanted to be home, under that thick stack of blankets, with the shades drawn tight.

"Let's just go," Naomi said. And whether it was the flatness in her voice or the heaviness to her eyelids, Sue shook her head twice as she studied her daughter.

But she did as Naomi asked.

Sue stayed quiet the entire ride home, even as tears slipped mercilessly from Naomi's eyes. The silence enveloping the two-door Toyota was anything but comfortable; it was heavy and dense, not worth wading through. Naomi didn't even bother to wipe away the rivulets of humiliation on her cheeks, not even when she sensed her mother's worried glances from the passenger seat. It was no small feat for Sue to hold her tongue so long, but Naomi was immensely grateful even though she knew it wouldn't last.

Yet her mother surprised her when they stepped into Naomi's apartment. She didn't rail nor did she lecture. There was no self-righteousness in Sue's firm grasp as she grabbed her daughter's limp hand and led her to the couch. Once they'd settled them-selves among Naomi's alarming number of throw pillows, she studied Naomi for a long time before speaking.

"I meant what I said, Peanut. I think you should come home. We can forget about all this. Leave it behind us."

Of course. The tried-and-tested Sue Kelly coping mechanism: run away, erase your memory, never talk about it again.

Something in Naomi pulled tight, but it wasn't a warning to slink away, to pull back, as she had with her mother so many times before. No, it was like a spring coiling to catapult itself forward, fueled by an emotion Naomi rarely gave in to when it came to her mother.

Anger.

"I don't want to 'leave it behind,'" Naomi said. With exasperated, graceless hands, she reached up to wipe her cheeks, sticky from the residue of salty tears.

"This place is bad vibes," Sue said. Already her mother was packing her mental rucksack, as if the weathered canvas were all the protection they needed. Cinch it closed, get moving. "We need a good cleansing."

Naomi dug in her heels. "I want to talk about it."

Sue's brow creased in confusion, and Naomi couldn't blame her. Talking things through was not part of their relationship: Sue filled the space between them with her opinions, lectures, and warnings, and Naomi listened quietly before moving on and doing whatever she felt was best.

But she'd never truly been able to move on, had she? Everything that had happened over the last three months—hell, over her life—was a testament that she was stuck in a past that she didn't know. Sue had never filled in the blanks and Naomi had allowed her to get away with it, absorbing the hurt but never prodding at the wound.

"Talk about what exactly?" Sue asked.

"I want to know about my grandparents. About your parents."

It was like releasing a storm cloud on a free spirit parade. Sue's face fell. "Why? Did Gia ask?"

"This has nothing to do with Gia," Naomi said. "*I* want to know."

"Why?"

The faint vibration in the base of her throat warned Naomi that her voice would quiver soon, and that fresh tears were not far behind. But for once, she didn't care. Let someone else clean up the mess for a change.

"Because they're my family, regardless if you want them to be or not. And you might shun your culture, but I want to decide for myself."

"I did what I felt was best for you," Sue said tightly. "That's what mothers do. I'm sorry if I embarrassed you at Diwali, but when your father mentioned you were attending an event like that, I knew you were getting in too deep."

Naomi shook her head impatiently, refusing to allow the full-bodied humiliation of that awful moment to waylay her from the conversation at hand. "I know cutting me off from my grandparents was your way of—"

"That's not what I—"

"—protecting me but—"

"It wasn't just me," Sue burst out. "They asked me to leave."

Everything in Naomi's chest drew taut. One deep breath and she would shatter. "What?"

Sue let out a heavy sigh before she replied. "Yes, I hated my childhood and yes, I was very unhappy. But I was also eighteen and pregnant by my high school boyfriend. I was scared."

"And they asked you to leave?" Naomi was incredulous.

"We were having an epic fight, which was nothing new. I always fought with them—I had never been the daughter they wanted me to be. But I threatened to leave, as I had many times before. Except this time, they agreed it would be best." Sue pulled a fuzzy throw pillow onto her lap and smoothed her hand over the top over and over again. "It sounds awful—and it was—but given the people they were, and the person I was, it was the best choice for both of us. And for you, I thought."

A dark, vile feeling crawled up Naomi's spine. Her grandparents had willingly disowned their daughter? *Agreed* to cutting ties? Like, *Sorry, you're not what we want in a daughter, so let's part ways*?

It was unfathomable. Disgusting. Wrong.

It's exactly what Dev worries about, a small voice reminded Naomi, and she cleared her throat. "Just like that? You make it sound so easy, like it was a quick, clean break."

A half smile quirked Sue's face. "No, it wasn't easy, at first. I think it was harder on them. For many years, they sent money. One of my cousins still calls every few months to catch up, and I'm pretty sure she does so because my parents want to hear about me." Sue's eyes softened. "And you."

"Why didn't you tell me any of this?" An errant tear slipped from Naomi's eye, but she impatiently swiped it away. "This is my history, too."

"Even though I looked at my life and knew I didn't want that for you, I never wanted you to hate my parents." Sue shrugged. "I still love them, even after all that."

Naomi studied her mother. The crystal necklace; her long, messy braid; healing beads around her wrists. Her mother had visited her only once before—a few years ago when she'd first moved to Kelowna—and had insisted on sage-cleansing her apartment and rearranging her furniture according to Naomi's chakras.

Was this the daughter her grandparents had known or was this part of Sue's rebellion, another backlash against cultural expectations? "How can you be so forgiving?"

Sue's lips lifted in a rare, self-deprecating smile. "Yoga helps." When she caught Naomi's stony face, she sobered. "It happened a long time ago, Naomi. It was almost a relief when they let me go— it would be worse if they were calling all the time, reminding me of their disappointment. Or worse, guilt-tripping me over how I was choosing to raise my daughter." Sue's gaze lowered. "I wanted a fresh start, and while the buildup was awful, my parents' decision allowed me to do that."

"So that's it. They don't want anything to do with us? With me?" Naomi bit her lip before she said something hurtful, but the words thrummed through her as they had her entire life: *I'm not you.*

"I don't know, Peanut. Everything I know about them is time-stamped. They care about their status in the community, they don't want to rock the boat, and they didn't know how to handle a daughter fighting like hell to break the mold. It was hard on all of us to have a kid like me in their community."

Naomi drew her knees into her chest and tried to sort through the riot of questions flooding through her from the answers Sue had provided. She had always considered her mother brave and independent, but a new, fragile respect was growing where impatience had once been. Because Sue sat before her, dry-eyed and accepting of the life she led. She might not have earned her spot on the podium, but she was unashamed of the race she'd run. For the first time in her life, Naomi envied her mother's too-calm, too-tranquil hippie persona. Sue, at least, was at peace.

There was only one question, really, that mattered.

"How can you not hate your parents even just a little bit?" Naomi asked.

"I talked about this at length with the guru at my annual meditation retreat," Sue said. Naomi heroically repressed an eye roll. "There's no handbook for immigrants and the generations that follow, Naomi. I think they did the best they could. They raised me according to what made sense to them. And I did the same for you." She offered a rueful smile. "We don't always get it right, huh?"

Had she heard this explanation three months ago, Naomi would've scoffed and written it off as a weak excuse for validating one's decisions. But after meeting Dev and learning about him, his family, and the never-ending demands circling his life, Sue's reasoning clicked. Sometimes children did not turn out the way parents meant them to.

Everyone just . . . tried. And maybe there were no absolutes in what was right, or authentic, or wrong. What Dev had introduced to Naomi about South Asian culture was beautiful and had filled her with a kind of joy she hadn't known was possible, but the more Naomi thought about it, that sense of fulfillment hadn't come from fitting in or receiving someone's approval.

It had come from sharing special moments with Dev, from exploring new things with him and living in the moment. From the little things, too: him dropping her favorite chocolate bar in her lap when he returned from paying for gas, the way he trudged after her in the paint store but never uttered a complaint when she loaded his arms with industrial-sized buckets to carry to the car.

Piggybacks in the rain because she was shivering in a waterlogged lehenga.

She wanted more of that—just feeling and basking in what felt right. Maybe it would be worth the awkwardness of fumbling through the pain. After all, even though her heart still ached from her fight with Dev, she didn't regret a single moment from the last three months.

Naomi cleared her throat. "What if I want to know them? My grandparents, I mean."

Sue gave her a long, searching look. "I can get their contact information for you. But, Naomi, I can't guarantee you're going to get what you want from them."

Undeterred, Naomi nodded. Maybe they would reject her or maybe they wouldn't fit in with her and the life she wanted to carve out for herself. But she knew, without a doubt, she would be okay either way.

She wanted to try.

chapter 27

I don't owe you shit.

Beads of sweat snaking into his eyes, Dev gritted his teeth and jabbed the speed up on the treadmill. But it didn't help. Since starting his run forty minutes ago, he'd been steadily increasing his pace, but between the pounding of his feet and the punishing slide of the running belt below, the words wouldn't go away.

I don't owe you shit.

When Naomi had hurled those words at him, they had drilled themselves into his brain and had been churning ever since. Dev didn't feel she owed him anything, but the question of *why* she hadn't trusted him enough with such an important part of herself haunted his thoughts and, try as he might, he couldn't outrun them.

With her, he had felt like a better version of himself, but she hadn't seen that. She had only seen someone who might turn on her or judge her for the slightest misstep. Someone she could spend time with in or out of the bedroom but not someone to trust.

And while that shredded his insides to bits, he couldn't help but be a little in awe of her: What must it be like to live your life with the confidence that you didn't owe anybody anything?

No family reputations to uphold, no demanding mothers to appease. No community to impress simply because you, more or less, shared the same ancestral country?

"Ahem," said a loud voice.

Dev's head snapped up to see Veera Auntie standing beside his treadmill, brows raised high enough to alert him that she'd been there for quite some time. He slowed his pace to a light jog while glancing around, half expecting to see his mother and aunt in eavesdropping distance.

Thankfully, it was just the two of them.

"I think we need to have a chat," the matchmaker said, her eyes pointedly skimming the length of the treadmill.

Dev resisted the urge to stop the machine and tightened his jaw. "I'm not done with my run."

Veera considered him for a long moment before circling around to the empty treadmill to his right. Her face set in determination, she hiked up the skirt of her beige sari and gingerly stepped onto the machine. She frowned at the panel for a moment before increasing the speed by three beeps.

"Your mother said I would find you here," she said conversationally, her hands gripping the safety handrail as she began her snail's pace workout. "I might as well get my money's worth. Eighteen dollars for a day pass! Can you believe it?"

At the sight of the blue veins in her wrinkled hands, Dev felt a twinge of guilt. "I can reimburse you."

Veera sniffed, the pallu of her sari swinging behind her. "A matchmaker's job is not for the weak-willed. Why don't you slow down so we can chat? You don't have to prove your stamina to *me*."

Once Dev had complied, she continued. "I think we're overdue for a check-in." When Dev didn't reply, she shook her head.
"For a few weeks now, I've been racking my brain as to why a handsome boy like you, with nice manners, a good job, and"—Veera
politely glanced at the ring of sweat around the collar of Dev's
shirt—"an interest in physical activity hasn't been able to successfully find a match, but the spectacle at the Diwali party clued me
in. You had failed to inform me that you already had a girlfriend."

"I didn't. I don't."

"You're not the first client to have a secret relationship, you
know. What do they call it? A 'side dish'?"

The current of heat flooding Dev's neck had nothing to do
with physical exertion. "I don't have a side di—I mean, a secret
relationship."

"Mmm, yes. It was clear that whatever was going on was more
than just an extra helping of chutney, if you know what I mean."

Christ. Dev tilted his chin upward, wondering where the nearest air-conditioning vent was situated, because if Veera Auntie
planned to continue down this line of bro talk, he would need it
on full blast.

"I wish you had told me, though," Veera added. "We could
have saved ourselves a lot of time."

"I'm sorry I wasted your time. But if you recall, I was against
this matchmaking idea from the start."

"Oh, no, dear, we still would have proceeded with finding you
a potential wife. I just would have scheduled this check-in much
sooner."

Dev swallowed a derisive snort; this felt more like an ambush.
"Auntie, I don't want to get married . . ." He trailed off. Funny how
the familiar phrase sounded hollow to his ears now. The conviction

that being alone was a foolproof method of avoiding living his parents' life without sacrificing his relationship with his family was no longer lodged deep in his chest.

Because he'd gotten a glimpse of what lifelong friendship and lighthearted teasing could feel like. Had experienced how casual, affectionate touch could awaken every single nerve ending. Dev had basked in the comfort of being part of a team, the opulence of relying on someone having his back whether he asked or not. It had all filled him with the kind of warmth he never thought was possible for a guy like him.

He was addicted and damn tired of acting like he didn't need it.

"Auntie," Dev tried again, his tongue thick and slow on the uptake, "maybe I don't want to marry the kind of woman my mother has preapproved for me. Maybe my list of must-haves are different than hers."

"You aren't the first person to feel this way, Dev." Veera's voice was kind but firm. "But young people don't think too far ahead when it comes to dating. They want someone they like spending time with, who makes them feel happy and attractive and special."

And that's a bad thing?

"But marriage is not dating. When a couple marries, everything changes. Things that might have not mattered will suddenly mean the world to both of you: life goals, expectations, family structures, children . . ." Veera trailed off and reduced the speed of her treadmill to zero. "Your mother is thinking about those complex matters and trying to improve your odds."

"I always assumed that marriage required compromise," Dev said, slapping his hand on the emergency stop button on his machine. His mother, after all, had capitulated to all her husband's wishes.

"Yes, it does. But it is not a bad thing for some things to line up between two people from the get-go. After all, how much can a person compromise in their life?" Veera's smile was patient. "I don't want to discourage you. I'm trying to explain that everything your mother and I are doing is meant to help you have a successful partnership with someone special."

Dev tipped his water bottle to his lips to hide his eye roll. It was hard to buy into the "someone special" line when said some-ones were reduced to one-page data sheets and a picture.

"And perhaps, if you feel very strongly that your mother's ideas for what you need in a life partner are wrong, then you should tell her so."

Dev scoffed. Because *that* had gone so well for him already.

"But remember," Veera added, peering at him over her glasses with a piercing stare. "Dating and having fun barely scratch the surface of what it means to be married. So instead of focusing on what puzzle pieces fit together right now, think about the big pic-ture. What is going to keep those pieces locked together for the rest of your life?"

Veera sure knew how to make a strong case for arranged mar-riage. And while she was right that he had no idea what life would throw at him and his future wife, he knew with absolute certainty that he didn't want to weather the storm with any of the smart, accomplished women Veera Auntie had tried to set him up with.

He could appreciate the big picture; hell, for the first time in his life, he wanted to work toward it, matrimonial fire and all. But he also knew what *he* needed so the smaller parts of the whole stayed fused together, strong and resilient in the face of life's trials. He needed warmth, casual affection, and an easy laugh teasing him out of a bad mood. Someone compassionate enough to stuff chewed-up food in his pockets to save an old woman's feelings and open-minded enough to try new things and embrace the parts of him that were complicated and tedious. He wanted a luminous, curly-haired goddess who was brave enough to go against the grain and call him out when he wasn't.

The future might be uncertain, but Dev had never felt more certain about anything—or anyone—in his life. He needed someone who brought the best out of him and loved him even when he was a grump.

And while his mother might not like it, might turn her back on a relationship that didn't check the right boxes, it wasn't Gia's approval Dev was interested in anymore.

When Dev returned to the bazaar from the gym, he knew Naomi wouldn't be there. It had been three days since Diwali, and even though they had planned a soft opening at the end of the week—with a guest list of family and close friends—Naomi had kept out of sight.

But she was still getting the job done, using Nick to complete the last finishing touches that the casual observer might not even notice but that were so undeniably Naomi, they made Dev's heart clench. Custom-printed napkins in a peacock design, a tiny plastic kitchen set pushed up against a wall so kids could "play" café in the café, and, Dev's favorite, a framed picture of a pregnant Gia standing in front of the bazaar around thirty years ago, looking unsure and nervous for what waited ahead. In the background, a young Neel was a blur as he ran out of the frame. Clutching Gia's hand was a two-year-old Dev, half hidden behind her leg, staring solemnly at the photographer. Beside the photograph, Nick had mounted a short origin story, also framed, about a newly married newcomer to Canada who had inadvertently created a sense of community in a bazaar selling everything from imported incense sticks to brown Jesus keychains.

Throwing a hoodie over his sweaty shirt, Dev stepped out of his vehicle to see Naomi's mother standing outside the bazaar, her loose genie pants flapping in the wind.

Was she here to wring his neck? Slap him for allowing his mother to talk down at her daughter? But when he caught a glimpse of the New Age crystal pendant hanging around her neck, Dev slowed his gait. Maybe she wanted to assess the bazaar's spiritual energy.

The only thing that he really cared about was if Naomi was nearby.

Sue must have guessed as much because her face was apologetic. "I came alone. Can we talk?"

He answered by slipping past her and unlocking the bazaar door. Once Sue had stepped inside, he gestured to a nearby table. "Have a seat."

Sue was busy looking around. "The energy in here is unreal."

With a half smile, Dev glanced around, too. Even though he had helped revitalize the space every step of the way, the results still impressed him. But as far as "energy" went, it was an empty café, devoid of pastries, tea, or customers. Unsure of how to respond, he gestured to the table again.

Sue waited until Dev had joined her at the table before folding her hands together on the table. "Naomi told me everything."

Dev couldn't help shoot a quick glance at the ceiling, where the bed he and Naomi had spent many, *many* hours was right above them. When he looked back at Sue, she raised her eyebrows.

"I know *everything*, Dev."

Dev cleared his throat uneasily and stared at the tabletop. Sue didn't *seem* like the traditional Bengali mother who would try to castrate him for sleeping with her daughter, but he was suddenly very grateful he knew where the first-aid kit was stored behind the counter.

"She's still hurt, you know. And angry with you."

Dev's gaze flew up. "You didn't have to come all the way here to tell me that."

Unruffled, Sue cocked her head to the side. "No, but I can sense the heaviness inside you, too. Your aura is bleak."

"You don't say."

Sue flattened her palms against the table and looked at Dev with such earnestness that, despite himself, he sat up straight in his chair and took notice. "My daughter lied to you, and while responsibility for that mistake falls on her shoulders alone, you should know where that lie comes from."

Dev shifted impatiently in his seat. His mother had already filled him—and Aashi—in on the conversation she had endured with Sue while Naomi and Dev had been outside the community center shredding each other to bits. Sue had revealed that she'd moved her family to another province to get away from people like Gia, and while the comment had offended and baffled his mother, Dev had put the pieces together.

"I know you moved to Alberta to get away from your family," he said.

"I didn't just do it to get away from my family. I didn't want to have anything to do with them anymore, to do with *any* of the members of the community. And I think . . . I think you can understand what that might feel like."

At Dev's imperceptible nod, Sue sighed. "I thought going the other way would make things easier for me. For Naomi. I wanted to provide her with everything I didn't have while growing up: the freedom to make my own choices, no forced ties to a culture I didn't embrace. No gossipy community members looking down on me for not doing what was expected of me." Sue's smile was bittersweet. "It never occurred to me that my daughter would want to learn about those things—that the culture might mean something for her. I guess, in trying to protect her from it, I took away the freedom for *her* to choose."

"Wait." Dev's mind raced. "You *never* talked about your culture? Your upbringing? You never exposed her to other Bengali people?" Having been immersed in his parents' culture his entire life, Dev couldn't begin to imagine the picture Sue was painting for him.

Sue ducked her head. "Aside from maybe ranting about them and all the injustices I lived through, not really. I thought I was doing what was best. It was selfish, too, I guess. I didn't want to revisit the past." Sue paused and her gaze wandered over Dev's shoulder. "Maybe I was afraid she'd want the things I ran away from. That she'd run away from me as a result. I tried to control her." Realization flashed across Sue's face and she chuckled. "Kind of ironic, huh?"

Dev wasn't about to touch *that* with a ten-foot-pole and decided to change direction instead. "But why would she lie to me about it? To everyone else, I get it. But why *me*?" He could barely croak the last words around the giant lump that had formed in his throat.

Sue reached forward to hold his hand, and while the multiple rings on her fingers shifted uncomfortably against his skin, he was grateful for the contact. "I can't say for sure, Dev. I raised a very independent, fix-everything-herself, ambitious girl. And I love her for it. But she's not used to sharing burdens, relying on others for help and security. She didn't have the same support system you probably grew up with."

Naomi's claim that she "wasn't Bengali, *not really*" replayed in Dev's mind, but for the first time, curiosity surfaced above the hurt and betrayal he usually felt when his mind revisited that horrible night. At the time, in the height of his humiliation, it had sounded like an empty excuse for her dishonesty. He had failed to understand that for someone like Naomi, who refused to accept that there were problems she could not overcome, her lack of ties to Bengali culture would be a serious source of shame. Especially next to his family, next to Gia, who cared so much about culture and reminders of home, she was oblivious to what was in front of her.

Because feeling Bengali wasn't something a person could fake or bluster their way through. Because he was a first-generation Canadian, everything Dev knew about his culture was passed down to him from someone else. Thanks to his parents, he was grounded in it. Sure, sometimes it was ugly, but it was beautiful sometimes, too, and he had *access* to it.

He had failed to be her support system when she had needed it most, probably confirming everything Sue had ever warned her about the community. She had stood in front of him, secrets bared, asking him to look past the shame and injustices that haunted her, and he had thrown it back in her face. He'd allowed his wounded pride to get in the way of what was really important: She wanted him to love her in return. Unconditionally.

"I fucked up, didn't I?" As soon as the curse word fell from his lips, Dev winced. He had never sworn in front of a Bengali elder before.

But Sue's answering smile was sympathetic. "You both did. But if I've learned anything from Naomi, there's always a way to fix things."

Dev studied Naomi's mother, trying to look past the crystal necklace and colorful headband holding back her hair. He'd never met someone like her, or anyone, who had left the community, whether voluntarily or by force. He'd heard rumors of it, but the fate of said person was only whispered about, usually from adult to child as a one-way lesson on the dangers of straying from the right path.

He had to ask. "Do you ever regret leaving it all behind? Risking your relationship with your family to pursue what you wanted?"

For several unblinking seconds, Sue stared at Dev as a myriad of emotions warred over her face. "I miss my family. I miss some of our traditions. But I did what I thought was best at the time—best for my daughter and for me—and I can't regret that. It may be too late for me to fix the mistakes of my past, but . . ." There was a flash in Sue's eyes and in it, Dev saw a piece of Naomi: the indomitable optimism that baffled him while drawing him closer, even when he tried to resist.

Sue's flair for drama was all her own, though, and she made him wait several seconds before grinning at him with a smile that was identical to Naomi's. "I think there's still hope for you."

chapter
28

As Naomi looked up at the gorgeous glass office tower in front of her, she suddenly realized why Cynthia walked around with a stick up her . . .

No, Naomi chided herself, *not today*. Not after her breakthrough with her mother. Naomi wasn't showing up unannounced at Cynthia's place of work for round two in the Thunderdome. She was there to clear the air, or at least speak up for herself—as civilly as possible—since their last confrontation had left her speechless.

Still, as Naomi stepped through the revolving door and received a cordial nod from the security guy whose polished black suit looked like it cost more than her monthly rent, she was glad she'd worn a flattering pencil skirt and her nicest blazer.

Although Cynthia worked independently as a brand consultant, her office was on the same floor as Kumar Construction, one of her father's many, many companies and, as such, any PR, facelift, or interior design needs went through Cynthia first, as she had often reminded Naomi.

"Hold the elevator, please!" a smooth baritone called, and

Naomi instinctively jammed her high-heeled foot forward to prevent the doors from closing just in time for a tall South Asian guy to slip inside, his arms piled with folders. Naomi caught a glimpse of his thick black hair and thought of the silky strands above the nape of Dev's neck, how he always pulled her closer when she gave the hair there a light tug.

The memory gave rise to an involuntary shiver, which the guy misread as an invitation to speak.

"Thanks for holding the door," he said, gesturing with his chin to the stack of files in his care. "Can you press thirty?"

Naomi glanced at the top folder in his hands. The Kumar Construction logo was stamped across the front. "I'm going to the same floor."

He cocked his head in her direction, interest clear in his eyes. "Oh, really?"

"Yeah, I'm here to see Cynthia Kumar."

"Are you a new assistant or something?"

Naomi's smile fell and she turned her eyes back to the elevator doors. "No. I'm her . . ." *Frenemy? Competition? Rival?* "Colleague."

"So you're a brand consultant, too?"

Naomi gave a curt nod even though her stomach turned at the assumption. Whether she'd continue to find work as a brand consultant in Kelowna and the surrounding area after the bazaar was said and done was another matter altogether.

The hint of flirtation in the guy's voice was unmistakable. "Well, I hope to see you around," he said as the doors slid open and he stepped out. "Don't be a stranger."

Naomi watched him leave. He was tall with broad shoulders and a charming smile. Undeniably handsome. But she felt nothing. Maybe if he had glared at her with a scowl, she might've felt a little flutter in her stomach.

But it was unlikely.

Naomi shook her head and approached the receptionist, who directed her to Cynthia's desk situated in a large corner office with floor-to-ceiling windows. *Of course.*

It was exactly what Naomi had pictured. Cynthia's workspace was a trendy oasis of clean metal lines, cool tones, and a glass desktop that would never dare to smudge. It was not a cozy little office by any means; the only décor items were an expensive-looking paper-weight and an abstract painting on the wall.

"Nice office," Naomi said from the doorway. She meant it. It suited Cynthia.

Cynthia's head snapped up and her eyes narrowed. "You're the last person I'd expect to see here."

"Can I come in?"

For several moments, Cynthia studied her in silence.

"I'm unarmed," Naomi added.

The corner of Cynthia's mouth twitched, and she gestured to one of the stiff ivory-white chairs facing her desk. "Have a seat."

Naomi perched on the edge of the chair and tried to relax her grip on her purse. "I want to talk about what happened at the grocery store."

"So talk."

She hadn't expected otherwise, but still, it miffed Naomi that Cynthia wouldn't even attempt to make this easy. From her slightly lifted eyebrow to the expectant set of her mouth, Naomi doubted that Cynthia believed she even owed her an apology.

But maybe Naomi didn't care. An apology from Cynthia wouldn't change anything, and Naomi was done feeling ashamed of her life. She was a poor, barely Bengali brand consultant with loose morals.

It was time she started owning it.

"You caught me off guard that day at the grocery store and I wanted to follow up."

Cynthia smirked, clearly expecting a concocted story that would cover Naomi's tracks.

But Naomi was done with lying, too.

"You were right. Well, kind of. I had been sleeping with Dev." Naomi shrugged against the tremor of shame slithering down her spine. "I'm in love with him."

All traces of arrogance flew from Cynthia's face. Naomi had stunned herself, too. On some level, she had suspected as much especially when, even after their awful fight, she kept waking up in the middle of the night to the rustle of her hand seeking through cool, empty sheets for his.

She loved him.

But she had never said it out loud before, much less to anyone else. Naomi had been too scared of the words, of how they might slice across her already bruised and battered skin. Now that she'd put the words into the world, she felt dazed like a gymnast pulling off the perfect floor routine to everyone's shock. Including her own.

"Hey, you're still here," a voice said from Cynthia's open doorway. It was the elevator guy.

Naomi squeezed her chair's armrest, praying her face didn't look like she'd just bared her bleeding heart in Cynthia's pristine, cream-carpeted, white-walled office. "Still here."

"What do you want, Rohit?" Cynthia asked sharply.

Elevator guy's easy smile fell like someone had cut the suspension ropes at the thirtieth floor. "Just making sure your guest hasn't frozen to death, Ice Princess."

Naomi turned wide eyes to Cynthia, who looked like she would happily ditch Rohit's unconscious body in a locked freezer.

"Don't you have somewhere to be," Cynthia snapped.

Rohit rolled his eyes. "Try not to get frostbite," he called over his shoulder as he walked away.

Clearing her throat, Naomi wound the straps of her purse around her hands. She wanted to say something comforting—women empowering women and all that—but, well, it was *Cynthia*. Rohit's nickname for her was kinder than comparisons Naomi had silently made in the past.

Cynthia, however, didn't need the reassurance. Instead, she pushed her chair back and stood up. "Let's go for a walk."

Although she was startled, Naomi followed suit, schooling her features when Cynthia slipped her feet out of a pair of sky-high heels for sensible sneakers instead.

She half expected Cynthia to give her a tour of Kumar Construction, to show off her connections and wealth as she so often had before. But Cynthia led her outside to the sidewalks snaking through one of Kelowna's more prestigious business districts. Very few people were outside today; by Kelowna standards, it was a blustery afternoon.

"Were you two dating before the rebrand?" Cynthia asked as if a full twelve minutes hadn't passed since Naomi's heartfelt declaration.

"No. And I don't know if you'd label what we did as dating, but it's over now. He . . ." Naomi's voice caught but when she glanced at Cynthia's uncharacteristically kind and guileless eyes, she shrugged again. "He doesn't feel the same way about me."

The admissions were so dear to Naomi that she regretted parting with them. She didn't want to talk about the pain of rejection and mistrust with anyone, especially not Cynthia.

But Cynthia surprised her, both by her abrupt decision to hang a sharp left at an intersection and by her next words. "I'm sorry, Naomi. I shouldn't have said those awful things to you."

Naomi's left heel skittered and she stumbled, but Cynthia did not slow down. "It was hurtful," she said, trotting to catch up, "but it wasn't that far off from how I was feeling about myself. I still can't believe I crossed that professional boundary for Dev."

"Was it worth it?"

Naomi hugged her purse to her chest and thought about his laugh, the way he tended to lean into even the most casual caress as if he were imprinting the touch onto his soul, his hand always finding hers in the dark of the night. His quiet way of taking care of her and everyone else around him.

The onslaught of memories was a fresh sting to the center of her chest, but the answer was obvious. "Yes."

"Well, if it's any consolation, I don't actually think the bazaar's success will have anything to do with Dev or your relationship with him."

Naomi's mind whipped back to their confrontation at the grocery store and Cynthia's accusatory face framed by overpriced packages of pasta. "Could've fooled me."

Cynthia's face twisted as if her next words burned her tongue. "You're good at what you do and I respect what you're trying to do with Gia's store. It just hit me pretty hard when I thought you might've been involved in some shady shit on the side." Cynthia's half smile was sheepish. "I *hate* being wrong. And you never struck me as someone who would resort to shady shit."

Naomi tried not to look too bowled over. "Thank you."

They walked in silence for a few minutes before Cynthia spoke again. "I have to admit that I was kind of jealous of you when we were in school together."

Naomi recovered from her feet tripping over each other with a weird sashay. "Are you serious?"

"Everyone seemed to gravitate toward you. I don't have that effect on people ... Not that I care," Cynthia hastened to add. "But you always kind of gave me the cold shoulder."

"I was intimidated by you."

Cynthia's half smile did not reach her eyes. "Everyone is."

After that admission, Cynthia came to an abrupt stop, shoving her hands in her pockets and looking down at Naomi, an unreadable expression on her face. Even without heels, she was a few inches taller than Naomi, and a few days ago, Naomi would have been as intimidated as everyone else apparently was. Not only because they were in an unfamiliar area—the perfect backdrop for Cynthia to murder her and dispose of the body—but also because Naomi had always thought she wanted, and needed, what Cynthia had: connections. A sense of belonging. The kind of success that fell into one's lap and made paying bills look like getting rid of chump change.

But now she looked Cynthia square in the eye, unashamed.

"Actually, after Garba," Cynthia explained, "I had an idea I wanted to run by you. As you might know, I get a lot of referrals through my dad's business deals."

"I'm aware," Naomi said wryly.

"Now, don't get me wrong, I'm up to any challenge, but sometimes clients are more interested in the kind of work you do."

When Naomi lifted an eyebrow in question, Cynthia waved an impatient hand. "Oh, you know ... They want *homey*. Touchy-feely. Knickknacks and crap like that."

"Thanks, Cynthia."

"You know what I mean. They want to run a business that gives people the warm fuzzies." Cynthia shuddered. "That's so not me. I also don't like working on those kinds of jobs. I don't find them . . ." Cynthia's nose wrinkled. "*Fun.*"

"So, what's your idea?"

"I thought maybe I'd send them your way . . ." Cynthia trailed off. "I know you're trying to build a portfolio, and a lot of those clients are acquainted with my dad. I'd feel better knowing they're in good hands."

The sound of rushing water thundered in Naomi's ears, pounding so furiously on her eardrums that her skin tingled in response. She looked down at her own hands like she couldn't believe they belonged to her.

Cynthia must have interpreted Naomi's stunned silence as disagreement because she added, "I don't expect you to do the same for me."

A small black scuff mark on the toe of Naomi's taupe heels suddenly caught her eye; the nail polish she had used to cover it up had chipped off at some point during their walk. As the magnitude of what Cynthia was offering her sank in, Naomi realized how much her feet hurt in these cheap, poorly constructed shoes. She'd worn them dozens of times, but her toes were pinched despite the rounded tip, and the back of her heel rubbed raw every. Single. Step.

These were her go-to adulting shoes. And they fucking hurt.

But she'd learned to ignore the pain, as well as the endless nights of ramen and sometimes wearing two layers of socks to bed to cut heating costs. Convinced that things would get better if she just kept going, Naomi had been running a marathon with no real end in sight.

Cynthia was offering her a finish line, one that she stood on the other side of, arms crossed and foot tapping. "I mean, I don't need any more referrals," she added, her patience for Naomi's silence tapering. "I've got more than enough to keep me busy."

"Of course you do." Naomi squared her shoulders. She was done running this race by herself. "I'd like that, Cynthia. I appreciate you thinking of me and trusting me. And . . ." With a deep fortifying breath, Naomi reached inside and loosened her grip on that part of her that was too proud, too self-reliant. "I could use the help. Times have been tough since I started my own business."

"Competition is rough right now." Cynthia gestured to the cityscape behind her. "And frankly, some of the brand consultants out there are straight-up assholes."

Naomi swallowed a smile. "Tell me about it. You seem to be doing really well. You know, *I've* always been jealous of the connections you get through your dad."

With a sheepish shrug, Cynthia tucked her hair behind her ear. "Well, if it makes you feel any better, he charges me to sublet my office space."

Naomi laughed for the first time in days. After months of wrapping herself in lies, it felt nice to shed her disguise, especially with a woman she'd often likened to a barracuda on the hunt. "You know what? It really does."

Cynthia nodded at the awning over Naomi's shoulder: New You Tailors. "It's a small, family-run place. They want to rethink their business model to bring in new clientele. You interested?"

Naomi surveyed the glass storefront where two mannequins, one in a red bridal sari and another in what Naomi assumed was a man's wedding suit, looked off into the distance. Even though she wasn't overly familiar with South Asian fashion, she knew she'd find her footing. She wasn't afraid anymore.

"Yes, I am," she said, following Cynthia inside.

An hour later, after a very successful client meeting, Naomi whipped out her cell phone as she and Cynthia parted ways and dialed Nick.

"I have a new client lined up," she said in greeting. "A tailor and a seamstress couple want a face-lift."

"That's great," Nick said. "I want to upgrade my truck."

"And that soft launch at the bazaar? I've changed my mind. I'm coming."

Naomi could hear Nick's smile through the phone.

"Even better," he said.

chapter
29

"Dev, we're here!"

Standing up from where he'd been sprawled on the couch for several hours, Dev frowned into his phone. With the soft launch for the bazaar planned for the following evening, he had invited Gia to come see the finished café and, hopefully, make a final decision for its future. But it wasn't like her to announce her arrival.

"So come in," he said, as he moved toward the stairs.

"Our hands are too full."

"Full? Full of what?" Dev paused on the rickety steps. "Wait, who all is with you?"

"Hurry up, would you? It's cold outside," Gia urged before hanging up on him.

Shy of the entrance into the bazaar, Dev shielded his hands in front of his body before realizing that the seashell curtain had been removed. Funny how pieces of the old store would always stick with him, maybe even inspire the odd twinge of nostalgia of how things used to be.

But it was time to move on.

Dev jogged to the bazaar's entrance to unlock the door, less than pleased when he realized that along with Aashi, his mother had also invited Neel, Priya, and their daughters. His nieces he wasn't so worried about, especially after they let out twin squeals of delight before running to the designated children's area closely tailed by their mother.

Neel was too busy surveying the redesign, arms folded in front of his chest like a land baron.

"Nice work, Downer Dev," Neel said. "This place looks pretty good."

"This place is beautiful!" Aashi called from where she and Gia were unloading the contents of various cloth bags onto the front counter. "Naomi outdid herself."

Dev nodded, slightly annoyed with himself that he hadn't been the one to credit Naomi first.

"Hang on a second," Neel said, jerking his thumb at the long family-style table. "I thought I told you to replace this with grab-and-go-type seating."

"That might have been what you wanted, but since Mom is the client . . ."

Neel rolled his eyes. "This again? We already discussed this."

"No, you—"

"Dev," Gia called from the register, inserting herself into a sibling argument as she had so many times before. "I forgot the matches at home. Do you have any?"

"Matches? What would you need those . . ." Dev trailed off when he saw what Gia and Aashi had set up on the front counter. A tiny shrine for the goddess Laxmi in the center, complete with fresh fruit offerings, tea light candles, and incense. He should have figured his mom would want to do a puja before the café was open to the public. Any time an important event—like moving into a new home, taking a big exam, or starting a new job—occurred, Gia always insisted on passing up prayers to whatever god or goddess she felt best to bestow blessings on her family.

Dev had always rolled his eyes at the ancient ritual, and yet, he felt something clench in his chest. These time-honored traditions might be dusty, but they were still a part of him and everything he knew.

"Found some!" Aashi called, pulling a lighter out of a drawer. She and Gia busied themselves lighting candles and arranging their offerings just so.

"This place is really something," Priya told Dev, materializing at his side. She smiled at where her daughters were pretending to make coffee. "The children's area is genius. And the colors . . . They're so cheerful and comforting."

"That's all Naomi," Dev confirmed, powerless against the proud smile spreading across his face.

"She's something special, too, isn't she?" Priya said gently.

With a deep breath, and a quick glance to where Aashi and Gia murmured prayers in front of their shrine, Dev nodded. "Actually—"

"This place is kind of frilly, isn't it?" Neel boomed, showing them his phone. On the screen was a before picture from when Neel had played amateur photographer when the bazaar had been newly renovated but with none of the accent pieces and customized flourishes.

"I think it reminds me of your mother," Aashi said as she and Gia joined them.

Neel shook his head. "That's not the kind of vibe we should be going for. Look, the bazaar was cute, but if we want to be taken seriously in the business community, we need to prioritize profit, not customers."

"And where do you think profit comes from, Neel?" Aashi asked with an indulgent little grin.

"They don't get it. This is a business, not your living room." Neel nudged Dev. "Tell them what I'm talking about."

The urge to belittle his older brother was strong, but instead Dev turned to Gia. It was time for her to choose for herself, to be the deciding factor over what happened to her namesake.

His mother looked a little embarrassed by the undivided attention. She glanced around at the beautiful café; it was hard to imagine that the dingy, tired bazaar had ever existed in such a vivid and coordinated space.

"It's a lot," Gia said softly.

"Yes, exact—" Neel said.

Dev's jaw dropped when Priya shushed him before he could.

Gia did a slow turn of the space, lingering slightly longer where her granddaughters were now bent over the same coloring book, hard at work. When she turned to face them again, a small smile graced her face.

"I'm sorry, Neel. I'm keeping the bazaar—I mean, the café. I'm keeping the café."

"Mom, you don't know the first thing about running a place like this," Neel protested.

Although the smile remained, a thread of steel ran through Gia's words. "I'll learn."

"I can help," Dev blurted out, "with the business side of things." Although he was momentarily taken aback by his declaration, a sense of rightness settled in his stomach. After three months of working on the rebrand with Naomi, the idea of staying connected

to it—even in a minute way—wasn't unappealing. He wanted to
see it succeed and to be part of its success. It meant something to
him now.

"You're an accountant, not a businessman," Neel argued.

"I'll learn."

"But I can take the bazaar to new heights. I have a vision!"
Neel turned imploring eyes to Gia. "Don't you want the family
business to be a respectable pillar of the community?"

Priya's hand clamped down on her husband's shoulder. "I'm
sure they'll appreciate you helping out when you're not pitching in
at home. With all this newfound ambition, you'll have plenty to
spare."

Neel's mouth opened and closed a few times like a fish stranded
on the shore. "But . . . But . . ."

"We'll all help," Aashi said with a nod, "where we can. This is
a family business, after all."

Neel stole one more glance at his mother, but something in the
set of her chin had him nodding grudgingly instead. Dev knew he
had assumed a responsibility that would ensure him a front-row
seat to endless Mukherjee family madness: conversations that were
half interrupting one another, half sly digs; well-meaning aunties-
turned-patrons who would provide unsolicited feedback on the
quality of food as if they were trained chefs themselves; and his
mom, bringing gossip home every day along with stale leftovers.

Yep. He had voluntarily signed himself up for this. And yet, if
he was being honest with himself, he didn't mind.

Aashi rubbed her hands together. "So, what are we going to call
this place?"

"Mukherjee Palace," Neel said right away. Behind his back,
Priya shook her head.

"Sweet Stop? The Sweet Spot," Priya ventured.

"Chai o'Clock!" Aashi laughed.

Gia examined every face staring expectantly at her before turning to Dev. "What do *you* think?"

It was Dev's turn to feel bashful under his family's scrutiny. Although letting them decide would've been a hell of a lot easier, Dev made his way behind the counter to pull out the sign he had stashed there. It was something he'd taken on in private, an independent contribution that now, when held between his hands for his family to judge, had his heart racing in his chest.

With uncertain fingers, he turned the sign so they could see its front: *Gia's*. Simple, bold white letters on a burgundy sign.

The scratches of the twins' crayons on paper were the only sound in the room until Gia said, her voice teary:

"Perfect."

At the ungodly hour of six thirteen on a Sunday morning, Naomi pulled into the bazaar's parking lot, a mixture of relief and disappointment burbling in her chest when she noted that Dev's car was nowhere in sight. He was likely at his weekly basketball game with his friends, affording her a few hours to make sure everything was ready for the soft launch. Naomi had already, with Aashi's help, ordered the food, created a playlist, and seen to the little odds and ends that she hoped would ensure that the guests left with a sense of satisfaction that would spread like wildfire when the café opened for real.

It had been a hard pill to swallow, physically avoiding the jobsite the week before its soft opening, yet another unprofessional taboo Naomi could add to her growing list of wrongs. She had justified it by telling herself that her pride was more valuable, that the last remaining touches could be performed as smoothly by Nick as by herself.

Protecting her heart, after all, mattered more.

Naomi let herself into the bazaar, already compiling a list of things she wanted to do. The peacock napkins should be artfully arranged on various surfaces, and maybe a *Please Don't Touch* placard should sit beside Aashi's pottery collection, and— Naomi froze in her tracks when she saw who was in the bazaar.

Gia. Sitting by herself on the burgundy couch, a wistful look on her face that dissolved into suspicion when she saw who had entered the premises.

"My son isn't here."

"I'm not here to see him," Naomi said even though the lump in her chest begged to differ. "I'm here to get things ready for the soft launch."

"Aren't you a little early?"

"The early bird gets the worm," Naomi chirped. Too bad that, in this moment, she felt more like the worm than the predator. She moved toward the creamer station by the front counter and began straightening its contents, placing a pink Post-it on the creamer to remind Aashi, who had said she would arrive at the café a few hours before the soft launch to receive the food, to fill it.

Gia ambled to her side, silent as she watched Naomi carefully arrange a small stack of peacock napkins in a perfect fan.

"These are beautiful," she murmured. "My favorite animal."

"I'm glad you like them."

"I suppose you're also here for your paycheck?"

Naomi turned to Gia, startled. "So you're happy with the result? You don't want to wait to see how the soft launch goes first?" Although she'd already received plenty of accolades from Aashi, this moment was what Naomi had been waiting for.

Or was it? Because when Gia nodded her confirmation, Naomi felt strangely empty.

Sure, a small part of her—the part that had pulled together a beautiful café in three months—glowed, but that sense of proving herself? Of impressing Gia, who had doubted her every step of the way?

Empty.

"Okay, great," Naomi said woodenly. "I'll email you my invoice next week." She forced a smile. "This place is going to be a success, you'll see." Although Naomi meant every word, it felt like she was saying it more for her own benefit than Gia's.

And Gia heard it, too. "What's wrong? Is this not what you envisioned?"

Naomi swallowed a bitter laugh as she looked around her; memories of the work she and Dev had put in coated everything like forest fire smoke. Instead of answering, she moved behind the front counter and began systematically opening and closing drawers and cupboards even though her brain barely registered their contents.

Gia moved to the other side of the counter and watched.

"I don't know if you're waiting for an apology," Naomi found herself saying, "for not telling you about my ethnicity. Or the fake-dating thing. Or for whatever my mother said to you at Diwali. If you are, then I'm sorry, okay? I'm sorry."

Naomi closed a drawer a little more forcefully than necessary and thanked the heavens that Nick wasn't around to see her abusing his craftsmanship. "I know you look at me and see failure. I'm the product of a teenage pregnancy. I don't know my grandparents, I don't know my culture, and I don't measure up to the standards you set for your son."

Gia's face was unreadable as Naomi bustled around, touching everything and completing nothing.

"But I'm done thinking I have to prove myself." Naomi stared into a cupboard full of oversized mugs. More fucking peacock designs. "I thought I had proven myself, and look where that's gotten me." She shut the cupboard and glared at the door handle before moving on. "It wasn't enough."

"I just said I'm happy with the work," Gia protested.

"Not you! Him. Dev! Your son. Dev." With her back to Gia, Naomi bowed her head, willing the tears threatening to shimmy down from her burning eyelids to stay where they were. She thought they had all dried out.

"In the end, the culture thing outweighs everything else, doesn't it?" Naomi said before sinking her teeth into her bottom lip. When she turned to face Gia, she didn't know what to make of her face, the hard and soft emotions warring for territory there.

"I admit it was stupid of me to lead you to believe I was something I'm not, to try to belong somewhere that doesn't want me. But my mother's decision to leave her family and shun the community? That wasn't my fault. My grandparents letting her go? Also not my fault. My dad not sticking around, being cut off from my culture . . . ? Not. My. Fault."

Immediately, Naomi felt lighter, as if saying the words had unburdened her of the dead weight of a past she barely knew. And yet her skin flushed cold, then hot with embarrassment when she realized what she had unloaded on Gia. It was the wrong dumping ground for all this toxic waste inside her.

But at least it was out.

Gia cleared her throat. "Well . . . Of course it's not *your* fault."

Naomi shook her head against the reassurance, so tentatively uttered. She didn't need Gia's approval anymore. Instead, she reached into her bag and pulled out her last contribution to the café: a tiny brown Jesus keychain that she carefully angled beside the cash register.

"I hope you know how lucky you are to have a son who would sacrifice everything for you," Naomi said.

"I'm doing what I think is best for my son."

Naomi snorted. "So did my grandparents, and look how my mom turned out."

"I would never let that happen—I love him too much."

Despite every brain cell commanding otherwise, Naomi's heart squeezed like it was wringing itself out. She needed to get away from here. "I'll send you my invoice after the soft launch," she said.

Naomi took one last look at the bazaar-turned-café and nodded. It was perfect. And while she might not be, she was okay.

"It was a pleasure working for you." She offered Gia a wobbly smile and let herself out.

Pulling down the visor in Nick's new black truck, Naomi examined her reflection, paying special attention to make sure no traces of her crimson lipstick had stained her teeth. As Nick pulled into Gia's parking lot, she turned to her friend and posed with her hand under her chin, angling her face like a Hollywood starlet.

"How do I look?" Naomi winced when she heard the note of vulnerability trembling just shy of a nervous falsetto in her voice.

Nick parked his vehicle before turning in the driver's seat to look at her. "You look hot. But maybe you should've toned down the boss vibe. This is a casual grand opening party."

Naomi smoothed down the front of her white blazer before brushing an invisible speck of lint from her matching pencil skirt. Perhaps she had gone a little overboard, but splurging on a power suit combined with her rarely touched but highly revered Whip It Red lipstick had not been unlike donning armor. Despite Nick's reassurance, the splash of color on her lips felt like a ghastly paint job, her new outfit stiff and scratchy against her skin.

But the costume was necessary. It had been almost a week since she'd seen Dev, and when it came to facing the man who had incinerated her heart, she was going to err on the side of caution. She wanted to be immune to those dark chocolate eyes, the ones that could see through her, turn her inside out, and set everything on fire. She just needed to get through the night in one piece. After all, it would likely be the last time she'd have to see him.

"This event might help me gain prospective clients," Naomi reminded Nick. And herself. "I wanted to look the part."

Nick half smirked. "Right. And this wouldn't have anything to do with a sexy, brooding ex who will definitely be in attendance?"

Heat crept up Naomi's neck, the rasp of her starchy skirt against the leather upholstery a dead giveaway as she shifted in her seat. "It might. Minutely."

Nick rolled his eyes and killed the engine. "C'mon, we're already late."

Naomi slid out of the vehicle and squinted in the direction of Gia's. The store's new sign, and title, screamed of Dev's handiwork: the no-nonsense name, the bold font. But there was a slight tilt to the gently curved letters, a hint there might be more beneath the surface for one patient enough to look.

It was perfect.

Nick had parked farther away than she would've liked, but out of the best kind of necessity—the available rows of parking facing the front of the store were packed. Even as Naomi hoped that the guest list wouldn't diminish the airy, open feel of the café she had hoped to achieve, a flutter of excitement glided across her chest.

She allowed Nick to take the lead as they snaked their way around cars to the entrance, which was propped open. Inside, a sea of excited faces filled the tables, leaned against walls, talking to one another in an overwhelming mix of English, Bengali, Hindi, and half a dozen or so other languages Naomi could not even begin to decipher. There were a few non–South Asian faces, including the Musas from next door who had staked their claim on the burgundy couch. They waved at Naomi and Nick enthusiastically, their excited smiles a welcome balm on Naomi's nerves.

Regardless of where they sat, stood, or lounged, every person held some kind of snack or dessert in their hand, and the heady smell of chai perfumed the air like a warm, cozy hug. The ambience in the room was perfect, right down to the number of children gorging on desserts. For once, Naomi's professional eye didn't see the tiny imperfections that required space on a never-ending to-do list. She only saw her vision come to life.

Triumph settled in the pit of her stomach, bookended by the din of people having a good time.

At the register, Gia chatted with various patrons, a wide smile on her usually dour face. Seated with a bunch of elderly ladies, Aashi shone even more brightly than usual, pushing plates of colorful mishti at them and chatting with her personal brand of gusto. Neel was here, too, looking a bit sulky seated next to his wife, who colored with her daughters with crumbs smeared across their faces.

"It's a full house," Nick announced, as if reading her mind. He, too, was taking it all in as only a contractor could, lingering on the brass light fixtures, the edges where flooring met baseboard.

When he nodded with satisfaction, Naomi couldn't resist giving his arm a squeeze. "Thanks for pulling this off with me."

He smiled. "The pace was ridiculous but worth it. Looks like everyone the Mukherjees care about is here."

Naomi wrinkled her nose as she moved toward the Musa family. She couldn't deny that, even with all the armor in the world, she was uncomfortable in the presence of all the people whose opinions mattered so much to Dev. These were the people he bent and curved his life for, the people whose respect he sought. Even if the events at Diwali had been different and he had been willing to make room in his hopelessly knotted life for her, she couldn't live her life like that.

But it wasn't the night for declarations of independence and zero fucks given. There would be time for Naomi to decide where she fit with this community, how she would incorporate it into her life. Whatever she decided, self-preservation came first, and right now, starting and ending the night with the Musas seemed like the safest option for her crumpled heart, prospective clients be damned.

But a familiar voice stopped her from the sweet relief of ano-nymity. "Naomi." That voice. Tangled sheets before sunrise.

Dev, annoyingly handsome in a black button-down shirt and clean-shaven jaw, moved to stand in front of her, his arms hanging awkwardly at his sides, hands clenching and unclenching to the apprehensive pulse spreading underneath Naomi's skin. Naomi fixed her eyes to the floor.

"I need to talk to you," he said in a low voice.

Ever so slowly, Naomi's eyes traveled upward, settling on a half-done button just above his clavicle. The imperfection on such a black-or-white, meticulous man inspired a swell of confidence. "So talk."

Dev's eyes widened. "Uh . . ."

She wouldn't give in, not to the discomfort clouding his beau-tiful features or the faint scrape of his feet shuffling boyishly on the floor. Her heart was absolutely *not* thudding against her rib cage at the sight of a nervous flush seeping onto the tips of his ears, where only a few weeks ago she'd memorized the outline with her tongue.

"Can we go somewhere private?" he asked.

With a scoff, Naomi glanced around them. No one was listening or paying them any special attention, but *of course* Dev would request they move somewhere where no one could see them, where no one could make assumptions.

Hidden away like a dirty secret.

"You know what, Dev?" The words came out deliciously challenging, and Naomi's spine straightened. "No, we can't go somewhere private. In fact, I don't want to talk to you."

His head reeled back as if she'd slapped him. *Good.* "Please, I—"

"No. I'm making it out of here in one piece tonight," she said, her voice emerging sharper than intended. When she saw guilt seep onto his face, Naomi couldn't help but gentle her voice, convincing herself it was more for her graceful exit rather than his feelings. "Now, if you'll excuse me, I'm going to go chat with the Musas. They, at least, won't be ashamed to associate with me in public." It was a petty dig, one that she knew she'd toss and turn over later tonight, but it did the job. Dev's mouth snapped shut and he stepped back.

A part of Naomi was disappointed, but she wasn't surprised. Backing down was what Dev did; he never made a scene or pushed the limits. He was a good, dutiful Bengali son, and although she'd once admired this kind of loyalty, in this moment she resented him for it.

She was halfway to the Musas when that same velvety voice stopped her again, this time in surround sound.

"Excuse me? Is this on?"

Naomi stopped in her tracks and turned to the source. Clutching a microphone in a white-knuckled grip, Dev stood at the cash register, and he was staring right at her. His intense gaze did not waver as conversations died down and everyone turned to the speaker, awaiting his next words.

Every muscle in Naomi's body clenched; now that the fight had been avoided, she was primed for flight.

Once he had claimed everyone's attention, Dev cleared his throat and looked around the room. "Thank you all for being here and supporting my family tonight." He gestured at his mom, who stood next to him, her arm threaded to Aashi's. Both sisters were beaming.

"This store has been a very special place to us, especially my mom. It's where she first planted roots in this country and built a home. It's also where she met many of you and found her first friends. It means a lot to her, and our entire family, that you all came to see what we have been working on these past few months. We are so grateful to have such wonderful people to call our friends."

Despite herself, Naomi felt a lump form in her throat at his heartfelt words. Dev was usually so reserved, even more taciturn in large groups, but she heard the emotion in his voice. He meant everything he said, and that stupid corner of her heart, the part that didn't care how hard she tried to cling to a cool and reserved exterior, was proud of him.

She wasn't the only one moved by his words. Enthusiastic applause met Dev's speech, and Nick let out a deafening whistle.

"When my mother asked me to help with the store's rebrand," he continued, "I admit that I wasn't sure what would become of the bazaar. I knew things needed to change, but everything you see before you could not have been possible without our brand consultant, Naomi Kelly."

Naomi's eyes widened in alarm as Dev gestured to where she

stood, turning the crowd's applause and murmur of appreciation in her direction. The loudest cheers seemed to be coming from the Musas and Nick, and while she was semimortified by the unexpected attention, Naomi pasted on a small smile and offered a small nod of thanks to Dev and his mother. If they asked her to speak, she would die.

Luckily, Dev didn't beckon her to the mic. But he wasn't finished. "Under Naomi's expertise, my mother's store took on a direction and purpose that celebrated many of the important parts of the bazaar that my mom held dear. I admit that I was skeptical at first, but I soon saw how invaluable Naomi is. She brought color and energy back to the bazaar. This beautiful café is her vision for the community. Naomi changed this place completely and for the better," he said.

Under the heavy stare of almost everyone in the building, Naomi's cheeks heated, but she was too spellbound by Dev's smooth voice to duck her head modestly. Or give in to the urge to run away.

He paused and stared at her with his familiar chocolate eyes, and Naomi allowed herself to melt, just a little bit. A small voice at the back of her head warned her to look away, but she couldn't. If this was the last time she would see him, it was a hell of a way to say goodbye.

In the short silence, the expectant audience turned back to Dev as if they could sense something big just waiting to tumble from his lips. Something important. Anticipation drizzled through Naomi, laced with something that was too raw, too deceptive.

Hope.

"And she changed me." Dev's voice thickened. "She imagined possibilities for my mother's store that I never would have dreamed of. And thanks to her, I've started imagining new possibilities for myself and what I need in my future."

In her peripheral vision, Naomi could see people whipping their heads back and forth between Dev and her, as if they were performing a skit and Naomi had the next line. It was laughable because from the way her heart was lodged in her throat, Naomi felt like she was on the verge of tears instead.

Dev paused to lick his lips, and in that moment everything faded away except the man in front of her.

"It might not be obvious at first, but Naomi poured herself into this store's rebrand," Dev continued. "All the incredible parts of her, like her ambition, optimism, and compassion, are all a part of Gia's now. And we are so lucky for it, because this place is a part of my family." And with a deep breath, he added, "And so is she. Naomi, I'm in love with you, and I want you to be a part of my family, too."

In the silence that followed, the only audible sound was a squeak from a wide-eyed Gia.

Beside her, Aashi's grin widened and she bounced on her toes.

"You should go up there." Nick's voice was low and excited in her ear—she hadn't even noticed him sidling up to her. His hand covered hers where, at some point, it had reached out and clutched the back of a nearby chair and was now squeezing it for dear life. Nick pried her clammy fingers loose. "Naomi, go. Do not deny me this real-life Bollywood moment!"

The café's guests began a scattered applause, the kind that followed an abrupt ending to a speech that had floored every single person in the room. Nick nudged Naomi forward, and as she made her way to where Dev stood, the applause grew in strength, coupled with whistles as Dev met her halfway, his gaze uneasy and tense.

This time, it was Naomi who reached for his hand and laced their fingers together. And it was all that Dev needed. He visibly relaxed and pulled her into his side.

"Hi," Dev whispered, his lips dangerously close to her earlobe. "If it wasn't obvious, that was me trying to say . . . I love you."

When she didn't respond right away, Dev's forehead wrinkled and he nudged her into facing him. "I'm really sorry about every—"

Naomi grinned and cut him off with a kiss. "Hi," she said, pulling back. "I love you, too."

As the bustle of patrons returning to their own conversations resumed, Naomi risked a quick glance at Dev's mother. Gia's lips were stretched into an uncomfortable smile but something in her eyes signaled acceptance. Or, perhaps, acquiescence. It wasn't the most encouraging face Naomi had ever encountered, but it didn't matter.

She had what she needed.

A few hours later, Naomi stood behind the counter where the last of the sweets had been laid on a large, silver tray for anyone to help themselves. Only one or two items of each variety remained, a sign that the food had been sampled thoroughly and enjoyed by many. Her mouth watered as she deliberated over which dessert would cap the night.

It would be a crime not to punctuate the most memorable evening of her life with something sweet and sumptuous.

"There you are," Dev said as he appeared next to her, satisfaction and something Naomi couldn't quite identify in his voice. Relief, maybe. Love.

"You knew just where to find me," she replied, gesturing at the sugary possibilities in front of them. But, as mint and pine overwhelmed her senses, she could focus on one temptation only: Dev. It had been her wonderful plight all night long. Between him greeting his family's friends and Naomi networking the room, Dev had faithfully returned to her side at every possible opportunity, squeezing her hand in greeting, often followed by a quick brush of his lips against her temple or a gentle tug to pull her closer to him, solidifying himself as her anchor.

And she as his.

Dev wrapped his arm around her waist, sneaking a quick nuzzle against her neck. "Careful," she teased, "or people are going to think we're a couple."

It was an empty threat. The café was nearly deserted, save for Gia, Aashi, and a few aunties who lounged like royalty on the burgundy couch. Dev, however, regarded Naomi in that familiar, intense way of his. "Sweetheart, people have been congratulating me on our engagement all night."

Naomi pressed her lips together to hide the goofy smile threatening permanent residency on her cheeks. *Sweetheart.* He'd called her sweet— Her face grew slack when the rest of Dev's words registered. "What?"

"I think my little speech might have given some people the wrong impression. One lady extended her best wishes because she thinks we're having a baby."

Naomi's blinked and glanced down at her stomach, speechless. Dev laughed.

"Did you set them straight?" Naomi asked, her voice weak. Most of the guests had left a half hour ago—who knew what kind of rumors had been hatched about them in that time span.

Dev shrugged one shoulder. "Does it matter?"

Something thick like molasses coated Naomi's insides, more

indulgent and sweet than gulab jamun could ever be. It was stronger than satisfaction, more potent than relief.

Love.

Naomi pressed her hands against Dev's chest, memorizing the rise and fall of his steady breath. "Have I mentioned just how much I love you yet?"

Twin dimples sank into his cheeks. "You have not."

"Well, I do." Naomi leaned closer to whisper in his ear. "I plan to show you how much later."

Dev's dimples disappeared, replaced by a wicked tilt to his lips. "I—"

"Devdas," Gia interrupted, ambling to the counter. Her eyes flickered to where Naomi's hands rested on his chest, but her face remained unreadable. "There's a lady on the couch who owns a small specialty tea company and wants to discuss partnership opportunities."

Dev exhaled a small, impatient huff before winking at Naomi, a promise for later. Dutifully he turned and went to where an elderly woman waited on the other side of the room.

Gia and Naomi stared at each other for a few moments of silence before Gia finally opened her mouth to speak.

"I don't believe I ever thanked you properly this morning," she said, her face devoid of any discernible emotion. "You really did work magic on my store." Gia gestured to the almost-empty room behind her. "My son was right. You breathed life into this place. I . . . I was wrong about you."

Naomi ducked her head. "Thank you."

Gia hesitated. "Thank *you* for what you did here." She peered at Naomi searchingly, her dark gaze, so like Dev's, speaking volumes. "It seems I needed to adjust my expectations all along."

It was clear that this conversation was difficult for Gia, but with Dev's speech etched across her heart, Naomi didn't need more from his mother at this time. Better yet, she didn't feel the need to reassure Gia that at Dev's side, she would try her best to honor all the important traditions and customs Gia held close to her heart and wanted to keep alive in her family. She would show her, in time.

Instead, Naomi offered Gia a warm smile and turned back to the dessert table. "I'm trying to decide which I'd like to eat." The assortment of sweets offered a range from various Indian cuisines, like jalabis, laddoos, gulab jamun, and others Naomi had never seen before. After a brief moment of indecision, she reached for one that was familiar to her: the sumptuous rasgulla, which she spooned onto her plate, paying special attention to also scoop the syrup they sat in to drizzle over the dessert on her plate.

When she realized Gia was watching her every move, Naomi smiled sheepishly. "This one is my favorite."

Gia's answering grin took her by surprise. "That's a famous Bengali sweet," she said. "It's my favorite, too."

epilogue

3 MONTHS LATER

As he pulled into the driveway of his mother's home, Dev checked his watch and grimaced. He was late. Dev jumped out of his car and booked it for the front door.

When he reached the kitchen, he found Neel standing in the kitchen, eating a bowl of daal with a length of four paper towels stuffed into the front of his navy blue kurta to protect from spillage.

"Late much?" Neel smirked before shoving another spoonful into his mouth.

"Kind of hard to duck out early when you're the new guy."

Neel shook his head, bewilderment competing for disapproval on his broad face. "I still can't believe you gave up your career at a firm to start at the bottom. In sports, no less."

"You're kidding, right?" Dev asked, heading to the stove. "I love my job."

"Seems like a dumbass move to me."

Several months ago, the comment might have nettled that

paper-thin place inside him that crumpled at the mere mention of doing anything that inspired his family's disapproval. But now Dev barely flinched. He'd lost track of time at a job he loved, doing things he cared about, for an organization that became more and more interesting every day. From how things were going, it was rumored that he would move up the ladder quite quickly, but for once, it didn't matter if Neel—or anyone else—knew that.

Dev was as interested in Neel's criticism as he was in pointing out that a fleck of lentil was hanging precariously in his older brother's beard.

"You better get ready or Mom is going to have a fit," Neel advised when Dev didn't respond.

Dev glanced through the sliding backyard doors to where Dhan was playing with their nieces. Priya, in a lovely purple sari, was hovering nearby, making sure the other three stayed clean and tidy for the event.

"We're going to an Indian wedding," Dev pointed out. "Why are you eating now? You know they're going to have a ridiculous spread."

Neel scoffed. "Bro, you know they won't serve food until, like, nine."

Well, at least his brother wasn't *always* in the wrong. Dev grabbed a bowl from the cupboard and scooped a spoonful of daal from the pot on the stove. It was a tradition in the Mukherjee household to gather at Gia's house before weddings so they could make an entrance together. And likely, too, so his mother could approve of everyone's choice of apparel. Ever since that one time Dhan had balked tradition and shown up wearing track pants under his kurta, gathering at Gia's house was a mandatory precursor to attending events as a family.

Even with a thriving business occupying her time, Gia still

liked to keep tabs on her brood. And she probably always would. As the shrieks of his nieces filtered into the house, Dev took a bite of perfectly spiced daal and realized he didn't mind.

"Where's Mom?" he asked.

"Probably in her room." Neel rolled his eyes again. "You know she takes the longest to get ready."

Dev spooned a few more heaping mouthfuls and went in search of his mother. As Neel had predicted, Gia was in her bedroom, but she appeared ready to go. Her sari was similar to Priya's purple one but simpler in design, the cut of the blouse much more modest. It was startling to see her hair part devoid of sindoor, the red powder Bengali women adorned themselves with to signify their marital status, which Gia only bothered with for larger events. It was also strange not hearing his father's impatient voice from downstairs, calling for everyone to hurry up, punctuated with the irritated jingle of his car keys. Gia, though, looked assured and at ease as she bustled about, safety pins tucked between her teeth as her hands moved in a flurry.

But what caught Dev's eye was Naomi, standing patiently under his mother's ministrations as Gia straightened the plum-colored sari pleats over her shoulder. Dev leaned against the doorframe, bowl of daal in his hands, as contentment pulled in his chest. Neither woman had noticed him yet.

"I like how you've done your hair," Gia murmured around safety pins, referring to the riot of curls that Naomi had styled to spill over one shoulder. "Very pretty."

"I can style your hair this way, too," Naomi replied. "Or show you how to do it."

His mother's hands self-consciously reached back to pat her low, understated bun—her usual hairstyle of choice for special occasions. "Oh no, I'm too old for that. What would people say?"

"You'd look great," Naomi said firmly. "What's wrong with do-ing things that make you feel beautiful?"

There was a hesitancy in Gia's voice as she ducked her head. "Maybe next time."

Dev grinned. Since the bazaar's reopening, Naomi had carved a place for herself in his family, a place that he knew sometimes baffled his mother. And yet every single time Naomi questioned, pushed back, or politely refused, Gia allowed her the room to be herself. He knew it wasn't always easy for Naomi to be the newcomer—in more ways than one—to his family, but it did not go unnoticed by any of the Mukherjees how eager she was to learn and understand all the customs they adhered to.

She was always respectful, always careful to communicate her opinion in such a way that Gia could bend. And so his family would not break.

"What are you eating?" Naomi asked, noticing his arrival and eyeing his bowl with interest.

"Daal."

"I want a bite!"

Dev stepped forward, ready to accommodate, as he often willingly—and, dare he say, cheerfully—felt compelled to when it came to Naomi, but his mother held up a warning hand. "No! Stay away. One drop on this sari, and she'll be ruined!"

Naomi and Dev exchanged private secret smiles over Gia's choice of words. They both tried to be open and honest with Gia, a united front in wanting Gia to accept them as a couple, as un-likely a pair as they were. But as far as people being *ruined* and such, Gia didn't need to know *everything*.

"I had your clothes dry-cleaned, Dev," Gia said. "They're on your bed. You should get dressed."

Without a doubt, Dev knew Gia had chosen blue. She liked the family to match, and while he would never admit out loud that his mother chose his clothes for events, he didn't mind.

"You're wearing navy blue," Naomi informed him, with a mischievous smile.

"I figured as much."

"And jutti," Naomi cackled, referring to the old-fashioned, curly-toed shoes that forced him to walk funny because the soles lacked any grip to them. A person could break a neck in those things.

Dev groaned. "Seriously, Mom?"

Gia shooed him away. "Go get dressed."

Shooting Naomi one last look of despair, Dev turned to go. But he didn't get very far when his ears perked to Gia and Naomi's conversation again.

"I'm not very graceful moving around in a sari," Naomi grumbled.

"You'll learn," Gia replied. "There are many events throughout the year for you to practice."

"But am I ever going to figure out how to put a sari on myself?"

"You'll learn that, too," Gia repeated, her voice brisk and firm. "Besides, a bride deserves to be pampered, so I'll be happy to help you when you marry my son."

Dev rolled his eyes. There his mother went again, planning his wedding without him, lining up his future according to what she felt was best for him. Here she was, talking marriage with his girlfriend before they'd done so themselves.

But, he thought with a smile, when it came to Naomi, he didn't mind.

Acknowledgments

I started my writing journey alone, on my living room couch, with very little idea of where my words might take me. But then some lovely, magnificent people walked into my life and . . . Poof! Everything changed.

I owe more gratitude than I can express to my fierce, magical agent, Jem Chambers-Black, for believing in my work and in me. You are a dream agent come true. And this profound appreciation extends to the Andrea Brown Literary Agency for their tireless work behind the scenes and willingness to walk this clueless Canadian through annoying and confusing international tax laws.

Thank you to my shining (and rising!) star editor, Sareer Khader, whose talent and keen eye shone so much light and love onto this novel. Thank you for championing Naomi and Dev—and me!—onto the bookshelves. I am so grateful for your guidance, kindness, and encouragement.

The same appreciation extends to the team at Berkley, including Kim-Salina I and Dache' Rogers. I know there is also a whole bevy of hard-working, amazing people who worked behind the scenes to produce this book—thank you, thank you, thank you for everything you've done!

To my mentors, Regina Black and Nikki Payne, I don't think I will ever find the exact right words to express my appreciation for everything you've done for me. Thank you for welcoming me into Team Soul Glo—I think a part of me is still (and will always be) in a state of shock that you selected my messy manuscript once upon a Pitch Wars. Your wisdom and advice went far beyond Naomi and Dev's story; you taught me so much about craft, publishing, community, and confidence. I can never thank you enough for propelling my novel and me into the publishing world, nor do these words properly capture the generosity of your beautiful souls.

I also owe a special shout-out to the members of the #BTeam— Sofia Arellano, Mae Bennett, Jessica Joyce, Rebecca Osberg, and Kate Robb—for being my first writing friends. I would be hard- pressed to find a better hype squad. Thank you for your firm belief in my writing and for keeping me upright through the hard times. There aren't enough gifs/questionable memes in the world to ex- press how I feel about all of you. The same goes for Alexandra Ki- ley who held my hand through this entire process. Thank you for being someone I can count on, especially when screaming into the abyss seems to be the only viable option.

There aren't enough trees on this planet (literally, but that's a topic for another day!) to list the many wonderful people in the writing community who have enriched my life, but to any writers or aspiring writers who stumbled on to this page, I cannot stress enough how vital it is to find your people. I am especially grateful to the Romance writing *and* reading community. I've met the best, most welcoming, and open-minded people in Romancelandia; thank you for embracing me in your smutty arms.

Thank you to my loving parents, who nurtured my love of reading with countless trips to the library. To Madame Arora for showing me that South Asian women are more than one thing. To Chris, for pushing me forward, and Chelsea, for pulling me back from the edge. To Aiden, for caring for my heart and Avery, for always making me laugh. To Paula, for helping me with translations. And to Laura Ly: thank you for telling me to stop talking about my story idea and "just write it down."

Finally, to you, the reader: I wish I had the right words to describe what it means to me that you are holding my book, right now, in your hands, but sometimes the simplest words are the best ones. Thank you so much. I hope you enjoyed the read.

Sunshine and Spice

AURORA PALIT

Behind the Book

I t's funny to me how off-hand, random comments can stick with us longer than we want them to.

In my early twenties, I was visiting family overseas when, after I correctly identified the Bollywood tune in someone's ringtone, one of my cousins remarked, "Oh, I guess there's some Desi in her after all."

The comment slid down my back like a half-melted ice cube, coolly reminding me: *You're not one of them*. I'd spent the entire trip trying to be friendly despite nieces and nephews shying away, to be easygoing even while culture shock slapped me in the face, and to be charismatic and fun with my rusty, cobbled together grasp of Bangla.

But it wasn't enough. Even submersed in the land of my ancestral roots, I felt like a guest. A well-meaning, respectful, oddball guest.

Some people laughed when the speaker called me out, others barely noticed. But it struck a chord with me. Even now, I remember exactly how I felt in that moment: uncomfortable, speechless, embarrassed. Maybe a little self-righteous?

It wasn't the first time I've felt that way as a South Asian person who, similar to Naomi, was raised in a homogenous "small town" with parents who encouraged us to speak English at home (so my mom could practice) and wanted us to fit in with our predominantly white community. Don't get me wrong, my parents tried to instill a lot of their cultural beliefs and traditions, but it was obvious—sometimes painfully so—that my upbringing was very different from the other South Asian first-generation kids I saw several times a year when we traveled to larger, more urban cities for Bengali celebrations and festivities.

Sometimes I felt like an outsider; other times I felt like I had found "my people." Even now, especially when I look at my mixed-race kids, I worry about their future and wonder how they'll navigate their own sense of ethnic identity.

Living in the in-between is confusing and shapes all of us so differently. And while *Sunshine and Spice* mainly focuses on the cultural in-between, we all deal with this space in some way or another: generationally, religiously, geographically, financially. It's a universal life experience that has the power to bring us together and create movements or alienate us and put up walls.

Sunshine and Spice is my love letter to anyone who has ever felt like they don't quite fit. I know it's not easy to feel confident and sure about who you are and where you belong all the time, but I hope Naomi and Dev's journey—both individually and together—inspires a sense of hope and optimism that we get to choose our own paths and decide what is the best fit for us. And that it reaffirms the fact that, despite where we are in those journeys, whether you're thriving and kicking ass or struggling and faking your way through, you will always deserve love.

Discussion Questions

1. Although Naomi's interest in rebranding Gia's Bazaar begins as a means of building her own business and paying the bills, it soon becomes much more than that. In what ways does the rebrand become part of her identity? What are the dangers/upsides of tying your professional life to your personal one?

2. How do Naomi's and Dev's complex relationships with their respective families shape them as adults? How can a person bridge the gap between the relationship they have with their families as children and the one they have with them as adults?

3. When Naomi meets the Mukherjee family, she decides to adopt the "fake it until you make it" philosophy to earn their trust and respect. Was this the right decision for her? At what point does this decision blow up in her face?

4. When the truth of Naomi's Bengali roots is revealed, Dev feels hurt and betrayed, prompting Naomi to tell him: "You know who I am. You know the parts that *matter*. I'm sorry that you feel lied to, but I don't owe you shit." What do you think of her

statements? How much of ourselves—like what we believe, iden-tify with, and feel—do we owe to other people?

5. A lot of the characters' relationships depend on how they identify with others, whether it's the color of their skin, cultural heritage, the way they were raised, current relationships with their fami-lies, etc. How much do these things matter in the relationships you have in your life? Do they define how you relate to others?

6. Dev spends a lot of time questioning what constitutes a lasting, happy marriage, and Veera Auntie, the matchmaker, tells him: "Dating and having fun barely scratch the surface of what it means to be married. So instead of focusing on what puzzle pieces fit together right now, think about the big picture. What is going to keep those pieces locked together for the rest of your life?" Do you agree with Veera Auntie's advice? What are the components that matter to you for a long-term relationship?

7. From everything Naomi and her mother, Sue, reveal about Nao-mi's maternal grandparents, do you think Naomi should attempt to reunite with her grandparents? How do you think it would play out if she did?

8. This novel explores how immigrants and first-generation off-spring navigate creating a sense of identity for themselves in a community/country that doesn't always feel like their own. Have you ever struggled with this challenge? What do you think builds the foundation for a person to feel acceptance, belonging, and security in themselves?

9. The epilogue of Sunshine and Spice offers a brief glance of how Naomi fits into the Mukherjee family. What message do you think the author is trying to inspire in the reader? What do you think Naomi's life with the Mukherjees will look like?

Aurora's 2024 debuts TBR pile consists of . . .

. . . sexy workplace rivals: *Let's Call a Truce* by Amy Buchanan

. . . gravitational love: *The Kiss Countdown* by Etta Easton

. . . steamy fairy-tale retellings: *Barely Even Friends* by Mae Bennett

. . . more romantic high jinks set in Kelowna: *Rules for Second Chances* by Maggie North

. . . Hollywood scandal: *When I Think of You* by Myah Ariel

. . . fake engagements: *Say You'll Be Mine* by Naina Kumar

. . . Scottish accents: *Kilt Trip* by Alexandra Kiley

. . . office drama: *I Hope This Finds You Well* by Natalie Sue

. . . more matchmaking fun: *Match Me If You Can* by Swati Hegde

Gabriela Cruz Photography

A first-generation Bengali-Canadian, **Aurora Palit** grew up in rural Alberta, where she was always the only South Asian student in her class. Her love of reading began at age four, but it wasn't until high school—when she wandered into the romance section of a bookstore—that she realized happily-ever-afters are her jam. Flash forward [an undisclosed number of] years and Aurora is now writing those stories with her own unique brand of humor, perspective, and belief that people of color deserve love stories, too. During her time pursuing a master's degree in English literature, Aurora was drawn to discourses on diaspora and identity, racism, and multigenerational immigrant experiences, topics she now explores in her writing.

VISIT AURORA PALIT ONLINE

AuroraPalit.com
Ⓞ AuroraPalit